Portia Da Costa is one of the most internationally renowned authors of erotic romance and erotica, and a *Sunday Times*, *New York Times* and *USA Today* bestseller.

She is the author of eighteen *Black Lace* books, as well as numerous short stories and novellas.

Also by Portia Da Costa

Master of The Game

PORTIA DA COSTA

BLACK
LACE

1 3 5 7 9 10 8 6 4 2

Black Lace, an imprint of Ebury Publishing 20 Vauxhall Bridge Road, London
SW1V 2SA

Black Lace is part of the Penguin Random House group of companies whose
addresses can be found at global.penguinrandomhouse.com

First published in 1996 by Black Lace

This edition published in 2016

www.eburypublishing.co.uk

A CIP catalogue record for this book is available from the British Library

ISBN 9780352347855

Typeset in India by Thomson Digital Pvt Ltd, Noida, Delhi

Printed and bound in Great Britain by Clays Ltd, St Ives PLC

Penguin Random House is committed to a sustainable future for our business,
our readers and our planet. This book is made from Forest Stewardship Council®
certified paper.

Prologue

It arrived, as momentous things so often did, amongst the cluster of files and documents in her internal mail.

Joanna Darrell picked up the small square envelope, which was undistinguished by any name or address, and felt herself tremble. She had a fair idea of what was inside, but still she held back from the moment of opening it, savouring a tension that she had come to relish over these last, strange months; a sense of expectancy that made her heart leap, and her loins grow hot and heavy.

What would he want this time? Something complicated and serious – involving long hours of preparation, and a solemn ritual? Or perhaps a lighter scene, something domestic, rather urgent and flirty?

With the envelope in the centre of her blotter, she sat quietly for a few minutes, occasionally touching her cheek, or her hair, or her thighs through the cloth of her skirt. She flexed her fingers. If she didn't open the envelope, but instead wrote a name upon it and returned it to its sender, nothing would happen. He had given her that option from the very beginning, but it was a right to refuse of which she had never taken advantage. She was an addict. He knew it and she knew it. What the envelope contained was a summons to something that was so much a part of her psyche that she could not even consider giving it up – now, or ever.

Reaching for the envelope, she felt an area at the very centre of her quiver and soften. There was a slight, warm rush between her legs. It was the effect he always had on her, even when he wasn't physically present. As she slipped a fingernail beneath the pristine white flap, she felt her panties grow sticky, and her nipples, dark and pink like two rosy plum stones, become puckered and hard beneath her blouse.

The message was terse, but that didn't bother her. Sometimes he was expansive, almost poetic in his communications, but when his words were short and sharp, he was at his most exciting – his most severe.

I will come to you tonight at nine. Be ready.

There was no signature, no mark, but who else would write to her like this? Who else would expect her to obey him?

Glancing at her Cartier watch – his gift – she suppressed a groan of longing. How could she last all those hours? She was ready for him now. Not ready in the sense demanded in the letter, because she was in her office, and empowered by her status, her expertise and her clothing. But her body was entirely prepared to receive him. His instruction, on the white paper, had made her wet. Anticipation of the words had begun the process, but reading the actual command had made her a helpless slave to her own raw desire. Shifting in her executive chair, she tried to ease the nagging ache in her genitals. Squeezing her thighs together produced a thin spike of pleasure.

This, she thought, smiling wryly as she wriggled like a horny teenager, was the reason he so often sent his summons this way. When a letter, or an e-mail arrived in the morning, she had the whole day in which to work herself up into a frenzy. It was an additional way of controlling her, she supposed. She was subjected to many long hours of unrequited passion and arousal, which was just as much of a torment as what would come later. Even masturbation couldn't help her, although she often succumbed to it several times a day while she was waiting. She would, nevertheless, become stirred again at the slightest thought of him. She would be working on a report, or be in a meeting, and she would suddenly think of his eyes, his narrow hands, or his cock. And she would be ensorcelled all over again: her heart pounding, her soul twisting with the simple fact of his absence, the folds of her sex slick and engorged, throbbing in readiness for his touch. Yet she had to endure so very much before actually receiving his touch.

'Damn you,' she whispered, smiling and wondering if she dared stroke herself through her skirt.

He would know, of course, if she had been playing with herself. He would suspect it, because – as he was fond of telling her – she was wanton and greedy for stimulation; and when he questioned her, she could conceal nothing from him.

She could almost hear his voice – the blunt question: 'Have you touched yourself today?'

'Yes . . . Yes, I did,' she would answer, quaking. Oh, how he delighted in wringing that first confession from her.

'How many times?' His stern eyes would flash.

'Three times.'

'And where did you do it? All this wickedness . . .'

'Twice in the ladies cloakroom, and once at my desk, when I was alone.'

'And did you climax each time?'

'Y-Yes.'

'And when you were in the cloakroom? Did you remove your panties, or keep them on?'

'I took them off. Both times.'

'And these times when you took off your panties – how did you do it?' He would be aroused by now, and she would feel him behind her, pressed against her, his cock hard and imperious through his clothes. He would push it against her naked bottom, or her thigh. 'Did you stand? Sit? Crouch? Kneel? Squat?' Emphasis would be on the last word, the most demeaning.

'Squat,' she might say, even if she hadn't. He enjoyed her verbal pictures, and the lewder they were, the more they entertained him.

'Both times?'

'Yes.'

'And did –'

The sudden ringing of the phone destroyed her fantasy.

'Hell's teeth!' she hissed, reaching for it.

The call was routine, but it reminded her of work to be done, and other phone calls that were required of her in turn. Still aroused, still wet between her legs, she slid her treasured message into its envelope, then into her attaché case, and prepared to return to the tasks and challenges of the real world. The continuum of dark pleasure would always be waiting for her because in a sense she could never really leave it. There was only a thin, illusory membrane between it and a mundane existence, and all it needed was a thought or word to break through . . .

The day, surprisingly, went well. Without false modesty, Joanna knew she was genuinely good at what she did, and her awareness of the letter secreted in her case seemed to act like a natural 'upper', sharpening her judgement and granting clarity to her thoughts. But it was late by the time she left the building, and she was glad of having her customary chauffeured car to take her home through the hassle of the city.

Her apartment, as ever, was a haven of peace and tranquility, its quiet orderliness preparing her for the long, ritualised hours ahead. Putting away her coat and her attaché case was like putting away the lesser part of herself, to leave a goddess, complete and shining, to wait in readiness. Feeling her excitement rise anew, she poured herself a drink. She only ever took one drink before he arrived, but even that was a part of the event itself, the first gathering and honing of her senses.

Sipping her gin, she relished its silvery bite on her tongue. It was a clean taste, but pungent, and it seemed to focus rather than befuddle or inebriate her. She took it with her into the bathroom, taking mouthfuls now and again as she undressed and showered, and went about her complex and very thorough *toilette*. When both the spirit, and her ablutions were done, she rinsed the glass, then returned naked to her bedroom.

In her long mirror, she studied herself critically, looking for any defect or shortcoming which might displease her coming visitor. She found nothing serious enough to worry about, but decided that she would soon need to have her hair cut. Her blonde curls were very soft and very fluffy when freshly washed; relatively short still, and looking somewhat ingenuous in the way they clustered around her ears, and across her brow. How now Shirley Temple? she thought, grinning at her reflection and wondering if America's Sweetheart had ever anticipated what was now taking such a grip on her senses.

Still assessing herself, she ran her hands over her full, bare breasts, her gently curved stomach and her long, well-toned thighs. Her flesh, all over her body, was firm and resilient. Smooth. Unblemished. A perfect canvas on which his whims might be painted. She turned, pirouetting on her toes, and looked over her shoulder at the cheeks of her bottom. At one time she would have said they were too round, too ample; but now she knew differently. Her lover was an artist who sometimes favoured broad strokes. He needed space, space on her body to express himself. Reaching round, she cupped herself, cradling the sleek, peachy globes in her hands. She experienced a frisson of fear – and pleasure – imagining how her buttocks would look and feel in an hour or two.

The carriage clock on top of the bookshelf chimed the quarter hour, and shook Joanna from her narcissistic musings. He was always prompt, and there were preparations yet to be made. Nude still, she sat at her dressing table and applied a little make-up. Just to her eyes, really, a touch of fawn eye-shadow, smudged; brown-black kohl pencil and a coat of mascara; all waterproof. She would cry before long, and runnels of paint on her cheeks were so unflattering. Her mouth she slicked with gloss, and this was colourless; there would be kisses aplenty amongst all the groans and tears.

Applying the make-up took but a moment, but she knew the next stage might take a little longer. She crossed to the wardrobes that covered the entire length of one wall, and pushed open a sliding door.

So much to choose from; so many beautiful things, all bought, but not all chosen, by him.

At first, Joanna had felt uncomfortable with the many gifts he gave her. She was used to paying her own way in the world, and to facing the consequences of her almost childlike extravagance; so to have so much luxury lavished upon her was an affront to her independence; her cock-eyed and rather accommodating form of feminism. But she had soon come to see that she earned every penny of her lover's *largesse*. Earned it in a way that would have found most other women wanting. Each exquisite item in this wardrobe had been paid for with her anguished cries, her sweat, her impassioned writhings over many, seemingly endless hours.

She pulled out an elegant, lace-encrusted nightdress in ivory pure silk. The light yet substantial fabric seemed to flow over her fingers, bringing a flood of sweetly poignant memories in its wake. He had presented this gown to her, that first time, in France, when he had revealed himself to her as he really was. She had worn it in bed, while he had made love to her, and she could still feel it sliding over the throbbing heat in her skin as he thrust deeply and joyfully into her sex. She had still been wearing it later, when he had leapt from that bed, his skin still scented with her fluids and her perfume, and knelt on the floor before her, then offered up his own naked body just as she had offered hers, earlier, to him. Nostalgia curved her lips as she considered the lovely gown.

Her lover could take it just as well as he could dish it out, she thought, smoothing her fingers again over the silk. This egalitarianism was one of his most endearing qualities.

The ivory gown was superb, but somehow it didn't fit her mood. She replaced it on the rack, and flicked further along the serried line of garments, some of which were more exotic than others.

Finally, she came to an old favourite, perhaps the least sultry item in her collection, but full – despite that – of its own particular symbolism. Aware that time was passing, and running out, she shrugged quickly into it, then hurried to the mirror.

The innocent, curly-top image was reinforced by her choice; a long, voluminous, Victorian nightie in the softest unbleached cotton. Its only trim was a network of fine smocking at the yoke, and a thin flounce around the cuffs and the collar. Her fingers trembled as she fastened the tiny mother-of-pearl buttons. There were only moments left before the pre-appointed time, and her lover was never, ever late.

Her feet bare, she scurried around the room, making some final adjustments to the décor. She turned out all the lights but the Tiffany lamp by the bed, creating soft pools of coloured radiance to illuminate the room. She lit an aromatherapy candle to provide a perfume for their diversions; the odour of patchouli soon permeated the expectant, silent air. Savouring the exotic vapours, she opened the top drawer of her dressing table, and took out certain implements which she laid out on the bed, their stark nature quite at odds with the satin counterpane. Her lover would appreciate the provision of a choice.

Finally, she stacked two of the plump, lace-trimmed and embroidered pillows, taken from the head of the bed, down at its foot and, feeling almost dizzy, she laid herself face down across them, her bare toes just touching the Persian carpet. With as much grace as she was able, she hitched up the long, flowing skirt of her nightdress and folded it as best she could into a roll that rested above her waist. At moments like these, she occasionally wished she had accepted his offer of her own personal maid, to help her prepare for him; yet there was a certain magic to these moments of solitary reflection. This heavy, almost charged time of waiting. She also knew that if there was ever anything particularly elaborate that needed doing, she could always call on her dear, dear Cynthia. Her handsome friend would be more than happy to do anything that required hands-on contact.

Breathing deeply, Joanna tried to centre herself, to assemble the wall of composure that would see her through what lay ahead. She could feel the coolness of the air against her naked bottom and thighs, and she relished it while she could. Soon there would be only heat. She folded her arms on the counterpane, encircling her head, her cheek against the satin. He might put her in restraints, later, when he really hit his stride.

There wasn't much time to settle herself, because a second or two later she heard a series of small sounds which culminated in footsteps outside her bedroom door. She could hardly breathe as the handle turned, and the door swung open. There was a pause, then a measured, near-silent tread approached her on the thick-piled carpet, and a potent presence filled every corner of the room.

A cool, slender hand settled on the curve of her right buttock, and into the stillness, she softly said:

'I'm ready . . .'

1

Get a Life

'Oh, get a life, you sad, sad bastard!'

Joanna Darrell couldn't believe she had actually said that. It had just leapt from her tongue as the very first thing in her mind; a release of pressure that had felt so good it was almost sexual. She had listened to her blood pounding through her veins in the following silence, and the moment after that she had slammed down the phone.

It was only afterwards, and more so now, that she had considered the ramifications of her outburst. There had been a major client on the other end of the line, a prime mover in one of the company's most lucrative accounts. The confidential file specified kid glove handling at all times. And she had called the man a 'sad bastard'.

It could have been worse, she supposed. She could have called him a 'sad fuck' instead. In fact now she wished she had done. Either way, it would have got her carpeted, so she might as well have made it worth the effort.

The company rule at Perry McAffee was to keep the client sweet at all times, and she had just broken it in fine style. It could possibly – no, would probably – mean dismissal.

Waiting in the lounge outside Halloran's office, Joanna had plenty of time to consider her *faux pas*.

The client had deserved her vituperation, she knew that. He was petulant, whingeing, a financial prima donna. A pain, in other words. He had always demanded more data than even the most talented analyst could supply or interpret, and Joanna had always done her best for him. Had stretched herself to her limits on his account. Even so, it had never seemed to be enough, and the client had not held back from letting her know that.

Why was it, Joanna wondered, that she had not let his complaints slide off her as they had always done in the past? Like water off vinyl. Harsh words meant nothing, it was part of the job when huge amounts of money were on the line. Discourtesy went with the territory. From the client, that was.

So why today? Why had she suddenly snapped and blurted out what she really felt?

With no real answer for that, she studied Halloran's personal assistant, who was sitting straight and perfect behind her desk, doing some apparently elaborate task that Joanna couldn't even begin to guess at.

Has she plucked that look straight from the pages of *Businesswoman*? Joanna wondered. The self-possessed young woman was so immaculate she might have been air-brushed, and just the sight of her made Joanna feel ill-kempt. Surreptitiously, she smoothed at a wrinkle that had appeared in her pencil skirt, and began to worry about the freshness of her white poplin blouse. She flared her nostrils, trying to detect sweat and other, more musky odours. She imagined the shock on that supermodel face across the room, if she should open her jacket and boldly sniff her armpits.

I'm going mad, thought Joanna, astounded at the tenor of her own thoughts. It's the waiting, it must be. I probably won't get near enough to Halloran for him to smell me. He'll just have me stand on that fancy rug of his – the oriental one the Zip Corporation gave him – while he calmly sacks me without turning a hair. Bastard!

But not a sad one, she reflected, as it occurred to her that, in a certain sense, she was looking forward to her ordeal. She enjoyed a battle. A challenge. In finance, life was just one long series of confrontations, and she relished each one she was involved in.

Halloran's ante-room was a blank, neutral expanse, designed to lull one into a false sense of security, no doubt. All beige, cream, and fawn shades; no-colours. Joanna suddenly wished she was wearing a suit in a brilliant primary colour, or at least a pair of red shoes to spice up her navy and white corporate look. Anything to break up the inoffensive monotony.

Had she felt this unsettled the last time she had waited outside an office? She didn't think so. She found interviews as stimulating as any other confrontation, and whenever she had been interviewed for a job, she had always ended up getting it. In fact, her success record was a stunning hundred per cent.

No, the last time she could recall feeling trepidation outside an office was back when she had been at school. In the sixth form. And even then her fears hadn't been justified – a light dressing down was all she had received, not the punishment she had imagined. Not a thrashing. Not being made to slip down her knickers and . . .

Dear God, where had that come from? What a bizarre thing to imagine. Her school had been modern, liberal, enlightened; corporal punishment in education had just been a horror from the dark ages, and she'd known that perfectly well at the time. Who was it who had now twisted her thoughts that way? she mused. Halloran himself, probably. He had very pure, stern features, and a vaguely autocratic demeanour – she could easily imagine him as a disciplinarian. His face would be a cool, handsome mask as he struck her tender flesh with blow after blow, his body as still as stone between each swing.

To distract herself, Joanna studied a print on the far wall. Unsurprisingly it was a sepia wash thing, suitably insipid, to match the rest of the room. Restless, she crossed her long legs, listening to the unnaturally loud rasp of one stocking against the other, and receiving a little shock when she realised she was aroused.

It must be all these weird fantasies, she thought, trying to adjust her posture without appearing to move. She was definitely a little wet between her legs, and she felt uncomfortable. Swollen. Engorged. It was a sensation she relished in its proper context, but it was unnerving to feel it here and now.

She glanced across at the PA and speculated. Did such bandbox grooming ever get ruffled by the absurdities of lust? Joanna couldn't imagine so doll-like a creature ever getting turned on, even by their handsome, stony-mannered boss, but then, suddenly, she remembered a story she had heard a few months ago. A choice piece of gossip exchanged between two giggly temps in the cloakroom.

According to the overheard whispers, someone had once forgotten to knock before walking into Halloran's inner sanctum – and had found 'Ms Perfection' face down across the leather-topped desk while her boss gave her an energetic shafting. The rumour went on to recount that he had said, 'Just a moment . . .' then climaxed, pulled out and zipped up, before smiling calmly and asking the intruder to take a seat.

It had to be purely apocryphal, surely, the product of the word-processing pool's fevered collective imagination, but Joanna had to admit the idea was hot. There was something quite compelling about the image of Halloran, all businesslike and formal, but with his bottom jerking as he fucked a willing woman.

Had he actually dropped his trousers and undershorts? Joanna wondered, picturing a pair of male buttocks tensing rhythmically. Would he have cried out as he orgasmed? It didn't seem in character. She imagined him to be as impassive in climax as he was in everything else; just a brief spasm distorting his fine, solemn features.

Lost in her musings, Joanna started wildly when the inner office door opened. She heard the tail end of a conversation – conventional pleasantries tacked on to business as a matter of form – then a familiar figure appeared on the threshold, before moving into the outer office, closing the door behind him.

'Hi! How are you?' said Kevin Steel, one of her colleagues, a freelance computer specialist who had been working in her division for several weeks.

To her chagrin, Joanna blushed. 'Fine, thanks,' she murmured, wishing Kevin hadn't chosen this particular moment to appear. He was another of her current preoccupations, and her heartbeat speeded up as he sat down beside her, placing the reams of printout he had been carrying on the floor at his feet.

'You're not in trouble, are you?' he said, his narrow face serious as he inclined towards her. He was an odd-looking man, and yet at the same time curiously attractive. His features were sharp and angular, almost pixie-like, and his eyes were a light, clear, bluish shade, sometimes stormy, sometimes limpid, always changing. His hair was dark golden blond, and very thick; the colour of overripe wheat. It was beautifully cut, but, though he always arrived at work with it brushed neatly into place, within minutes his boyish fringe would be flopping into his eyes. Just as it was doing now. With a swift, unconscious gesture, he swept it back.

'Nope. There's no problem,' Joanna lied, silently begging Kevin to go about his business and leave her alone. The fact that they had been to bed together a week ago made him one of the last people she needed to see right now. She wanted her wits about her when she went in to see Halloran, and thoughts of sex – more thoughts of sex, that was – would distract her. Kevin Steel was a conundrum she had not yet had a chance to decipher.

'I don't believe you,' he said, his concerned expression shifting into a slow challenging smile. 'You've got that "I'm about to get a rollicking" look to you.' He waggled his expressive blond eyebrows. 'What did you do? It must've been pretty bad . . . I would've thought you, of all people, could get away with just about anything in this place.'

Before she could challenge this statement, Kevin leapt lightly to his feet, scooping up his sheaf of paper as he rose, then patted her encouragingly on the shoulder. 'Look, I've got a meeting like ten minutes ago . . . But I'll see you later and you can tell me all about it.' He flashed her a knowing wink, then was gone almost before she could register its impact, his exit as quick and mercurial as everything else about him was.

'Bastard,' Joanna muttered, adding him to the growing list under that heading. She was aware of the cool eyes of

Halloran's PA sweeping over her, and she wondered if she and Kevin were the subject of salacious whispering too. It had been purely a once only thing, so far, and they had been careful and made no reference at all to it at work.

Without conscious volition she found herself remembering . . .

It had started when they had worked late together. Working late wasn't an unusual occurrence at Perry McAffee – far from it – but it was the first time she had stayed behind with Kevin. She had needed a new way to present the data in a crucial report and, with his expertise, he had been the ideal man to call on. The task had taken longer than either of them had expected, and when it was done, Joanna had suggested dinner, purely on a whim. She hadn't been entertaining any specifically seductive intentions, but the light in Kevin's eyes had been so immediate and so gratifying that Joanna had suddenly wanted him.

Kevin had countered her suggestion of going to a bistro with the proposal that he come back to her flat and cook for her. And the idea had been so unexpected that she had agreed.

Perhaps it was the same sense of novelty that had caused them to end up having sex. Kevin Steel certainly wasn't her usual type. She generally preferred tall, dark, very grown-up men. Like Halloran, she observed ruefully. But somehow, it had seemed quite natural to invite Kevin to make love to her. In fact, looking back, she couldn't remember if she had even asked at all. It had come about almost instinctively, in the way the whole evening had done. One minute they were eating, talking, and getting on so comfortably with each other that they might have been friends for years, and the next they were kissing wildly and searching for gaps in each other's clothes.

Or, at least, she had been searching.

'Hey, steady on,' Kevin had said, laughing, as he grasped her wrists and kept her still. 'What's the hurry?'

Joanna blushed, aware that she was dishevelled and breathing heavily. She felt mortified at having seemed so keen. She usually played the self-possessed, hard-to-get hand with men, and it usually worked. It was only because she was tired and disorientated that she had let herself rush things.

Frowning, she jerked free of him, then clutched at the gaping neckline of her blouse.

'Hey,' he said again, softly this time, cajolingly. Then, like quicksilver, he caught hold of her by the upper arms, and leant forward to kiss her slowly on the mouth.

For the first few moments, he simply pressed his lips to hers, letting her enjoy the warmth of the gentle, quiescent contact. Joanna had closed her eyes, automatically, but now she opened them and found that his, too, were open. Blue and placid, they were level, intent, lazily watchful. She tried to pull back, but his hands whipped up from her arms to cradle her head. Her eyes widened, and she tried to struggle, but before she could achieve anything his tongue flicked between her lips like a small, hot serpent. He continued to watch her as it probed and darted lewdly.

For a reason she didn't quite understand, Joanna found it impossible to move. She stood, almost limply, her head still lightly gripped in Kevin's hands, while his tongue flashed around her mouth and explored its inner membranes. She closed her eyes, but sensed that his were still open.

The kiss went on for several minutes and throughout it Joanna remained passive, letting Kevin take the initiative for them both. His hands moved constantly in her soft blonde curls, adjusting the position of her head; gently tilting it, occasionally stroking it. It was as if he were a sculptor creating the kiss as a work of art. Joanna had never been kissed that way before.

When his lips finally left hers, she swayed slightly. Though her eyelids felt weighted she opened her eyes just as Kevin released her head and, as she focused on him, she realised he was stripping off his clothes. Torn between anger and desire, she let the latter win, and began unfastening her blouse. She was astounded, however, when Kevin – his tie, shoes and socks already flung about him, and his fine cotton shirt undone – grasped her hands again, and squeezed them, as if to hold her still. She was even more surprised that, when he let them go, they stayed where they were – clasped against her chest, the fingers curled, while he continued.

In a moment or two he was naked and, almost reluctantly, Joanna was impressed. Wearing clothes, Kevin was an appealing man, for all his unusual, pointed features; without clothes he was something else entirely. Wiry almost to the point of thinness, his body was nevertheless hard-muscled like a dancer's or an athlete's, exuding physical power without the slightest trace of vanity. He was not particularly hairy, with just a few sandy wisps across the centre of his chest and a larger, thicker mat at his groin, but his cock was unexpectedly distinguished. Not wanting to fall into the trap of appearing visibly awed, Joanna was still forced to stare at it – with hunger. Kevin himself seemed to have no special pride in his genitals – unlike a lot of men of her acquaintance – but, even so, his erection was sizeable, both in terms of length and, more importantly, of girth. He was circumcised, she noticed, and his glans was rounded and glossy, with a clean and succulently ruddy glow. A small amount of moisture was already seeping from the little eye at its very tip and, as Joanna watched, it swelled to a pearl-sized drop.

Meeting his eyes again, she found him studying her. She coloured hotly, and he glanced down at his prick, shrugging dismissively. She half expected him to take her hand and close her fingers around it, but instead he took her in his arms and kissed her again, the same deep, involving kiss as before. He seemed almost oblivious to his own state of nudity.

Joanna wasn't oblivious to it, though, especially when she slid her arms around him in response, and felt the smooth, almost glassy texture of his skin. Running her hands up and down his back and his buttocks, she heard, and even felt him make a gruff sound of appreciation in his throat. His cock leapt against her thigh, and she could feel its heat clean through the fabric of her skirt. She imagined his pre-come oozing freely over the fine linen, and as – ludicrously! – her mind drifted to the resultant cleaning bill, she felt Kevin's hands slide to her waistband, and unfasten the button. Before she knew what was happening, her unzipped skirt was in a pool around her ankles and he was teasing down her satin half-slip as well. When that had been dispensed with, he suddenly nipped playfully at her tongue, and then, while she was distracted, he sank to his knees on the carpet before her, deftly skinning down her tights and panties as he went.

Laughing softly, he probed her crotch and gently opened her, parting her blonde curls and exposing her inner wetness. Joanna moaned as his thumbs peeled back her outer labia and the tension made her clitoris rear up proudly – a fat red bead in the coral setting of her sex. Hobbled by her clothes around her ankles, she struggled to part her legs and give him better access, but all she could manage was an ungainly, bent-kneed crouch.

Kevin seemed unperturbed. His thumbs pressed in more determinedly than ever, as if he were attacking a particularly juicy fruit, then, darting forward, he took her clitoris between his lips.

'Oh God!' Joanna began to pant, then almost to grunt, uncouthly. He was sucking hard now, drawing the tiny, sensitive organ as deeply into his mouth as he could and mashing his face against her swollen, moistening vulva.

The stimulation was too much, too soon, and too fierce. Or maybe Joanna had been wanting him for far longer than she had realised. Her knees went weak and she suffered a sudden, juddering climax that was so sharp and unexpected it almost hurt her. She grabbed Kevin's head, meaning to pull him off her but, of their own accord, her hands only clasped him closer.

Even though her intimate flesh seemed to be on fire, she was still keenly aware of the soft, almost baby-like silkiness of his hair around her fingers, and of the scent of herbal shampoo that rose up from it.

'No! Please! Kevin, it's too much!' she cried, wriggling frantically as the suction on her clitoris increased.

But instead of letting her go, he released her labia and slid his hands quickly around her hips until he was clutching her surging bottom. His grip became unyielding as he continued to plague her core.

'No! Oh Jesus God!' she yelped, experiencing another huge orgasm. Her hips bucked and jerked, but Kevin clung on tenaciously, his fingertips deep in her bottom cleft, pressing and probing as he lashed her clitoris with his tongue. 'Oh God, no!' she cried again. His fingers were on either side of her anus now, stretching it open with tiny, pulsing tugs that were timed to the frenzied jabbing of his tongue in her sex.

'You can go in now, Ms Darrell.'

Joanna started violently at the sound of her name. She had been so entranced by her memories of being with Kevin that the real world – Halloran's outer office, and her forthcoming disciplinary reprimand – had lost all substance. It seemed incongruous to be sitting here, outwardly calm, decorous and untouchable, while, between her legs, she could almost feel the stroke of a man's nimble tongue.

'Ms Darrell? Are you all right?' enquired the sleek PA, looking faintly pleased by Joanna's confusion. 'Mr Halloran will see you now. If you're all right, that is?'

'No problem. I'm fine,' Joanna answered curtly, wary of this smooth, unruffled young woman, whose faultless grooming and creamy pallor made her feel sleazy.

'Go straight in, then,' said the PA, adding 'please', after a moment, and somewhat grudgingly. Joanna was suddenly struck by the thought that the other woman might be jealous.

Straightening her jacket and putting on her airiest, and most indifferent expression, she attempted to banish her memories of Kevin Steel's exquisite way with cunnilingus, then opened the door that led to Halloran's spacious office.

'Ah yes, good morning, Joanna.'

'Hello, Joanna, how are you?'

The presence of two men in the room, as opposed to the expected one, disconcerted her somewhat, but, composing herself carefully, Joanna gave no sign of it. Instead, she took the seat in front of Halloran's desk, that was so obviously meant for her, and crossed her legs with an elegant deliberation. In the brief hiatus that followed, she studied her inquisitors.

Halloran looked the same as he always did; dark and imperturbable in his Savile Row suit, his calm face a perfect picture of corporate authority. For her part, Joanna had always found him sexually intriguing – and now, more so than ever, after all the scurrilous talk. She tried to imagine him leaning across the broad expanse of desk that stretched between them, with a pliant female body bucking ecstatically beneath him. In her current frame of mind, it didn't take much effort to put herself in the place of his PA.

About his companion, she had no such stimulating thoughts.

Davidson – who was slouched in a leather chair at a right angle to her – was the fancifully titled 'Human Resources Coordinator', seconded to London by their transatlantic masters, to oversee the utilisation of personnel in their UK establishments. The common opinion of him was that he was also a spy, a snooper, reporting to the New York office on matters relating to far more than just the purely personnel matters. His smooth, almost glib persona certainly added weight to the notion. It also gave Joanna the creeps. It wasn't that Davidson was an ugly man, or repulsive in any way – quite the reverse. But there was definitely something not quite right about him. He was 'soft' somehow, his voice quiet, and strangely light. She would have categorised him as effeminate, but there was nothing concrete about him that deserved the tag. He was tallish and dark-haired, with a good physique and, like Halloran, he dressed well but conservatively. He should have been a turn-on, but he made Joanna's hackles – rather than her libido – rise.

'So, what can I do for you?' she said in an even tone, aiming her attention pointedly at Halloran, and not at the closely-watching American.

'I think it's more a case of what we can do for you,' said Halloran, steepling his fingers before him. He cocked his head questioningly to one side, and the light overhead glinted on his severely gelled hair. Something about his manner reminded Joanna of a benevolent schoolmaster, and she had to choke back a gurgle of amusement, recalling her peculiar notions of a little while earlier.

'Are you OK, Joanna?' enquired Davidson, leaping to his feet and stepping towards her. 'Can I get you a glass of water or something?' He gestured towards the carafe and glasses on a side table, the model of solicitude, but Joanna still found his languid style unsettling.

'I'm fine thank you, Mr Davidson,' Joanna replied sweetly, matching his smile with one of her own. She was aware of Halloran watching her, observing the interplay between herself and Davidson. He was probably wondering if she could be goaded into calling the American a bastard too.

'Please. It's "Denis",' Davidson murmured, returning to his seat. As a faintly complicit look passed between the two men, Joanna suddenly had a rather ominous thought.

Did they want her out of the company in any case? Not just because she had called a client a bad name, but because she didn't fit the job profile in some way? Perhaps she was too good at what she did, and was making one of the Americans' pet employees look inferior? It could be for any of a multitude of such reasons, in a company like Perry McAffee, and it must have a personnel angle if the 'Human Resources Coordinator' was present at the interview.

Davidson lolled back in his seat, and with a discreet cough Halloran took things over once again. 'I think we all know why I've asked you to pop in and see us, Joanna,' he said suavely but not unkindly. 'Your little outburst with the representative of Vale Associates.' He paused, then looked a little regretful. 'It just wasn't like you at all, was it?' He fixed her with a thoroughly understanding smile. 'You work hard for this company – very hard. And you produce superlative results. But I, that is *we* –' he glanced towards Davidson, who nodded '– think that for the last few months you've been working *too* hard.' He studied his fingernails for a moment. 'When did you last take a holiday, Joanna?'

'I went to France last year,' she said. 'For a whole month. It was great.'

'Do you like France?' Davidson enquired, something sharp in his eyes making Joanna suspicious. For all her vague dislike of him, she readily conceded that he was a good-looking man nevertheless, and his strange, silky aura had a disquieting effect on her.

'Yes, like I said, it was great,' she snapped. 'What's it to you?'

'We think you need another holiday,' said Halloran, gently, picking up the thread of the conversation. 'A complete break. A change of scene.' His tone hardened. 'In fact, we think it would be a good idea if you left straight away.'

Joanna sprang to her feet. 'You're sacking me, aren't you, you bastard?' She saw Davidson roll his eyes and her fury mounted. 'You're giving me the push! Just because I told that old fart at Vale a simple home truth!' She stood there shaking, her heart racing, astounded that her anger could feel so erotic. 'Well, you can stuff your bloody job!' she cried, turning on her heel and heading for the door. 'He needed telling. Everybody knows that account is more trouble than it's worth!'

In a few seconds, she would have been out of the office, and probably out of her job altogether, but with a turn of speed quite unexpected in a man so seemingly laid back, Davidson darted across the room again, took her quite firmly by the arm and led her back to her chair. Joanna wasn't sure why she allowed him to do this; it was as if something primal in her responded to his strong male grip, a part of her personality that she disliked and usually kept hidden. The need to succumb to a man, to submit to him, that usually only surfaced in bed. As she sat tensely in her chair, glowering at Halloran and then accepting the glass of water that Davidson seemed set on her drinking – as if she were a fragile Edwardian flower with the vapours – she found herself suddenly thinking of Kevin, and remembering again how he had so easily overwhelmed her.

After sucking her to a climax, he had drawn her down on to the carpet, then entered her where she lay, still in her clothes.

'Nobody is sacking you, Joanna,' she heard Halloran say, as if from a great distance. 'But I think we must insist that you take a break now. Before – well, we won't be able to overlook another, similar incident so easily.'

He continued to speak, but Joanna hardly heard him. She felt like a hart cornered by two wolves, and the sensation was scary. Doubly so, because she never usually let men in the workplace intimidate her. Trebly so, because she still couldn't work out why she was finding her state of vulnerability to be so arousing.

'I think you'll enjoy yourself,' Halloran was saying as she tuned back in to his discourse, realising she had just nodded her head in agreement with something. 'Whiteoaks is a superb facility. They employ all the latest relaxation therapies, and there are sports facilities if you're feeling energetic.'

'Oh – Er – Yes, thanks. It sounds first class,' she muttered, trying to snap back to a state of full attention. Both men were on their feet now, signifying that the interview was over.

Davidson in particular was looking unpleasantly pleased with himself, his sharply-defined, almost voluptuous lips curving in a way that produced thoughts she preferred to reject.

'Lisa will make all the arrangements,' Halloran continued, escorting her to the door now, guiding her with a hand on her elbow. 'And we'll see you back here in a week or so, hopefully with all the stresses and strains worked out of you.'

'Don't worry, Joanna. It'll make a new woman of you,' murmured Davidson, just as Halloran opened the door for her. The American's tone was unctuous, yet somehow mischievous and exciting, too. As she left the room, Joanna wondered what he had meant, and just what exactly it was that she had so unresistingly agreed to.

2

A Sabbatical

'Whiteoaks, he called it. It's a health farm or something. Have you ever heard of it? I thought Littlebourne was just a place people retired to.'

'No, it doesn't mean a thing to me,' replied Kevin, taking a sip of his wine. 'I have a hard enough time getting to my own health club.' He shrugged. 'I'm the world's worst when it comes to serious workouts.'

'Oh I don't know,' said Joanna, feeling the effects of her own wine. She was already on her third large glass. 'I've seen your body. You look in good enough condition to me.'

Kevin grinned, his thin, well-shaped lips curving sexily. 'A little goes a long way,' he said, his eyes twinkling and looking even bluer than usual. 'But thanks anyway. You don't look so bad in the buff yourself.'

It was the first time, since it had happened, that Kevin had referred directly to their lovemaking, and Joanna felt relieved. It hadn't been a disappointment, or a non-event, far from it, and the fact that he hadn't mentioned it had perplexed her. She wouldn't have liked him to have bragged about it to all and sundry, but between themselves, she felt a need to address the matter.

'Oh, so you do remember that we went to bed together, then?' she enquired, pointedly. 'I was beginning to think it had completely slipped your mind.'

'Oh no,' he said softly, flicking his fringe out of his eyes. 'I've been thinking about it quite a lot. I just got the impression that you wouldn't want to make a big deal about it at the office.'

He was quite right, of course, but his diffidence was irritating. Joanna sipped her wine again, and decided to change the subject. Kevin seemed as reluctant to be pinned down about sexual matters as she herself was, and to harp on about them now might sound possessive.

'So, do you think I should go to this Whiteoaks place, then?' she asked. 'I mean, all the way to a neither dead nor alive place like Littlebourne when I'm a member of a perfectly good health club here in town?'

'Why not?' replied Kevin reasonably. 'It's all expenses paid. It's a change of scene; sea air and all that. Plus the fact you'll be on salaried leave. Take advantage; it's not often the company offers something for nothing.'

'True,' she answered doubtfully. 'It's just I don't like to be outmanoeuvred by the likes of Halloran. And as for that creep Davidson? Ugh!' She shuddered expressively, remembering the American slouching languidly in his leather office chair.

'What's wrong with Davidson?' Kevin looked puzzled. 'He seems OK to me.'

'He would. You're a man!'

'What's that got to do with it?'

How could she describe it? Why did she need to? She would have thought that Davidson's ambiguous smoothness would have thoroughly spooked a red-blooded heterosexual like Kevin.

'He's weird,' she said, aware that the word was inadequate. 'He's too smooth. He's a creep,' she finished, spurred on by Kevin's look of curiosity.

'If you say so,' he conceded, reaching out to top up her wineglass.

They were in a wine bar near the office, and it was well past lunch time. Joanna had decided that regardless of whether or not she went to Whiteoaks, she would still take the rest of this annoying day off. Kevin had dropped by her desk not long after her interview, and had cheerfully announced that he might as well join her, giving Joanna no real opportunity to refuse – making him yet another man who had pushed her into something she wasn't sure she wanted!

Joanna studied the brimming glass, aware that she was already more than a little drunk.

'I do say so!' she proclaimed, in answer to Kevin's easy-going observation. 'And even if he was a paragon of sweetness and light, I still wouldn't want to be told what to do by him! Or bloody Halloran, for that matter!'

'Well, don't go then,' said Kevin, still logical.

'I have to,' she said, through gritted teeth, then tried to describe the subtle ultimatum she had been given in Halloran's office; the unspoken threat that, if she didn't take this break now, and take it where they had specified, she might find herself out of a job.

Kevin shrugged. 'You'd better go, then,' he said. 'But pretend it was your own idea. Enjoy yourself.' He looked thoughtful for a moment. 'I'd offer to come with you; you know, make a bit of a dirty weekend of it –' His eyes lit up wolfishly. 'But I've got a lot on at the moment. I can't get away. I shouldn't really be here now.'

'Well, you'd better get back then, hadn't you?' Joanna said tartly, although inside, the idea of a dirty weekend with Kevin had a powerful effect on her. He was a bit of an odd cove, really, and she hadn't the faintest idea where she stood with him, but he was, she had to admit, a remarkable lover. One of the best she had encountered in ages. She thought back to the feel of his mouth against her vulva; to the way he had sucked her to climax after climax.

And he hadn't been a slouch when it came to the actual fucking, either. He had exhibited an impressive endurance when he had first taken her, on her sitting room carpet, and had then been able to get a second, sturdy erection only a few minutes later, when they had finally got as far as her bed.

Meeting his eyes, she drained her glass of wine, then licked her lips, knowing she was being so damned obvious that she might as well have shouted, 'I want you!' at the top of her voice, but not caring at all.

Kevin smiled a slow, impish smile that said, 'you're on!'. Then he rose to his feet, took out his wallet, and tossed a handful of notes on to the table in a gesture so cinematic that – if Joanna hadn't already wanted him – would have rendered her amorous enough to receive him straight away.

'Come on,' he said, then turned and led the way out of the darkness of the wine bar and into the sunny day outside.

Gathering up her bag and her trenchcoat from the banquette seat, Joanna felt thoroughly confused. A second ago, she had been desperate with lust for the man, but now he was behaving like just as much of a high-handed macho shit as Halloran and his ilk. Sweeping out of the wine bar like a maharajah, and expecting her to follow meekly and dutifully in his wake.

When she reached the pavement, Kevin had already hailed a taxi, and the black cab stood at the kerb, engine running, like a magic chariot to take them to God alone knew where.

'Changed your mind?' Kevin fixed her with glittering eyes, having registered her hesitation. His look challenged her and, remembering again the pleasure he was capable of inducing, she strode forward, accepting his dare. She wanted to get either to her home, or to his, fairly quickly anyway. Three large glasses of wine were beginning to play havoc with her bladder and, as she sat down on the back seat of the cab, she felt a nasty little jolt. It was with some care that she arranged her legs, her coat, and her bag.

Kevin gave the cabby her address.

'Assuming a lot, aren't we?' she said as the glass partition slid up to give them privacy.

'I could just drop you there and go back to work,' Kevin observed.

'I'd prefer it if you didn't,' she said, trying for an imperious tone, but not quite achieving it. She suddenly felt very, very unsettled. The heavy drag of her bladder seemed to impose itself upon her like a presence. Yet another controlling entity to modify her behaviour; just like Kevin and, before him, Halloran and Davidson. She shifted her thighs cautiously against the leather, glad that she had her trenchcoat spread across her lap to mask her wriggling.

'So would I,' said Kevin softly, then suddenly his arm was around her waist. The hold was light, and not even possessive, but somehow it seemed to exacerbate her plight. She moved again, uneasily.

'Is something wrong?' he enquired, his voice strangely loaded.

'No! No, I'm fine!'

'Sure?'

Joanna turned to face him in the gloom of the back of the cab, and to her horror saw that his eyes were as bright as torches.

Dear God, he knows! The bastard! He knows!

As Kevin smiled slyly, she recalled how eager he had been to fill up her wineglass each time. It had occurred to her while he was doing it that he might be trying to get her tipsy so he could also get her into bed – but could he really have had a far more sinister motive? His hand, on her thigh, beneath her coat, seemed to suggest the latter.

But what if it was all just relatively innocent sexiness? His hand was moving now, deftly edging her skirt up her thighs at the front. It was a slim-cut skirt, but its satin lining betrayed her, allowing its hem to slide right up to her crotch.

Expecting him to finger her immediately, Joanna almost sighed with relief when Kevin touched one of her suspenders. His expressive eyebrows showed his preference for the stockings she had on today, over the tights she had been wearing the last time he had explored her.

Joanna held her breath as Kevin's fingers began to move again, tracking inwards towards her panties – and towards her problem. Should she tell him? Ask him not to touch her just yet? Beg him not to put pressure on her bladder?

Damn! she thought, in torment. She had been manipulated yet again. Put into a man's hands, and at his mercy. She gnawed her lip as he reached her *mons pubis*, his fingertips brushing across the flimsy, damp lace. His arm around her shoulder urged her to lie back against the seat, and she felt his breath like a hot wind against her throat. When he pressed lightly on the pit of her belly she almost choked.

'Kevin! Please don't!' she cried, experiencing daggers of fierce sensation. A feeling that was half discomfort, half delight.

'Hush,' he whispered, nodding towards the cabby in front of them as he pressed down again, and she bucked up from the seat.

'Oh no,' she hissed as his fingers circled in her pubic hair, then slid down into the brimming channel of her sex.

'Oh yes, I must,' he said, his voice as intent as his probing fingertips. 'You're such a beautiful girl, Joanna. So tempting. You almost force me to touch you.'

'Please . . .' she murmured incoherently, feeling him massage the area above her pubic bone with his thumb, while his nimble fingers strummed her throbbing clitoris. The tension inside her was almost unbearable now. Every time he bore down on her distended bladder a delicious wave of pleasure-pain swept through her loins. Her legs were kicking now, involuntarily, as he fondled her.

'Please, Kevin, I'm going to wet myself,' she groaned, feeling her face flush hot with embarrassment.

'No, you're not,' he said gently, adjusting his hold on her. Withdrawing his thumb from its devilish ministrations against her belly, he used it, and his slim forefinger, to pinch her clitoris. 'You can hold it. Don't worry,' he said, speaking now in a perfectly calm and ordinary tone, just as if he wasn't pulling and flicking at the most sensitive part of her body at all. As if he didn't have his whole hand stuffed inside her panties, and it wasn't wet and thoroughly sticky with her juices.

'We'll soon be home,' he said, then kissed the side of her face before nibbling at her earlobe. Beneath her clothing, he rolled her clitoris from side to side. 'It'll soon be better. Just try to hold on.'

Beside herself, plagued almost to madness, Joanna fought hard to clench every muscle in her body. She was desperate to climax, but she knew that if she did, she would pee all over Kevin's intruding hand. Not to mention her clothes and the back seat of the taxi. She felt sweat break out in her armpits, between her breasts and in her groin, and she guessed she must be scarlet in the face from her efforts. She moaned like an animal as, delicately, he pinched her.

Joanna had no idea how she got through the rest of their short journey without disgracing herself. Never before had she actively had to resist an orgasm. Kevin had two fingers inside her, and his thumb squarely on her clitoris when they drew up outside her building, but when the cabby turned their way, to collect the fare, he calmly withdrew them. And using the same, sex-scented hand he proffered the payment.

Flinging open the cab door, Joanna shot from the interior of the vehicle, then ran inelegantly inside, clutching her crotch, but no longer caring if anybody saw her. Panic flared when she reached her door and realised she had left her coat – and, more importantly, her bag, containing her keys – in the taxi. She had to dance from one foot to the other while she waited on the landing. After what seemed like a millennium, Kevin came trudging slowly up the stairs.

'My keys,' she groaned, as he reached her. She was cupping herself with both hands now, convinced that she was already trickling, but hoping that the moisture she felt was merely coming from her sex.

Smiling broadly, Kevin rummaged through her bag and, when he pulled out her keys, she snatched them from him, unlocked the door, fumbling in her haste, then almost flew through her flat towards the bathroom.

'Oh God. Oh, please, no!' she whimpered when, finally sitting on the loo, she found she was too tense and too aroused to relax and urinate. Tears sprang into her eyes, and she rocked to and fro, but nothing happened.

'There, there,' said a soft, soothing voice, and suddenly Kevin was crouched beside her, his arm around her shoulders.

Beyond shame, Joanna slumped against him, resting her hot face against his soft, silky hair. There was one simple way now to start her flow and, without hesitating, she reached for it. Taking Kevin's hand, she drew it determinedly towards her vulva.

Dropping his arm around her waist again, he began, with the utmost gentleness, to stroke her. His fingertips moved in small, careful circles, caressing both her clitoris and the entrance to her urethra. With nothing to fear now, Joanna gave in and accepted the pleasure.

Pleasure indeed. Her orgasm, so long denied, crested through her like a huge, descending wave and, as her loins relaxed, her pent-up water was finally released. She laughed with relief, and with pure *joie de vivre*, as it splattered and tinkled around the pan. Kevin's hand was deluged, but he continued to rub her until the flow was all but gone.

'Good God,' she said eventually, when a stunned kind of silence fell around them. 'That was – God, I don't know what to say.' Now that the actual pleasuring was over, the lewdness of her situation reasserted itself, and her embarrassment became a flaming red miasma. Making a sound of disgust, she looked downwards at her body.

Her spread thighs accused her, as did the nectar-soaked knickers around her ankles, but most damning of all was Kevin's hand, still curved around her crotch. His tapered fingers were as soaked with fluid as her sex was. Unable to look him in the eye, she watched as he reached, unconcernedly, for a sheaf of toilet tissue, then blotted the evidence both from his hand and from her pubis.

'Hup!' he said next, slinging his arm round her waist again, then helping to her feet. After a second or two, he calmly pulled the flush. 'There. All done. Nothing to worry about.' When she finally caught his eye, he appeared serene, but still excited.

'What do you mean, "nothing to worry about"? That was . . . that was grotesque!' Shaking free of him, Joanna struggled to pull up her panties and straighten her skirt. 'I haven't urinated in front of anyone since I was a tiny child. That was the most mortifying thing that's ever happened to me!'

Kevin's lips twisted in amusement. 'Maybe so,' he said, after a moment, 'but you enjoyed it. You can't deny that.' He took a step forward to close the distance she had put between them. 'Don't try and kid me that was a faked orgasm.'

Joanna had no answer. Her own feelings confused her. She turned towards the washbasin and ran some water, then took the soap and worked up a thick lather between her hands, rubbing them compulsively, massaging the foam carefully between her fingers and beneath her nails.

'Hey! You're not upset with me, are you?' asked Kevin, coming up behind her, slipping his arms around her, then prising the soap from her grasp. 'I didn't mean to embarrass you with all that.' His breath was warm against the nape of her neck, ruffling the soft fronds of her hair in a way that soothed her. 'I thought you seemed to want it. I'm sorry if it wasn't really good for you.'

Joanna remained silent, but for a different reason now. Kevin might have certain sexual foibles, but she sensed a genuine kindness in him, too. She pressed back against him, and observed – from within the circle of his arms – as he followed her example and rubbed soapsuds over his hands.

She began to relax even more as the lather was rinsed away, and as Kevin took a towel from the rail and dried them both. He moved the soft terrycloth very gently but thoroughly over her fingers, in a way that was sensual yet understated and, as she leant against him, Joanna's desire awoke anew. She could feel his erection nestling snugly between her buttocks, its vigour undiminished by the layers of cloth between them.

'I don't really want to move,' he said, almost apologetically from behind her, as he replaced the towel on the rail. 'This feels too nice.' Shifting his hips, he rocked his hardness in her furrow, delicately caressing her anus with the knot of his desire. Joanna reciprocated, swirling her bottom against his groin.

'How do you feel about finishing what we've started?' he suggested, letting his hand fall on to her belly, then remain there. As if awaiting her permission to venture lower. 'I mean, if you don't feel like it, just say so, and I'll go.'

'No! Don't do that!'

The idea of his leaving her was unexpectedly harrowing. She could feel her sex beginning to engorge again, to flow. She imagined his penis forging into her, pacifying both the furore between her legs, and its own aching need. Her entrance fluttered as if he were already demanding admittance.

'Can I have you, then?' questioned Kevin, pushing more determinedly.

Something in Joanna's psyche protested faintly at his choice of terminology, but was instantly shouted down by the voice of lust. This was not a moment for feminist semantics.

'Yes. Yes, I do,' she answered. 'Shall we go to bed?'

'No time for that,' he gasped, already rucking up her skirt, 'I'm too far gone . . . Let's do it here.'

Joanna felt an immediate and violent increase in her excitement. She remembered Kevin's stunning performance in the sitting room, the sensation of his lips and tongue working on her clitoris. She knew that wasn't what he wanted to do right at this moment, but the frisson, the delicious thrill, was just the same.

'Oh yes,' she whispered, almost choking on her own desire as he hauled up her tight skirt again. He touched her briefly through her panties, and she couldn't help but cry out, astounded at the speed of her own rousing. Just the lightest brush against her sex and she had almost come.

As Kevin moved a little way away from her, to unzip himself, Joanna peeled her knickers down her thighs as far as her knees. She was just about to slide them the rest of the way off, and step out of them, when Kevin suddenly gripped her arm and stopped her.

'No!' he gasped, 'I like them there. You'll be tighter when I push into you. Just leave them. Please!'

Confused, and hampered by the bridge of cloth around her knees, Joanna let Kevin take control and arrange her to his liking.

Moving her by the hips, he placed her parallel with the side of the bath, then encouraged her to lean forward and take her weight on her hands, her body forming a right angle. Closing her eyes, she could imagine what he would be seeing – her bare buttocks framed by the arch of her ivory suspender belt; the soft, coral slash of her pouting vulva at the heart of things. She moaned as she felt him delicately prising open the ruffled folds of her labia with his fingers, then grunted a welcome when he pressed his smooth, hot glans inside her. The fact that he had to use his hands to guide his stiffness into her made the sensation of being entered feel twice as titillating. She cooed with instant pleasure as his firm length breached her.

He was right. She was tighter, and her own close hold on him exquisitely excited her. He was jammed into her, lodged inside her. There was limited scope for movement, but what little he achieved felt magnified. He bucked against her in a volley of short, staccato shoves, each one seeming to touch a brand new point of sensitivity. She became aware that she was mewling like an animal in heat, and that Kevin, too, was emitting a series of expressive snarls. The noise in the small room was as incredible as it was almost bestial but, at that moment, it was the sweetest music to her ears.

Oblivious to the discomfort of the position, and to the fact that their combined weight was being rocked against the brace of her arms, Joanna felt her pleasure descend upon her with alarming suddenness. One second the wild tension was building, then the next her body was spasming around Kevin's penis. Insensible with delight, she lost her hold on the bath, but somehow she didn't fall. Perhaps it was a miracle? Perhaps an angel had taken hold of her?

'Oh God! Oh yes!' she crooned, the sensations reawakening as she felt Kevin beginning to come. He was gripping her strongly by the hips with his slender, supple hands, while his own pelvis hammered powerfully against her. When he reached his peak, his fingers flexed and he sobbed her name.

The last thing she remembered was collapsing backwards, his cock still in her.

*

'Mmm . . . White chocolate ripples – my favourites,' murmured Kevin appreciatively, as he appeared in the kitchen doorway, a towel slung around his neck.

Joanna had undressed and grabbed a robe after their tempestuous coupling, and had come through to make some coffee while Kevin had a wash. As the percolator had bubbled merrily, something about the occasion had demanded biscuits – the luxurious, continental kind, a secret vice of hers she had never revealed to anybody.

'You struck me as a chocolate biscuit man,' she replied, watching him saunter into the room and sit down at the breakfast bar, perfectly at home.

'Do I get a pipe and slippers, too?' he enquired, starting on the biscuits. His eyes were twinkling again, and his air of relaxation seemed to tease her.

'I didn't mean a chocolate biscuit man in the comfycosy, fireside and feet under the table sense,' she retorted. 'To me, chocolate is pure self indulgence. A pleasure. Something sensual.' She saw him grin, and felt herself getting cross with him, and then, with herself for letting it happen.

'Oh, that's me. Definitely,' replied Kevin, finishing one biscuit and reaching for another. 'What was it old Oscar said? "I can resist anything but temptation".'

Joanna poured the coffee, considering his statement. 'Yes,' she said after a moment, settling on the other stool. 'I think I'm going to be more like that from now on. Halloran's right. I *do* work too hard. I'm going to loosen up a bit. Try new things.' The more she thought about the idea, the more she liked it.

'Like Whiteoaks?' suggested Kevin. As Joanna watched him, his gaze left her face, on which it had been focused, and slid lower, settling on her thighs, which were revealed by her loose, slippery robe. As she tried to cover herself, the silk fabric slithered further, and the golden curls of her pubis came into view. Twitching the robe back into place, she gave Kevin an old-fashioned look, which he answered with a grin.

'This is torture.' With a heavy sigh, he reached for his coffee and drained the cup. 'All that and I have to go back to the salt mines. It's a sin!'

'I'm sure you'll survive,' Joanna said, wishing suddenly that he didn't have to go, and that he would be free tomorrow, so they could sample Whiteoaks and its amenities together.

You're right, Kevin, she thought later, after he had finished his coffee and left with an almost theatrical show of reluctance. Who did know what Whiteoaks would have to offer her? If there was anything – or anybody – there who was even half as unexpected and perplexing as Kevin Steel was, then she certainly had a challenge lying ahead of her.

Okay, so I'm on a sabbatical, thought Joanna the next day, as she settled down into her first-class seat on the coast-bound flyer. As the firm was paying, she had decided not to deny herself any indulgence, and had gleefully begun amassing her expenses. At the newsstand, she had asked for a receipt, and now had a choice of two newspapers and three magazines for her journey, even though, feeling strangely dreamy, she suspected she would probably read none of them.

The only fly in her self-indulgent ointment was the lack of Kevin. She would have liked to have flirted with him as they travelled; perhaps paid him back a little for yesterday's games. She was also curious to see what he looked like when he dressed casually. So far, she had only ever seen him in a business suit. Or naked.

She saw him as a denim man. The stone-wash blue would be perfect for him; it was the cloudy colour of his large, expressive eyes. And he had the ideal shape for clinging jeans, too; narrow hips and long, lean legs. She imagined him sitting beside her, the rough fabric of a pair of 501s stretched tightly across the hard bulge of his penis.

Don't do this, Joanna, she admonished herself silently, feeling the familiar tingling of arousal beginning to plague her. The first-class compartment was relatively empty, compared to the bustle and activity of the other sections of the train, but there were still ticket collectors, refreshment stewards, and other commuters in search of lavatories and the buffet car, passing to and fro from time to time. She was not alone enough to do anything about her physical urges, especially as this was the prosaic normality of a British Rail journey, and not *Le Train Bleu*, bound for the decadent South of France.

Still, Kevin in denim was a mouth-watering concept. She moved his phantom image from beside her, to opposite her, so she could kick off her deck shoes and massage his crotch with her bare toes.

Retribution would come in the form of the refreshment trolley, pushed by a pretty stewardess, and this time Kevin would be the one forced to put his coat across his lap. To hide the fact that he was being masturbated, and that he was dangerously close to a climax.

Joanna laughed huskily, enjoying Kevin's illusory predicament, then fell silent again as an unmistakable rattling and trundling announced the arrival of the very trolley she had been imagining.

'Would you care for any refreshments, madam?'

Joanna looked up to find herself being addressed by a handsome steward. He was tall and dark, and looked good in his bow tie, crisp, white, short-sleeved shirt and black trousers. When she smiled back at him, she felt herself blushing, as if though, by some unexplained trick of the mind, he could discern the erotic tenor of her thoughts.

'Er . . . Yes,' she faltered. 'But what have you got?'

Her innocent enquiry sounded like an obscene suggestion, and made her blush harder. Fortunately, or perhaps unfortunately, the young steward remained unperturbed and began to list the contents of the trolley.

Not really hungry, Joanna took a packet of cheese biscuits, and was about to ask for a soft drink when she spotted individual bottles of wine on the lower shelf. Let Perry McAffee pay through the nose; they can afford it, she thought. As the attendant pushed away his trolley, she eyed his buttocks in his neat, black trousers and toyed with the fantasy that she had also paid for his services, later, in the cramped seclusion of the nearby toilet cubicle.

The wine was indifferent and none too cool, but it felt quite strong on Joanna's empty stomach. A few sips imparted a pleasant glow but, mindful of her experiences the day before, she drank slowly. There was no Kevin here to touch her, and embarrass her, but she still felt wary of the effects of alcohol.

What was all that about, anyway? she mused, pushing her plastic 'glass' to one side, out of harm's way. What she had done, at Kevin's behest, had been one of the kinkiest things she had ever done. Letting him play with her while she was desperate to pee, then urinating to order, while he was stroking her clitoris. Letting him control both her actions, and the functions of her body.

'Ugh,' she murmured, shuddering half in excitement, half in horror. Her state of light arousal had intensified at the thought of being manipulated. Were all men into games like that? Did they all have a 'nasty little boy' streak just below the surface? She had never really encountered it in her previous lovers, but that didn't mean that it wasn't there. What if they were all entertaining strange and grubby thoughts about the women they courted? Ideas involving embarrassment and distress?

Moving from the general to the specific, she wondered about Halloran and Davidson. They had clearly found it diverting to intimidate her.

She imagined being called into Halloran's office at a split second's notice, her bladder as full as it had been in the taxi, with Kevin. Heat rushed through her as she envisaged them staring at her knowingly, making her aware that they knew she needed to pee, and that they were thoroughly enjoying themselves. That her plight excited them. Made them hard . . .

Stop it! Don't be stupid! You're depraved! she told herself. With a sigh, she reached for a magazine, a trendy women's glossy she usually read and thoroughly enjoyed.

Today, however, the journal seemed boring after just a few pages. It was full of glib advice to career women, and the usual incessant urgings to buy over-priced cosmetics and chic but ugly clothing.

The second magazine, a businesswomen's quarterly, entertained her even less. There seemed to be nothing in either publication with which she could identify; no reference to either the strange, semi-sexual dissatisfaction that had brought her on this journey, or to her bizarre thoughts and the experiences of yesterday. It suddenly dawned on her that she was – actively – looking for something but to her dismay she couldn't work out what it was.

The third magazine seemed more promising. She had picked up *Luscious* purely on impulse, as an act of defiance against the company. It was a new women's monthly, and something of an innovation – a well-produced title devoted primarily to sex. Thumbing through the pages of near-the-knuckle articles, explicit fiction and daring photographs, Joanna suddenly froze, catching her breath, when an image and some text struck a chord.

This month's theme was 'women in the office', and the editorial examined the traditional gender rôles, questioned the political correctness of the traditional boss-and-secretary, man-and-woman rôles. One set of photos in particular illustrated a popular female fantasy.

A transgressing secretary was facing an angry boss, in his office. But what made this scenario more telling for Joanna was the presence, in all of the pictures, of a second man. Almost instantly she was transported back in time, to Halloran's plush sanctum. The two men facing her were not the two impossibly handsome models in the photographs, but her real-life inquisitors, with their flawed good looks and their genuine air of menace. She could still feel the dark, almost baleful intensity of Halloran's watchful eyes, and the slyer scrutiny of the louche, disquieting Davidson.

Of course, yesterday, in the real world, there had been no impropriety, just their peculiar insistence that she take this trip, this unexpected holiday. There had been none of the delicate soft-porn activity portrayed in these pictures. The female model in the photographs ended up stretched out on the desk in her disarrayed scanties, while one man, half-dressed, kissed her throat, and the other – completely naked – worshipped her navel.

Joanna's imagination struck out on a new track altogether.

'You've let us down, Joanna,' said the make-believe Halloran, the words as clear in her mind as if they had actually been uttered. 'Disappointed us. You must make amends.' His face, too, was clear to her, and completely impassive. He – or more properly 'they', because Davidson seemed his equal in this scenario – were going to elicit from her something that she would not normally give them, and yet Halloran's cool features showed no excitement, no passion, no feeling. Davidson's precocious leer suddenly seemed preferable.

As if thinking of him was a cue, the American, in his phantom form, now spoke to her. 'What can you give us, Joanna? What can you offer us in return for being so bad?'

In this storyline, her two adversaries suddenly had every material thing that life could offer, while she had no asset but herself.

'Only my body,' her imaginary self whispered. Or was it a new imaginary self, one not a bit like the usual, dynamic Joanna who demanded equality in every arena? As she listened to this submissive inside her, Joanna realised it wasn't this creature's first appearance. This other Joanna had already emerged in earlier fantasies. She was the one who dreamed of headmasters; of being punished. It was this woman who had allowed Kevin to embarrass and control her; this one who had just been waiting for a chance to show her pliancy.

In the quiet, air-conditioned peace, the train's gentle motion lulled her further. Closing her eyes, she let the magazine slip from her fingers, its purpose served, and watched the two men in her fantasy close in on her. Halloran came around to the front of his desk, just as Davidson rose from his seat and stood behind her. Her insides shuddered as he settled his hands on her shoulders, and when he pressed down on them, she suppressed a whimper of desire.

How could this happen? demanded her higher brain, the thinking, analytical cortex that still functioned normally. How can it be happening? she corrected it, realising that here, in the real world, she was aroused, intensely aroused, and at a speed that astounded her. Her nipples stood out beneath her T-shirt and seemed to prickle; they were so hardened, so puckered. Between her legs, her sex-lips softened and began swelling, their ruffled surfaces thickly coated with running juices. Shifting in her seat, she parted her thighs to ease the growing discomfort, and shivered again as her labia slipped and slithered.

Hearing footsteps pass alongside her in the aisle, she kept her eyes tightly shut, hoping that whoever they belonged to didn't look at her too closely. She felt hot now, in that distinctive way that accompanied arousal. She knew that her chest and her throat would be visibly flushed, and her condition apparent to even the most casual observer, given that the scooped neckline of her T-shirt was quite low. But, riding the crest of her growing dream, she couldn't leave it.

Becoming her own alter-ego, she sank gracelessly to her knees, unable to resist the surprising power of Davidson's hands. 'Good girl,' whispered the American into her ear, with the silky voice of the smoothest of all smooth operators. She tossed her head, trying to resist, but his fingers gripped her, spread around her ears like a cradle, and forced her to be still and to look up at Halloran.

Was there a spark in those calm eyes now? A tinge of response to her predicament? To her suddenly available beauty?

Locked into her daydream, she could almost feel the coarse weave of the carpet chafing her knees, smell the heady blend of two different, but equally extravagant men's colognes. Halloran was standing right over her now, looming. His expression was still unreadable, but he was extracting his penis from his beautifully tailored trousers. Davidson, strangely, was on the carpet with her, kneeling against her back, and fondling her body roughly through her clothes. As the frozen frames of her fantasy began to roll into full, multi-sensory action, his elegant hands began to play havoc with the executive look she had strived so diligently to achieve. One slid into her suit jacket, and grasped her breast cruelly through her blouse and her bra; the other began hiking up her skirt. As it reached her panties, Halloran liberated his impressive cock before her.

This was the mighty phallus that shafted willing women over the desk behind him. The raw symbol of maleness that sat at the core of all he was; the motivating force beneath the sophisticated gloss.

In both worlds, Joanna's mouth watered, and she pictured a reciprocating moisture forming at the tip of Halloran's cock. A clear, jewel-like droplet that cried out to her tongue that she lick it.

As she leant forward, Davidson's foraging hand became impatient with her blouse and tore it open. Gasping, she felt him dig into her brassière and lift one of her breasts free of it. Taking her nipple in a firm grip between his finger and thumb, he seemed to drag her inexorably towards Halloran.

'Yes!' said both men simultaneously, as her lips touched the hard flesh before her. And, as it slid into her mouth, their hands were all over her.

Halloran grasped her head for purchase and pushed himself deeper – chokingly deeper whilst Davidson squeezed her breast and pawed determinedly at her panties. Within seconds his whole hand was inside them, his fingers dividing her sex lips. She ran her tongue eagerly around Halloran's cock as Davidson took possession of her clitoris.

'This is all that clever little hussies like you are good for, you know,' he growled into her ear, the suave tones all gone now, as his long fingers pincered her pleasure bud. 'A cock in your mouth and a hand inside your pants.' He exerted pressure, above and below, and Joanna tried to groan because the sensation was so strong.

But no sound escaped her lips. In the shadow-world of Halloran's office, her mouth and throat were too crammed with him to utter a sound, and, in the hushed but rhythmically moving comfort of a British Rail first-class compartment, she bit her lip – hard – to keep in her cries. In both realities, her sex began to flutter but, just as an orgasm, an amazing, spontaneous orgasm, raced through her, a polite voice from quite close to her said: 'Excuse me, are you all right, madam?'

Joanna's eyes snapped open, and her hands flew in horror to her red face. The handsome steward was leaning over her, his face full of a mixture of concern and amusement.

'Madam?' he prompted, when Joanna found herself entirely unable to speak. 'I thought I'd better wake you. We arrive at Littlebourne in two minutes.'

'Th-thank you. I'm fine,' Joanna finally managed to utter. 'Thank you.'

As the young man moved away, he nodded cheekily, his smile all-knowing.

3

The Major's Lady

Apart from the fresh ozone tang in the air – which Joanna smelt with every breath she took – she could detect nothing particularly remarkable about Whiteoaks. It was just a medium-sized country house, in undistinguished grounds, no more than a fifteen minute taxi ride from Littlebourne station. It didn't look special enough to have travelled all this way to.

'I'll get you, Halloran,' Joanna muttered, hoisting her holdall on to her shoulder, and pushing through the swing doors that led into the lobby.

The reception area itself was much like the exterior of the building; pleasant but uninspiring. A smartly-dressed receptionist sat behind a long, low desk, and there were several comfortable-looking leather lounging couches, as well as a crowded notice board, some potted palms, and a glass display case full of a variety of sporting sundries, presumably for sale. One or two of the club's patrons were either sitting or standing around chatting, some dressed for exercise and others in ordinary clothes. A set of glass swing doors led to a conservatory-cum-bar.

Joanna introduced herself to the receptionist, and explained the nature of her booking. As she spoke, she could see the young woman's pretty face becoming more and more puzzled and, by the time she had finished, it was patently clear that she wasn't expected. The receptionist looked down at her book, frowned, flicked a few pages back and a few pages forward, then looked up again, wearing an apologetic expression.

'I'm terribly sorry, Miss Darrell,' she said. 'I don't seem to have a booking for you at all. Not under your own name, nor under the name of your firm.' She shrugged her shoulders in her white cotton dress.

Joanna frowned too. She was hot, and she felt sweaty and dishevelled from her journey. She wanted to wash her hair, have a shower and change her knickers.

'Try the name Halloran,' she suggested, watching the receptionist run her finger down the names. 'Or Davidson. One's my boss and the other's a personnel officer. Either one of them might have booked it in his own name.'

The receptionist drew a blank, but continued to be sympathetic. 'You're welcome to join the club as a temporary member, and to use the facilities –' she quoted a string of charges that seemed cheap by London standards '– but I'm afraid all our accommodation is taken at the moment. I can suggest a good hotel nearby, but it *is* the busy season . . .' Obviously unhappy, she let the sentence tail off, unfinished.

'Oh, that's just bloody marvellous!' Joanna snapped, then immediately felt chastened by the receptionist's crestfallen expression. 'I'm sorry. It's not your fault. It's just that those idiots at my firm have sent me all the way here when I could just as easily have taken a few days off at home and worked out and had a sauna at my usual place.'

Cheering up, the receptionist apologised again and offered to ring round a few likely hotels, but, just as she was about to begin, one of the women who had been chatting – a rather striking middle-aged brunette – approached the desk and smiled at both of them.

'I'm afraid it's awful of me to eavesdrop –' the newcomer said cheerfully, '– but I couldn't help but overhear that you're in a bit of a pickle. Perhaps I can help?' She held out her hand to Joanna. 'I'm Louise Walker. I live quite close to the club. Perhaps I could offer you a room for a few days?' Her smile widened, and she looked unusually hopeful. 'If you like, that is?'

For a moment, Joanna was taken aback, both by the offer, and by the woman's avid, almost acquisitive expression. Louise was staring at Joanna almost as if she wanted to eat her and, instead of being irritated, Joanna found the sensation strangely stirring.

'Joanna Darrell,' she replied, gripping the proffered hand, and making an instant decision. 'Your offer's very kind –' she glanced down at Louise Walker's left hand '– Mrs Walker. I must admit, I'm really very tempted to take you up on it.'

'It's Louise,' said the other woman. 'And I meant it. You're more than welcome to stay with us. My husband doesn't mind; in fact, I'm quite certain he'll be extremely pleased to meet you.'

Joanna felt a moment of disquiet, full of thoughts of lecherous old men with rheumy eyes and wandering hands, then told herself not to be so suspicious. She smiled warmly. 'Well, in that case, thank you very much. I'd love to stay with you,' she said, then realised she was still holding on to Louise Walker's well-manicured hand.

'Let's go then,' said the older woman briskly. 'Unless you want a workout straight away, of course?' Her bright eyes seemed to challenge Joanna, as if suggesting that to linger here at Whiteoaks was the less testing option of the two.

'Er . . . No, it's all right,' Joanna said, wondering, for just a second, why she was trusting this total stranger so completely. 'I can always come back here later. Or tomorrow?' She turned to the receptionist, who nodded approvingly, and appeared to exchange a knowing look with Mrs Walker.

'Come along then, my dear.' Louise Walker reached for Joanna's bag and whisked it up proprietarily. 'It's only a few minutes' walk to where I live, and I'm simply longing to introduce you to my husband!'

'Oh, Christopher! She's so beautiful! Quite delicious! It was all I could do to keep my hands off her!'

Louise Walker sauntered into the potting shed and stood behind her husband, sliding her arms around him and pressing her body against his strong straight back.

'I'm working, my dear,' her husband said quietly, but with an authority that made her insides quiver. 'I'm sure that Miss Darrell is quite charming, and every bit the prize we've been led to believe, but I think I can just about bear to wait until dinner to make her acquaintance.'

This was a downright lie, and Louise knew it. She could sense his impatience through the tension in his body. Christopher was never happier than when he was about to get his hands on a toothsome young woman for the first time. One who was new to his special erotic preference – a girl whose mind was virgin, even if her body was experienced. Louise slid her hands downward across the front of her husband's twill gardening trousers, then crowed softly when she discovered his erection.

'It doesn't feel as if you want to wait,' she said, smiling against his shoulder, then planting a quick kiss on the back of his neck, between his collar and his crisply trimmed hair. 'It feels to me –' she squeezed his penis through the fine cloth of his trousers '– as if you want to get to know her straight away.'

'Louise, I'm warning you.' Her husband abandoned the trowel he was using to bed small plants into individual pots, and placed his hand over hers. Encouragingly.

'She's got the most beautiful bottom, Christopher,' Louise persisted, circling her pelvis against her husband's own neat, male backside. 'She was wearing a thin cotton skirt, and the breeze blew it against her. I could see the shape of her cheeks. They're very firm, Christopher. All rounded and gorgeous. Just the way you like them.'

'I shan't tell you again, Louise,' Christopher Walker warned, his hand belying his words as he held her palm against him.

'And her thighs are lovely, too,' Louise continued, knowing he would be able to hear the hunger in her voice. 'Long and toned and lithe. Plenty of scope to get creative there, my love.'

'I don't need pretty young house-guests in order to be creative,' Christopher observed, his voice steady and controlled; and yet excited. 'As well you know.'

Louise now knew she had crossed the rubicon. She had been pushing for it and, having achieved it, her heart sang with trembling expectation. Unable to help herself, she shimmied against Christopher's bottom again, aware that, at any second, he would curtail her shameless gyrations and

turn around. Ready to attend to her. She caught her breath
as he dashed her fingers from his groin.

'And I think that there's a certain matter we ought to
deal with here and now,' her husband continued, shaking
her clinging arms off him, and turning towards her, just as
she had known he would. 'You're too forward, Louise. And
impetuous. If we're too hasty now we could ruin everything.
For everyone, not only for ourselves.'

His eyes glittered coolly in the subdued light of the tiny
shed. Louise felt the pit of her belly go soft; all golden and
melted like syrup. She clenched her fists to keep her hands
from exploring her own body; she clenched her jaw to keep
her wayward lips from moaning. In compensation, she let
her gaze travel wantonly over Christopher – her handsome
husband – admiring his noble, supremely fit body, his tanned
face, his thick, silvery-grey hair. But, most of all, she looked
at his hands. His strong, graceful hands that could wreak
such havoc, in so many ways, across her flesh. She watched,
hardly daring to breathe, as he took a cloth from the counter
and wiped the last traces of soil from his fingers, preparing
those deadly weapons for their strange but loving task.

'I think you ought to prepare yourself, my dear,' he said,
his voice mild as he studied his fingernails meticulously.

'H-how do you want me?' She felt almost beside herself
with longing now. Longing for her ordeal, and what lay
within it and beyond it. Her own hands were shaking so hard
she had to grip a fold of her skirt to keep them still. She was
the very antithesis of Christopher's unruffled calm.

'Should I really have to ask?' he said with a sigh, playing
the game with all his customary cleverness. There were
a score of different positions in which he might want her
to arrange herself and, beyond that, yet another score of

dispositions of her clothing. She might stand, bend, or kneel. He might want her naked, or in just her stockings, or half exposed, her skirt up, her pants down.

'I . . .' she began, but her voice petered out. His implacable eyes left her speechless.

'Remove your skirt, your slip and your pants,' he said, enunciating each word with great care. 'Then I'll have you across my knee.' Without further elaboration, he moved across the tiny, claustrophobic space of the garden shed, and sat down on a sturdy old kitchen chair which he had brought from the house for just such occasions as these.

Despite the fact that they had been married for over twenty years, it still thrilled Louise to disrobe before her husband. Especially when she was commanded to take off only some of her clothes. Partial nudity was more titillating to her, somehow. She was at a loss to understand why, but just accepted the effect it had upon her. She could feel her body reacting as she unzipped her sober, pleated skirt and let it drop to the earth-strewn floor of the shed. Her breasts felt bloated inside her brassière, straining against the lace and the lycra. She was no sylph – she accepted that fact with equanimity – but her ample form was shapely and well-proportioned. Her bosom was large, and her nipples were firm and acutely sensitive; a quality that Christopher was wont to exploit when she had been more than usually wilful.

Striving for maximum grace, she slid down her peach satin slip, then stepped out of it and kicked it away to follow her skirt. She paused for a moment, in her matching panties, knowing that Christopher could clearly see her dark pubic thatch through the sheer fabric, then hooked her thumbs into the waistband and pulled them down.

'I've changed my mind. That's far enough,' her husband ordered, when the panties were around her knees. 'Come to me now,' he said, holding out his hand.

Louise swallowed. Her lips and mouth were dry. This was a moment that had never once lost its exquisite, sensual charge. Shuffling a little, she crossed the small space towards her husband, then, drawn by his guiding hand, she lay across him. Her head went down; her bottom stayed high; her legs stretched out. While it was the most basic pose, it could still be difficult, but Christopher's strong, braced thighs made a stable platform.

He didn't begin immediately, but instead, did something that often seemed crueller than the thing she was waiting for. His fingers settled on the lush, white flesh of her bottom, and began to explore it slowly, and methodically, just as a blind man might have done if it had been a page of Braille before him.

The pads of his fingertips went everywhere. The full surface of her lavishly rounded cheeks where they bulged from within the arch of her lycra suspender belt; the deep creases where her buttocks joined her thighs; the central cleft, first into the slippery, spongy convolutions of her engorged vulva, then into the drier, darker crease of her bottom, where her anus pouted and tensed against his touch.

Involuntarily, she tightened her muscles when he touched her there, and she felt his instant and demanding reaction. He pressed insistently at the tiny, clenching portal.

'Yield,' he hissed, pushing harder, and forcing a digit through the muscle ring and inside her.

Louise groaned and began to squirm. Sweat pooled in her armpits, and in her groin. The nerve-endings inside her bottom were entirely confused by the determined intrusion, and sent scrambled messages speeding to her brain. She wasn't sure whether she was going to soil herself, or whether she was going to erupt in a different way, and orgasm hugely. After a few seconds of terror, she did neither of these, but still teetered dangerously towards the latter.

The finger inside her twisted slowly, and the explosive, embarrassing sensations roiled again. 'Please, no. Oh no,' she moaned, unable to keep her hips still and beginning to slide off Christopher's knee. His free hand settled squarely on her back, steadying her, while the stiff finger continued its lewd swivel.

'Do you deny me, my dear?' he questioned her, his voice sly, but as sweet as the rich touch of velvet.

'No! Oh no! Never!' cried Louise, no longer sure whether she was begging for a cessation, or for the torment to continue. Holding her breath, she fought to stay still and to master her own responses. Her whole vulva seemed to be hovering on a knife edge between bliss and perfect anguish, and her clitoris was a throbbing knot of stress.

All this and he hadn't even struck her.

A situation that was reversed with no discernible warning. One second her husband was teasing her rudely with his finger in her rectum, and the next the invasion was gone, as if it had never been there, and his flat hand was impacting severely on her bottom.

'Oh! Oh God! Ow!' she yelped, even as a second blow fell – on her left cheek, to match the first on her right.

'For Heaven's sake, Louise,' said Christopher sharply, applying a crisp volley of slaps to each buttock alternately. His hand felt as hard as a thick slab of wood. 'Don't make such a fuss,' he went on, slapping, slapping, slapping. 'It's only a spanking. If you don't shut up, I'll have to use my belt.'

I'll get that later anyway, thought Louise, gritting her teeth to stifle the loudest of her protests. A session with his belt was Christopher's favourite pre-bed activity; he preferred it to even a whisky toddy, or straight sex. And tonight, with an attractive female guest in the house, he was more likely than ever to want to thrash his reckless wife.

The smacks began blending into one big sore mass. Louise's bottom was a very hot object indeed, but the heat was having its usual delicious effect on her. Where her sex had been twitchy before, it was volcanic now, and each blow knocked her clitoris against the lean male thigh beneath it. Fighting not to cry out became a losing, and then a completely lost battle, and Louise keened loudly as her climax triggered suddenly. She stiffened and arched across her husband's rock-like lap, and her legs kicked up wildly from the floor.

When the tumult inside her had settled, Louise realised, to her surprise, that her husband had ceased to smack her bottom. She gasped when he summarily tipped her off his lap then, just as quickly, lifted her up and pushed her across his work-bench, face down, her white blouse rubbing against stray scatterings of earth, and the sap-filled cuttings of his plants.

'You've ruined my blouse,' she mock-protested, knowing he would most likely buy her a dozen blouses to replace it. What really mattered now was to have him.

'A pity,' he murmured, as Louise listened for the almost inaudible sound of trouser fly buttons being dealt with. 'It was rather a lovely one.'

Something slick, rounded, and delightfully hard presented itself at the entrance to her vagina and, with a glad cry, Louise pushed back against it, smearing yet more earth and plant fragments against her ravaged blouse.

She laughed with pleasure as her husband's cock possessed her.

*

'What the Devil's going on?' whispered Joanna to herself as she sat in the window-seat of the pretty, light-filled bedroom she would be occupying for the next few days.

Briar Villa was a large, graciously proportioned residence which stood on a promontory, overlooking the town of Littlebourne and its bay, and which had been decorated and furnished with a very obvious loving care. There were two other guest bedrooms, Louise had told her, but Joanna couldn't imagine either of them being more welcoming than the one she had been shown to. Its view of the extensive and fanatically well-kept garden was a pure delight – but at the moment it wasn't the flowers that held Joanna's rapt attention.

Below her, and oblivious to the fact that they were being watched, Louise Walker and a tall, good-looking man of a rather military bearing – presumably her husband, Christopher – were walking arm in arm across the shrub-encircled lawn, coming from the direction of a small shed at its further end.

About three quarters of an hour ago, Joanna had seen Louise slip into the same shed, with an expression of mischief on her broad, handsome face. Now, however, her hostess was still smiling – she looked radiant, in fact – but she looked as if she had been dragged backwards through a jungle. Her thick brown hair was sticking up and dishevelled, and her white blouse was heavily marked with smears of mud.

As they reached the terrace, the Walkers hesitated and turned to each other; then their lips met in a long and lingering kiss.

'Good grief!' murmured Joanna, her own jumbled feelings confusing her. Louise Walker, though well preserved, was in her mid to late forties, Joanna guessed, but her tall husband appeared considerably older. And yet the couple were kissing each other like a pair of sex-starved teenagers, their mouths in constant motion, their tongues clearly duelling. Then again, there was no reason why the couple shouldn't still feel passion for each other, and Joanna felt ashamed, as she watched them, that it should have seemed so unexpected. She only hoped that she, too, would feel so full of desire in another ten or twenty years.

As Joanna continued to observe them, Christopher Walker's hands began to travel possessively over his wife's lush body, squeezing first her breasts, then sliding down to cup her bottom. As he squeezed her there, Louise Walker began to wriggle like an eel, her pelvis circling and thrusting crudely against her husband's crotch, as if she were trying to reach orgasm by the friction of their bodies alone.

After a few moments of this, the Walkers broke their kiss, and Louise threw back her head, her face contorted.

Dear God, she's coming! thought Joanna, feeling suddenly disturbed by sensuality below her. As a cry of pleasure drifted up towards her, she moved away from the window, feeling aroused and vaguely guilty.

Sitting down, she tried to make sense of her reactions. Why should she feel ashamed of having watched the Walkers? Presumably Louise had told her husband they had a house-guest by now, so wasn't the performance they had just put on a case of pure exhibitionism? They must know that their lusty kiss, and Louise's response to it, were likely to be observed.

What have I got myself into? Joanna asked herself. She felt restless and fidgety and, as she hugged herself, rubbing her hands over her upper arms, she had an uncanny feeling that her presence in the Walkers' house was not an accident. The thought seemed irrational, but the more she dwelt on it, the more it obsessed her. In fact, the whole sequence of events – her interview with Halloran; her trip here, to Littlebourne; Louise turning up so conveniently at Whiteoaks – had a flavour of having been planned about it.

She had no concrete evidence, but it seemed unlikely that the usually faultless machinations of Halloran could have backfired. His precious Lisa was too efficient to allow that to happen.

And what of the Walkers? They had to have been expecting her. This charming room was too well prepared for it to be otherwise. The bed was made up with sheets so crisp and fresh that it could only have been hours since they had been laundered, and every convenience and practical item had been supplied for her. Fresh towels hung over the rail by her washbasin, and a spray of mixed garden flowers stood in a delicate crystal vase. There was even a selection of toiletries on the dressing table, along with an unopened box of tissues, and cotton wool balls in a coloured glass jar.

She *was* expecting me!

There was a less Machiavellian explanation though; the simple possibility that Louise Walker might be an exceptional hostess, and always kept her guest room so well appointed. It seemed only logical if she took in Whiteoaks's patrons fairly often.

Which accounted for almost everything – except for Louise's tousled hair, and the mud-streaks on her blouse.

'And do you enjoy your job?'

Joanna had to stop and think for a moment, and then said, 'Yes, Major Walker, I really do. A lot of the time it's a challenge, and mostly it's damned hard work, but on the whole, I'd say I'm very happy.'

'Glad to hear it,' said her host, reaching for his glass of wine as they sat chatting over dinner. 'But please, call me "Christopher". There's no need to stand on ceremony here, you know.'

Now why don't I believe that? thought Joanna, smiling back at him.

Between them, the Walkers had served the meal with an almost intimidating precision, and the table was set with the finest bone china, heavy silver cutlery and the appropriate crystal glassware for each very carefully chosen wine. Louise Walker had turned out to be every bit as good a cook as she was a hostess. The food – smoked salmon mousse followed by medallions of pork in a cider and peppercorn sauce – was *cordon bleu*, mouth-wateringly delicious and exquisitely presented yet, as far as Joanna could tell, there were no domestic staff in the household. Just the Walkers, on their own, looking after each other.

'How long is it since you were in the army, Mr-sorry, Christopher?' Joanna enquired, seeking a topic of conversation that might take the edge off her awareness of being scrutinised. Both her host and hostess seemed constantly to be watching her, albeit quite subtly and for a reason she couldn't fathom.

'Fifteen years,' he answered, smiling slightly. 'I retired quite early. Came into a little money and decided to resign my commission. Life's too short not to do exactly what you want to do.'

'But you did have quite a distinguished career, didn't you, my love?' interjected Louise, her smooth, unlined face aglow with genuine fondness.

'Not all that distinguished,' the Major observed wryly. 'I could have gone further. Much further. But I wasn't driven in the way that the best soldiers are. I lacked the proper discipline.' He paused, and an odd expression passed across his face; a look of half-humour, half wonder which seemed to light up his features and make him appear a decade younger. 'That's something I really only discovered after I'd left the army.'

Restraining an urge to ask him exactly what he meant by that, Joanna reached for her wineglass and took a sip of the excellent Chardonnay they were drinking. She had the distinct impression that the Major's enigmatic statement was a message of some kind, and one aimed squarely at her. She looked again at the immaculate table, and at the remains of their sublimely cooked food. Everything was in perfect, apple-pie order. Was he attempting to hint to her that such perfection was attained only by means of discipline? That his wife might perhaps not be so efficient and accomplished without – without certain incentives?

Joanna stared at her glass, and at the golden wine within it. Were they trying to drug her? Or was it her own mind positing such an outlandish theory? The weird thoughts that had begun outside Halloran's office, yesterday, had suddenly surfaced again. She seemed to see Louise Walker in a similar ante-chamber, awaiting the consequences of an untidy room, or an improperly cooked meal. Or perhaps, even, of a less than pristine blouse?

And yet she sensed no coercion, no oppression. Quite the reverse, in fact. This was most definitely a happy house, and a harmonious relationship. There was a sense of specialness and excitement that seemed out of all proportion between a couple so long married, and so clearly well accustomed to one another. Louise in particular seemed so animated she almost sparkled.

The Major's lady wore a cowl-necked dress in a fine knitted fabric of royal blue tonight, ideal for a cool summer's evening. Its relaxed cling flattered her Juno-esque figure, accentuating her good points, and cleverly skimming over those that were less than perfect. Her high, rounded breasts looked especially splendid and, as Joanna noted them, she also realised that Louise knew she was being studied.

Joanna blushed and reached for her wine again, then remembered her resolution not to drink too much – not after what had happened yesterday with Kevin.

'Do you have a boyfriend, Joanna?' asked Louise suddenly, as if she were attempting to divine the cause of Joanna's sudden rush of colour. 'I'm sure a beautiful young woman like you must have scores of admirers.'

'Well, sort of.' Joanna felt the heat in her grow. 'It's not a steady thing. Not really. We've only seen each other a couple of times.'

Would a 'boyfriend' do the things Kevin had done? she wondered. It was the wrong label for him entirely; it sounded faintly pejorative and, at the same time, far too possessive for what he was. They had had sex together – some of the most intense and satisfying sex she had ever had – yet, despite that, he was little more than an acquaintance. She wasn't quite sure she could even call him a friend.

'Tell us about him,' urged Major Walker, lifting the wine bottle and topping up Joanna's glass. Suddenly the table seemed smaller and more intimate than it had before, and the Walkers themselves seemed to be sitting uncomfortably close to her.

'Yes, please do,' echoed Louise. 'I'm sure he's delightful. A real catch.'

Joanna looked from one handsome face to the other. They both looked benign, but intent, as if the state of her love life were a matter of crucial importance to them. And strangely, it seemed important to her that she confide in them. She looked at her wine, wondering again if it were laced with a drug.

'Well, like I said, it's a fairly new thing. We've known each other a while, at work, but only just . . . got together, I suppose you'd call it.'

It was more difficult than she had anticipated to describe her unstructured relationship with Kevin. There wasn't much more to it than the sex. And slightly kinky sex at that.

'Is he good in bed?' enquired Louise, her eyes frank and bright.

'Louise!' said her husband sharply.

'It's a valid question,' the older woman protested. 'Sex is important. And I'm sure Joanna isn't a prude. She doesn't strike me as being in the least bit shy about describing her boyfriend's performance.'

The Major gave his wife a very focused look, as if he were transmitting instructions in a private and secret code. There was a complicity between the couple, the like of which Joanna had never seen before. It was an electricity, a sexual charge, and its fallout was strong and heady around her. Dismissing her good intentions, she drank deeply from her glass of delicious wine, then licked her lips.

'Yes, he's very inventive. He doesn't always want to do it in bed.' She paused, considering ways in which she could describe what she had experienced. 'He seems to like . . . um . . . Variety, I suppose you'd call it.'

'Indeed,' murmured Major Walker, his interest clearly as avid as his wife's but more subtly expressed.

Louise's brown eyes were as bright as stars, and Joanna sensed a dozen questions hovering on the woman's full, softly painted lips. Yet all she asked was, 'Is he firm with you?'

Joanna shrugged, sensing again the edge of something momentous swirling close to her. She suspected very strongly what it might be, but was afraid to trust her suspicions. Did such things really happen?

Feeling vaguely disappointed with herself she said, 'No, not really. He doesn't order me about or anything. In fact he's very egalitarian. A New Man, I suppose you'd say.' She hesitated, knowing that she was deliberately dancing around the real meaning of Louise's question. 'But he's not a wimp.'

Louise laughed softly. 'Well, at least he sounds promising,' she said, leaving Joanna even more confused than ever, and vaguely aware that an opportunity had been missed.

The feeling of lost chances intensified as the evening wore on, and the talk slid imperceptibly on to matters less contentious. Both the Walkers were consummate conversationalists and afterwards Joanna wondered if she had imagined the peculiar moments of tension and promise around the table. They retired to the sitting room with liqueurs, and she found herself describing more of her life in the financial world of the City, and her interests and pastimes in general. Louise Walker responded with tales of a pleasant but purely conventional existence, which were witty and amusing, and held no hint of anything bizarre beneath the surface.

When finally it was time to retire, Louise led the way upstairs whilst her husband set about locking up the house.

'We lead a quiet life, really,' said the older woman as she preceded Joanna up the stairs. 'Not much partying and very few visits to nightclubs, I'm afraid.'

'Oh, I don't go out all that much,' replied Joanna, unable to stop herself from staring at the curvaceous bottom swaying just inches away from her nose. It was clear that Louise wore no girdle, and neither did she display any discernible panty-line.

Is she naked? thought Joanna, feeling a wild urge to lift the knitted fabric of Louise's dress and discover the truth. Or almost naked, she amended, observing the sheer, dark nylons which encased her hostess's legs.

'Well, I'll wish you goodnight,' said Louise as they reached the landing, her voice rich and warm, and her body suddenly far closer than was normal, and deep into Joanna's personal space. Before Joanna could move away or protest, the older woman kissed her, very gently, on the mouth.

It lasted no more than a few seconds, yet felt full of meaning. When Louise stepped away, her eyes were as brilliant as they had been at the table, when the questions had been at their most probing. 'Sleep well,' she whispered, then turned away and walked off along the landing, leaving Joanna nonplussed, and touching her fingers to lips that seemed to burn.

4

A Cry in the Night

Joanna lay awake for a long, long time that night, thinking over everything she had heard and seen since she had stepped off the train.

The bedding was smooth and fragrant, and the mattress firm; in fact the bed was more comfortable than the one she had at home. It was just her vivid imagination that kept her from sleeping.

Had the Walkers really been suggesting what she thought they might have been? All that talk about 'firmness' and 'discipline'? Had it been an opening gambit of some kind? An *entrée* into something she felt confused even to think about? She had seen the edge of it in the media, and in her uninformed fantasies – particularly in the last day or so – but she had never, ever expected to encounter it for real.

She wondered what would have happened if she had called their bluff. Would she have been laughed at, or looked at with horror or pity? She could imagine them now, chatting quietly together before they went to sleep. 'What a peculiar young woman,' they might say. 'What a thing to suggest!' 'Good grief, what depraved things they get up to in London!'

Sighing with exasperation, Joanna sat up, punched her pillow into a slightly different shape, then lay down again.

'But I'm not. And I don't,' she whispered to herself. 'Not really. It's just the unexpected things that have been coming into my mind lately – And Kevin.'

The Walkers are just nice people, she told herself, stretching her legs down to the bottom of the bed, her toes flexing restlessly. They're hospitable. Civilised. There's nothing kinky here, Joanna, except your over-active mind!

And yet still she couldn't stop reviewing the conversation over dinner; looking for clues, secret signs, and heavy hints. After what seemed like an hour of this, she decided to get up and go to the window. A breath of fresh night air might clear her head.

But just as she was about to rise, a faint, but intriguing sound broke the ever-repeating cycle of her quandary.

It was a human cry. A woman's cry. And it was coming from within the house, not from outside in the garden or the lane.

Oh dear God! thought Joanna, her heart beginning to race. Like an automaton who had ceded control to a higher force, she slid herself out of bed, then stood up and went to the door. With a stealth that would have done a cat burglar proud, she silently pushed open the door, then squeezed through the narrowest gap she was able to, before stepping out on to the landing. At the furthest end of it, a second door stood slightly ajar.

I'll get caught for sure, she thought, padding along on the rectangle of fine Persian carpet which covered the landing floor. But the thin slice of light, another soft, evocative cry, and a new sound which had preceded it were suddenly irresistible to her. The heart that had pounded so hard seemed to have lodged itself somewhere in her throat, but still she crept covertly towards the radiance. She was now almost completely certain of what she would see when she reached the Walkers' bedroom door, and she simply prayed that she had sufficient self-control not to give herself away.

Within the room, Louise Walker was kneeling on all fours, facing towards the foot of the large, satin-quilted marital bed and away from the door. Apart from a pair of hold-up stockings, her high-heeled shoes, and a thin, black velvet choker around her throat, she was naked. Her full, voluptuous bottom was thrust into the air as if she were a mare or a she-cat about to be serviced, and at the crown of each perfect, white buttock was a bright patch of red.

Christopher Walker, standing slightly behind his wife, but to the side, had, by way of contrast, shed only his jacket and his regimental tie. In his shirt sleeves, and with his thick, silvery hair only the slightest bit dishevelled, he was engaged in the most strenuous physical activity that Joanna had yet seen him perform. He was striking out, at his wife's bottom, with a belt.

There was a loud crack.

The impact of the sturdy strip of leather across Louise's opulent buttocks sent the woman pitching forward and brought a thin, heartfelt whimper to her lips. Joanna winced in sympathy, and clapped her hand across her mouth but, after a moment, her gasp of shock became a silent exclamation of wonder.

With her white flesh more vividly marked than ever, the beautiful victim heaved herself up off the bed, and offered up her body again, willingly, to the lash. Her back was an elegant, deeply curved arc, and she seemed to be raising her rump even higher than before. She was inviting the blows, teasing and taunting her husband, luring him into executing yet more severe and telling strokes.

The belt whistled down again, and this time struck lower, across the tender margins where Louise's thigh and bottom cheek merged. Louise's reaction was a low, sobbing howl, but yet again, after a moment, she resumed her pose.

She loves it, thought Joanna, feeling amazed – on one level – that anyone in their right mind could court such obvious suffering so eagerly.

And yet in another, more visceral way, a tiny light of understanding dawned. Joanna had had no directly comparable experience herself, but the shame, and the delicious discomfort that Kevin had inflicted on her yesterday, gave her a sense of kinship with Louise. For herself then, and Louise now, the prime emotion was an intense awareness of yielding, a submission of the will, and it clearly aroused Louise every bit as powerfully as it had stirred Joanna herself yesterday. As she curved her back and lifted her behind higher, the Major's lady also proffered her naked sex. Her lush, convoluted niche was glistening with a clear, silvery fluid, and the fleshy outer lips were visibly swollen. She was an invitation, pure and simple; a flower of lust.

And her noble, strong-armed husband wasn't immune to the situation. As he turned to one side, to take a greater, more effective swing at his wife's bare bottom, Joanna observed that the front of the Major's trousers was clearly distended. And, even as she admired the vigorous bulge, she saw him touch it. His firm, ascetic mouth curved into a sly, secret smile, an expression of relish that again took a decade from his age.

This really is their pleasure, thought Joanna. Their preference, their secret, their shared, defining passion. It was a painful activity for Louise – Joanna didn't deny its severity – but it was about as far away from the grim tabloid exposés of wife beating and domestic violence as one could get. The Major was thrashing his wife out of the deepest of love for her, that was obvious; and she was taking it as an expression of her devotion. Proof came even as another powerful, cracking blow blazed its reddening trail across Louise's naked bottom cheeks. Her resulting cry was both jubilant and adoring.

'Have you had enough?' asked the Major, leaning over his wife's trembling, sweating form, and making her moan brokenly as he rubbed the belt against her buttocks. He was stirring the agony, Joanna could see that, but he might as well have been caressing Louise's sex. As the leather moved slowly over her soreness, her cries became cruder, more choking, and she gyrated her ample rump in response.

'More,' she gasped. 'I need more. I was greedy. Lewd. I asked too many personal questions. I wanted her.' She shuddered, almost choking as her husband used his hands too, drawing his nails over the crimson soreness of her behind. 'I *still* want her! Oh, please. Oh God, Chris, hit me hard!'

With one last squeeze of his wife's tormented lobes – which made her yelp – Christopher Walker rose to his feet and took a couple of steps away from the bed, giving himself space to wield the leather belt at its fullest extent.

'So, my dearest, are you sorry for your misdemeanours?' he asked, his voice full of affection and humour. 'Are you penitent? Do you repent for the sin of asking indecent questions of our pretty young Joanna? Are you sorry for your prurient interest in her sex life? For lusting after her? For wanting to touch her the way you touch yourself?'

There was a long, taut silence.

'No! I'm not!' cried Louise at length. A second later the belt was flying through the air again, at incredible speed, and a second after that, her face was buried in the counterpane as she muffled a shrill wail of agony.

The belt whistled again, hitting lower this time, clear across the writhing woman's anus, then again, catching her squarely across the sex-lips. Her moaning, gobbling cries were barely subdued by the cloth against her mouth.

'Are you sorry?' demanded her husband, sending the cruel leather slicing diagonally against her thighs, and eliciting yet another stifled shriek.

There was a second excited pause, then, still hiccuping and wiping her tearful face on the bedcover, Louise muttered, 'Yes. Yes, I'm sorry.'

'Then you shall have your reward for that, my darling.' Dropping the belt to the floor, Christopher Walker was suddenly all over his wife, drawing her punished body against him and kissing her hair and her neck. Her breath hissed through her teeth as he flipped her on to her back and on to the raw soreness of her bottom, but she still tried to pull him to her. Even while he was tearing off his clothes.

All his military meticulousness forgotten, the distinguished Major undressed with a speed that would have put younger men to shame. And when his garments were scattered on the carpet and he was moving over his wife again, his naked body would also have shamed younger men. His physique had a hard, toned quality that spoke of a man who understood discipline in all its guises, and Louise cooed with joy – and pain – as he pressed it against her, pushing his long, elegant, circumcised cock immediately into the opening that desired it.

For a second, Joanna turned away. Then she turned back again, wondering why she was embarrassed to see the older couple fucking. She had just watched them engage in a far more deviant pursuit, so why should good, honest, normal intercourse bother her? It was clear that the thrashing with the belt was just as much a communion for them as the passionate entwining of their bodies.

'Oh God, Chris, that hurts!' Louise half-groaned, half-laughed as her husband shafted her with obvious ardour. 'That hurts!'

'Does it really?' His hips moved faster, then paused, and Joanna saw the firm rounds of his buttocks flex as he held himself above her. 'Then how about this?' he enquired, thrusting forward and down, penetrating his wife's willing channel to the greatest depth possible, and jamming her bottom against the mattress in the process.

Louise Walker howled. 'You beast! You bastard!' she growled, churning her hips beneath him, then freezing, her thighs splayed, her toes visibly curling with ecstasy. 'Oh God! Oh dear God, Chris! I'm coming,' she cried, still motionless, until the next heartbeat, when she locked both her arms and her legs around him, and pounded her pelvis against his as if the punishment to her rump had never happened.

'Louise! Louise, my love!' crooned her husband, his own body stiffening revealingly as the tumultuous climax became patently mutual. Then their mouths met, and there were no more groans and cries, just sub-vocal meandering that expressed far more than words.

On rubbery legs, Joanna staggered away from the door, no longer with any fear of discovery. It was obvious that the Walkers' senses were tuned only to each other now, and a score of heavily armed intruders could have crossed the landing without their noticing.

In the sanctuary of her room, Joanna flung herself on her bed, her mind whirling. Now she was away from the scene, a part of her could barely believe what she had observed.

Yet it had to be real. The pictures were etched on her brain with more clarity than any erotic image she had ever seen. She couldn't deny the validity of her senses.

He had hurt her, but she had wanted it, was Joanna's simple analysis. The belt that had impacted on Louise Walker's bottom had been a thick strap of heavy duty leather, and it had been applied with the utmost force by a strong, supremely fit man. The woman's bottom must have been in some pain right from the first stroke, and yet she had still sought more punishment, lifting her flesh towards the blows and inviting them.

But how could that be sexy? thought Joanna, knowing that the very heat between her own legs made the question redundant. She didn't quite understand the cause – at least, not yet – but the effect was self evident. Her own quim was as puffed and slippery as Louise's had clearly been, and her clitoris was a hard, aching knot. A faint, blissful cry came floating to her from the Walkers' bedroom, and she longed to be Louise, squirming in orgasm beneath her beloved Christopher. Or even just to be herself, Joanna, being soundly fucked by some, or even any powerful man.

But . . .

As she slid her hand into the bottoms of her silk pyjamas, she shook her head, irrationally denying the thought that had suddenly come to her. It had to be a man who had just beaten her, a man who would use his weight, as he moved inside her, to stir the pain while he filled her with pleasure.

Closing her eyes, she tried out mental images while her finger found her clitoris.

Christopher Walker, would he do?

The Major was handsome, and she found him desirable but somehow she could not find it in her heart to claim his phantom at the very moment he was making love to his wife. Joanna knew, even as she swirled the tiny, hard bud of her pleasure, that one day she would fantasise about Louise's husband, but right now, for some reason, she couldn't.

So who then? Her mind offered Kevin, then Halloran, then even – to her amazed horror – Davidson; but somehow none of them was right. There was a man out there for her; she knew that. A man who might do to her, and for her, what Christopher Walker had done to Louise, but she sensed, instinctively, that she did not yet know him. Nor was she quite sure she wanted to.

Circling her buttocks against the quilt, she scrubbed at her clitoris, trying to imagine herself feeling pain as well as pleasure; feeling the thrust of some mystery man inside her, his possession of her body made all the more significant by the fact that he had just finished lashing her bottom.

The sensations of approaching climax began to amass at her centre but, frustratingly, she couldn't create the accompanying pain. She slapped clumsily at her thigh, but she felt nothing more than an annoying, momentary sting. Filling her mind with the picture of the Major's belt arcing towards his wife's crimson bottom, Joanna reduced herself to the rôle of observer and, in so doing, triggered her own orgasm.

Rolling waves of heat washed through her crotch, and seemed to fill her up as if she were a golden, brimming vessel. She bit her lip to keep in her fevered groans.

Something's changed, she thought, a moment later, collapsing on to the quilt that smelt so delicately of some pleasant, flowery essence. It's not the same; I need to know. I've got to know.

*

The next morning, Joanna woke up muzzy-headed from her disturbed sleep. Giving herself a climax had always ensured a refreshing, untroubled night for her, but now this no longer seemed to be the case.

She realised that some restless part of her consciousness had still been listening as she had slept; keeping her on alert for the slightest sound that might indicate more activity in the room along the hall. What was more, while she was showering and dressing it became increasingly obvious to her that Louise – or Louise *and* her husband – had fully intended her to hear them.

Thinking back, the noise had been phenomenal. Only the dead-to-the-world tired, or the deeply drugged could have slept through it. Had they been hoping she might join them? she wondered. The idea dismayed her, and the prospect of facing her hosts over breakfast was daunting. Was there any way she could pretend she hadn't heard the cries? The whistle and snap of the descending belt? No, not really. But if she admitted it, she was opening a door that she wasn't sure she wanted to open – even though it intrigued her. That way led to a loss of control and, as her entire life was built on the premise that she alone directed her destiny, to change now was scary to say the very least.

And yet, oh, how that weird scene had aroused her! It had been frightening, but she longed to understand it.

'Good morning, Joanna,' said Louise warmly as Joanna entered the dining room, dressed in leggings and a baggy top, ready for Whiteoaks and the healthy break she was supposed to be taking.

'Oh – Yes, good morning,' replied Joanna, as an unpleasant sense of *gaucherie* enveloped her. 'A lovely day, isn't it?' she went on, disgusted by the craven feelings that drove her to take refuge in the weather.

'Yes, glorious!' replied Louise, gesturing Joanna to a seat facing the window, and the verdant glories of the garden. 'Help yourself to toast and cereals. Or I could cook you a breakfast, if you'd like? We've got sausages, bacon, eggs, whatever you prefer.'

'No, toast is great,' said Joanna, quickly reaching for a slice. 'Thank you. It's what I usually have anyway.'

'Sensible girl,' observed Louise with a smile, heaping thick, dark marmalade on to the side of her plate, to accompany the several pats of butter that were already there. 'I'm afraid I like a full English breakfast now and then. More often than I should, really.' She looked ruefully at the over-indulgence on her plate. 'I'm very lucky to have Christopher to keep me in line.'

Oh God, thought Joanna, feeling butterflies racing around inside her, and suddenly losing her appetite. She dabbed nervously at the butter dish, and captured a pat for herself. She could not look her hostess in the face.

A little silence gathered around them; frantic on Joanna's part, and seemingly completely serene on Louise's. To her horror, Joanna found herself wondering what her hostess's bottom looked like this morning. And how it felt.

Louise showed no sign of discomfort. On the contrary, she appeared relaxed and full of the joys of life. Her voluptuous body was swathed in a loose silk robe, the casually arranged neckline of which displayed quite a lot of her lovely cleavage. With this, and the sexily tousled state of her thick, dark hair, 'blowsy' was a good word to describe her, and she certainly looked like a woman well-loved and without a care in the world. It was only when she reached across with the coffee pot, to fill Joanna's cup, that she exhibited the slightest trace of discomfort.

'Did you sleep well?' Louise suddenly enquired, making Joanna drop her knife with a clatter.

'Er . . . Yes, thank you,' she replied, blushing. As she retrieved her knife, a heavy, peculiar feeling settled in her solar plexus; the awareness of a moment of truth approaching.

'Nothing disturbed you then? No bumps in the night or anything?'

She's laughing at me, thought Joanna. She knows that I know. That I spied on her.

Joanna placed her knife carefully against her plate. Do it! she told herself. Do it now! Tell her!

Yet even as Joanna's tongue froze in her mouth and her heart seemed to stop, Louise set aside her plate, propped her elbows on the table and leant forward, resting her chin on her loosely-clasped hands.

'I left the door open on purpose, you know,' she said, her voice soft, husky, and very gentle.

So, it was true after all.

Joanna rearranged her plate and her knife, positioning them as if her life depended on them not being even a millimetre out of place. 'I did wonder,' she said at length, feeling, as she did so, that a great weight seemed to lift from her chest. The strain of trying to act normally in an abnormal situation was gone, but she still couldn't bring herself to speak.

'I expect you've got questions,' prompted Louise, unfolding her clasped fingers, and attacking the toast on her plate with great enthusiasm. She took a large bite, then smiled, sweeping a droplet of marmalade from the corner of her mouth with her finger, and then sucking it off voluptuously.

'I – I've got a hundred questions, but I don't know where to start,' Joanna said at last, eyeing her own toast nervously. 'I suppose "why" is the one that puzzles me most.'

Louise laughed throatily. 'And the one that's most difficult to answer.' Her eyes sparkled as she spread her hands in a helpless gesture. 'I don't really know the answer myself. I can't begin to describe why it is that I want what I want. I only know that if I wasn't beaten regularly there would be an empty space in my life. It's as simple and as complicated as that.'

'But doesn't it hurt?' Joanna drank some coffee, and felt grateful for its bracing, aromatic richness. Her mind was whirling, and her thoughts lacked structure, but the caffeine boost seemed to sharpen her focus.

'Of course it hurts,' replied Louise cheerfully, reaching beneath her bottom as if to test the fact, then hissing between her teeth at her own touch. 'It hurts like hell. Both at the time, and afterwards if he uses something like his belt. Dear God!' she exclaimed, and Joanna realised she must have squeezed her punished flesh.

Louise brought her hand up to the table again and reached for her cup, her fingers shaking visibly. 'But there's something else at the heart of the pain; an excitement that's hard to describe until you feel it. It's like magic. A sort of transformation. A pure pleasure from the most frightful of suffering.' She took a long drink of her coffee then poured more for both of them. 'I'm no philosopher –' she shrugged and smiled '– I'm not really a very bright woman at all. But, when Christopher spanks me, or whips me, or canes me, it's as if that contact between us – the bond, the very pain itself as it comes from him to me – It's as if it takes me out of myself. Makes me more than I was before.' She straightened up, wincing slightly, and made much of adding milk to the coffee and offering sugar. 'It sounds silly; I told you it was hard to explain,' she said, grinning and setting about her toast again.

'No, it doesn't sound silly,' Joanna answered.

But did it? Nibbling the edge of a slice of toast, she compared what Louise had described to her own transient feelings, last night, when she had wanted – briefly – to take her hostess's place. She had no doubt now that there was a feedback, and that the experience – or even just the anticipation of it – would arouse her.

'Do you get beaten often?' she asked, after a few moments.

'I usually need some kind of seeing to every day,' said Louise, matter of factly, pushing her plate away and drawing her coffee cup forward.

'Because you've done something wrong?'

'Well, technically, yes.' The other woman seemed to consider. 'But I often have to manufacture something, if you get my drift?' She looked at Joanna very levelly.

'I-I think so,' said Joanna. 'Is it always like last night?'

'Oh, heavens no!' Louise laughed again. 'I'd be black and blue all the time.' She reached down, touched her bottom once more and caught her breath. 'No, more often it's a hand spanking. They can be pretty painful – especially from a master like Christopher – but the effects don't last all that long.'

'Oh,' said Joanna, nonplussed again at the relaxed way in which her new friend described her frequent punishment.

'Hand spankings are convenient, too,' continued Louise, blithely, warming to her theme. 'There are no special preparations needed. You can have one anywhere. No need to take an implement when you go out; it's just skirt up, pants down and across his knee. Wherever and whenever it's necessary.'

Joanna absorbed the statement. 'Do you mean to say you've been punished in public?' The concept was horrifying, yet she felt an immediate and unsettling surge of yearning. In her mind she saw a flash frame of an assembly of some kind.

Eager, expectant faces watching a woman's bottom being revealed, then struck repeatedly. She didn't know whether the bottom was hers or Louise's.

'Oh yes, it's a treat.' Louise hesitated. 'Well, more for Christopher than for me. It's something I have mixed feelings about. It's very shaming to be exposed that way, and to cry in public. And yet, weird as it seems, it makes me even more randy. By the time it's finished, I'm usually screaming more from need for an orgasm than from the pain. If, that is, I haven't climaxed already because I just can't help myself.' She touched her fingers to her lips, frowning, looking suddenly a little bemused. 'And *that's* even more embarrassing than ever, so therefore it's more arousing. It feeds on itself.' She paused, shrugging her shoulders. 'I told you I didn't really understand it.'

The two women stared at each other for a moment. Louise, to Joanna, seemed wise and knowing despite her self-deprecating comments. She was a woman who had discovered herself, who understood her own needs and who accepted them happily, despite their strangeness. She had reached a place that Joanna had only just discovered existed.

I'm in the wilderness compared to her, thought Joanna.

I think I'm so sophisticated, but I'm really just a child. I haven't even started on the grown-up games yet.

Looking at Louise, she wondered how to broach the obvious question.

It took her quite some time to ask.

The perfect hostess, Louise showed Joanna round her large and beautifully tended garden after breakfast, pointing out the many rare plants that her husband spent so much hobby time nurturing. The Major was away for the day, attending what was apparently one of his very occasional business meetings. Although retired from the army, he was on the board of several companies, each of which furnished him with a stipend to top up an already very comfortable income.

A nice life, thought Joanna, stuffing her sports gear into her holdall, ready for the brisk walk to Whiteoaks with Louise. The Walkers were affluent, their time was their own and, far from letting themselves sink into a long, bland well-off middle class middle age, they still pursued an active and imaginative sex life. They were still in love, she realised, feeling a faint wistfulness. It wasn't clear whether the spanking was the operating factor in maintaining that love, or whether it was because they loved each other that they had sought out something new to keep them fresh.

Whichever way, it worked.

The longer she spent with Louise Walker, the more Joanna liked her and, at the same time, vaguely envied her. She watched the older woman closely as they worked out together in the superbly appointed gym at Whiteoaks. It was clear that Louise's tenderised behind gave her trouble as she went through her exercises. Yet, despite this, she seemed to wear the suffering like a proud badge of courage, an expression of her natural superiority over younger and fitter women. Joanna could do nothing but admire her.

When it came to the time for a massage, and various body treatments, Joanna expected Louise to decline and opt for a shower, alone, in a private cubicle. However, to her great surprise, Louise slipped off her clothes without hesitation, and with only the slightest of blushes when her sore buttocks were revealed.

'My colours,' said Louise softly, turning gracefully to better show off what her husband had done with his wicked, swinging belt.

Joanna glanced around nervously, but the two female attendants who had come to give them their massages seemed unperturbed by the vivid sight of Louise's bottom. It was clear that the Major's wife often sported such telling evidence of her unusual relationship, and, if anything, Joanna detected a touch of the same envy in the Whiteoaks women that she felt herself.

When she finally lay down, Joanna enjoyed her massage, but wasn't able to relax quite as much as she normally would have done. Louise's soft, purring moans, as she was treated, were distracting. The sound of them brought back all the arousal Joanna had experienced the night before on seeing the marks inflicted, and she felt very aware that her nipples were stiff and her quim was slick and juicy. As it was an all-woman environment, she and Louise were completely naked for their treatment and, as the massage was full-body, and very thorough, she couldn't hide her tell-tale state from her masseuse.

'I see that the Major was on form last night,' she heard the girl working on Louise say, her murmuring voice intimate, almost arch.

'He was indeed,' answered Louise creamily. A second later she yelped as strong fingers pounded her martyred bottom.

Joanna was relieved when her own massage was over. As she sat up, her own girl smiled slightly, and asked, 'Will there be anything else?'

For a moment, Joanna was puzzled, then suddenly the question's meaning was apparent. 'Er . . . . No. No, I'm fine,' she stammered, then hurriedly grabbed her towel and turned towards the showers. Out of the corner of her eye, she caught a brief glimpse of Louise, still on the massage table.

The older woman's face was contorted, and her punished body was moving rhythmically. As well it might have done with the masseuse's hand between her legs . . .

5

Lessons and Lovers

'Do I shock you?' asked Louise, later, as they were walking back to Briar Villa.

Joanna glanced at her companion. Had she been shocked? Or was she jealous? Envious of Louise's ability to take exactly what she wanted, when she wanted it, and without a single trace of inhibition? She had been aroused herself after her massage, and the attendant had offered a solution. But she hadn't had the courage to accept it.

'A bit,' she conceded, swinging her sports bag and feeling just as she had done as a girl – during similar confessionals, after games. 'But . . . I don't know. It's all more of a surprise than anything. I thought I was a sophisticate; completely liberated. So worldly.' The words wouldn't come out properly, and Joanna kept hearing some of the things Louise had admitted, last night, under duress. 'I don't disapprove – at least, I don't think I do,' she finished, becoming less and less sure of what she thought.

'I was like that at first,' said Louise, her voice gentle and nostalgic. 'Only I was *completely* naive. I was a virgin when I married Christopher. I knew nothing and he knew everything.

He opened my eyes.' She hesitated, a far away look in her eyes. 'I remember one of the first parties I went to . . .'

They were rounding the corner onto the lane on which Briar Villa stood, and they were alone. So alone that there might not have been another person alive in the whole world. Louise turned to Joanna, her eyes questioning.

Without thinking, Joanna nodded.

'I'd thought it was just a cocktail party we were going to, but when I got there, I discovered it was quite a bit more than that.' She paused, as if deliberately trying to pique Joanna's interest. 'I didn't know any of the people there, but I soon realised *what* they were. They were like Christopher, they were into doing anything and everything in the pursuit of sex. Bondage. Exhibitionism. Punishment. And I was a special treat for them. A relative innocent, but the star of the show.' She smiled, as if amused by her own beginnings. 'Anyway, first Christopher caned me, quite hard, in front of everybody, and that got me into quite a state, I can tell you. I was crying with the pain, but as randy as hell, and I wanted him to take me away, to one of the bedrooms, and give me a really good seeing to. Pain or no pain. But instead, he made me climb up on the table and spread my legs, then close my eyes. I was embarrassed to do it, but there was no way I could refuse. I was dying for an orgasm, and I suppose I was expecting him to fuck me there, in front of everybody. I lay there, with my thighs wide open, and after a second or two, I felt someone move between my legs, then kneel down and start licking my clitoris. Tiny fast licks, then darting, stabbing. It was gorgeous. Gorgeous. I came in seconds, so hard and fast that I wanted to grab Chris's head and pull his mouth even closer against me but, when I did, I realised it wasn't Chris that was licking me at all, but the hostess. The woman who had thrown the party. She was really beautiful; long red hair, green eyes, white skin. What she was doing to me was incredible, but I panicked and tried to pull away, so Chris grabbed me by the shoulders and made me keep still while this glorious woman that I hardly knew just went on sucking me and licking me until I started to come again. Then he kissed me, and kept on kissing me while this woman – Beatrice, I think they called her – brought me to about half a dozen orgasms. It was incredible, unbelievable, and all this time, there were about thirty other people standing around watching.' She stopped to unlatch the garden gate, which they had just reached. 'So, what do you think of that, Joanna?' she finished, turning to Joanna, who was following her up the path.

'I don't know,' Joanna said. 'I think I'm out of my depth.' She paused, feeling dazed. 'It's like an entirely new world. I'm just a novice.'

'Well, somebody must think you have potential or you wouldn't be here –' they were in the lobby by now, and Louise stopped short, dropping her bag on the floor. '– Ooops!' she said softly, turning towards Joanna, her eyes wide with a sudden, guilty amusement.

For a second, Joanna's dazed state turned to genuine dizziness. It felt as if the world was shifting around her like a circular stage, and the scenes were being changed by some unknown, godlike hand.

'What do you mean I "wouldn't be here"?' she said tightly, trying to control a sense of growing panic. 'What "somebody"? Are you trying to say I was *meant* to stay here instead of Whiteoaks?'

Louise remained silent. She slid off the cardigan she had been wearing slung around her shoulders and twisted it in her hands.

'Well, was I?' demanded Joanna, her mind flying back to Halloran, in his office, and to Davidson. Was this something cooked up by them? And if it was, then why? She could see no link between Perry McAffee and the Walkers.

'In a sense.' Louise continued to mangle her woolly. 'We know people. People who have similar interests . . .' She faltered.

'What people? You mean people who are into the same things as you . . . Punishment? Kinky sex?'

'Yes, sort of. It's all inter-related. Just variations on a theme.' Louise began folding her cardigan decisively. 'Look, let me prepare us a bit of late lunch, and we'll sit on the terrace. And I'll tell you what I can; it isn't much, though,' she finished, half defensively. 'People have to keep secrets when they're into – well, what we're into. They don't always use their real names. It's all rather clandestine.'

Lunch sounded like a good idea to Joanna. It would give her a chance to gather her wits, to formulate questions. Ones that would cut to the heart of the matter.

'Okay, I'll buy that,' she said, trying to disguise her disquiet and sound businesslike. 'Just let me slip upstairs first, though.'

'Right,' replied Louise, looking relieved. 'I'll be on the terrace when you're ready.'

In her room, Joanna pulled out her mobile phone and started dialling Halloran's number. Then she stopped, and cancelled. What if it was Davidson? The creep! Should she phone him instead? But if she did, what exactly was she going to accuse him of?

The only special reason she could have been sent here, to the Walkers' place, was to discover their secret sexual pastimes. There seemed to be nothing else to account for it. And yet it still seemed preposterous. Bizarre. Incomprehensible.

Dropping her phone on to the bed, Joanna went through into the bathroom, still considering her dilemma.

Maybe I should phone Kevin? she thought, running a comb quickly through her hair. She didn't know him all that well, but he was friendly and basically on her side. Also, and more importantly, he seemed to be something of a sexual experimenter, and probably wouldn't be too surprised by what she had to tell him. He might even know some of the same people as the Walkers did. Perhaps he could make some enquiries?

Pleased that she had a strategy, Joanna decided to defer the call to Kevin for a little while. Knowledge is power, she thought, checking her appearance before going down to lunch. First, she would hear what Louise had to say.

On the terrace, Louise had excelled herself. There was a tempting selection of cheeses, pâté and assorted savoury biscuits and breads set out upon the garden table; a spread which she seemed to have assembled in no time at all. Olives gleamed in a small china dish, and sticks of crisp celery were clustered in a tall jar. A bottle of white wine stood chilling in a cooler, and beside it was a soda siphon, and ice in a heavy glass bucket. Good, thought Joanna. She could dilute her drink, stay sharp, and find out what she needed to know.

'Dig in,' urged Louise, a little warily, and neither of them spoke until their plates and glasses were full.

'So,' said Joanna at length, savouring the tingle of wine, ice and soda on her palate. 'Who sent me here? And why?'

'Would you believe me if I said I don't know?' Louise twirled a celery stick between her fingers.

'No.'

The older woman frowned. 'It's all very peculiar really.' She took a bite of her celery and chewed it thoughtfully, for a second. 'It was done anonymously, but that's not unusual. The people we meet, the people we play with . . . Well, as I said, they often don't use their real names. The secrecy is part of the allure, part of the fun.' She looked far away for a few moments, her face rapt and dreamy, then squared her shoulders and sat up straight, as if detecting Joanna's growing impatience. 'A few days ago, Christopher received a fax with your photograph on it, that's all, so we knew to expect you, and that you'd be crossing our paths sooner rather than later.'

'That's stupid!' Joanna reached for the wine bottle and stiffened her drink, her good resolutions abandoned.

'Yes, I suppose it might seem that way,' observed Louise, with a sudden, almost smug smile. 'To an outsider.' She, too, poured more wine into her spritzer. 'To someone who's never played the game, or felt the thrill.'

'What do you mean? What is it I'm outside of? I don't understand!'

Louise seemed to think deeply for a moment, then spoke. 'Having said that, though, you're not really on the outside any more. Someone's seen you, and decided that he – or she – wants you on the inside. On the scene. A part of everything.'

'You're talking in riddles. Inside what? A part of what?' Joanna drank more wine, even though her insides were fluttering, and her pulse racing. She could feel something, some discrete state or condition hovering just beyond the reach of her imagination. She sensed – knew – that it was bound up with sex, with punishment, and with any number of weird and wonderful perversions that she hadn't yet encountered, but she also knew it was more than that. 'What do you mean when you say "the scene"?'

'I don't really think I can describe it. It's one of those things that don't seem to exist when you try to define them.'

'Jesus Christ, Louise; don't you know yourself what you're involved in?'

'It doesn't have a name,' the other woman said, beginning to look as puzzled as Joanna herself felt. 'But there's a sort of group within a group; an élite, if you will, but if you try and pin anyone down as a member, they deny it. And the whole thing disappears and you're out again.'

'But *you're* in it,' persisted Joanna. 'Now . . .'

'We seem to be; we must be, or you wouldn't have been sent to us.'

'Oh, I give up!' Joanna plonked down her glass, and began buttering some French bread.

'But you mustn't give up,' said Louise, catching Joanna by the arm. 'You'll regret it. You'll always wonder what you missed.'

'What? Having my bottom smacked? Ending up black and blue, and being used?' She took a bite of bread as Louise released her, then plastered the rest crossly with cream cheese. 'Big deal!' she exclaimed, then munched the rich morsel without really tasting it.

'How can you know until you've tried it?' Louise seemed to have lost her confusion again now, and had become, once again, the sly, seductive advocate. 'And, after what I've told you, and what you've seen, you're surely not going to dismiss the chance to try it for yourself? You don't strike me as a coward, Joanna. Not at all.' She gave Joanna a burning sideways glance. 'You're bold. You're daring. And you're greedy.'

I used to be, thought Joanna, suddenly glum. But lately my life has just been work, work, work. Plod, plod, plod. Fucking Kevin was the first risk I have taken in ages.

Thinking of the man who either was, or wasn't her boyfriend, she turned to Louise, realising that, subconsciously, she had already taken up the gauntlet. 'So how do I start? Do I get the man I'm currently involved with to spank me? He seems pretty adventurous.'

'Yes, that might be all right,' replied Louise, thoughtfully. She was clearly aware that Joanna had 'come over'. 'But if I were you, I'd–I'd take advantage of the situation I was in now.' She shrugged, then made a loose, open gesture that seemed to take in herself, her home, and her absent husband. 'Let someone experienced introduce me.'

'You mean I should do exactly what this mysterious person whose eye I've caught wants me to do?'

'Why not?' said Louise, smiling creamily. 'We know what we're doing here. We have the expertise, the equipment. Even literature you can read if you want to.' Shifting in her seat a moment, she gave a little gasp, then reached beneath herself, grimacing ecstatically. 'And Christopher's a perfect master of the art; he would never do anything to you that you're not ready for.'

Joanna took a deep breath. She could try it once. Then she would know.

'Okay,' she said firmly, looking at Louise – who seemed to be squeezing her bruises and going off into another reverie. 'But I'm going to need to drink some more of this first –' she nodded towards the now empty wine bottle '– and I want to see some of that literature you mentioned. I believe in thorough preparation, and extensive research. In anything I do!'

'You're absolutely right,' replied Louise, snapping out of her fugue and leaping gaily to her feet. 'You wait here and I'll get everything you need!'

In the end, Joanna didn't drink a great deal. The magazines and books Louise brought out, in abundance, were so absorbing that the wine remained forgotten.

The pictures were a revelation. It seemed that if the journals of perversion and punishment were to be believed, there were women like Louise – that was, those who were aroused by being punished – in every walk of life, and on every social stratum. All over the country – all over the world, even – women were baring their bottoms and allowing them to be thrashed.

And not just women. There were men who enjoyed being chastised too. Joanna entertained a fleeting fantasy of making Halloran bend over his own desk while she lashed him. Wouldn't that just teach him to play games with her life! If, that was, he was the one who had sent her to the Walkers.

Louise had claimed she had chores to do inside, and had left Joanna alone with her reading.

It must be the vulnerability, the submission, thought Joanna, staring hard at a flamboyantly posed photograph of a young woman bending over a kitchen table, her plump bottom offered naked to the lash.

The picture was crude in some ways, nowhere near as well composed as those in the magazine she had studied on the train yesterday, but there was something in the angle of the body, and in the fact that only the victim's buttocks were uncovered, that made Joanna tingle in the pit of her belly. Involuntarily, she put herself into the place of the model. She could almost imagine the wooden table against her belly, and the coolness of the air as it flowed across her bare skin.

A man would come into the kitchen. Not the undistinguished, slightly overweight nonentity in the picture, but someone dark, mysterious, and commanding. Trying to conjure more from the image, she expected to see Halloran, but the face of her unknown master wouldn't form. He was simply Everyman; tall, handsome and strong. He carried a strip of leather, coiled around his fingers, but then allowed it to hang loose as he took his place behind her.

Looking to the photograph for prompts, Joanna tried to envision her own bare rump, instead of that of the sagging, sluttish young woman in the picture. Her own backside would be finer, its shape pert and well-toned; its nakedness more alluring. She saw the pallor of her skin there; the pout of her sex, where it nestled in plain sight, at the junction of her thighs.

Would she be as aroused, when the time came, as she was now? Lying on the sun lounger, reading and wondering, she suddenly wished again that she had allowed the masseuse to follow through on that final offer. Frustration then had primed her for an even greater degree of yearning now. Inside her cotton panties, her vulva was a river, its engorged banks overflowing with desire.

Did she dare touch herself? The state of her body seemed to command it, just as surely as the master – in the magazine – ruled his slave. Her hostess was busy inside, preparing something delicious and elaborate for dinner no doubt, and there was nobody else around. It would be simplicity itself just to ease up her skirt, slip her hand into her pants and rub her clitoris.

Joanna turned the page, saw a girl kneeling on a wooden form in what looked like a mocked-up schoolroom, and her decision was made.

The picture had captured the young woman just after a blow had fallen, and her face, turned to the side, was contorted in pain. But it wasn't this that was so exciting. It was the fact that even though a set of clear weals was visible on the girl's rear cheeks, she was still curving her back and lifting her bottom towards the cane that had struck her. She was suffering but despite that she wanted more.

Staring intently at the girl's attitude, and at her marks, Joanna tugged at the fullness of her soft, flower-printed skirt, and raised it to the tops of her thighs. Still cataloguing the nuances of the image – the girl's tense thighs, her gleaming vulva – Joanna slid first one finger into the leg-opening of her panties, then two, working them quickly through her sticky pubic hair.

'Yes!' she whispered, finding her clitoris. It was a swollen, taut knot beneath her fingertips, and her whole sex flexed as she began her favourite rhythm. Closing her eyes, and still rubbing, she saw herself on the wooden classroom form, her body naked, her bottom raised, all her muscles tensed in readiness. She had no idea quite what the pain would feel like, but just to hold the position in preparation for it was enough. Beneath her fingers, her clitoris leapt and she orgasmed strongly.

The spasms were fierce, and as she lay gasping – and enjoying the way the ripples seemed to tumble in on themselves, like a hot syrupy wave – she realised with some shock that a familiar man-shaped shadow had fallen over her.

'I see you're enjoying our magazines,' observed Major Walker calmly, dropping his lanky frame on to the adjacent lounger. His eyes, thankfully, were hidden behind a pair of opaque sunglasses, which made the fact of what he had clearly just seen a little less mortifying.

But only a little. Joanna could say nothing – nothing at all – but, to her horror, she did emit a moan, and her fingers still moved wilfully inside her panties.

The moment seemed frozen, etched indelibly in time, completely unreal yet palpably happening. Her sex was still pulsing; she still felt exquisite pleasure. When it began to ebb, she turned away, her face doubly crimson with both shame and her climax. Reluctantly, she withdrew her hand from beneath her skirt.

After another unnatural pause, she felt her companion reach forward and take her wrist. Although she still couldn't look at him, she felt him lift her fingers towards his face, then felt the waft of his breath against their tips. He breathed in deeply, then laughed. Joanna sobbed, still speechless with guilt and embarrassment.

'I suppose this would make a perfect beginning,' observed the Major, his voice urbane, knowing. 'I could accuse you of being a dirty little girl and suggest that I punish you accordingly.' He paused, making Joanna quake as he brushed his lips against her musky fingertips. 'Or would that seem too contrived to you?' he asked.

'I-I don't know,' said Joanna, finding her voice at last, and hearing tones that were made husky by sex.

'I've used flimsier excuses,' replied Major Walker wryly, his fingers smoothing hers to relax them. 'And had them taken deadly seriously.'

'By Louise?'

'And other women,' he said, releasing her hand. 'Women who share – shall we call it – our "interest".'

'Did you know them beforehand?' Even though she still couldn't look at him, Joanna felt curious. Her intense need to know was still with her.

'Sometimes . . . Though not always,' he said slowly, as if reminiscing. 'Sometimes, I've found myself spanking a woman I've never met before. Either she's offered herself to me at a party, or a smaller gathering, or she's been sent.' Significantly, he fell silent, and seemed to be listening to the soft swish of the lawn sprinkler nearby, and the chatter of the birds in the drooping alders at the bottom of the garden.

'You mean like me?'

He said nothing, but she sensed the question didn't perturb him.

'Do you know who's behind this? Who it is that's set me up?' she persisted.

'Louise is supposed to have dealt with that side of things,' he said, his voice giving the impression that he was trying to sound impatient, and perhaps a little testy, but that somehow that, too, was another contrivance. Maybe he really was impatient? Impatient to get her pants down and start spanking her?

'Why keep asking questions, Joanna?' he said suddenly. 'Don't you like mysteries? Does everything have to be explained? Accounted for?'

'It's my job,' she said, feeling a surge of defiance, 'to analyse. To account for things. To know the whys and wherefores. The causes and effects. I can't help doing it, it's what makes me what I am.'

'Well, if it's understanding you're after –' He paused, slid off his sunglasses and looked at her very directly. His eyes were filled with the same fire-like intensity that had pervaded

Louise's expression earlier. '– I can help you. You know that, don't you?'

'Yes,' she said, her heart full of butterflies, her head full of fear and trepidation.

'But "yes" in what sense?' he asked, his voice so soft she had difficulty hearing him.

'In every sense,' she said, feeling a safety net slip away from underneath her.

'Come on then,' he said crisply, rising to his feet and holding out his hand to her.

Joanna took it and let herself be helped up and led into the house.

'We won't be long, my dear,' said the Major to his wife as they passed the kitchen door. Joanna looked into the light, airy room, and saw Louise, in an apron and with floury hands. The other woman smiled complicitly, then ran her tongue slowly over her lower lip as if expressing a hunger.

'Don't worry,' she called out to Joanna. 'He knows what he's doing.'

Which is more than can be said for me, thought Joanna, as she realised they were going upstairs to her bedroom.

'Has anyone ever seen to you before?' Major Walker asked as the door closed, and they were alone in Joanna's room.

She was puzzled for a moment, then understood. 'Seeing to' didn't mean sex in this context, but was yet another term for punishment. It had a vaguely benign sound to it, invoking a sense that a spanking might be thought of as a therapy of some kind. Something beneficial that might be performed on someone you cared for.

She shook her head.

'Wonderful!' The Major's voice was full of warmth and genuine happiness. 'There's nothing nicer than an initiate.

A tender, untouched bottom.' He crossed to the windows, and drew the curtains slightly. 'There, that's better. Subdued light might make things a little easier for you.'

It was like the first time you found yourself in a bedroom with a new lover, thought Joanna and, on reflection, she supposed that was exactly what it was. Eroticism, but expressed in a different way. For an instant she thought of Kevin, remembering what had happened the first time she had been with him. That certainly hadn't been an average occurrence, either. What would it have been like, she wondered, if he had wanted to smack her bottom instead of to lick her sex, then fuck her?

'Are you quite here?' queried Major Walker, shaking her from her thoughts. He had removed his jacket and folded it neatly over the edge of the bed and, as she regarded him warily, he sat down on the edge of the mattress – his body sternly masculine against the softness of the Victorian chintz.

'I'm sorry,' said Joanna, aware that subconsciously she was already halfway into her rôle.

'What were you daydreaming about?'

'About a man I've been seeing,' she admitted.

'A man you've been having sex with?'

'Yes.'

'What were you doing? Imagining that he was the one who was going to spank you?'

'No! Yes! Sort of.'

'Well, you'd better come over here, then,' the Major said evenly. 'I'll soon focus your attention for you.' When she reached him, he took both her hands and made her stand before him, like a recalcitrant child before its guardian. 'Look into my face first, Joanna,' he instructed her. 'Make sure you know who it is who is going to punish you.' He paused; looked thoughtful. 'I'm sure this man will get his turn soon enough, as will others, I suspect. Many others.'

What others? I'm only going to try this the once, she wanted to say, but couldn't, knowing that it might not be true. She felt his hands around hers like a pair of steel bracelets, felt his eyes boring deep into her soul.

'Now, my dear, dear Joanna,' he said, his voice strong yet somehow also coaxing. 'Let's have you across my knee.'

He wasn't rough, he wasn't forceful, and he didn't even seem to push or pull her at all, but, almost before the words were out of his mouth, Joanna was face down across Major Walker's lap. In the first few seconds she felt unsafe, with her weight precariously distributed, but then, with a clever shift of his thighs, he steadied her.

He patted her back in a gesture of reassurance. 'There, now; let's see what we've got, shall we?' His voice was warm, almost avuncular, and it regressed Joanna to the days of her childhood. Or at least to a version of her childhood. There had been no spankings in her home, and none necessary. The only discipline had been that which she had imposed upon herself, a regimen purely figurative, not physical.

Beginning to shake, she felt her thin skirt being lifted away from her legs and her buttocks, then folded neatly at her waist, out of the way.

'Lovely,' murmured the Major, touching her once more, his fingers drifting meditatively across her bottom cheeks. He seemed to be testing the firmness and resilience of the flesh he was about to belabour, assessing its sensitivity and its likely tolerance of suffering. She caught her breath when his fingers hooked the elastic of her knickers and began to tug it over her buttocks to uncover her. 'Lovely,' he whispered again, the task completed.

Joanna stared fixedly at the carpet just inches from her nose, concentrating on its elaborate Gothic lily design as if it were a mandala containing the secret of all existence. It was either that or laugh – or perhaps cry – at the predicament she found herself embroiled in.

'Ludicrous' was the best word to sum up the situation. She was face down over the knees of a man she hardly knew, waiting to have her bottom smacked. It was like a scene from an inferior Sixties farce, and the sooner they started, the sooner the whole silly business would be over.

'Are you going to get on with it, then?' she enquired tartly, twisting around to glare up at her would-be chastiser.

His eyes twinkled in the subdued light, and his puckish smile gave his face a younger look. 'Certainly,' he said, and then commenced.

The first slaps were gentle, little more than pats, and strangely sensual. For a moment, Joanna wanted to laugh, thinking how foolish she had been to be frightened, when the sensations were more pleasant than painful. The acute arousal she suddenly felt was disturbing, though, and involuntarily, she began to work her hips and sigh.

'Are you enjoying yourself?' enquired the Major, catching her with a stroke that was real this time, and much harder.

'Yes!' she gasped. The pain had taken her by surprise . . .

'I see.' Almost contemplatively, he caught her with another heavy spank. 'How about now?' He hit her again, twice in quick succession this time, and with increasing force.

'Yes!' she cried defiantly, her bottom-cheeks stinging.

The blows continued, in a stately, even tempo, getting sharper and sharper each time they fell. He was hurting her now, making her bottom jounce and smart as he covered its whole surface in a methodical circular pattern.

'Are you still enjoying yourself?' he asked again after a couple of minutes, continuing to smack her with relish and vigour.

Was she? She couldn't tell any more. Her buttocks were glowing, throbbing; pounding with the hot blood that raced through her beaten tissues. It *did* hurt, more than she would have thought possible, yet she still couldn't give a simple answer.

'No!' she yelped.

A resounding, square-on spank hit her right on the join of her left buttock and her thigh.

'Yes!' she cried wildly as its impact resounded through her, then was lost in the shock of the next blow. He had caught her on her right side with a perfectly matched stroke, exhibiting an artistry she admired despite the pain.

'I don't know,' she finished, choking in horror at her own pathetic tears.

Why am I crying? she thought, while the spanking went on evenly and inexorably. All through her life, she had been brave, tough almost; not one to fall apart in times of stress. Least of all when it was inflicted by a man.

Yet she couldn't help herself. The shame and ignominy of her position, the pulsating inflammation in her buttocks. These were upsetting her, but they didn't explain her sobbing. The weeping, she realised, came from an anger within her. She was furious with her own weakness, and confused by it. She was cross because the pain had turned her on.

But I'm not a submissive! I'm no man's slave, no weak and wimpish bimbo who gets off on being dominated and exploited. So why is my sex all wet and running again? Why am I aching more between my legs than I am in my buttocks? Why do I want this man so much, this stranger who is old enough to be my father?

As if aware of her every thought, Major Walker suddenly paused in his unrelenting rhythm. 'Are you all right, my dear?' he enquired, his hand resting caressingly upon her, its heat matching the heat it had created.

His hand must hurt too! The sudden thought amused her, shook her out of her self-pity and confusion.

'Yes, I-I'm okay,' she said, keeping quite still lest her movements reveal her passion. She really did want Major Walker, she realised, but there was also Mrs Walker to consider. It was a moot point as to whether allowing a man to fondle her bottom and spank her could be classed as seducing him, but allowing him to penetrate her was fairly unequivocal. She would feel truly guilty if she bedded Louise's husband.

'How do you feel?' the Major persisted, leaning closely over her. She could feel the brush of his well-pressed shirt against her soreness. 'Tell me honestly. No white lies.' His lips were almost touching her ear, and his hand, which was still against her buttocks, flexed and gripped.

A fresh jolt of sensation rippled through her; a new heat from his clasping of her bottom. Sinking into her vulva, his fingers made her gasp, and ripple there, too. She felt her labia engorge and her clitoris jump and stiffen.

'Joanna,' the low voice prompted as the fingers plagued her.

'It hurts!' she keened, her breath catching as his hold tightened and his thumb-tip brushed her anus. Trying to shift her hips and get away, she felt herself being poked in the abdomen by the bulge of his erection, then heard a ragged gasp as she moved herself against it.

The Major did not lose his composure, however, and his voice, when he spoke again, was quiet and calm.

'That isn't all though, is it?' he said silkily, his thumb relocating against her tender rear portal. When she didn't answer he pushed insistently against it.

'When you allow a man – a Master – to spank you, Joanna, you must yield all to him. Surely you realise that?' he went on reasonably. 'Half measures could be construed as fickleness. Wantonness. Entrapment.'

'But–'

'But what?' The pressing thumb seemed a mile wide now, and twice as determined. He was working it against the tight muscle ring, rocking it insistently.

'I only agreed to a spanking,' she hissed, her jaw clamping tightly as the thumb went right inside her and his fingers spread out across her bottom cheek, curving inwards to create four foci of heightened pain.

'I said I'd help you, Joanna. That I'd see to you,' he purred. 'I don't recall either of us setting any limits.'

6

Looking for Limits

There had been limits, of course, but neither she, nor Major Walker had set them, Joanna realised. The boundaries of what could and could not be done to her had been decreed by an outside agency, the same unnamed controller who had sent her to the Walkers in the first place.

Was it Halloran? Or was it Davidson? It could be either, or both, or neither one of them. There could well be some other figure who stood beyond them, wielding his – or her – power from the shadows. Someone she hadn't yet encountered. Someone whose dictates had made the Major contain himself.

After her spanking, Major Walker had urged her back on to her feet again, with his intruding thumb still lodged inside her body. She had been deeply ashamed at how pleasurable that had felt, and had turned away from him to hide her scarlet face.

'You're very aroused now, aren't you, Joanna?'

The question had been redundant. She had revealed herself completely throughout the spanking, and during its interstices. Her visible wetness, and her sensuous moans had been too conspicuous to mistake. Her skirt had dropped back down around the site of the insult now, but her heaving chest and her erect nipples still betrayed her.

So why then, when her arousal was so evident to both of them, did she find it so impossible to admit to it?

'Joanna,' he had prompted softly, tightening his grip upon her body. His thumb moved inside her, making her groan aloud with desire, while his nails raked the redness of her bottom.

'Yes! All right! I *am* aroused!' she proclaimed defiantly. 'Can't you tell?'

'So what is it that's made you aroused?' he enquired, ignoring her bravado. His free hand settled just above the tangled bunch of her panties where they rested at her knees, then slid up and around to touch the soft hair at the juncture of her thighs. 'The spanking? Or what I'm doing now?' He wiggled his thumb and at the same time sought her clitoris, working his fingers through her sticky pubic bush.

'I don't know – both!' she gasped, as his fingertips found their target. When he started rubbing her, she swayed and almost fell.

The strokes that passed across her clitoris were light and shallow, and diabolically teasing; yet they seemed to rebound off the obstruction in her bottom. The presence of Major Walker's thumb managed to both agitate and pacify her at the same time, setting a torch to something that was already dangerously sweet. Without thinking, she bent her knees to improve his access.

'Oh, yes . . . Yes . . . Yes . . .' she chanted, her excitement growing, but, as her orgasm loomed, he withdrew his hand from her quim.

This retreat seemed to hurt more than the soreness of her buttocks did. 'What's wrong?' she demanded, her voice a strangled squeak. 'Why have you stopped? Oh God, I need to come . . . Why have you stopped?'

'You must ask for what you want, Joanna,' the Major said quietly, his thumb rocking. 'Say "please"; it's merely a matter of simple good manners.'

Suddenly, Joanna's mettle was stung. He was enjoying himself, the bastard. He had broken their unspoken ground rules, and was subjecting her to a gross indignity. And, on top of that, he expected her to plead with him!

'Go to hell!' she said, trying to shake herself free and only making matters worse. His rigid thumb jiggled in its lewd, dark niche, making her almost choke with reluctant pleasure. At the same time, he dug his fingers into her bottom cheek.

'Temper, temper,' he chided, using his crude grip to turn her sideways and pull her back against him. His lively, bulging hard-on was a brand of fire against her and, hissing with fury, Joanna tried to hit out and force him to release her.

'Will you stop that?' he said suddenly, his voice calm yet menacing. For a moment, she seemed to see him clad in khaki, his fine eyes narrowed beneath his dapper officer's cap, his aura of command complete and unrelenting. Her body went limp, and she dropped her hands to her sides.

'That's a good girl,' he said, still holding her but no longer so fiercely. 'Now I want you to reach around and unfasten my trousers, if you will? I'm feeling a little uncomfortable, although I expect you've already noticed that?'

Not as uncomfortable as I am, thought Joanna, as she swivelled round – still speared – and obeyed him. It was impossible to look her captor in the eye, so she concentrated on the area of operations, watching her own hands as they negotiated his clothing. She fumbled a little – never having had to undress a man under such duress – but soon she was easing his erection from the fly of his white briefs.

And a handsome erection it was, too. Major Walker sported a stand more vigorous than many of the younger men she had had sex with. His shaft jutted proudly from the opening of his flannels, its rosy tip swollen and shiny with clear juice. She was just about to fondle it, when he caught her hand in his.

'No no, that's not what I want this time, young lady,' he said genially, directing her hand downwards. 'Pull your skirt up for me again, will you?'

Again, one half of her wondering why she was suddenly so compliant, she obeyed him, lifting her thin cotton skirt to her waist.

'There, that's it. Now hold it up with one hand –' He paused, then slung his free hand around her, pulling her close to press his penis against her thigh '– and use the other between your legs, the way I did.' Already breathing heavily, he leant his head against her arm.

What an odd tableau this must be, thought Joanna dreamily, as she began to slick her clitoris. A middle aged man and a younger woman, half entwined, yet not fucking; each rubbing themselves to pleasure in different ways. There was something almost tender in the way Major Walker held her, his silvered head resting against her body; a feeling quite at odds with other aspects of their pose. His thumb still plugged her, its mass rude and thrilling in her rectum, and his prick jerked and plunged against her thigh. With each thrust it rubbed against her pulled-down panties. In wordless submission, she leant inwards to increase the friction.

Between her own legs, the fires were burgeoning too. It was difficult to masturbate the way she usually liked to, but the awkwardness and constriction of her position seemed to enhance the sensations. Her quim aflood, she swirled her clitoris in tiny ragged circles, then cried out when a sudden climax claimed her.

The pleasure was brief and sharp, spiked by her throbbing bottom and the living bung inside her and, as it began to fade, she felt the Major coming too. His penis jumped against her body like a captive serpent, and after a second or two, warm semen kissed her thigh. As it trickled over her skin and on to her panties, he sighed and hugged her to him, slipping his thumb out of her bottom to hold her better.

Sitting up now, on the high old bed, Joanna looked down it towards the spot where her disciplinarian had sat earlier, and where she had stood, like a helpless plaything, between his thighs. When pleasure had run its course for both of them, Major Walker had given her a chaste, almost paternal kiss, then – whilst refastening his trousers – he had suggested she take a rest before dinner. Joanna wondered if he knew just how much she needed one.

What had happened here in this room could not be glossed over. All parties in the house were aware of her spanking, even the one who hadn't participated. How on earth could she face the Walkers over dinner after this? Slipping down on to her feet, Joanna hoped – no, more than hoped – that Louise was accustomed to such arrangements. Things could be awkward if this was some sort of lapse on the Major's part.

But what about all that business with the masseuse? reasoned Joanna, as she unbuttoned her skirt and let it slip to the floor to join her panties. She moved to the elegant cheval glass in the corner of the room, and studied her reflection. She was completely naked below the waist and, pivoting like a dancer, she presented her bottom for inspection.

A veil of pink lingered where the Major had smacked her but, to her surprise, it was already fading.

An expert, eh? she mused, reaching around and running her hands sensuously over her slightly glowing buttocks. There was still a transient, almost ghostly tingle in the flesh there, a faint warmth that was erotic when she fingered it. On an impulse, she raised her hand and brought it down in a fierce slap across the already punished area, then yelped like a scalded puppy when hot pain flared once again.

Why do I like this? she wondered, admiring the increase in radiance. The heat, and the simple fact that she had smacked herself had made her feel aroused once more and, when she parted her legs and touched her vulva, she found it wet.

It doesn't make sense, she thought, still entranced by her own lewd reflection: her long legs, her sticky thighs, her bare and pink-tinged bottom.

'It doesn't make sense,' she repeated aloud, beginning to stroke herself slowly, almost absently, making a slicking noise with her own flooding wetness. With her left hand, she landed another slap against her buttocks, hitting the other cheek this time, and caught her breath as her arousal ramped up sharply.

'Oh God,' she moaned, slapping again, and speeding up her rubbing. Her movements were clumsy and uncoordinated now, but still effective. Tension was building in her sex, and she was getting wetter and wetter – and it was the renewed heat in her bottom that was doing it. Sliding, half falling, to the floor, she felt the soft carpet beneath her face as she contorted. 'Oh God,' she whimpered again, and kept on smacking and rubbing in graceless hunger.

As she orgasmed, she dug her nails into her pain.

*

'So, how are you feeling *now*?'

Joanna didn't quite know how to answer the Major's question. They were on the terrace together, taking the evening air before dinner. Below them and to their left, Littlebourne's short promenade was a necklace of winking jewels in the twilight. The town's fanciful illuminations were nothing special, really, but to Joanna, at this emotive time of day, they suddenly seemed magical.

'You keep asking me that,' she said, still staring at the lights, as if their multi-hued radiance might serve as a meditation aid and grant her mental clarity.

'At such an early stage, you need constant monitoring,' observed the Major mildly. He had changed his clothes since they had been together earlier, and was wearing a dark, polo-necked sweater with a blazer and dark trousers. It was an ensemble which only increased his subtle dominance.

'I feel all right,' she said, still looking towards the lights but not really seeing them any more. 'A little sore, but good, in a strange way.'

'I'm glad,' said the Major, giving her a quick smile and then turning towards the patio table and taking a bottle of champagne from the cooler that stood there. 'Glad that you enjoyed the experience. Not every woman does. Sometimes even the ones who come to spanking voluntarily don't like the real thing when they get it.'

Do women really seek out something as bizarre as this? thought Joanna, watching her companion deal deftly with the champagne, popping the cork and pouring the wine with no spillages. She tried to imagine a situation in which a woman, perhaps even herself forty eight hours ago, might have a sudden, but compelling urge to experience pain.

'It doesn't make a lot of sense to me, though,' she mused aloud, as the Major handed her a glass of the sparkling, straw-coloured wine.

'Does it have to?' he countered, touching his own glass to the side of hers in a gentle toast. Joanna realised she was just standing there, holding the champagne flute, still trying to analyse what it was that had changed inside her. She took a sip of wine, wishing there was self-knowledge within its bubbles.

'I think I'd feel easier with myself if it did,' she said at length. For the first time in her life – or perhaps the second or third, she thought, remembering Kevin – she was caught up in something beyond her control. The idea made her shiver.

'Are you cold?' enquired the Major.

'No. Thank you,' she murmured. Her summer dress was light and floaty, with a drop waist and cap sleeves, in a soft shade of lemon, but it was perfect for the balmy summer night. She wore only a G-string beneath it, but she was perfectly warm. 'I'm fine.'

The Major eyed her speculatively, but said no more. Instead he retrieved the champagne and topped up her glass.

'Are you sure you can't tell me who's behind all this?' Joanna said suddenly, just as recorded music began to play somewhere within the house. Louise had put on a CD or a tape, something delicate yet stately played by a small chamber orchestra.

'I wouldn't even if I could,' replied the Major, catching Joanna's eye, his expression wryly amused. 'As I think my wife has already told you, the more one pushes, the less one discovers. The only way is to go with the flow, and let things happen.' He took a sip of his wine, then stepped forward and touched Joanna's arm encouragingly with his free hand. 'Come along, let's go in and enjoy our dinner. You must be hungry and if the smells of cooking are anything to go by, we're in for a treat.'

It was a diversionary tactic, but Joanna realised she was hungry – famished even – and allowed herself to succumb to it. There seemed no way to prise any additional information from either her host or her hostess, so all that was left to her was to follow the Major's advice, and let events unwind at their own pace. For now.

Louise had excelled herself again, and the meal they now consumed was light, beautifully cooked and perfectly presented. As she enjoyed a chilled consommé, then a delicately sauced fillet of sole, Joanna was aware, once more, of a strange, pervading sense of dual reality.

On one level she was eating delicious food in the company of urbane and convivial new friends, and discussing music, the theatre, and current affairs; on another, purely emotional level, she was conscious of being constantly scrutinised. From time to time, she would look up from her plate and find the eyes of both the Walkers on her. They seemed to be watching for any changes in her behaviour; in her responses. In Louise in particular, she perceived an excitement, an expectation. It was as if her hostess were just waiting for her to make any reference to what had happened earlier, in Joanna's bedroom.

I shan't tell you, thought Joanna, steeling herself. I'll just act normally, as if it were nothing new; just another kink amongst many.

And yet the precarious interpersonal tension was exciting. As the conversation turned to Joanna's work, and her thoughts on investments and financial trends, she grew increasingly scared of letting her poise falter. Of letting slip some word or phrase that could be construed as a *double entendre*, or an allusion to what the Major had done to her.

In the end it was Louise who asked the question, when they were settled in the sitting room with coffee and a selection of liqueurs.

'So, what did you think of your first spanking then?' she enquired, her voice level, almost casual. She was sitting very far back in her armchair, her shapely legs crossed, her body sensuous and relaxed beneath a full-skirted black silk dress.

Joanna almost choked on her Tia Maria, and had a great fight to retain her equilibrium. The sense of anticipation, and scrutiny, seemed to thicken and intensify exponentially. The Walkers, such a civilised and well-mannered couple, suddenly seemed to become a whole legion of salacious degenerates hanging on her every word. Waiting for titillation; and for a breathless confession.

Swallowing the sweet, fiery fluid, Joanna paused, and let it calm her. 'I enjoyed it,' she said boldly, admitting the truth.

'Oh, I thought you would,' replied Louise smugly, adjusting her position slightly in her chair, as if she were suddenly uncomfortable. Joanna watched as her hostess recrossed her long, stocking-clad legs, then sipped her own liqueur, her eyes closing in appreciation. Or excitement. Or something.

She's as aroused as I am, Joanna thought, as the truth of her own condition came home to her. In the bodice of her light dress, she could feel her breasts slightly swollen, the nipples peaking and, between her legs, her flimsy G-string was getting wet. The feeling of being watched was a piquant spice to her senses.

'And would you like more?' enquired the Major, from across the room, his quiet voice only heightening the stimulation.

Would she?

Joanna raised her glass to her lips, then realised it was empty. Feeling bemused, she looked at it, then put it on the occasional table beside her chair. Immediately, Louise rose and fetched the decanter to provide a refill.

No one prompted her to answer, but Joanna felt the Walkers' expectancy pressing down on her like a weight. Did they mean *now*? She suspected that they did. And that Louise should remain, and watch the procedure.

Yes, Joanna thought, looking at the smiling faces of her host and hostess. That was it. She was to repay Louise for the performance of last night with one of her own. Here and now in this room. If she said 'yes', if she so much as nodded her head, they would expect her to comply immediately by going over the Major's knee.

Would they also expect her to strip? she wondered. Or just to lift her skirt? She coloured with embarrassment, wishing she hadn't chosen such abbreviated underwear, then realised that, subconsciously, she had worn the G-string on purpose, for just such an eventuality. She imagined the sight of the thin, silk cord passing up between her buttocks, and she knew it would turn Louise on. Increase the arousal that was so evident already.

Joanna swallowed, feeling as if she were about to perform some great feat of bravery or exertion. Her heart was pounding in a way it had not done almost since girlhood. She suddenly pictured herself on the games field, about to launch herself forward for the long jump.

'Yes!' she said, the single word almost robbing her of energy.

Before she could backtrack, before she could renege, she brought her balloon shaped glass to her lips, and swigged down the sweet liqueur within, letting the rich, coffee aroma revive her strength.

'Yes,' she reiterated, rising to her feet and handing the glass to Louise who still hovered beside her. 'I'd like to try again; right now, if you're willing?' She glanced across at the Major, who had also now risen to his feet.

'I am willing,' he said, with a little nod of affirmation, 'But sadly it is not my turn.' He gestured towards his wife.

'I-I . . .' Joanna faltered, feeling her small fund of confidence begin to melt. 'I meant –'

A woman. She was going to be spanked by a woman. More than ever, the act of punishment became, in her mind, an act of sex. And though she herself didn't have lesbian tendencies, at least not overt ones, Louise certainly did. The Major's wife was going to touch her, to handle her body, to lay a strong hand across her flesh in a fierce caress.

'What's this?' The Major's voice was gently taunting. 'A lack of nerve? Surely not?'

Joanna straightened her stance. She was a sophisticate, wasn't she? She could do this. It wouldn't be difficult. In her mind she could make Louise Walker into a man.

'No, I'm fine,' Joanna said, making her tone as calm as she could, despite the beating of her heart and a feeling of light-headedness. 'But I will have a little more of that.' She gestured towards the decanter of Tia Maria.

When Louise had poured the liqueur for her, Joanna drank it down rather quickly. She was aware that a new boundary was about to be crossed. Her previous limits exceeded. She put aside the glass, hoping her determination was sufficiently stiffened.

The Walkers both sat down again, the Major returning to his armchair, and his wife taking position on the sofa, where Joanna had been seated, smoothing her black silk dress across her knees as she did so.

'Come here,' said Louise, patting her lap.

Joanna took a step, then laid herself gingerly over the other woman's thighs. As she adjusted her balance, she felt a hand stroke her bottom, and she quivered in dread anticipation.

'No need to worry,' Louise murmured, then in a quick, businesslike movement, she uncovered Joanna's all but bare bottom. 'Oh, my dear, this is so naughty,' she continued, touching the narrow silk thong of the G-string. 'Do you often wear undies like these?'

'N-no,' answered Joanna, her voice trembling, too. Louise was caressing her now, sliding knowledgeable hands over her naked bottom lobes, and occasionally tugging on the cord that nestled between them. 'Only on special occasions.'

'Well, we'd better make this a really special one, hadn't we?' said the Major from his seat a few feet away.

And, as Joanna looked up and sought his laughing eyes, the first smack fell like fire across her buttocks.

'So what happened next?' enquired Kevin, easing forward in his garden chair, his eyes luminous.

'She spanked me, of course,' said Joanna, pausing to sip her tea.

They were sitting in the communal garden to the rear of Sweigert Mansions, where Joanna's flat was situated, and she had been back from Littlebourne just half a day. She had left the Walkers far sooner – she suspected – than she was supposed to, but the need to know who had sent her to them in the first place was so insistent that she couldn't stay any longer. No matter how much she liked them, and their strange and painful games.

'And?' prompted Kevin.

'And what?' she replied, being deliberately obtuse. Kevin was doing his best to control his eagerness to hear her account, she could tell, but if he got any keener she could swear he would soon be drooling.

'Well – was it different? Was she better at it than her husband, or worse?' His teacup rattled in its saucer, and he put it aside, as if his body were too keyed up to continue to hold it safely. 'Did you have sex with her when she'd finished spanking you?'

'Is that any of your business?' Joanna observed sharply, although inside, she too felt excited.

'Well, you were the one who started telling all,' Kevin countered, grinning.

He's right, Joanna realised. Somehow she had moved from the general to the specific – and the intimate – with no particular encouragement on his part. It was only when the narrative had already become sexual that he had prompted her to expatiate in full and lurid detail. If she balked now, he could accuse her of being the worst kind of cock tease. An obscure sense of honour stabbed her conscience and, staring fixedly at the reports scattered on the grass around her chair, that she had promised herself she would work on, she began speaking in a low voice, acutely conscious that her neighbour from the flat below was pegging out her smalls on the shared washing line close by.

'Louise was far crueller than her husband, actually.' She paused, thinking of the keen, sharp pain that Louise Walker had inflicted. The Major's wife had possessed an exquisite awareness of which areas of Joanna's buttocks were most susceptible to the hand. Stroke after stroke had landed on the tender underhang, or found the inner slope of her bottom crease. Or even the sensitive lips of her vulva, revealed where her G-string had been pushed sideways by her wriggling.

'She knew exactly where to hit me,' Joanna continued, 'and she didn't hold back like her husband did. The Major tempered his smacks; he curbed his arm, I'm certain of it. But Louise just let rip as hard as she could.' She began to shift her body in the chair, still feeling a phantom trace of the spanking's pain, but more aware of other sensations the thought of it induced.

There had been a scent in the air, that evening at Briar Villa. Mainly Louise's pungent perfume, but laced with female sweat, and a musky sexual ichor. The awareness of this last aroma had troubled Joanna more than the punishment itself. The odour of arousal had come mostly from her own body, she realised, and the Major's lady must have known exactly how excited her victim was. The sights and the smells were unmistakable. When the spanking – which had been long, and agonisingly thorough – was over, Joanna had waited in fear and an agitated stillness to be touched.

'And when she'd finished, she told me to go and stand in the corner, facing the wall, and hold my skirt up in a bunch, so my bottom was on show.' The memory made Joanna's heart race. She could not look up at Kevin, and instead, she reached down for one of the reports, and flicked at its pages, over and over, seeing nothing. 'Then she pulled my G-string down to my knees, and just left it there. Somehow, that was the most embarrassing thing of all.' She tried to swallow, finding it difficult to proceed. When she spoke again, her voice sounded thin and wavery. 'I had to stand there, for about half an hour, with my bottom bare and this ridiculous scrap of lace stretched between my legs. Then I had to listen to her groaning and creating while her husband fucked her. It just went on and on. She was shouting; thrashing about. I could hear the settee creaking and protesting with each thrust.'

'God, I wish I had gone with you, now,' said Kevin after a moment, his own voice audibly affected. Out of the corner of her eye, Joanna saw that he too was moving slightly in his seat, and that his hand was on his thigh, near his crotch. She hoped earnestly that her neighbour wasn't watching.

'If you had gone to Littlebourne with me, we would probably have gone to a hotel. And then I wouldn't have met the Walkers.'

That was a point, thought Joanna suddenly. If Kevin had been there, Louise would most likely not have intercepted me. And what would have happened to my secret admirer's plans then?

So far, Joanna had not revealed that particular aspect of her trip to Kevin. It seemed too weird and unlikely. He would probably laugh in her face at the idea of a covert society that changed the course of people's lives.

'That would have been a shame – I think.' He looked confused for a moment. 'What I mean was that it would have been a shame for you to miss something so wild and kinky. We could have had a good time, but different. Sort of.' He was still clearly uncomfortable, and Joanna could now see the major cause of that. He had an erection that was pushing hard beneath his jeans.

'Although, it would probably have come out later,' he went on, adjusting the way he was sitting yet again, 'this masochistic streak of yours, I mean –'

'Not necessarily,' demurred Joanna, trying not to look as if she were too obviously studying his crotch, but still seeing a vision of his penis bare and rampant. 'I might never have realised that people really do such things. I might never even have thought of it.' She felt sweat trickling down her back, beneath her T-shirt, and a different moisture leaking slowly between her legs. 'I needed a trigger, really; someone to point me in the appropriate direction.'

'I wish you'd point me in the right direction,' said Kevin plaintively, glancing quickly at his groin, then looking up again to catch Joanna's eye. He shrugged and his grin widened, as if he were challenging her to ogle him blatantly.

Joanna gave a short, nervous laugh, then felt angry with herself. It was ridiculous. Why was she embarrassed? It wasn't as if she hadn't seen him naked before.

'Let's go to bed,' she said shortly, already on her feet and gathering up her papers. Giving herself no chance to change her mind, she began walking purposefully towards the back door of the building, not looking to see if Kevin was following. After about two seconds, she heard his footfalls just behind her.

Once they were through the lobby, and up the stairs and into her flat with the door closed behind them, her confidence failed. She hesitated, again not daring to look at Kevin, but this time he took the initiative. Removing the bundle of files from her arms, he dropped them on the settee, then took her face between his hands and started kissing her roughly, with his tongue deep in her mouth.

Joanna just let him devour her. She felt as if she were hanging from his grasp, her body helpless against both his strength, and the power of her feelings. She wanted him to a degree that almost shocked her. Though she had experienced orgasms during her short stay with the Walkers, there had been no simple, straightforward penetration. No fucking. And she had missed it. Missed it while she had stood, exposed and burning, listening to Louise caterwauling with pleasure as her husband reamed her body on the sofa. Missed it as she had lain in her solitary bed each night, speculating and brooding, with only a discreetly loaned vibrator to ease her yearning. She moaned around Kevin's tongue as she thought of that, feeling her vagina flex and ache with yawning emptiness.

'Please . . .' she gasped as he released her, and his long, capable hands dropped to her breasts. He squeezed her quite forcibly, his fingers pressing into her resilient curves, examining her shape through the slight barrier of her T-shirt and her light, silky bra. Her eyes were closed, but she sensed him watching her face. She wanted to touch him, but her arms seemed to have no life.

'Come on,' he said suddenly, letting her go and turning away from her. Numbly, she watched him walk across the room towards the hall; she felt bereft, her body abandoned, her will forgotten. When she followed him into the bedroom, he was already half-stripped, his trainers and socks, and his powder blue sweatshirt flung across the floor, and his deft fingers working quickly on his zip.

The speed at which things were happening was alarming, dizzying. Joanna reached for the hem of her T-shirt, then flinched when Kevin said, 'No! Wait! I want you to strip for me.' She hesitated, lost, while he climbed swiftly out of his jeans and shed his briefs. Granting her only the most fleeting view of his enormously erect cock, he flipped up the duvet, and then slid into her bed.

'OK,' he said, pulling the quilt over himself, and lying back against the pillows.

Bastard! thought Joanna, feeling rage race through her as she came back to her senses. One minute he was gentle, almost sensitive, a friend who seemed to take her seriously; the next he was behaving like the most obnoxious kind of macho recidivist. Expecting her to perform for him, to obey his juvenile commands. And the worst thing about it was the way her body – against her will – was thoroughly aroused by him.

Struggling for composure, she made her movements steady and measured. First she stepped out of her sandals, then she took hold of the hem of her T-shirt and drew it slowly over her head, very aware that the bra beneath it was soft and sheer, and showed her nipples.

She took a pause then, and drew in several deep breaths. Her breasts lifted as she inhaled, and she could almost feel the surge of approval this evoked in her watching lover. The awareness of his desire, and of how such simple movements of hers could stoke it, made something flip inside her. Her anger inverted suddenly, and she realised that she was as much in control of this situation as Kevin was. Against her own current inclinations, she was temporarily enslaved by him, but by the same token, he was a hopeless minion of his own consuming lust. They were a matched pair and, accepting that, she smiled.

'God, you're beautiful,' said Kevin, almost seeming to acknowledge this finely balanced arrangement. She could see that he had slid one hand beneath the cover of the duvet and, though there was no motion there, she knew he was holding his cock.

'You think so?' she answered, her spirit rising. Turning away for a moment, she let him watch her unclasp her bra, then lean forward cradling her own breasts. As the narrow straps slithered from her shoulders, she turned back towards him, holding the soft orbs of her own bosom in a cupping grip.

Enjoying herself now, she began squeezing and lifting, not handling her body as rudely as Kevin had, but still exerting an exciting degree of force. Not looking at him any more, she tipped her head back, and threw herself into her performance, relishing the way in which the pressure on her breasts sent shivers of reciprocal sensation to her vulva; the way her sex-lips grew heavy with blood and her clitoris pulsed. Rolling her hips, she gasped with delight. In her belly, there was a delicious, dark drag as her sexual hunger massed.

'Let me see you, Joanna. Please!' entreated Kevin, an expression of strain on his face. The pendulum had swung the other way entirely.

After one last, circling squeeze, Joanna let the bra drop away, exposing her breasts. Looking down at herself she saw that her nipples were tightly puckered, their colour deepened by arousal, and as ripe and firm as two berries. Breathing in, she found enjoyment in her own display.

'Joanna! Come here! Please!' cried Kevin, reaching out towards her.

'In a minute,' she murmured, unfastening her skirt in a leisurely fashion. 'I thought you wanted a slow strip.'

'I've changed my mind,' he answered quickly, making as if to climb out of bed and fetch her.

'Too bad. Stay right where you are; I won't be hurried.' Placing her hands flat on her hips, Joanna eased the skirt down slowly, inch by inch, allowing her panties to snake downward with it. When her pubic curls came into view, she heard Kevin draw breath. Knowing it would drive him crazy, she rocked her pelvis to and fro, very slowly.

'Joanna!'

Allowing her skirt and underwear to drop to the carpet, Joanna stepped free of them, one pace towards Kevin. With her knees flexed, and her thighs slightly open, she slid her hand between her legs and touched her quim. When her finger found her clitoris, she sighed.

'Joanna!' Kevin repeated, throwing back the quilt, then reaching out towards her.

Still touching herself, Joanna met his gaze and held it. She felt a wild desire to tease him, to stroke herself where she stood, to slick her flesh to a tumultuous orgasm without him. But the sight of his handsome body was too tempting, and far too much of what she wanted to resist. His prick was rigid; it seemed to call her; she had to have it. She gave him a narrow, warning smile then darted towards him.

As she reached the bed, Kevin tried to pull her down on to the mattress and roll on top of her, but somehow that wasn't what she wanted. Evading his grasp, she positioned her hand on his warm, muscular chest and pushed him down instead. When he was flat on his back, she slung her thigh across his lower torso, quickly reached between their bodies, and guided his penis into her entrance as she sank down on him.

Her impalement was almost instantaneous and quite complete. Kevin cried, 'Oh God!' and grabbed her hips for purchase and, as he held her, his fingers gouging, his hot flesh seemed to swell inside her.

I'm going to come, thought Joanna almost detachedly, her eyes closing. If I move, even in the slightest degree, it will happen. She felt like a soap bubble, a precarious sphere of swirling iridescence. One minute shift in position, one jot more pressure, and the surface equilibrium would shatter. Holding her breath, and with the sinews in her stretched groin beginning to ache, she remained as still as a saint carved in stone.

'Did you do this with the Major?' enquired Kevin, his voice devilish and, as he jiggled his hips, Joanna opened her eyes. And climaxed.

7

Experiments

'You bastard!' Joanna hissed again, collapsing forward, and Kevin felt the tremors begin to lessen. She was still fluttering and contracting around the whole length of his penis, but the force and rhythm of the delicious undulations were rapidly fading. He let out his breath in a sigh of relief. The moments of most critical danger were now in the past. Or at least he sincerely hoped they were.

'I don't know what you're complaining about,' he said, laughing to hide how close he had been to coming. Reaching up, he slung a hand around her head, and drew her lips toward his for a kiss. For a second she resisted him, then her mouth softened and admitted his tongue. He tasted her quickly, then pulled back, sensing her irritation at her own acquiescence. 'I made you come, didn't I?' he pointed out as he let her go, jerking his hips – carefully – to remind her of his lingering erection.

'Yes, but you also seem to have a knack of making me dance to your tune,' she said, then made him gasp by gripping him tightly with the strong muscles of her vagina.

You hellcat! he wanted to shout, but maintaining control seemed to consume all his energy. He wished there were some way to hide the effects of what she was doing to him, but it wasn't possible. He clenched his jaw and gouged the mattress with his fingers.

'But I thought you were getting to like that sort of thing?' he muttered through gritted teeth, almost choking as she bore down again, massaging his flesh with her hot and wet interior. Back on the very precipice of ejaculation, he groaned and tossed his head.

'Not all the time,' she answered, apparently recovering fast from her own recent pleasure. The tables had turned completely now, he realised, and the ascending power he sensed within her was pure and awesome. Her quim was a furnace, but her eyes were cool and level and when she swirled her hips he couldn't contain a crude profanity.

Not sure how long he could fight her, he nevertheless tried. 'But surely,' he persisted, 'if it's to be real, you have to be ready at any time? Always susceptible to it?'

'If what's to be real?' she said, beginning to circle, and making his bursting heart pound faster.

'Damn you, you witch!' he shouted as she pressed down on him again, squashing her sex against him to engulf his cock more deeply.

'If what's to be real?' she persisted, gripping his hips, now, as he had previously gripped hers. Right at his centre he felt an enormous climax massing.

'This submission thing. The spanking. Obedience.' As she drove downwards, he arched his back and rose to meet her. He could feel fresh perspiration popping out in his groin and his armpits, and see a sheen of it on his own chest. But these sure signs of effort seemed to please Joanna immensely, and she hunched forward to lap the sweat from along his collarbone.

Kevin seized the moment. In a swift, all but unthinking action, he slapped her left buttock with the flat of his right hand.

'You pig!' she shrieked, but before she could retaliate he slapped her again, harder this time. Then he felt his loins surge, as Joanna's body betrayed them both.

Fire seemed to tear down his spine then spew into the very heart of her, the pulsating cauldron that now clasped him harder than ever. Her inner contractions were so pronounced he almost passed out.

Returning to his senses afterwards, Kevin felt like a mariner washed up on a beach after a tempest at sea. He had no strength in his limbs, and had to content himself just to lie, panting and with his body bathed in lassitude, while Joanna lifted her hips from his pelvis and released his softening cock.

'Dear God,' he heard her mutter confusedly as she lay down at his side.

There was a period of silence then, although Kevin could swear he could almost hear the hiss of heat dissipating from both of their bodies, and the sweat, and the various other fluids, drying swiftly on their skin.

'What the hell did you do that for?' demanded Joanna as she sat up suddenly. Kevin watched her eyes zero in on the window and the undrawn curtains, and smiled to himself as she reached awkwardly for her robe – which lay on the floor, having slid off the bed – keeping low to avoid being overlooked from adjacent buildings.

'Well?' she prompted, nominally decent again as she sat down on the edge of the bed beside him, yet still a temptation in the thin silk cling of her multicoloured robe.

Why had he hit her? It hadn't been a planned thing. His intention had been to draw them both into a long, slow duel of sensation, to tease her to her limits and coax the very best out of her and himself. He had wanted to watch her writhe above him, her movements heavy and voluptuous. He had wanted to make her breasts sway while he held her down firmly on the rigid prong of his cock; he had wanted to feel the inner ripples of her not-quite-orgasming channel as he flicked lightly at the pushed-out prominence of her swollen clitoris. He had wanted to float at the edge of his own climax for as long as was humanly possible, savouring the delights of this sublime, extraordinary woman.

He had wanted to make it last, basically, but in one mad, instantaneous impulse he had totally blown it.

'I don't know,' he said, shrugging and sitting up. There was no way a passer-by could see his groin from that angle, but he didn't particularly care if they could. 'It was just a whim, really.' He paused, feeling an urge to reach out and touch her again, to mould her silky wrap to the opulent curve of her beautiful breast. Instead, he touched himself, running his fingers over his soft, sticky cock in a gesture of displacement, a form of comfort. He saw Joanna glance down quickly at what he was doing, but perversely, he carried on with his casual fondling.

'I suppose I wanted to see what it felt like; how you would react.' He flexed his back, stretched his shoulders; amazingly, he felt his penis rouse again. 'It sounded so sexy, the way you described your spankings. I was turned on. I wanted to try it for myself.' It was the truth, and now he wanted to try again. His swelling cock confirmed the simple fact.

'But it wasn't like that!' protested Joanna, still watching his hand. 'It's a ritual. It's formal. Elegant. Civilised. You don't just land a stray wallop whenever you feel like it. The preparations are a part of the whole experience.' She frowned, then nibbled her lower lip. His penis had grown beyond the grip of his fist now, and she was eyeing it as if it were a cobra. 'You've got it completely wrong, Kevin. You don't know anything.'

He was intrigued, and excited, by her sudden air of authority. Joanna Darrell had the keenest mind of anyone he had ever met – she was certainly the shining star at Perry McAffee – and it was clear now that her perspicacity extended far beyond the commonplace realms of financial and business analysis. She was a quick study in everything, it seemed.

'Then tell me more,' he said, gently stroking his new erection.

'I've told you it all,' Joanna answered, then passed her tongue over her lower lip, her attention still centred on his penis.

'No, you haven't,' he said, shifting his bottom a little on the bed. It amazed him how with Joanna he could get hard again so soon; his powers of recovery were good, he knew, but no other woman had brought him back to life this quickly. 'You finished, as I recall, with you standing in the Walkers' sitting room, with your knickers at half mast while the Major gave his lady a good seeing to.' He let his hand fall still on his penis. No use going too far and wasting all his work. 'You haven't told me anything of what happened afterwards. You were there four days; surely there was more to it than that? Did you do anything with Louise, or didn't you?'

'No. We never quite got around to it,' she said quietly, and then, to Kevin's astonished delight, she began to blush again. 'I got a spanking each day, but no sex.' The pinkness was spreading visibly over her throat and her cheeks; even the soft lobes of her ears were colouring.

Joanna's obvious embarrassment was as arousing in its own way, Kevin reflected, as any of the tall tales she had just told him. And he could see the answers to the rest of his questions writ large in the rosy bloom that stained her skin.

She had wanted Louise Walker. She had been brought to a high pitch of passion by the spankings and the humiliation. And she was heading for the same exalted state now, here with him, just from thinking and talking about her experiences.

'No sex at all?' he queried, keeping his face impassive, though inside him his desires were wild and surging.

Joanna hesitated, her face peony pink. 'N-not with other people.'

The image made his cock lurch perilously. Joanna, masturbating. What a delectable thought. Would she do it for him now, if he asked? He looked down at her slender fingers, each tipped with a short, but neatly manicured nail, and pictured one – no, several of them – jammed between her thighs. He imagined her so hungry, so far gone in lust that she couldn't keep from slicking herself over and over again to repeated orgasms, each one slaking only a fraction of her ever-growing desire.

'Ah, I see,' he said evenly, watching her gaze flit about but keep returning to his penis.

'Well, I had to do something!' she said defensively, meeting his eyes for the first time in minutes. 'They kept exciting me, then they left me hanging. It was worse than the spankings; far worse.' Her eyes skittered away again. 'And they . . . she . . . Well, somebody had left a vibrator in my bedside drawer. It seemed a shame not to use it when I needed it,' she finished, her voice low, petering out, almost to nothing.

It was too much. Throwing himself forward, Kevin took hold of her, kissing her mouth as his head filled with fantasies. The idea of her pleasuring herself with a vibrator, a vulgar plastic facsimile, made his real, rigid penis ache with longing. He was harder now than he had been before, he was convinced of it, harder and more unyielding than any dildo. He needed release, and he needed it to be inside her. There would be time for complicated games and experiments later, but at this moment, he had to have her around his cock.

'Joanna!' he gasped, covering her face with kisses, as he drew her down and parted her robe. Too impatient with the firmly knotted sash, he simply wrenched apart the flimsy panels, leaving the belt still circling her slender waist. Manoeuvring her on to her back, he presented the head of his penis at her entrance, then sighed happily as she pulled him down and into her, wrapping both her arms and legs around his body to urge him on.

'Oh, God, Joanna,' he groaned as she began to squirm. 'Now, tell me everything. Start at the beginning. The whole damned lot!'

But she hadn't told him everything, had she?

It was late at night and Kevin had just gone, but instead of lying in her bath, luxuriating in the afterglow of some unconventional, but truly inspired lovemaking, Joanna was staring down at a small rectangle of stiff white card, and wondering why she hadn't revealed its existence to him. What was printed on the rather innocuous business card was both a clue to the identity of whoever had sent her to Littlebourne, and the next step in her voyage of strange discovery.

'De Rigeur,' she murmured, running her fingers over the embossed, calligraphic script. Beneath the two stark French words was an address – 6a, Portmeirion Gardens, NW6 – but no telephone number or personal name of any kind. Louise Walker had slid the card into Joanna's hand when they had parted on Littlebourne station, but, when pressed for further information, the Major's wife had been uncharacteristically evasive.

'For if you want to go further,' she had murmured, kissing Joanna's cheek with considerable enthusiasm as they had stood together on the platform.

'Who are they? What do they do?' Joanna had demanded, but just then the guard had blown his whistle and she had been forced to turn and run towards her train.

'Oh, you'll find out,' Louise had called out laughingly, in the direction of Joanna's back.

The simplest, least disruptive thing to do would be to rip up the card, fling it away, and to chalk up the whole Littlebourne and Briar Villa episode to quirky experience. Part of life's rich tapestry, and all that. She had a suspicion that, if she didn't rise to the bait, the mysterious manipulator behind all this would realise she couldn't be played with, or manoeuvred into any more perverse and compromising situations, and then, perhaps, would leave her alone to get on with her well-ordered, and successfully work-based life.

And she didn't particularly need to go elsewhere to get kinky thrills if she wanted them, anyway. Kevin was shaping up quite nicely in that department, and had a good deal more sexual imagination than the rest of her previous lovers put together. He would even, it seemed, be glad to spank her if and when she finally worked out why she wanted it.

But a profound curiosity piqued her. She had seen the leading edge of something dark but alluring. Thanks to the

Walkers, she now knew of a secret world, a second continuum which existed alongside the life she had always been used to. Anyone might be in it, anyone at all. Even people she knew. She already had Halloran, and perhaps Davidson, pencilled firmly into the frame, but not knowing for certain annoyed her. She could easily confront either of them at work, but where was the real thrill in that? She could already see Halloran's cool, impassive face as he murmured, 'I'm afraid I don't know what you're talking about, Joanna.' Davidson would probably treat her accusations as a huge joke – whether he was involved in the secret continuum or not.

To obtain unequivocal proof, she had to pursue her perverted admirer into his – or her – own lair. There could be no denials if she faced her nemesis *in situ*.

Tossing the card on to the bedside table, she said, 'All right, whoever you are, you're on!' then shrugged off her robe and climbed naked beneath the sheets. The scents of sex drifted around her like a miasma, but she felt too tired to do anything about them. Catching a thread of Kevin's cologne amongst the raunchier, more pungent odours, she smiled.

Perhaps after tomorrow she would have even taller tales than those of Littlebourne to tell him?

The next day, Joanna did not go in to Perry McAffee. Halloran had banished her, so she would stay banished for a while and, for the first time in years, she realised she wasn't all that worried about the work she had outstanding. What was happening to her personally was infinitely more stimulating, and seemed to demand that she move the process forward. She had no option but to visit De Rigeur.

With what she had said to Kevin about form and ritual in mind, she dressed soberly for the occasion. From her selection of officewear, she chose the ensemble she felt most expressed a disciplined mind – a sleek, but shapely Anna Sui suit in soft charcoal wool gabardine. Its clever cut suggested the lines of her body, yet was restrained, and beneath it she wore no blouse, only underwear: a perfectly plain set of bra, suspender belt and panties in white stretch satin. Her stockings were sheer grey and, recalling her maverick notions outside Halloran's office, what seemed like a century ago, she dug out a pair of party shoes she hadn't worn in ages. They were red leather, outrageous without being fancy, and their spiked heels were the highest she possessed.

Studying her reflection in her bedroom mirror, she felt her heart flutter. What the hell was it she was dressing herself up for?

To go further, Louise had said. But how much further? thought Joanna, flicking her blonde curls into place, then applying a coat of red lipstick to her lips, and blotting it carefully. Her eyes she had kept subtle, grey to match her suit, with no other trace of colour.

As she snapped the cap back on to her lipstick, a sudden vision made her sway in her daring high heels. For a moment, she seemed to see herself bent over, draped across a bench, the back of a chair or something.

Her bottom was bare, but she still wore her bra, her suspenders and stockings, and her high heels. The exposed globes of her buttocks were striped with the same red as the leather of her shoes, and she was crying. And aroused. From the rear, a stern, dark clad figure was approaching her, but the impression was vague, almost formless. She couldn't tell if it was a man or a woman; she only knew that she wanted this stranger – who was the same one who had lashed her bottom – to touch her sex, and grant her the blessed release of orgasm.

'Oh God,' she whispered, feeling sensation already flaring between her thighs. For a moment, she considered tearing off her suit, kicking off her shoes, and climbing into easy summer clothes. It would be so much safer just to go for a walk, take in a gallery or a concert, or perhaps waste an hour or two shopping. To escape into normal life and reject this nebulous compulsion to be punished. The temptation was strong, but before she could succumb to it, she reached for her phone and punched in the number for a taxi firm, citing her destination as Portmeirion Gardens. It was the only way to keep herself on track.

The journey was short, and it was only as she travelled that she realised how close to home the mysterious De Rigeur was. She might even have walked past it, she postulated, then realised, as the taxi slid to a halt, that she actually had, on a number of occasions. At the far end of Portmeirion Gardens – an irregular, tree-shaded square comprising a number of austere but obviously expensive Regency houses – lay a pleasant park through which she occasionally walked or jogged.

Number Six was one of the larger houses, and its many polished nameplates indicated multiple occupancy – a mix of private apartments and the offices of smallish firms. Joanna felt deflated as she stood beneath the imposing portico; there wasn't even a 6a in the building as far as she could ascertain, and the names listed were fairly ordinary and unexciting. There was no mention whatsoever of De Rigeur.

She pushed a button at random.

'Yes?' said a young female voice, faintly accented, possibly Italian, or Spanish.

Feeling foolish, Joanna asked for De Rigeur, quoting the precise address from the card as she did so, even though she knew she had not been mistaken.

'I am sorry,' replied the unknown female, 'I have never heard of such a name.'

Joanna frowned, wondering if there was a camera focused on her. Most probably there was; places like this were well protected by security.

'Are you sure?' she demanded, feeling all the thrill, and all the resolve she had amassed earlier seep away. 'What about the other apartments?'

'No, Madam, I am sorry. There is no such name used in this building.'

Suddenly infuriated, Joanna tore the card in two and swore. It was obviously a servant of some kind she was talking to, yet the intriguing foreign accent also carried an annoying hint of superiority.

'Are you quite certain?' insisted Joanna, additionally rattled by the fact that a car had just drawn up somewhere behind her, and swift, light footsteps were approaching. 'I have a card here with the address printed on it. It must be here somewhere!'

'No, Madam, there is no-one –'

'Is there a problem?' interrupted another voice, from a point somewhere close behind Joanna, a voice that was low, husky and even more intriguingly accented than the one that issued from the speaker-phone.

Joanna whirled around. Standing just a couple of yards away was an unusually tall, very smartly dressed woman, whose face was all but obscured by a heavy veil of fine black mesh. The veil was attached to a chic black felt hat and, from beneath this, the woman's hair – impossibly shiny, and a rich brown the colour of conkers – swept down in a thick, 'forties' fall that caressed her broadish shoulders.

'I'm sorry, I think someone has played a joke on me,' said Joanna, suspecting as she spoke that it was the literal truth. 'I was given this card – ' Feeling a fool, she proffered the torn halves towards the mysterious figure who loomed over her like a shadow clad in black suede and heavily draped silk crèpe. 'But the – the establishment or whatever it is doesn't seem to exist.' She could barely see the upper part of the woman's face, but she sensed dark eyes narrowing attentively beneath the veil. 'Well, at least, not at this address.'

She made as if to stuff the bits of card into her shoulder bag, but the veiled woman took them from her, then flicked them dismissively between her gloved fingers. Joanna felt the scrutiny focused on her intensify, and – just beneath the edge of the obscuring black net – she saw the ghost of a smile form on the woman's firm and very smoothly painted lips. She had a large mouth, and had coloured it subtly with a matte lipstick in a flattering brownish red.

All of a sudden, the woman leant past Joanna, making her flinch, and spoke quietly into the speakerphone.

'It's all right, Mercedes. It's me.'

There was the clunk of a mechanism, and the door before them opened slightly. The veiled woman then nodded to Joanna and indicated that she should go inside.

As they passed into the building, Joanna was acutely aware of her unknown Samaritan, just behind her, and caught the trailing edge of a powerful, exotic perfume. As she breathed in, to try to identify the scent, it began to seem familiar somehow, as if she had encountered it before in another, quite different setting.

In a cool, sparsely decorated entrance hall, lit by narrow windows and with gleamingly polished tiles underfoot, they were met by a dark-haired young woman in a maid's uniform of a black dress and white apron. She smiled warmly at Joanna's companion, who was presumably her mistress, but seemed to look straight through Joanna herself, while at the same time exuding a faint contempt. It was almost as if the maid was fully aware of the purpose of Joanna's misdirected presence in the building, and her pink lips quirked when her employer handed her the two pieces of the torn white business card.

What the hell am I doing? thought Joanna as the three of them proceeded in silence up the wide staircase that faced the front door. The veiled woman had said nothing after her initial enquiry on the porch, but even so she seemed to expect Joanna to follow her. And at a loss to know what else to do, Joanna did so.

On the landing, the maid darted forward and threw open the door to what was clearly a self-contained residence and, still unspeaking, the three of them trooped inside: first the tall woman, then Joanna, then the maid.

The flat was decorated in the same light, spare, almost timeless style that the hall had been and, as she was led through several different rooms until they reached what seemed to be a boudoir, Joanna reflected that whoever owned it was clearly not short of money. The location, though close to her own flat, was far more desirable, and the sheer size and number of rooms spoke of a price tag in many, many figures.

And yet the boudoir they had ended up in was almost homely. A little smaller than the previous rooms, it had a cosier, more period feel to it, and the presence of an inviting, deeply upholstered settee, as well as an exquisite, galleried *chaise-longue* seemed to add to its appealing air of feminine intimacy.

Pausing by the window, the veiled woman looked out for a moment, then turned and spoke quietly to her maid. 'I'll have a bottle of gin, Mercedes. With ice, and two glasses, please.'

Once again, Joanna was intrigued by her mysterious hostess's voice. The woman spoke in deep, slightly gravelly tones, and each word carried an indefinable accent; which, though attractive – erotic even – gave Joanna the distinct impression that it was assumed.

In fact, standing as she did in the full focus of the veiled woman's scrutiny, Joanna was able to observe that everything about her companion was informed by an exotic sense of drama.

The woman was extremely tall, for one thing, possibly six feet even without the benefit of her elegant black suede court shoes. And her build was on the large side too. She wasn't fat, or in any way heavy, but instead had a rather athletic frame; strong and rangy, with big, lengthy bones. When she moved across the room, to take a seat on the sofa, her stride was long, yet graceful, and when she sat down, she descended lightly, crossing her legs with a deliberate elegance.

Unexpectedly, she did not offer Joanna a seat, but simply said, without preamble, 'Why are you here?'

Not knowing whether to sit or stand, or what to do with her hands or her bag, Joanna felt the beginnings of a hateful, rising blush. 'The card,' she began, shifting from one foot to the other. 'I was trying to-to get in touch with the people on the business card. Some friends gave it to me and – '

'No. Forget the card,' the woman said, still staring, but still not removing her heavy veil. 'I don't mean why did you turn up on my doorstep, I mean what are you doing here, inside my home? In my most private room?'

'I don't know,' said Joanna, aware that she still had no concrete idea why she had followed this strange woman inside. It was like a compulsion; as if she had been hypnotised. It felt, silly as it sounded, as if it had all been pre-destined, and she suddenly knew that – regardless of what the maid and her tall mistress had said – she had found De Rigeur.

Certainty flooded back into her now she realised she was in the right place. She lifted her chin boldly, and looked directly into the faintly discernible eyes of her inquisitress. 'No, that's wrong,' she said, trying to seem uncowed, yet respectful. 'I think I am in the right place, and I think you're the person I'm supposed to meet. The card's not important; it's just a means to an end.'

The well-shaped lips curved slightly. 'So, what is it you want from me?' the other woman asked.

Joanna's fragile confidence wavered. She wished she could see the woman's eyes, and read their expression. The veil made it impossible to gauge the woman's response to her, and with no feedback it was hard to judge whether she was on the right track or not.

'I want to learn,' said Joanna, crossing her fingers behind her back, just out of the seated woman's sight. 'Someone I met recently said there were ways to find out more about a-a new interest of mine.'

'And you think I could educate you?' The voice was challenging now, and touched with a faint, ironic humour.

'Yes, I do. I think you're meant to do it. Somebody's sent me to you specially.' Pursing her lips, Joanna wished she could just make herself say exactly what she meant. But it was so difficult, such a preposterous thing to ask for out loud.

'And which somebody might this be?' The veiled woman was being arch now; she was definitely amused. Joanna felt like a cornered mouse being eyed up by a sleek black cat.

'I'm not sure. I think it's a man I know, or perhaps one of two men. They both work for the same company that I do. They're both my superiors.' She paused, swallowing, her mouth suddenly excruciatingly dry. 'And I think that whichever one it is, he wants to – to extend that relationship beyond work. To control me in a sexual sense, too.' By beating me, she wanted to add, but couldn't. Which is OK, she thought, but I don't really understand why.

Before the veiled woman could answer, there was a soft knock at the door, and Mercedes, the maid, reappeared, carrying a bottle of gin and two glasses on a silver tray. Without waiting for instructions, she placed both bottle and glasses on a handsome sideboard, which stood against the wall, then poured a largish, neat measure and presented it to her mistress. After a second, she glanced quickly at Joanna.

'You may serve her, Mercedes,' her mistress said, allowing herself a small, controlled smile. 'I think she needs it.'

Almost grudgingly, Mercedes complied, handing Joanna a drink just as generous as the one the veiled woman was now sipping.

'Will that be all, Mistress?' enquired Mercedes, her eyes lowered, her demeanour more demure, more subservient, as if they had – all three – moved into another dynamic stage of the meeting.

'For the moment,' replied the veiled woman, studying the crystal clear fluid in her glass. 'But remain on hand. I may need you.'

Mercedes walked silently back to the sideboard and took up a clearly pre-defined station beside it.

Watching this interchange, Joanna felt her spirits coagulate like a heavy mass inside her. Mercedes, whose opinion of her was clearly low, was to remain throughout the interview and consequently would hear, and observe, a variety of hot, embarrassing secrets. All of them Joanna's.

'I'd drink that now,' said the veiled woman, nodding at Joanna's glass of gin. 'I might not allow you to later.'

Joanna took a large sip of the raw undiluted spirit, and only just avoided choking on its cool, intense fieriness. Gin had never been a favourite of hers, but somehow it seemed to suit the moment, its strength and clarity unremitting. She took another drink and felt her stomach warm, and her head become perceptibly lighter.

'Now, where were we?' her veiled inquisitress prompted, her lips just a little moist from her own gin. Joanna imagined she could see eyes twinkling behind the obscuring veil, suggesting a sense of mischief as well as one of power. 'I believe we were discussing your interests; and a certain special man.'

Joanna drank more gin before replying, then wondered if there might be repercussions from delaying her answer. From not obeying the 'Mistress' straight away. 'Yes,' she began slowly. 'I believe that this man wants to test me; to see if I'm – I'm up to what he wants from me.'

'And what is it you think he wants?' enquired the veiled woman, rising quickly to her feet, and making Joanna jump and almost spill her drink. Without a word to Mercedes, the woman pressed her shoulders back and, with a ballerina-like gracefulness, let her black suede jacket slide off, down her arms, behind her. As the dark garment reached her hands, the maid sprang forward and took it from her, folding it neatly, then laying it across a nearby upright chair, one of a set of several. As she returned to her spot by the sideboard, her mistress smoothed the black leather gloves she wore, seating the leather more snugly over her fingers. Joanna thought suddenly of an executioner, and shuddered.

The abandonment of the jacket had revealed the beautiful, sumptuous blouse that had been hidden beneath it – a construction of slim, fitted sleeves and a full and flowingly draped bodice, that hung in heavy folded ruffles designed to flatter its wearer's rangy figure.

The veiled one cocked her head on one side as she resumed her seat. 'Well?' she reminded Joanna, who had been so engrossed in watching the woman remove her jacket that she had almost forgotten the question.

'I think he wants to punish me,' she replied, her voice small in a vain attempt to prevent it carrying across the room to Mercedes. 'To spank me. To beat me.'

'Not an unreasonable expectation,' observed her companion, touching a ruffle of her blouse, rearranging it.

'What do you mean "not unreasonable"?' demanded Joanna, straightening her shoulders and standing taller, unconsciously squaring up for a fight. She sensed that total subservience was not quite what this enigma required of her. 'Up until a few days ago, I never realised people hurt each other for pleasure; it seemed entirely unreasonable!'

'But now you see things differently?'

'Sort of; I don't know. I've only really scratched the surface so far.'

'Which is why you're here?'

'Yes.'

'Well, then,' said the veiled woman, draining her glass and setting it aside. 'Let's see what we can do, shall we?'

Joanna finished her own drink, then allowed Mercedes – who had darted forward – to take it from her. 'May I ask one question?' she said, her heart pounding and seeming to rise into her throat. 'Before we start?'

'Of course,' the other woman replied, letting her gloved hands rest upon her lap, clasped like an elegant black flower.

'Who are you? What's your name? What do I call you?' She sensed the almost-invisible eyes narrow inscrutably.

'I think for the purposes of this visit – ' the veiled head lifted slightly, '– you may simply call me "Mistress" . . .'

8
Mistress

'Yes, Mistress,' whispered Joanna, momentarily amazed at how easy the word felt on her lips. It should have seemed silly, pretentious, a contrived protocol; but instead it sounded just right.

'Any more questions?' Mistress's husky, accented voice sounded amused.

'Yes . . . er, please . . . Mistress,' answered Joanna, feeling her natural boldness fight the persona she knew was now expected of her. 'Who are you?' she repeated.

'You'll come to know me soon enough, Joanna,' said Mistress, laughing softly.

It took a second or two for the significance of the statement to sink in. 'My God, you know who I am! How the hell is that?' She paused, blood racing through her veins, possibilities teeming through her mind. 'And I must know you too! Who are you? Who are you?'

'Enough!' said Mistress, her tone still quiet, but changed. Joanna felt an icy finger trace the length of her spine, then change to fire as it sank through into her belly. Heat gathered in her loins, in her crotch. A heavy heat that was both delicious and gnawing. Her knees trembled, but she braced them, determined to avoid showing weakness.

'All your questions will be answered in the fullness of time,' went on Mistress, still sitting, apparently composed and unperturbed, yet seeming to loom over Joanna like a nemesis. 'In the meantime, you will remain silent. Mercedes!' She turned to the motionless servant. 'Will you take Ms Darrell's bag?'

Maybe she's the one? thought Joanna as she held out her shoulder bag. It could be Mistress herself. Yes! She's probably seen me somewhere. Perhaps she's a client of Perry McAffee? She could be anyone behind that veil and that put-on voice. Anyone.

Torn between staring, and keeping her gaze respectfully lowered, Joanna ran her mind back through recent work meetings with clients. There were plenty of powerful people amongst them, but she could remember no women who were especially tall, or who were as elegant and mysterious as Mistress.

There were a few moments of total silence in which the tension in the room grew. Joanna was aware that Mercedes was still standing next to her, and that from behind the heavy black net, Mistress was regarding the two of them speculatively, her curvaceous, sculpted mouth faintly smiling. For a split second, the shape of those painted lips seemed obscurely familiar, but then the recognition was gone again, too ethereal to tie down and keep a hold on.

'Will you remove your panties now please, Joanna?' said Mistress into the quietude, speaking as normally as if she had requested Joanna to sit down or to help herself to another drink.

So it begins, thought Joanna, wondering whether to lift her skirt or just slide her knickers off from beneath it. Would she be expected to keep herself exposed, as she had done for Louise Walker? She suddenly realised she was automatically assuming that Mistress was a lesbian, and would find the sight of a woman's naked crotch appealing. But what if she wasn't gay, and felt only contempt for a woman who was submissive before her? What if all she felt was a single-minded desire to inflict pain?

'Joanna. We haven't got all day,' said Mistress evenly, making Joanna realise that she had been putting off the fateful moment of revelation.

Embarrassed by her own clumsiness more than by what she was actually doing, Joanna hiked up her skirt only as far as was necessary to reach her panties, then tugged on them until they slid down her thighs. She was aware of her pubic hair being on show for a fleeting moment, as she wriggled, but having no instructions to the contrary, she let her skirt drop back into place and cover her. The expected command to expose herself did not come, surprisingly, but even so, as she stood there, bunching and crumpling her panties in her fingers, the bareness of her vulva beneath her skirt made her nervous.

'Put the bag in a safe place, Mercedes,' said Mistress, still calm, still pleasant. 'Then bring me the choice item which Joanna is presently mangling, would you?'

There seemed to be a sudden lack of oxygen in the room. Joanna felt her breathing go shallow, and her head undergo a curious expanding sensation as if she were suffering from vertigo. This is really happening, she thought, letting Mercedes take her creased-up panties. I'm not dreaming. I'm actually here. It's all true.

Watching, but wondering whether she should be, she saw Mercedes stretch the knickers between her two hands, smoothing the fabric, then deftly turn them inside out before presenting them to Mistress. The significance of this little act made Joanna feel almost sick with both mortification and excitement. There was a clearly visible sticky patch that had spread almost the full length of the cotton-lined gusset, and it was this that the maid was displaying, her glee obvious in the smug smile on her face.

'Well, it's quite obvious that none of this is going against your nature, Joanna,' commented Mistress, taking the garment from Mercedes, studying the betraying evidence for a moment, then lifting it closer to her veiled and hidden face. Joanna heard Mistress draw breath, inhaling deeply as if she were sampling an expensive designer fragrance or the scent of a hot-house rose, but the knowledge of what she was really smelling made Joanna's face redden with the hot blood of shame. Her whole body seemed to boil as Mistress sniffed again, then placed the panties on the arm of the settee, the telltale mark on the gusset significantly uppermost.

'So, tell me what you've already learnt,' Mistress said, gesturing to Mercedes to bring her more gin. 'What discipline have you received, and what did you think of it?'

Joanna glanced automatically towards the maid, and saw Mistress take note. 'No secrets from Mercedes, Joanna,' she said, smiling slightly beneath her veil. 'In fact, revealing your most intimate secrets before a servant is a useful test; a part of your education, you might say. Please proceed.'

Joanna thought of what had happened at the hands of Major and Mrs Walker. The exposure, the ignominy, the pain – and the delicious, unexpected pleasure. To detail it would take far more nerve than having to take her knickers off. Far more than having to strip entirely even.

'I met some people; a Major Walker, and his wife Louise . . . I was staying with them for a few days, down in Littlebourne, and one night I heard a noise when I was in bed,' she began haltingly. 'A cry. I went to investigate, and discovered the Major was beating his wife.' She saw again the explosive, unthinkable images. Louise naked, with her bottom striped and burning. The Major swinging powerfully with his fiendish leather belt, then using his lean body and his stiff, noble penis with an equally impressive power. 'I was shocked at first. Flabbergasted that it was happening.' She paused, remembering. 'Then I realised that they were doing it for pleasure; and that Louise wanted it.'

'Ah, the Major and his good lady,' murmured Mistress, reclining languorously in her seat as if she too had exotic scenes with the Walkers that were worth remembering. Joanna wanted to ask her how well she knew them, but decided she had probably run out of permission to pose questions.

'Go on,' instructed Mistress, her voice dreamy.

Growing more and more self-conscious, and feeling more aware, by the second, of the hidden nakedness between her legs, Joanna continued her faltering narration. She described every particular of her punishment at the hands of the Major, but her throat seized up and it became difficult to speak, when she reached the point of recounting what had followed it.

'Come along, Joanna, this is no place for prudishness,' said Mistress sternly when Joanna fell silent. 'Did he masturbate you? Did he put his hand between your legs and bring you off?'

'I –' Joanna fought to get the words out, but her own sense of shame, and the presence of Mercedes seemed to choke her.

'You're surely not going to tell me he didn't finger you,' persisted Mistress, shifting her long thighs ever so slightly beneath her tailored suede skirt as if she were as aroused and aching as Joanna was. 'I can't for the life of me imagine any red blooded man who wouldn't want to!'

At this, Mercedes, still in her corner, sniggered loudly. Mistress glanced towards the maid, and the set of her beautiful, painted mouth seemed to indicate that Mercedes, too, might experience a punishment of some kind. Later.

To her surprise, Joanna experienced a sudden jolt of jealousy. 'Yes, he touched me,' she said quite loudly, to draw Mistress's attention back to her. 'He stroked my crotch, and he . . . he . . .' It was too late now to backpedal, she realised, but how could she speak of that rude thumb that had wiggled inside her? 'He touched my bottom too,' she finished, her face scarlet.

'Well, he would have had to do that to spank you, Joanna,' observed Mistress smoothly, her slight smile returning. Joanna had a sudden, sharp longing to see the rest of her face, her eyes, the entirety of her. She realised that to know Mistress, and to discover her secret identity, would be worth far more than she had endured with Major Walker.

'I think you meant something else, didn't you?' continued Mistress, her voice unequivocally arch now, taunting and teasing. 'Why not tell us the whole story?'

Joanna shifted her weight from one leg to the other, horrified by the way a single viscous trickle of her lubricating moisture began to slide down the inside of her thigh. She was so full of dark desire she was overflowing.

'He put his thumb inside me,' she whispered.

'Detail, Joanna,' prompted Mistress softly.

'It was in my bottom. He put his thumb inside my bottom.'

'Ah,' murmured Mistress, her deep voice little more than a sigh. A tiny sound that seemed to express appreciation. 'And did you enjoy that? Answer honestly, Joanna. We deal in nothing less than the truth here.'

Staring at her toes, as if her polished red shoes might supply some fortitude, Joanna answered, 'Yes', then braced her psyche for the inevitable reaction.

Mistress, however, seemed to digest the response rather slowly. Although Joanna did not dare not look up into the other woman's veiled countenance, she sensed a mood of measured speculation.

What is she going to do? thought Joanna wildly. Is she planning to do something to me that's similar? Her mind offered up a new set of images. Mistress, peeling off her black leather gloves. Herself, bending over, everything intimate exposed. A slender thumb, its nail painted a beautiful, softly pearlised crimson, pushing slowly through the muscle-ring of her anus.

'Food for thought,' said Mistress quietly, as if she, too, had seen the perversity within Joanna. Behind her veil she seemed to be contemplating, planning, making choices but, after a few moments, she spoke again, briskly. 'But first things first. I think it's about time we got down to some spanking. After all, it is what you're here for.' She rose swiftly, moving with an energy that made her fine nylons rasp against each other, and some satin undergarment rustle beneath her skirt. 'Do you have any preference as to the implement?'

Surprised, Joanna tried to recall her reading. In the Walkers' magazines, it had appeared that all manner of devices – either specially fashioned 'tools', or common objects with useful properties were employed in the dispensation of corporal punishment. For her own part, she had experienced only the hand, but instinct told her that it was probably the least severe item on any notional prospectus. Louise Walker had shrieked and yowled under the application of her husband's leather belt, but Joanna couldn't imagine that anything else – either the cane or slipper or birch rod – would be any more benign.

'I – I don't think so,' she responded cautiously. 'I've only been spanked by hand. I don't know what anything else feels like.'

'In that case,' said Mistress, sounding distinctly pleased with herself, an impression that made her seem far more human than Joanna had yet perceived her, 'I'll choose something. Mercedes!'

The summoned servant hurried to her mistress's side, then leaned close to her black veiled face for a whispered instruction.

If she would let me get that close, I might be able to work out who she is, thought Joanna as Mercedes slid quietly away, taking her silver tray with her. Mistress settled herself comfortably, on the *chaise longue* this time, half-sitting, half-lying, her head tilted back and her attitude one of silent meditation. The exposed lower half of her face was still and tranquil, almost Madonna-like, and her lips formed a soft, relaxed line. A lovely curve that once again seemed familiar.

To distract her mind from her growing excitement, Joanna studied her companion carefully, cataloguing every feature and characteristic that was on show to her. After a few moments, a startling conclusion began to form.

Mistress was tall. Mistress was big-boned. Her hands and feet, though graceful, were extraordinarily long for a woman and, beneath her blouse, her shoulders were broad, and well-defined. Furthermore, the portion of her face below the veil was distinctive in a most particular way; the set of her jaw was powerful and resolute, her throat was strong, almost muscular and, in addition to her lipstick, she wore a smooth but fairly heavy layer of make-up. When she spoke, her voice was deep, with a dramatic accent.

Dear God, she's a man! A transvestite – it's so obvious. Why on earth didn't I cotton on to it before?

The abrupt realisation brought even more confusion in its wake. Joanna could no longer quite categorise her feelings. There was a sense of slight relief that it was a member of the opposite sex that she felt so enthralled by, but, by the same token, it was Mistress's very femininity that made her so alluring. *Him* so alluring. And, even though only half of Mistress's face was on show, she was beautiful. Or *he* was beautiful. Joanna sighed, trying to make sense of the wildly disparate facts.

'Have you figured me out yet?' Mistress said suddenly, and Joanna realised that the eyes beneath the veil had not been closed, as she had assumed.

'Partially,' she replied, with caution. So far, she only knew 'what'. 'Who' was still a nagging mystery.

'And does it bother you?'

'I don't know.'

This was true. The very ambiguity of what Mistress was had an excitement all of its own. The mix of genders produced a mix of emotions; revulsion and desire in almost but not quite equal parts. Not quite equal because Joanna could feel that lust was winning. For a moment, she imagined Mistress's cock, rampant inside a swathe of delicate lace and satin; and between her own legs the liquid heat grew thicker.

'Are you wet?' enquired Mistress, as if she had seen the fluid phenomenon for herself.

The question made Joanna hotter than ever, but even as she felt sweat pool in the creases of her groin and trickle down to join her other juices, her rational mind drew attention to something curious.

Despite what she had learnt, she was still thinking of Mistress in terms of 'she' and 'her' and femininity.

How odd. She now knew full well that the individual lounging so elegantly before her on the *chaise longue* had a penis and testicles beneath that chic suede skirt, and that, in a matter of hours, that meticulously painted, half hidden face would sport a shadow of tell-tale stubble; but it didn't make any difference. The persona who was taunting her was a woman.

'Yes,' said Joanna, answering the question.

'Well, there you are then,' drawled Mistress, her accent a little heavier, as if it were now more than her identity she was trying to hide. 'When the effect's right, who cares about the cause?'

As Joanna absorbed this pearl of wisdom, there was a knock at the door and, when Mistress bade her enter, Mercedes came back into the room. The dark and sultry maid was carrying before her the gleaming, chased silver tray again, and what was on it now eclipsed the puzzle of Mistress's gender.

'Isn't this a little beauty?' observed Mistress, lifting up a heavy, rather plain, wooden-backed hairbrush – which, to Joanna's eyes, was neither little nor beautiful – and balancing it thoughtfully in one long, black-gloved hand.

Hairbrushes had featured prominently in her reading at the Walkers'. She recalled a photograph, bland and awkwardly posed, yet still powerful, which had shown a serious, bespectacled, academic-looking man apparently striking a middle-aged woman's buttocks with a particularly heavy and fearsome brush. There had been no red marks on the woman's flesh – Joanna had got the impression that it was probably against the law to show them – but something in the woman's posture betrayed a knowledge of the real thing. The real thing, which Mistress was about to inflict on her.

The matte mouth beneath the veil was smiling slyly. 'Come here; take a closer look. Feel the weight of it.'

Joanna took a step closer to Mistress and, at a prompting nod, reached out to take the brush. It was just as solid and substantial as it looked, she found, and the polished wood was strangely warm to her timorous touch. She swallowed, trying to imagine the impact of its hard, smooth surface against her bottom, but finding it impossible to gauge. There was no knowing until the actual moment, she realised and, while one half of her was terrified, the other half was insatiably curious. To her surprise, she found the curiosity far outweighed the terror, and she ran her thumbnail along the close grain of the wood.

'Superb, isn't it?' said Mistress, stretching out her hand to retrieve the brush.

Joanna nodded.

Mistress flicked her tongue across her lower lip. 'Oh, yes, I can see they were right about you; you're a natural.'

Joanna wondered who 'they' were. The Walkers, she supposed, despite the fact that Mistress wasn't necessarily supposed to be the personage they had sent her to. It was all a part of the game, a way to unbalance her.

'Now, to business,' said Mistress more seriously. 'As it's your first time with me, I'll give you a few choices. Would you prefer to be beaten naked, or to keep some of your clothes on?'

Flustered, Joanna felt her blush heat up again. She had expected, once things were underway, to have the burden of all responsibility taken away from her. It was something she had almost been looking forward to, and now, the element of preference seemed an awe-inspiring burden.

'I don't know,' she muttered, feeling a self-directed anger at being so suddenly indecisive.

'Well, why don't we start by taking one or two things off and seeing how you feel then?' said Mistress reasonably. 'What do you say to that?' Her hidden eyes seemed to bore into Joanna, expecting an answer.

'Y-yes, Mistress,' she replied, her fingers going quickly to the buttons of her jacket.

'No! Leave those! Mercedes will undress you.'

Shocked by the unexpectedness of the order, Joanna froze, watching in horror as the Hispanic maid put aside the silver tray, then approached her. She closed her eyes when the girl reached up and made her put her arms down by her sides, feeling her blushing face seem to get even hotter than it had been already.

Swiftly, and with a slight, almost malicious roughness, Mercedes relieved her of her jacket and then her slim, grey skirt. Joanna expected a comment from Mistress at the lack of any blouse or camisole or slip, but then decided that young women must often present themselves in this room in all shades and degrees of dress and undress, and her own choice to wear only undies was probably not remarkable. She was, though, intensely aware of her own lack of panties.

'The slave says she's wet, Mercedes,' said Mistress after a short pause for scrutiny. 'I wonder if you'd confirm that fact for me, my dear? I wouldn't want to think that I'd been lied to.'

Mercedes obeyed immediately, and with obvious relish. Joanna groaned as the dark girl's hand delved peremptorily between her legs, first in a single, unkind squeeze, then in a more complex and intimate action, seeking out her clitoris and flicking and pinching it cruelly. For the second time, she felt her knee joints weaken dangerously. 'Oh, no, please,' she whimpered vaguely, as the inspection went on.

'The slave will keep quiet from now on,' said Mistress, her voice as soft as velvet. The concept of choice was clearly a thing of the past. 'Unless I specifically instruct her to speak, or give permission for her to cry.' She rose, unfolding her long legs like some fabled, regal bird, then stood before Joanna, cupping her chin while Mercedes still cupped her sex. 'That's what you are now,' she said, so close that Joanna, forced to look at her, could nearly discern the features behind the veil. 'A slave.' In the midst of embarrassment and arousal, a shred of recognition tried to stir, but went under again, sinking down beneath the weight of roiling emotions. 'My slave; to use, and punish, in any way I please.'

Releasing Joanna's face, Mistress turned away and picked up the brush again, her leather-covered fingers caressing its shiny, unyielding surface. 'Well, Mercedes, is she wet?' she enquired, still handling the brush, turning it this way and that as if practising her action.

'She runs like a river, Mistress,' replied the maid, her tone suggesting that she despised such a copious, uncontrolled response. 'It is oozing down her thighs, and into the crack of her bottom. Shall I fetch a cloth and wipe her?'

'Yes, please do,' Mistress said, still fondling the brush, but more provocatively now, running her fingertips up and down its handle, as if she were stimulating the male organ that lay hidden beneath her skirt. 'We wouldn't want to make a mark on this beautiful upholstery, would we?' She nodded towards the roll at the end of the *chaise longue*.

So, the game continues, thought Joanna, shaking in just her bra, suspenders and stockings as, at last, the spiteful maid released her. It was just another ploy, she realised; a further reduction in her status. But why, oh why, did being treated almost as an incontinent child turn her on so very strongly?

She moaned again when Mercedes passed a soft cloth between her legs, and around the tops of her thighs, then felt a jolt of even greater shock when the maid grasped both her wrists and, quite without warning, snapped handcuffs securely around them.

'No!' she cried, struggling. This wasn't at all what she had expected.

'I'm afraid it's "yes",' murmured Mistress, close again, her rich, evocative perfume tickling Joanna's nostrils. 'And it's time now, my pretty slave. We must get started.'

As Mercedes arranged Joanna over the end of the *chaise longue*, her bottom high, legs straight, and her toes – still in her high red shoes – meticulously pointed, Mistress slowly peeled off her leather gloves. From her awkward position – canted forward, and with her cheek pressed against the soft, yet scratchy surface of the upholstery – Joanna saw that at least one of her notions about Mistress had been accurate. The nails that tipped those long, flexible fingers were beautifully lacquered, and the thought of being touched by such well-kept hands made Joanna quiver.

But she's not going to touch me, she's going to beat me! The thought was both chilling and enflaming. Joanna shifted her body against the firm, upholstered edge of the *chaise longue*, then realised, to her even greater shame, that what she was really doing was massaging her aching crotch.

'Be careful. Be very, very careful,' said Mistress, her voice even and measured as she took up a position a little way to Joanna's rear. Joanna imagined her waiting, her hand outstretched, for Mercedes to pass the brush.

'You might find the brush very different to what you're used to, you know,' Mistress continued, pressing the cool, flat back of the brush against Joanna's finely trembling backside. 'It's really quite a spectacular sensation – Feel!'

Joanna did feel. The first whack seemed to come out of the blue, pounding into her almost while Mistress was still speaking. It was hard, very heavy, and quite breathtaking; the sensation was so intense that, for a few seconds, Joanna couldn't quantify it, but, when her nerves fired up again, she let out a yelp of anguish.

Dear God, it was terrible! And terrible again and again and again as, in a strict, metronomic cadence, the stunning wallops continued to fall and fall and fall. With each one, Joanna could not prevent herself from yelling. Each hefty slab of pain brought a sharp cry to her lips, regardless of Mistress's earlier dictum, and the silent, unsettling presence of Mercedes.

After about ten strokes, Mistress hesitated. 'You're not doing very well, are you, slave?' she said, touching her fingertips to the sizzling crown of Joanna's left buttock. 'I never gave you permission to make such a fuss, did I?'

The taunting questions seemed to exaggerate the suffering, and Joanna fought hard to keep in her sobs and snuffles. Her bottom was a mass of torment; it felt as if it were swollen to twice its normal size, and almost audibly pulsating. Its colour she hardly dared begin to guess at. Flaming crimson? Rose pink with livid, purple, brush-shaped weals? A uniform magenta?

'Slave, I'm talking to you!' persisted Mistress, making Joanna yelp again, by pinching her raging flesh. 'Did I give you permission to yell?'

Joanna could only shake her head.

'Well, then.' Mistress paused again, her fingers still palpating the damage the brush had done.

Joanna bit her lips, and clenched every muscle in her body in an attempt to suppress her own reaction. She had been determined to be brave, to be impressive. It had been her aim to put up such a magnificent show of stoicism that whoever was behind both this, and the greater game beyond it, would be awed and dazzled by the strength of her performance.

No such luck, she thought, her head filled with the echo of her bottom's livid throbbing. I'm a broken whinger, and the beating has barely started.

'Things might be easier for you if you were gagged,' suggested Mistress and, without thinking, Joanna answered with an eager nod. If her mouth was stoppered, she wouldn't be able to shout and yell.

Dear God, what am I doing here? Joanna asked herself in the short hiatus while Mercedes brought a gag. Why have I let this happen? Again?

Strangely, though, she could not seem to adequately answer her own question. For all the pain, for all the humiliation, there seemed a certain perverse appropriateness to her condition. She had been allowed small choices – in the matter of clothing and gags and suchlike – but the big issues, which were whether or not she should hurt, or become aroused by it, were out of her hands. The loss of responsibility was a strangely blissful feeling, and she began, to her own astonishment, to feel relaxed.

'What are you feeling?' asked Mistress suddenly, bending close, her hand still resting on Joanna's bottom. 'Tell me. It's all right. I allow you to speak.' Joanna felt the brush of the net veil against the side of her face, and knew that if she looked now, through the gauzy barrier, she would easily be able to see her tormentor's features.

'I hurt,' she whispered, her eyes closed. The scent, and something in the voice, were beginning to bring an identity to the surface of her consciousness, but if she accepted it fully, this game of cat and mouse, of pleasure and pain, would be at an end. Ignoring the gathering facts, she let the game continue. 'My bottom feels as if it's on fire, and my arms are aching.' She wriggled her wrists in the cuffs. 'And all the blood seems to be rushing to my head.'

'From where I'm standing,' said Mistress, straightening up, 'I'd say it's rushed to quite a different place entirely.' She laughed softly, and touched the heated place once more.

Joanna tossed her head, but stayed silent. Acceptance was one thing, but her pride called for a small show of spirit.

'You're good, slave,' murmured Mistress, almost dreamily. 'So very, very good. If it was up to me, I would really test your limits.' She sighed, a real breathy woman's sigh, that denied the true fact of her masculine sex. 'But alas . . .' Joanna sensed a regretful shrug.

Again, there was just a hint of that person in the background. The Master – or Mistress – of the dark continuum. Were they all doing this to tease her? Or were they all truly in awe of this person? Joanna longed to ask but, at that moment, Mercedes returned – presumably with the gag.

Almost immediately, Joanna felt a thick wad of rolled silk being passed between her lips, then looped around and tied behind her head. It was a scarf, and a very expensive one, that had been worn very recently by Mistress. Joanna could both taste and smell the transvestite's distinctive and beautiful scent.

'Are you ready?' asked Mistress, almost kindly.

Joanna nodded her head, feeling the lingering gnaw of pain in her buttocks, and trying to remember what the shock of each spank had felt like. After a moment, her memory was refreshed, and the slow, steady whacks of the hairbrush began again, meeting her tender rump in a series of measured impacts.

Again, after the first outrage, Joanna found the even, almost languid rhythm of the strokes almost lulling. Her buttocks were growing fierier and fierier, and attacked, it seemed, in a way that sank deep into regions of her body that she had never thought had any connection to her bottom. She was being belaboured, and yet she seemed to be floating like a cork on the sea of her own rising passion, her sex – against the upholstery – wide and throbbing. When a stroke was slower in coming, she found, to her astonishment, that she raised her hips, automatically, to meet it.

Then, without warning, the punishment was over and, opening her tearful eyes, Joanna saw that Mistress was standing closer, much closer than before. After a second or two, she felt the transvestite's body curved over hers, almost back to front, then she groaned as the gauzy, black veil moved delicately across her smarting buttocks, its fine mesh like barbed wire against her soreness.

'Oh God. Oh please,' she tried to entreat, the words muffled by the silk in her mouth. She was, she realised in a second of pure longing, just a heartbeat away from orgasm. Her clitoris was a fat, swollen berry between her labia, so sensitised that it would probably need little more than an increase in tension to tip her over. She gasped around the gag, then mewled and pleaded incoherently, begging, against the instincts and inclinations of a lifetime, to be brought to climax, to be released from her cage of misery.

Deliverance came in a most unexpected way. One moment she was in pain, in torment, and engorged; and the next she was still hurting, but her loins were contracting exquisitely, grabbing and pulsing around a solid obstruction that had been pushed into her vagina.

At first, as she writhed and shimmied and almost sang her joy and her thanks into the scarf, Joanna thought that Mistress had whipped up her smart suede skirt, become a man, and started fucking her. But, after a moment or two, as she regained some scraps of her critical faculties, Joanna realised that the object that was thrusting inside her was a very odd shape for a man to be. Even a rather peculiar man like Mistress.

It was the handle of the hairbrush. The object of her agony was now the instigating source of her pleasure. Mistress was using it slowly, and with skill, in a perfect mock-copulating action.

Eventually, when Joanna felt almost too exhausted to come any more, the wet and slippery brush-handle slid out of her. She sighed, as much with weariness as anything, then felt her nerves beginning to register the aches and pains that her orgasm had nullified. Slumped over the *chaise longue*, she let herself sink into the soreness and accept it, her brain too numbed by all the sensations to think further than the next second, the next breath.

'Joanna?' said someone softly, after a while.

At first, the significance of the voice's timbre didn't register.

'Joanna, honey, are you with us?' the inquisitor persisted.

In a split second Joanna was awake, fully aware, and torn between laughter and rage. With help from the suddenly solicitous Mercedes, she struggled awkwardly to her feet, and then – when the scarf had been removed from her mouth – she turned to face the source of the distinctive accent.

'Mistress' was standing a couple of feet away, her arms elegantly lifted, deft fingers prising the long pins from her hat. As, with the utmost care, she lifted the chic veiled creation from her head, she turned away and to the side, then jabbed the pins into the hat again and tossed it across the room.

And when 'she' – 'Mistress' – turned around again, her silky hair swinging softly with the motion, Joanna found herself facing a set of features that were quite familiar beneath their paint.

Regarding her with a wry, mischievous triumph were the brown, twinkling eyes of Denis Davidson.

9

Sundry Revelations

'You! Bloody hell, I might have known!' cried Joanna, struggling against the handcuffs, and ignoring the pain in her buttocks as she tried to launch herself forward. 'You slimy creep! It's you who's behind everything, isn't it? You're the bastard who sent me to Littlebourne on a wild goose chase!' She jerked harder as Mercedes gripped her elbows.

'Tut tut!' said Davidson, still grinning, his man's face made extraordinarily pretty by his skilful, flattering make-up. 'Language, Joanna.' He stepped forward, relieving Mercedes, and holding Joanna in a surprisingly strong grasp. 'And I really don't know what you're bitching about. It felt to me –' He glanced quickly towards the abandoned hairbrush, still gleaming with her juices '– as if you were having a great time. If you were a lady, you'd thank me for making you come.'

'I'm no more a lady than you are,' proclaimed Joanna, still trying to shake him off.

Davidson ignored her efforts, his grip like iron as he nodded for Mercedes to leave the room.

'Maybe you're right there,' he admitted, his smug, but somehow appealing smile very close to Joanna's scowling face. 'But admit it; you were enjoying yourself. You get off on pain.'

Aching, Joanna ignored the truth of the last statement. 'Why do you have to play these games? Be so sneaky? If you wanted me to get into some kinky sex with you, why couldn't you just say so? You could have asked me out; suggested something outrageous over dinner. I'm a grown-up, Davidson; I'd probably have said "yes" anyway.' For the first time since she had stepped over Mistress's – correction, Davidson's threshold – she thought of Kevin, and of how easily and naturally they had slid into bizarre sex-play. She realised that what she had just told Davidson was most likely the truth. And for all his chicanery he was a genuinely attractive man.

Feeling her resolve slipping, and undermined both by her own helplessness, and the proximity of Davidson, Joanna went back on the attack again. 'There was no need to play all these silly, "Evil Mastermind of Sex" charades, you know.' She narrowed her eyes, trying to look dismissive. 'You've been watching too many Bond films, Davidson. You're not Mr Big. You're not even Miss Big,' she said, casting a glance over his smooth wig and lovely, no doubt designer labelled, clothing.

Infuriatingly sure of himself, Davidson let go of her arms. Then, before she could stop him or protest, he kissed her lips, and cupped her breast with his hand.

Contrary to her will, Joanna felt herself melt again and instantly respond. Her mouth opened beneath his, and she moved against him, not sure whether it was his masculinity, or his femininity that stirred her. He was just Davidson, whom she had once loathed, but now suddenly desired.

But, just as she was beginning to really enjoy him, her tormentor withdrew his mouth and pulled away. 'You're right, Joanna,' he said, his eyes bright with laughter. 'And you're wrong, too. There *is* a "Mr Big", if that's what you want to call him – but it's not me.' He lifted his skirt a little and, pointing one toe, made a smoothing gesture along the length of his nylon-clad leg. 'I'm just a foot soldier who likes to wear high heels.'

The gesture was so female, and so natural, that Joanna felt a kick of lust in the cradle of her belly. Wanting him, but not knowing quite how, her confusion grew. She started shaking, even though the room was warm.

Is it him I want? she asked herself, as Davidson straightened up, patting his skirt into place. Or is it still 'Mistress'? And if it is, does that mean I'm a lesbian? Or bisexual? Once again, her thoughts flew back over the recent past, fixing on her temptation at the hands of Louise Walker.

With a gasp of impatience, she banished her seaside aberration, and returned her attention to Davidson, who had retreated to the *chaise longue*, and sat down again. As he crossed one leg over the other, with all the cool poise of a supermodel, his suede skirt edged discreetly up his thighs.

'Who is it then?' she demanded, returning to her early point. 'Who's pulling the strings? I need to know!'

'I can't tell you,' said Davidson, brushing an imaginary speck from his immaculate skirt, and suddenly looking vaguely awkward. The poise was still there, but so was something else – and in a flash of insight, Joanna realised what it was.

'I-I could make it worth your while,' offered Joanna, mellowing her voice, and letting her gaze settle around the area of Davidson's black-clad lap. She thought again of a hard cock enrobed in softest satin and, to her surprise, found the prospect enticing. Maybe he didn't even have to tell her anything. She took a step forward, unconsciously licking her lips, then realising how obvious that seemed.

Davidson seemed to read her mind. He laughed, and adjusted his chic skirt. 'Is that a fact?' he murmured, his transatlantic accent thickening.

'I think so,' went on Joanna, marshalling as much *sangfroid* as she could. 'I think you probably need me to.' She licked her lips again, enjoying her own gambit. 'You can't tell me all this dressing up and spanking doesn't turn *you* on.'

'What had you in mind, Joanna?' he drawled, re-crossing his legs elaborately, and confirming her observations with his own shudder of patent arousal. 'Were you thinking of blowing me in return for the identity of "Mr Big"?'

'I wouldn't phrase it quite so crudely,' replied Joanna, feeling the excitement surge deep down inside her. The fact that he had spoken crudely was exciting. 'But yes, that's essentially the offer.' She shifted from one leg to the other, her naked vulva swelling.

'No dice,' said Davidson with a shrug. 'My word is my bond; I made a promise.' He paused, and shifted again, evocatively, on the *chaise longue*. 'But if you let me come in your mouth, I will set you free.'

'But you'll have to do that anyway!' protested Joanna, half afraid he wasn't joking.

Davidson merely arched his painstakingly pencilled brows.

Joanna struggled again with the cuffs, wincing as she jolted her glowing buttocks in the process. 'Davidson!' she muttered, through gritted teeth. 'What the hell are you playing at?'

'I don't have much time to waste, Joanna my love,' he said suavely. 'I'm due in a meeting in three quarters of an hour, and I have to transform, as it were, before then.' He lifted one long, effete hand and stared, with mock regret, at his nail polish. 'I could just leave you here with Mercedes all day, if you like? Still in the cuffs.'

'All right, you win!' said Joanna, eyes downcast, suppressing a smile. It wouldn't do to let him know that, suddenly, and serendipitously, she actually wanted precisely what he wanted. She turned her back to him and shook her shackled wrists, aware that she was also displaying her heavily becrimsoned buttocks to him too.

'Oh, no,' purred Davidson, staying exactly where he was. 'I think afterwards would be better.'

'Davidson!' she snapped, spinning around again.

'Call me – Call me "Denise",' he urged, then pouted outrageously, making Joanna laugh despite her discomfort and her acute vulnerability.

Awkwardly, hampered both by the handcuffs and by the rapidly stiffening muscles in her buttocks, she descended to her knees before him, and watched, in fascination, as Davidson parted his legs and slid his shapely black skirt the rest of the way up his stockinged, and no doubt meticulously waxed legs.

Like her, he was wearing suspenders. But that was where all similarities ended. Dear 'Denise' also had on a pair of black silk French knickers – from one leg of which poked a magnificently rampant and neatly circumcised penis.

Not as big as Kevin, thought Joanna absently, leaning forward for a better view as Davidson edged the constricting silk out of the way, allowing his erection to rise to its full stretch.

'Oh, baby,' he moaned, as Joanna closed in and took his glans into her mouth.

Oh, Denise, thought Joanna, smiling greedily around his flesh, then launching herself – with vigour – into her delicious, self-designated duty. As her tongue raked his frenum, his painted fingers caressed her head.

Out in the fresh air of Portmeirion Gardens, Joanna felt dizzy. A taxi bowled along the road, the sun was shining; the whole scene was so absolutely commonplace and unremarkable that it seemed difficult to credit what had just happened to her inside. The whole business of 'Mistress' seemed like a weird, attenuated dream.

A painful one too, thought Joanna, touching her bottom through her skirt and flinching. On her tongue, she could still taste Davidson's semen.

She was more confused now than she had been before her encounter with the Human Resource Manager's astounding alternate persona. Fragmented thoughts and images passed through her mind. Things that first Mistress and then Davidson had said. Joanna still wasn't sure that she/he hadn't been lying through her/his teeth all along, and that the lovely 'Denise' wasn't the lynchpin of the continuum.

Dithering on the pavement, Joanna found herself thinking, 'What the hell am I doing?' again, and realised just how many times she had asked herself that question in the last few days. It was as if she had been suddenly cast adrift from the normal, in-control life she had been leading for longer than she cared to remember. She felt like a cork again, this time skittering along on a white water torrent, and racing pell-mell towards God alone knew what. Half of her liked the feeling, but the other half was scared. Scared stiff.

You've got to get a grip, she told herself sternly, still unsure what direction to take. Her bottom throbbed, her head was light, and she suddenly felt swamped by emotions and drained of all purpose. To her horror, she felt tears welling up in her eyes.

Almost automatically, she began walking, taking the direction of the little park at the far end of Portmeirion Gardens, drawn by a green jewel of peace in the midst of the grey and somehow forbidding lines of the tall period houses. When she reached it, and found a tolerably clean bench, she sat down, hissing through her teeth at its hardness against her hot, maltreated buttocks. But what else could she do? Just stand around, blubbering? Adjusting the way she sat, she found a slightly less painful position, her legs crossed and to one side, in – she realised – an unconscious imitation of Mistress's elegant posture.

Damn, why am I crying again? she demanded, fishing a handkerchief out of her bag and blotting her eyes. The tears she had shed for Mistress had possessed a validity, a purpose, a higher cause that had created a common effect. While this, however, was just a childish, pathetic grizzle.

It's a catharsis, her more rational side announced, surfacing through the confusion and surfeit of emotion. You've had another very radical experience; passed another watershed. You have got to vent the tension somehow, or the whole thing will drive you round the bend.

Feeling slightly better, she continued to cry, but very quietly. Her eyes on her mangled hankie, she reviewed all the strange events that had led her to this moment of tears and reflection.

It's Davidson, it's just got to be, she thought, still seeing Mistress with the hairbrush in her hands. She had felt uneasy with the American from the moment she had very first met him and, with hindsight, his watchfulness and his knowingness were sure indicators of a dark, concealed agenda.

'Excuse me – are you all right?' a voice suddenly enquired from just beside her.

Looking up, her hankie still twisted in her fingers, Joanna found an attractive and vaguely familiar young woman standing over her, her wide hazel eyes full of curiosity and concern.

'I'm sorry; I don't mean to pry, but I noticed you crying,' said the woman, pushing back a stray strand of her rather beautiful long red hair. 'And I thought, "hang on a mo, I know her".' Smoothing out her summer-printed cotton skirt, she sat down beside Joanna. 'Is there anything I can do to help? I'm Cynthia Russart, by the way. We go to the same health club. You know, Bodyline in Tobias Shaw Street?'

'Yes. Yes, of course,' replied Joanna, dabbing her eyes again as she recalled seeing the handsome redhead quite a few times lately, both in the changing room, and during step and circuit training sessions. 'I do know you, don't I? I'm Joanna Darrell,' she said, stuffing the disaster of a handkerchief into her bag and holding out her hand. 'But I'm not at my best at the moment, I'm afraid.'

The hand that took hers was very soft and cool, and its light, fleeting touch seemed to soothe her overheated emotions in an instant. She experienced a frisson of something dangerously delightful, and felt Mistress's baleful presence beginning to fade.

'You look OK,' said Cynthia Russart cheerfully, turning over Joanna's hand and patting it as if it belonged to an emotionally wrung-out mental patient in need of humouring. 'I was a bit worried; I mean, when I see you at Bodyline you always look so, you know, "together". So unapproachable. It was a bit of a shock to see you in tears.'

Feeling strangely reluctant to do it, Joanna withdrew her hand, then twitched at her jacket hem in a nervous, unnecessary gesture. 'It was a bit of a shock to me too, but – well – something very weird just happened to me,' she said, wondering just how much she should tell this relative stranger. They were both women, but there was nothing to say that Cynthia wasn't a hard-line feminist, or a born-again Christian or something. The tale of Mistress and her trusty hairbrush might disgust her. 'And the thing is, I really don't know whether I hated it or enjoyed it,' Joanna finished, turning away from the other woman's look of interest.

'Really?' replied Cynthia, her light, almost musical voice hinting that she too had had weird things happen to her; that she understood. 'Do you want to talk about it? It might help.' She cocked her head a little to one side, and Joanna noticed delicate filigree earrings dangling amongst the ruddy waves of her hair. She also noticed that Cynthia didn't appear to be wearing a bra beneath her thin, white T-shirt, and that her small, dark nipples were tumescent. She felt a disquieting tension in her own breasts, in response.

'Sometimes it's easier to talk to a stranger,' the redhead continued, her smile pleasant and guileless, completely unmanipulative.

'I-I don't know,' replied Joanna, looking around and realising that the little park was rapidly filling up with what appeared to be office workers liberated for their lunch-breaks.

Cynthia glanced around at the newcomers, then returned her attention to Joanna. 'Look, if you like, we could go to my place? I only live around the corner. We could have a glass of wine; maybe a bit of lunch, if you're hungry? To be honest, it would be nice to get to know someone else who goes to Bodyline; a lot of the others seem a bit stand-offish. I've been wondering whether to change clubs and find somewhere more friendly.'

It all sounded so reasonable. So inviting. The effect of the gin that Mistress had given her was wearing off now, and a glass of wine might be just what she needed to unwind and think more calmly.

'Yes! Great! I'd like that,' she said, feeling energised by her own positive decision. 'Lead the way,' she said, springing to her feet, then grimacing when the stiffened muscles in her sore bottom reasserted themselves.

'Are you in pain or something?' asked Cynthia, clearly a practised people-watcher, who had noticed Joanna's quick frown.

'No . . . er . . . not really,' lied Joanna quickly, suppressing a groan. Her brief sojourn on the bench had caused her to seize up with a vengeance. 'It's nothing. Let's go. I'm all yours.'

Now that was a strange thing to say, thought Joanna as she struggled to walk normally – and not hobble – alongside Cynthia. Not so long ago, she had been 'all' Mistress's. How was it, that after a life of self-sufficiency and self-determination, she was suddenly so excited by the idea of putting herself into the hands of other people? She had never seen the appeal of it before.

Cynthia's home – which was indeed just around the corner – consisted of a large apartment, plus a studio on the top floor of a fairly modern, but understatedly genteel block of flats. It was immediately apparent that they were in the abode of an artist of some kind, because the studio-cum-main room was huge, with an illuminating bank of skylights above them, and at one end of it was a drafting table and stool.

'Do you think I might use your bathroom?' asked Joanna, gazing around her and looking for the appropriate door. It had suddenly dawned on her that her mascara might be running.

'Of course,' replied Cynthia gesturing to a heavy, velvet curtain at the far end of the room. 'It's behind there.'

Cynthia Russart's bathroom was as unique as the rest of her living space, with vast, clumpy, Victorian fittings, and enough overgrown potted plants to furnish a medium sized garden centre. Joanna even had to brush away long strands of trailing foliage to see her reflection in the mirror, but she was relieved to discover her makeup unravaged.

'This is a marvellous place you have here,' she exclaimed, returning to the studio room and feeling the heat from the sun overhead pouring down on her. The room was so warm and light-drenched that they could almost have been in the tropics, and she felt a pang of irritation that she couldn't remove her jacket. It was true that Cynthia had already seen her quite a few times in skimpy sports gear and various stages of undress, but somehow it didn't seem quite right to sit around in her bra with a woman she had only just spoken to, for the first time, today.

'Yes, I like it,' said Cynthia, who had kicked off her sandals and was pottering around in her small kitchen area. When she returned, she was carrying a bottle and two glasses. 'Just plonk, I'm afraid,' she said, easing out the plastic 'cork' and pouring each of them a large measure.

'You're an artist, obviously,' said Joanna as they took their seats – in her case very carefully – on a long, shabby settee which overflowed its frame like a badly set blancmange.

'What sort of work do you do? Will I have seen any of your stuff?'

'I don't know,' said Cynthia, her eyes twinkling as she looked back over the rim of her glass, then took a quick sip. 'I do a lot of magazine work, and coffee table books. Specialised stuff. It all depends on how broad-minded you are.'

'Fairly,' replied Joanna slowly. 'Well, very, really. In a way. Just recently, I've rather had it broadened for me. Especially this morning.'

Studying Joanna closely, Cynthia took another drink of wine, then put her glass aside. 'I'm intrigued,' she said, her intent face indicating she meant it, then rose to her feet and walked lightly across the room to her work area. After a few moments of rummaging amongst assorted artistic paraphernalia and a number of large folders, she returned with an ink drawing on a page of A3 paper.

'What do think of this?' she said, holding up the work for Joanna's approval.

'This' was a very detailed, yet delicate study of a naked young woman, depicted in a pose that made Joanna catch her breath. She was kneeling on a sofa – possibly the very one they were sitting on – with her hands tied behind her and her mouth securely gagged. There was a curious, enigmatic expression in her eyes, half fear and half hunger, and her abundant bottom was clearly marked with thin, dark lines.

'I see what you mean about broad-minded,' Joanna said quietly, unable to stop identifying with the model. She wondered what it was that had caused such vivid marks.

'This is a commission,' said Cynthia, unperturbedly. 'For a friend who's a connoisseur of sights like this.' She touched the paper where the woman's backside was striped.

Continuing to study the image, Joanna sipped her wine. Ideas turned over relentlessly in her mind; events, coincidences, connections. How was it that, at this particular juncture, she had just happened to come into contact with an erotic artist? And one who clearly excelled at depictions of punished women.

Was this a pure, but unlikely fluke? she wondered, then dismissed the idea. Cynthia must have been waiting for her to arrive in the park, or perhaps had been somewhere close by, discreetly watching, when she had emerged from the door of Mistress's building.

Or maybe Mistress had phoned her?

'It wouldn't be for someone called Denis Davidson, would it?' she asked, keeping her voice light and casual, and watching Cynthia's face carefully. The woman had the most beautiful veil of freckles across her nose, Joanna noticed, detachedly. Like sparks of gold in her otherwise creamy complexion. 'It's just that I found out recently that he's into this sort of thing.'

'Davidson? Hmm . . . No, this is for someone else,' Cynthia said, still studying her own work. 'The name rings a bell, though. What's he like? I may know him.'

I'm being toyed with again, thought Joanna. The experience was gentle and non-threatening this time, but nevertheless, she was still being given the run-around. 'He's American. In his thirties. Tall, dark and handsome.' She paused, thinking fast. 'Very handsome indeed. Almost beautiful, I'd say.'

'Sounds familiar, actually,' said Cynthia, looking up, her expression open and innocent. 'I think I've met him at one of my art shows. Rather fanciable, I thought,' she finished with a smile.

'Just an acquaintance then?' prompted Joanna.

'Oh, yes,' replied Cynthia evenly. 'One of many; I meet all sorts of people, being in my line of art – you know, a special interest.'

'I can quite imagine,' observed Joanna, taking another sip of wine. It was one of those situations in which there were actually two conversations going on at once. The innocuous pleasantries on top, but beneath a subtle joust. Advance and retreat. Thrust and block. Hints, half truths, intimations.

'Would you like to see some more of these?' said Cynthia suddenly, flicking her long hair out of her eyes with one hand, making it ripple like dark amber shot silk.

'Yes. I would,' said Joanna in reply. After all, it was one of her own special interests now, wasn't it?

Leaving the commission on the coffee table, Cynthia rose, crossed the room, then came back with one of the A3 folders.

The drawings were all more or less in the same vein. Girls naked and half dressed, and in a variety of different poses, but every one of them with marks of some kind on her bottom. And in each case the posterior itself was displayed as the most prominent portion of the anatomy; the focal point of the composition. The very emphasis reminded Joanna of her own rump. It was still stinging and glowing, but the sensation of pain was fading now. What remained was more pleasant than distressing, and she kept feeling sudden, intense urges to touch it. To explore the heat with her fingers, to press it and test her own limits.

'You'd make a good model, you know,' said Cynthia suddenly. 'You've got just the figure for this sort of thing; slim, but not skinny.' She cocked her head on one side, assessingly. 'A nice rounded bottom.' She grinned, her eyes twinkling. 'Yes, I can just imagine your pretty cheeks all pink and sore and burning.'

This is it. Here we go again, thought Joanna. She was now so obviously in a set-up that it was superfluous to protest it as such. Cynthia Russart was as much a part of the continuum as Denis/Denise and the Walkers of Littlebourne were. Joanna felt a momentary pang of anger at being manipulated. Again. But then she reminded herself of the fact that, almost from the start of things, there had always been ways out. She could back off now, if she wanted to. The trouble was she didn't particularly want to. After what she had experienced earlier, with a counterfeit woman, she felt a sudden, sweet urge to try a real one.

'Yes, I've always fancied modelling,' she lied, attempting to sound nonchalant, but feeling butterflies dancing in her abdomen. The delicious urge was not without its fears.

'Really?' said Cynthia, evincing such mock surprise that Joanna nearly laughed aloud.

'Yes, really,' she confirmed, already itching to be out of her clothes and displaying herself. It would be the second time within the space of just a few hours, she realised, thinking of just how much she had changed within the space of the last week or so. It was almost as if she had become a brand new person. Would the old Joanna have been so keen to strip? Would she have been scared but longing? Would she truly have wanted to have sex with another woman?

'Why don't you slip off your suit, then?' said Cynthia, her voice brisk now. Encouraging. Excited. 'Come on, let's have a proper look at you.'

Joanna stood up. 'Just the suit?' she asked, her fingers already working on the buttons of her jacket.

'Oh, go on! Let's go mad! Take the lot off,' said Cynthia, cheerfully, placing all the pictures in the folder, then putting it aside.

Feeling herself to be rushing, Joanna made a conscious effort to slow down. This wasn't an all-girls, changing room strip she was effecting, she reminded herself. This was an effort to please, and to seduce; and every bit as much a one as it would have been if Cynthia had been a watching man. Allowing her jacket to swing open and reveal her bra, Joanna turned her attention to her skirt, unzipping it, and sliding it off in one reasonably smooth action, whilst still teetering in her super-high red heels. She had finally managed to reclaim her panties from Davidson, and she smiled slightly as she remembered him watching her put them on. He had seemed to enjoy it just as much as he had enjoyed watching her taking them off. But then again, he was unusual to say the least.

As Joanna stepped out of her skirt, Cynthia moved forward and took the garment from her hands, then folded it neatly and put it out of the way. She did the same, next, with Joanna's jacket, then repeated the process with the rest of her clothing. Within the space of a couple of minutes, Joanna was standing there quite naked, but still wearing her fancy scarlet shoes. The fact that her bottom was red was more embarrassing than its being bared.

Not knowing what to do with her hands, Joanna clasped them in front of her, at the level of her midriff, and fought off the urge to cover her breasts and her crotch. That she display herself seemed to be an integral part of these weird new experiences. It was as if her bosom, her sex and, in particular, her buttocks were no longer hers but belonged to the continuum – and she was obliged to make them available at all times.

Will she want to beat me, too? thought Joanna, lowering her eyes. She had found that modesty seemed to be the best policy. And if she does, can I take it? she asked herself. It wouldn't take much to stir the existing pain to agony.

Cynthia's next words seemed to confirm her fears.

'Bend over please, sweetheart,' the artist said softly. 'Let's have a look what they've done to your lovely bottom.'

Unsteadily, because of her heels, Joanna bent over, and felt a sharp jolt as her punished muscles stretched.

'Good, very good,' murmured Cynthia, while Joanna struggled to hold on to her equilibrium. Swaying, she watched the other woman's trim ankles flash beneath her skirt as she circled swiftly round her 'undraped' exhibit. 'But part your legs a bit, Joanna,' Cynthia urged. 'I need to see everything if I'm going to do you justice.'

She'll see how wet I am, thought Joanna, edging her feet apart carefully, almost tottering, then clasping her ankles to hold herself steady. And what exactly does she mean by 'do me justice'?

'Are you going to draw me now?' she asked, finding it difficult to keep her voice even. The question she had really meant to ask had been, 'Are you going to spank me?', but she was afraid that the word would invoke the deed. Even so, Cynthia paused directly behind Joanna, where only a portion of her floaty skirt, her lower legs and her feet were visible.

'No, not today,' said Cynthia and, as she spoke, her bare toes curled against the carpet. 'I just want to get an idea of you.' A white T-shirt fluttered to the floor and was kicked to one side. 'The texture of your skin; your musculature.' The skirt itself slid down now, and was nudged out of the way by one slender foot. 'The way you mark so exquisitely when somebody's punished you.' A tiny pair of peach-coloured panties joined the heap of crumpled clothing.

Joanna wondered whether she dare straighten up. She really wanted to see Cynthia completely naked. Even at Bodyline, the other woman hadn't exposed the whole of her body, just given tantalising glimpses from behind towels and from under her sports gear. Would her pubic curls be as auburn as the beautiful, glossy fall of her head hair? Desperate to know, Joanna pulled on her own ankles, stretched down lower, then craned her head to see a little more of Cynthia's body.

Yes! At the apex of the other woman's thighs was a little 'V' of fluffy, russet curls. The hair was very soft and fine, and clung close to the shape of Cynthia's labia. It was one of the prettiest sights Joanna could have imagined.

'I have a photographic memory, you know,' said Cynthia, almost conversationally, then began to pad across the carpet. Joanna swivelled her head to follow the view. 'I can fix an image of you like this in my head, then summon it up and draw you later, when I've got more time.'

Cynthia was standing directly in front of Joanna now, and by craning her neck, Joanna could look straight forward towards the other woman's groin. When Cynthia grabbed her head, and pulled her closer, she almost fell.

'Lick me, Joanna,' ordered the artist quietly, as she parted her thighs.

Knowing it would be almost impossible to do as she was told in her current position, Joanna sank down on to her knees and edged forward, to bring her face to Cynthia's crotch. At such close quarters she could smell the woman keenly. She discerned a flowery perfume and the sharp tang of musk.

Not quite sure how to proceed, Joanna touched Cynthia's inner thigh, then slid her fingers upward until she was brushing the flossy hair. Though very fine in texture, the reddish strands were abundant and, using both hands, Joanna dug through them, very meticulously dividing Cynthia's thatch. When revealed, the flesh within was very wet. Wet, sweetly aromatic, and convoluted. Joanna was so enchanted by Cynthia's structure she could only stare.

'Oh please, Joanna, lick me,' pleaded the artist, swaying forward and almost butting Joanna's face with her mons. 'I can't bear it. I can't wait any longer.'

The intensity of her plea galvanised Joanna. All day, she seemed to have been the supplicant, the submissive, the under-bitch, but now – although she was the one who was kneeling – she realised that it was she who was in command of the situation. She could either grant Cynthia's pleasure or deny it. She could even get up, put on her clothes and leave. It was as simple as that.

But instead, she chose to stay. And to lick.

Thumbing apart Cynthia's sex lips, Joanna stuck in her tongue and went straight for the other woman's clitoris, which was very prominent, cherry pink and softly glistening. The juices that coated it were very salty, musky and marine-flavoured – quite delicious in an unexpected way. Joanna lapped instinctively like a kitten drinking milk.

'Oh God!' shrieked Cynthia, grabbing Joanna's head and tugging her hair to urge her onward. 'Yes! Yes! Oh God, you angel . . . Do it harder!'

Aware of the pain in her abused scalp, but somehow detached from it, Joanna plunged into her task with force and vigour. First, using her tongue in long, flicking strokes, she lashed at Cynthia's clitoris almost roughly – and was rewarded with even more impassioned shouts and cries to Heaven. Cynthia's hips were bumping now, jerking forward involuntarily but, though it was difficult, Joanna clung on like a succubus. It seemed to her as if all the sustenance in the world lay between those slender, freckled thighs, and there was no way, barring a loss of consciousness, that she would relinquish it. She would hang on, and keep on working, until exhaustion claimed her.

It was like being in a trance. In a dream. There seemed to Joanna to be no reality at all except the fragrant, running crevice where her mouth now lodged. In a moment of inspiration, she took the fat, swollen bead of Cynthia's clitoris between her lips and sucked it as she might have sucked a nipple. Cynthia's own nipple. Drawing on it as if there were indeed a sustenance to be derived from it, she made it her mission – of this moment – to torment her beautiful new friend with so much erotic stimulation that the woman capitulated her free will completely.

This was a turnabout. A switch. A payback for the sumptuous cruelty of Mistress.

I can do both, thought Joanna, her spirits soaring as Cynthia almost collapsed on to the carpet, and she herself followed, her mouth still buried in the redhead's sex.

'Stay there,' she ordered, and rose briefly from her feast to grab loose cushions from the settee, then brought them back and jammed them beneath the artist's bottom. Her eyes closed and her shell-pink mouth slack with passion, Cynthia lay there, exactly as she was bidden.

Entranced, Joanna had rarely seen a sight that looked more lewd. With her pelvis raised by the cushions, Cynthia's long, athletic thighs gaped open, revealing the gleaming scarlet chasm of her sex. Her face was red, too, and her throat and chest were blotched raggedly with pink. She was blatantly pinching her own nipples with her fingers.

Remembering the prim, clean woman she had encountered at their health club, Joanna laughed softly as she crouched between her lover's outspread legs. Never believe anything you see, she told herself, thinking briefly of Davidson, then inclining downwards towards Cynthia's running quim.

Except perhaps this, she amended, scrutinising the swollen topography of an arousal so extreme it seemed to be on the point of spontaneous climax.

Yes! Always believe this, she thought, drawing the bud of Cynthia's clitoris back between her lips, then pursing her mouth to compress it with a sly and subtle tension.

As she began to suck again, her happy victim howled.

10

With a Capital 'C'

'And do you know a man called Halloran at all?' enquired Joanna, squirming idly as long fingers strummed her soreness.

'No, I can't say I do,' replied Cynthia, pressing harder and making Joanna jerk and hiss and grind her pelvis against the mattress. 'But then again there are a lot of people I sort of know, but without knowing their names.' She paused, bent down to kiss the place she had just abused, then went on, 'What does he look like? Describe him to me. I might know him then.'

'Tall. Black hair; brushed back and gelled usually. Sort of stern looking. Cool, dark grey eyes. Always dresses immaculately. Classic stuff, not flashy. Usually a dark suit, white shirt, striped tie.'

'Stern looking?' said Cynthia thoughtfully. 'He sounds nice; I don't know if I have met him, but I think I'd like to.'

They were lying together on top of Cynthia's bed which – Joanna had discovered while her new lover had still been almost insensible from their lovemaking on the rug – was in a curtained-off corner of the same large room. They had both retired here when Cynthia had come back to her senses, and she had repaid Joanna's compliment by licking her to orgasm. This had seemed as natural as if it had been happening all her life.

I am bisexual then, she thought, laughing softly.

'What's so funny?' enquired Cynthia. 'I should think, given the state of your bottom, that you'd understand the attractions of stern men?'

'Oh, it wasn't a man who did that,' gasped Joanna, looking over her shoulder to where Cynthia was delicately nipping at her pink and punished bottom cheeks. The pain was quite strong, but somehow it was rapidly turning her on. 'Well, not exactly. Sort of . . . Oh God,' she moaned, arching her back to press her mons against the bed.

Why does being hurt arouse me so? she asked herself, circling her hips as Cynthia's deft fingertips worried and tugged at her beaten flesh. She had experienced the phenomenon enough times now to accept it as a valid part of her sexuality, but she still didn't understand the mechanism. In her mind, she was still a baby, afraid of pain, and with a childishly low tolerance of it; but her body and her subconscious had other ideas. On a purely genital level, being punished made her throb.

'Hold that thought,' said Cynthia, suddenly, making her yelp with a particularly fiendish tweak of the tender inner slope of her buttock. While it was still stinging, Cynthia stretched across the bed, and opened a drawer in her bedside table. Not wanting to see what the artist was fishing for, but with a good idea anyway, Joanna buried her face in the heap of goosedown pillows.

The next thing she knew she was being pulled up, by her thighs, into a crouch, then something smooth was being pressed to her vagina. Something smooth, and very big. Very

very big. She groaned and struggled as the intrusion pushed inside her.

'I can't! It's too big!' she protested, rubbing her face against the linen pillowcase.

'Yes, my love, it's an absolute monster,' said Cynthia with a giggle. 'But you can take it, I know you can. Just relax . . .'

Relax? But how, when something so huge was threatening to split her open? When something so immense was being slowly fed inside her?

'Relax,' urged Cynthia again, inexorably pushing.

Inch by inch, the awesome dildo went into her body, its progress becoming easier when her mind-set began to change. Her flesh was elastic, she knew that; it did possess the ability to encompass this leviathan. As her psyche accepted that fact, the sense of pressure became delightful.

'Oh God,' she groaned, feeling her stretched channel being caressed along its every inner surface. The thing was vibrating now, and emitting a muted, whirring drone.

'Is that nice?' enquired Cynthia, her voice as much a purr as the vibrator.

'Oh yes, oh God, yes,' croaked Joanna, hardly able to move because of the obstruction in her body, yet driven to writhe by its insistent pulsation.

'And how about this?' asked Cynthia, bending low over Joanna's back, and letting her silky hair trail languidly against her skin. She made a swift adjustment to the vibrator's oscillation, increasing its speed, then, a second later, she began drawing the tips of her nails across the sore globes of Joanna's bottom.

Unable to articulate her mad mélange of feelings, Joanna let out a cry that was half shriek and half gurgle, its pitch increasing as her tormentress scratched her harder.

She was on fire now, and plagued a thousand ways by her stuffed vagina and the anguish in her buttocks. The tension was so great she was convinced she might explode.

'And finally *this*!'

With only this perfunctory warning of her intentions, Cynthia reached underneath Joanna's body, and took her jumping clitoris in a delicate, pinching grip.

As Joanna climaxed, she began to squeal; then she passed out cold.

'Look, I know this is going to sound stupid,' said Joanna, cradling her mug of tea in her hands and studying Cynthia's face carefully. 'But are you by any chance a member of a secret society?'

Sipping her own tea, Cynthia stared back guilelessly. 'I don't think so,' she said, placing her mug on the table before her. 'What a strange idea. If I am in one, it's so secret that no one's ever told me.'

Above them, and through the skylight, the sky was already well on its way to getting dark. They had spent the whole of the afternoon and evening making love, but had got up at last, both in robes, to prepare a meal. Their plates – emptied now of cholesterol-laden egg and chips, which was the one dish they had both really fancied – lay before them, and they were sitting drinking mugs of strong, dark, Assam tea with milk. Beneath Joanna's bottom was a soft foam-filled cushion, even though by now the once-fierce ache was quickly fading.

'Well, that's rather odd,' observed Joanna, still scrutinising Cynthia's face for any sign of a reaction, 'because you seem to know, or have met, a lot of the people I'm pretty sure *are* in one.'

'I don't think it's all that odd,' Cynthia said cheerfully. 'In my line of work –' She hesitated, and nodded towards her drafting board, on which lay preliminary sketches for a study, albeit anonymous, of Joanna. The angle of the naked, proffered body ensured that the face and most of the head were hidden. '– I tend to meet all sorts of weird and wonderful people anyway. I wasn't joking; I might be part of this group, or whatever it is, without knowing.'

Pondering this, but quite sure Cynthia was flannelling her, Joanna remembered what Louise Walker had said about being in the continuum. The more you tried to find out, the less you were able to. Someone who claimed to know nothing at all might well turn out to be at the very centre of the mystery.

Taking another swig of the full-bodied, invigorating tea, Joanna maintained her observation of Cynthia. What if *she* were the mastermind? What if she had recruited all the others when they had gathered to admire her erotic art? It would be an efficient way of drawing like minds together.

'Does this club or whatever have a name?' asked Cynthia after a moment.

'Well, nobody I've met seems to think so,' said Joanna cautiously. 'Or if it does have a name, they haven't told me it yet.' She paused, and thought for a moment. 'I tend to think of it as the "Continuum".'

It was true, she realised; she had unconsciously christened the mysterious association 'the Continuum'. The word had crept into her mind gradually, at the same time as her suspicions had been growing, but it was only now, on revealing it to another, that the name had acquired its capital 'C'.

'Sounds rather posh, but I like it,' replied Cynthia. 'What the hell does it mean?' After a second or two, she pushed aside her mug, leapt to her feet and darted away, crying, 'Hang on a mo!'

When she returned she was carrying a thick book with a tattered red and blue dust-jacket. 'Here we are,' she said, after thumbing swiftly through the dictionary's pages. '"Continuum" – "a continuous series or whole, no part of which is perceptibly different from the adjacent parts."' Chuckling, she snapped the heavy book shut. 'Well, that makes me a lot wiser!'

'It's one of those words whose meaning you *think* you know –' Joanna laughed, too, at her own pretentiousness. ' – right up until the moment you try to define it.'

'Seriously, though; I think I know what you're getting at,' said Cynthia, her face suddenly soft and rather dreamy. 'It's a society whose members look just like all the normal people around them but really they aren't a bit like them at all. It's a world within a world within a world.'

My thoughts precisely, reflected Joanna, staring hard at her beautiful new friend, and elevating her to the top of the list of suspects. She had a sudden and powerful urge to talk with Kevin about Cynthia, and to get his sharp but wry opinion on her suspicions.

Could it be that 'Mr Big' was actually 'Ms. Big'?

Later, lying in the bath, she tried to phone Kevin. She had taken a shower with Cynthia, but there was something in her that craved a long, relaxing soak. The residual soreness in her buttocks had tingled with the heat when she had first immersed herself, but she had loaded the water with a supposedly miraculous new bath essence. Herbs, flowers, God knows what. Would any of these ingredients really do anything for a spanking? Or for a vagina that still felt faintly stretched?

Still, whatever was in it was sweet-smelling, soporific and soothing both to nerves and skin. She felt so full of ease and satisfaction, she almost dozed; then she remembered her desire to speak to Kevin. Having plucked her mobile phone from the bathside shelf, she dialled his number. As it rang, she took a sip of wine from the glass that she'd also brought into the bathroom with her.

I'm turning into a drunken sot, she told herself, as she listened to the steady ringing tone.

But I need it, she excused herself. I've had a gruelling day. I doubt if anyone ever had a day quite like it.

The ringing tone went on and on with no response and, expecting the answering service to cut in at any second, Joanna decided to switch off and abandon the call. She was just about to press the appropriate key, when a voice crisply answered, saying, 'Steel'.

'Kevin. Hello. It's —'

'Joanna,' he finished for her. 'So what's up? How was your day? Did you . . . er . . . find out anything interesting?'

'Interesting! You would not believe the things I found out today. Never in a million years.' She realised she was gushing like an over-excited schoolgirl and slowed down, taking a sip of her wine. 'Well, one of the things is truly astonishing. It'll kill you, honestly.'

'I'm intrigued. Go on.' Kevin's voice was warm, encouraging.

The secrets, the details, the whole exotic story hovered on her lips, ready to be told. Then the old Joanna, the pre-Continuum Joanna, whispered caution. The implications of 'outing' Davidson could be serious, and not only for the man himself. Could she really trust Kevin so completely?

'Joanna? Are you all right?' he prompted, and Joanna wished he was there with her, so she could see his face. See his clear blue eyes, so open and honest, and know that she could trust him. She also wished – in spite of every weird pleasure she had enjoyed today – that he was close by so he could come and share her bed. It would be uncomplicated, she would make sure of that. Just plain sex, no frills, as simple and wholesome as eating freshly baked bread, warm from the oven, with nothing on it.

'Yes. I'm just tired. It's been a weird day.'

'How weird?' enquired Kevin, his tone playful. Joanna heard a faint rustling sound in the background as he spoke.

'Very,' she said shortly, pressing the phone as close to her ear as she could. Was he in bed, she wondered? Was he naked? Was he touching his penis?

It occurred to Joanna then that she hadn't even told Kevin about De Rigeur. She would have to explain that before she went on to tell the tale of her exploits with 'Mistress'. And with Cynthia.

Pre-empting Kevin's questions, she asked one of her own, hoping to retain her control of their exchange. 'Did you go into Perry McAffee today?'

'Yeah, I was in this morning. Why do you ask?'

There was more rustling, and the image of him naked and touching his body grew irresistible.

'I just wondered.' She paused, sipped her wine. 'Did you by any chance see Denis Davidson at all?'

'No, I can't say I did. But then again our paths don't cross all that much. Why?'

'His path crossed with mine today, actually.'

There was a long, taut pause. She could almost hear Kevin's brain programming in the possible combinations.

'Are you trying to tell me what I think you're trying to tell me?' he said at last.

'I didn't fuck him, if that's what you're thinking?'

There was the sound of a small exhalation of breath. A sigh of relief? A gasp of excitement? The line was clear but it was still impossible to tell.

'Something happened, though, didn't it?' said Kevin, his voice frustratingly neutral.

'It's a long story,' she said, her heart suddenly skipping alarmingly.

'That's okay; I'm sitting comfortably. Or, should I say, lying comfortably.'

'I'm not,' she said, realising that the water that she was wallowing in was getting cool. 'I'm in the bath and the water's gone cold. Hang on a minute.' Abandoning her glass, and the phone, she rose from the water, stepped out and swathed her body in a thick, fluffy towel. 'That's better,' she continued, retrieving both phone and glass and walking through into the bedroom. Lying down, she began the tale of De Rigeur, describing Mistress only as a tall brunette who wore suede and a veil.

Her account was punctuated by more gasps from Kevin, and the occasional terse question. She was pretty sure he was masturbating now, and she couldn't blame him. Even in retrospect, what had happened turned her on. Opening her towel, she cupped her breast and flicked her nipple, pursing her lips – in a moment of silence – to contain her own gasp.

'And sh-she put the brush inside you?' asked Kevin, his voice wavering.

'Yes, right in. It was warm, where she'd held it. It felt good. Even though I was in pain. *Because* I was in pain,' she said with emphasis, reaching around and feeling the ghost of that agony in her buttocks. 'Then she used it like a dildo. She screwed me with it. In and out, in and out until I climaxed.'

'Oh, dear God!' Kevin's cry was choked, almost strangled, then faded away shockingly into the distance.

He had dropped his flip-phone and was using both hands on himself.

In contrast, Joanna gripped her own phone so tightly she nearly snapped it into two pieces. With her free hand, she pressed hard into her crotch, feeling an ache that was low and gnawing, but also welcome.

Never having been in Kevin's bedroom, the image she formed of him was tightly focused. Just a man, with an erection, on a bed. It would make a marvellous photoset for *Luscious*, she thought – remembering the magazine she had so enjoyed on the way to Littlebourne – or even a subject for Cynthia's fine artistic eye.

He would be naked, she decided. Definitely. She, or perhaps they – herself and Cynthia – would pose him undraped, on a gleaming black silk sheet, to highlight his creamy skin and his shock of wheat-blond hair.

But would he be tense, or languid? The pictures she was seeing now, she realised, would never be accepted for publication in a magazine. His flesh was far too stiff for the image to be legal, and he was gripping it, like a weapon, with his fist. In the rise towards orgasm, his body rose up too; arching up, on heels and shoulders, like a bow. His pointed, boyish features were distorted, barely recognisable; his lips were thinned in a helpless snarl of lust.

'Oh God,' she whispered. After all that had happened today, she was still so aroused she couldn't think straight. She could see her vision of Kevin masturbating so clearly it stunned her, as if he were with her, in the room, and on her bed.

'Joanna?' queried a small voice, breaking into her fantasy, and she realised that she too, like Kevin, had dropped her phone. Picking it up, and flipping her towel across her glistening, fragrant crotch, she held it to her ear, but couldn't seem to find the words to form an answer.

'Joanna, are you still there?' asked Kevin, his voice calm now, perfectly normal and unflustered.

'Yes. Of course. Where were you?'

He laughed, unabashed. 'I kind of lost it, I'm afraid,' he said, still chuckling. 'That story of yours was so steamy I got a hard-on. Have you ever thought of writing porno for a living? You'd make a fortune.'

'I'm a numbers person, not a words person, Kevin,' she said primly, reacting instinctively, and with anger, to his flippancy. 'And that wasn't a story; it all happened.'

'Maybe you should write your autobiography, then?' he suggested.

Joanna's finger hovered over the 'receiver down' button. Why was she letting him get to her again?

Because she probably liked him far more than was good for her, she realised. Kevin was a friend with whom she just happened to have amazing sex, too. He had never suggested they make things more serious. They were lovers, but nothing more than that.

'I haven't told you the best bit yet,' she said, lightly. 'But it's getting late. And I'm really, really tired.' To her surprise, she suddenly had to quash a yawn.

'I'm sorry, I'm a pig. Please go on.' Kevin's voice was gentle and genuinely contrite.

'After I'd – I'd settled down after my spanking – and the consequences – well, I found out who "Mistress" really is.' She paused, for effect. 'And you'll never guess who it is.'

'Well then, who is it, Joanna?'

'I'll give you a clue; she told me to call her "Denise".'

There was a short silence, then Kevin said, 'Davidson?' His voice sounded strangely unperturbed.

Joanna was puzzled. She had expected an outcry; something laddish and derogatory. How typical of Kevin to surprise her yet again.

'You don't sound as if it's much of a shock to you,' she said.

'It isn't, I suppose . . . In a way,' said Kevin thoughtfully. 'He's a good-looking man. He's got great presence. Fabulous bone structure. And he moves well. If I had to pick out any man as a cross dresser, it would be him.'

Joanna stared at her phone, surprise changing rapidly to astonishment. And approval. What a reasoned response; so accepting. It was incredible; every time she thought she had the measure of Kevin Steel, he showed her a new face, a new level of complexity.

'You almost sound as if you admire him,' she said, and, after a moment, added, 'As if you're attracted to him.'

Too much, Joanna, she told herself in the protracted silence that followed. It was one thing to applaud a man's tolerance, another to suggest something that to most men was a slur on their manhood. Just because *she* had discovered a new and expanded sexuality, it didn't mean that Kevin felt the urge to expand his.

'I am,' came the answer, the words tranquil.

Joanna sat up, her desire for the moment forgotten. Her towel slithered away from her body.

'Have I shocked you?' enquired Kevin, with a smile in his voice.

'I'm surprised,' she said, rising from the bed, picking up her glass, and walking through to the kitchen, naked, as she continued to speak. 'But I feel a bit guilty, too. I shouldn't make assumptions.' She reached her destination and poured more wine, feeling vaguely numb, but in a pleasant way, as if she were cushioned in some soft, voluptuous substance. 'It's as bad as passing judgements. I'm sorry, I just didn't know.'

'No reason you should,' said Kevin. 'It's not an issue that's arisen between us yet.' It was his turn to pause and, straining her senses, Joanna imagined she could detect a trace of apprehension. 'Does it bother you?'

Did it?

No. No, it didn't. Not at all! But how could she tell him?

'Joanna?'

She hesitated, in the middle of the living room. Her nipples were tingling, she realised. She felt sleek and fiery, like a mutable new woman. Whole new worlds seemed to be opening up to her; new ways to enjoy herself, new ways to take her pleasure.

'No, Kevin, it doesn't bother me at all –' she strode forward into the bedroom, her excitement rising '– apart from the fact that it turns me on like crazy!' Having put her glass down, she flung herself backward on to the bed and kicked her bare legs exultantly in the air. 'Tell me all about it. It's your turn to tell *me* a story!'

'A story, eh?' Kevin mused, wondering whereabouts in her flat Joanna was.

The bedroom, he supposed. Was she naked perhaps? Or in a robe or a night-gown? For a moment, he imagined her in a soft, pretty Victorian night-dress. Something in white or cream, complete with flounces and lace and embroidery.

Down boy, he thought, as his penis grew frisky again, and he felt an unbearable urge to touch it. He wanted to last this time, to extend his own pleasure and to induce an equal sensation in Joanna – as he told her a tale of his exploits with other men.

'Kevin. Are you still there?' she queried.

Kevin said, 'Yes; just thinking,' then placed the receiver of his phone on its hands-free mounting, and settled down more comfortably. He was lying on a leather chesterfield, in the study of his small London house, wearing an open towelling robe, and with a glass of whisky placed to hand on the rug beside him. Perfect bliss, save for the lack of another body.

'I'll tell you about the last time I was with a man,' he said at length, adjusting his position on the couch. He felt a ghostly sensation in the crease of his buttocks, as if just referring to the event produced a resonance. It had been good, a sweet act of pleasure between two longstanding friends.

'It was about eight or nine months ago, before I met you,' he went on. 'With a man I've known for ages. A friend. We have sex sometimes, but we're not an item as such. I like him. He likes me. It's nothing heavy.'

'What's he like?' asked Joanna suddenly. 'I need to be able to imagine him.'

Kevin sensed that she was also dying to ask if the man was someone she knew herself, and he admired her restraint when she didn't.

'I'm not that good at descriptions,' he said thoughtfully, 'but you could imagine a man like Davidson, perhaps. That type. You know; dark, very sure of himself, very hip.'

'A transvestite?'

'Oh no, not in this case,' replied Kevin, drifting back. 'I was staying at his house, it was evening. We were both casually dressed. Jeans, T-shirts – a bit scruffy really. We were drinking beer, and watching sport on the television. Real

Boy's Own stuff. But I happened to look across and notice he had an erection.'

'And he looks like Davidson?' persisted Joanna, doubtfully.

'Yes. Definitely.' Kevin thought fondly of the man he had spent that night with. His thick, brown hair, unstyled and a little tousled where he had run his hand through it in exasperation when his team had missed an easy point; the pleasant, almost ordinary face that came alight when he smiled.

'I can't imagine a man like Davidson wearing jeans.' Joanna seemed to ponder. 'Especially not now.'

'Well, just give it a try,' urged Kevin, grinning to himself. 'I'm sure even Davidson himself doesn't always wear Armani.'

'OK.'

'He was hard, that was obvious,' said Kevin, picking up the story. 'But he was either trying to ignore it, or he was genuinely unaware of the fact. This is a very sexy man, Joanna,' he emphasised, 'the sort of person who spends a lot of his life turned on. He's probably used to being stiff at odd, unexpected moments.'

'What did you do?'

'Well, for a start, I got hard myself . . .'

'Then what?'

'I started touching myself,' he said, letting his hand brush momentarily against his penis. It had been rising even as he spoke, the warm flesh filling with blood and jerking upwards from where it had rested against his thigh. 'To show him it was OK; that I was turned on too, and that I wanted him.'

'Did he see what you were doing?'

'Yes. But neither of us was in any great hurry, so we just went on watching the game. Both holding, and occasionally rubbing ourselves. It was nice. Sort of companionable. Neither of us spoke, but we didn't seem to need to.

'Anyway, the sport finished, and some other programme came on, but by then neither of us was really watching the box. After a while, he closed his eyes, let his head loll back, and ignored the screen. And I watched him.'

The memory was keen now. He saw again the moment when his lover had unselfconsciously unzipped himself, then taken the waistband of his jeans and his boxer shorts in a bunch, and pushed the whole lot down to his knees, baring both his penis and his bottom in one move.

'He uncovered himself,' Kevin said quietly, savouring even the words. 'Pushed his jeans and shorts down, the whole lot. Then he started wriggling, massaging his arse against the chair, and squeezing his cock with his fingers. It was one of the sexiest things I've ever seen –' And he had seen some sexy things in his time, he reflected, smiling to himself.

'And what did you do then?' Joanna's voice was very breathy all of a sudden, and Kevin permitted himself a moment's diversion. Instead of his male lover, he saw Joanna – her pelvis jerking, her legs tense, her soft breasts bouncing as her fingers rode her clitoris.

'Kevin?'

'I got down on my knees and crawled across the room to him. I had my cock out and it hung down as I crawled. I was so turned on it felt like a slab of lead.' His fingers flickered up and down his penis, dancing over tender spots, taunting and teasing. 'He looked so beautiful I just wanted to worship him. My cock was really hurting me, but I was glad of it. I was suffering for him. And the more it hurt me, the more tribute I gave to him.'

As he spoke, he wondered how well Joanna understood that concept. Quite well, it seemed, because very faintly, he heard her whisper, 'Yes . . .'

'I felt constrained by him. Bound by the sight of him. I wanted to touch myself. I wanted to wank myself senseless. But I knew instead I had to deny myself. And serve him.

'He made me watch, for what seemed an age, while he caressed himself. It was all very unhurried. He seemed to be denying himself, too; keeping his touch light, squeezing the head of his penis carefully to stave off his climax. After a while, I couldn't bear not to touch him any longer. I shuffled forward and began to kiss his thighs. I tried to move upwards, to get my mouth around his cock, but he wouldn't let me. When I got too close, when I nudged his shaft for a second, he slapped my face.'

'He hit you?' Joanna sounded entranced, not horrified, as if she too were responding in the way Kevin had. With, that was, a wild rush of fresh arousal to her genitals.

'Yes. And hard, too. My cheek was stinging. It brought tears to my eyes. But I nearly shot my load on the carpet.

"Not until I tell you!", he said, then grabbed hold of my hair, and wrenched my head back. He was still holding his own shaft with the other hand. I thought he was going to pull me down on to him then; to make me suck him. Instead, he just twisted his fingers into my hair and pulled it. It really hurt, but I didn't dare say a thing to him.'

Kevin remembered a pair of brown eyes studying him disdainfully, and a slow, smug, almost spiteful smile. His scalp had been on fire, but it had been the ache – the sweet, heavy ache – in his cock that had pained him the most.

'"You're such a slut," he said to me. "You really want it, don't you?" He raised me up by my hair then, and I thought he was going to kiss me, but instead he just flung me away from him. I grovelled, but I couldn't take my eyes off his penis.

'The next thing I knew, he had kicked off his trainers, and was gesturing for me to remove his jeans and shorts. I did so gladly, trying my best not to touch him in the process. Because he'd told me I shouldn't. That I didn't deserve to.'

What a sight it had been. His beautiful male lover, naked from the waist down, with his shaft rearing insolently from his groin. The tip had been very red and engorged. Oozing with the thinnest sheen of crystal fluid, the tiny aperture pouting. He had wanted to lick it, but he had known that that was forbidden, too.

'He told me to stand, then, and to remove my lower clothing in the way I'd removed his for him. I sprang to it, as fast as I could, feeling embarrassed by my rigid, swinging cock.

'Not that it seemed to make much of an impression on him. He hardly even seemed to look at it, as if it were so undistinguished he couldn't be bothered to take notice. "Turn around," he said, and I obeyed him. I could feel his eyes almost feasting on the view there, on my bare arse. I knew what he wanted, and I wanted it too. I struck a pose, legs apart, backside thrust out, to show him what I had to offer.'

There was silence, now, from Joanna's end of the line, but Kevin knew her attention was still riveted on the sound of his voice.

'He leapt up then, and pushed me down on to the carpet, making me crouch, like a bitch, on my hands and knees. I was panting hard as he knelt down behind me and began to massage my bottom, his fingers dipping greedily into my crease. "You slut!" he said again, stroking my anus and making me whimper like a child. I was helpless now; I could barely control myself. I pushed back against him and swivelled my hips. Then he shoved me over again and made me kiss the rug.'

Kevin looked down at his own body. His penis was just as hard now as it had been on the night he was describing, and his glans just as slippery with silky juice. But it hadn't been his own hand that had triggered him then.

'I suppose you can work out what happened next,' he said, the tenor of his voice growing shaky.

'Yes. I can,' came the reply, full of warmth and excitement. 'But that doesn't mean you don't have to tell me.'

'All right! All right! But don't blame me if I sometimes have to stop.'

He heard her laugh softly just as his fist closed round his shaft.

11

Overload

It was a condition she had always called 'overload', and she had it now for the first time in ages. And, for the first time ever, it was over her private life, not about work, as was usually the case. Joanna looked up, across the tube compartment she was riding in, and stared at her fellow travellers as if she were an alien fallen by accident to Earth.

Kevin. The Continuum. Spanking. Cynthia. The Walkers. Davidson. Denise, for God's sake! It was all too much for a normal person to absorb in a year, never mind within the space of a week. Joanna was confident of her own ability to cope with pressure, but this was entirely different. She couldn't think about it, and them, all at once. It was difficult even to think about one of them, at any one time, without feeling a dangerous urge to panic. The only answer, she realised, was to distract herself with work; fresh, different work, not the collection of uninspiring project files she had already lost interest in. She knew there were a couple of new reports in her pending basket – ones which had just come in when she had been ordered to take her sabbatical – and she had decided to take a chance and to go into Perry McAffee to collect them. A phone call had revealed that Halloran wasn't in the office today, so it should be possible to slip in, get the files, and get out again without too much notice being taken of her. Having dressed casually, she could always fob off enquirers by saying she had called for some personal item or other.

But the journey in was making her feel strange. Shifting in her seat, she felt the residual tenderness in her bottom as it chafed against the inside of her jeans. It was nothing now, really, and yet just the fact that it existed reassured her somehow. She had tangible proof that she had visited Mistress yesterday, and had had her buttocks thrashed with a hairbrush. And if that was true, so must everything else be. She really was bisexual, and she really had made love with Cynthia Russart. And, by extension, what Kevin had told her last night, during their phone call, was also a reflection of true fact.

You're doing it again, Darrell, she told herself as the credits of her bizarre inner movie began to roll for the twentieth time that morning. Seeking distraction, she stared around the compartment.

Did the parallel world – the Continuum – also exist in these grubby surroundings? Of course it did, even if she were its sole representative. Which she might not actually be, at that.

Surreptitiously, Joanna studied a woman sitting opposite her. She looked shy, almost scared, as if she were an out-of-towner and the metropolis intimidated her. Her frequent, nervous glances at the tube map indicated she was terrified of missing her station.

But what if this modest, middle-aged creature were on her way now to meet a 'Mistress' of her own, or perhaps a

'Master'? Joanna could almost taste the woman's imaginary trepidation; the delicious, weakening shock when she was ordered to take her knickers down and bare her bottom before some fickle power figure. She closed her eyes, lost in the moment of shame the woman would experience when it was revealed that she was not only fearful, but also drippingly aroused. She imagined a gag, a blindfold, shackles; the flash of pain as the hairbrush, the hand, or the slipper, or whatever it was, crashed down upon a defenceless white bottom.

The carriage rattled and swayed and Joanna almost whimpered.

For goodness sake, there I go again, she thought, taking a deep breath to bring her back to reality. The timid-looking woman was by the sliding door now, clinging on tightly to the rail, and Joanna wondered for an instant where she was really going. Then she hoped that it was at least half as exciting as her own daydream.

At Perry McAffee, Joanna got in without attracting much attention, and strode through the open plan offices, hoping that her jeans and leather jacket might act as a camouflage. She got to her desk without encountering any problematic faces, although she knew already that Halloran was out, and that Kevin was elsewhere today. Sifting swiftly through the items in her tray, she flipped open one or two files, then slipped them discreetly into her tote bag.

'Hey, what's this? Industrial espionage?' said a familiar drawling voice from just behind her, making her drop one of the bulging folders on to the floor. 'I thought you were supposed to be taking a holiday?'

Oh no. Not him!

Joanna crouched down to retrieve the scattered papers, but didn't turn round. Apprehension was a solid mass inside her chest and, as a long, elegant hand reached from behind her, and lifted the manila folder she had been scrabbling for, she felt so giddy that she almost toppled over.

'Steady. Take it easy. Are you okay?' said Davidson, kindly, as he helped her to rise to a standing position, then began slotting the papers neatly back into the folder. He was wearing a dark suit today, something loose and Italian, which made her think of Kevin's jibe about Armani, but which also flattered his cryptic looks to perfection. She had never seen him looking so strong and dark and male.

He studied her with mischievous brown eyes as she clutched her bag against her for protection. 'Come and have coffee with me,' he said suddenly, then grinned. 'We can have a little chat; you look to me as if you need one.'

A few minutes later she was standing in Davidson's spacious office, feeling as jittery as she would have done if he had been some unprincipled South American dictator, about to extract secrets from her by the foulest of foul means. Either that, or he was suddenly going to don a dress, high heels, and full make-up.

'You shouldn't really be back here yet, you know,' he observed, leaning back in his massive leather chair. Ludicrously, Joanna felt unable to take a seat herself, until he had granted her permission.

'Really?' she countered, feeling a small amount of confidence return, and with it a frisson of desire. She thought of the penis that lay within those dark, modish trousers. 'And what are you going to do about that?' She glanced at his desk, which was uncluttered apart from one slim file and a blotter edged in tooled green leather. 'Put me over the end of your desk and spank me?'

Davidson laughed, the distinctive shape of his mouth curving exactly as it had done when it had been coated with red-brown lipstick. 'Tempting,' he murmured, his voice carrying a faint echo of Mistress as he steepled his fingers and looked thoughtful. 'Very tempting; although, right at this minute, Joanna, I'd far rather fuck you.'

Joanna realised her surprise must have shown in her eyes, because he went on, 'Oh, I can act incredibly macho when I feel like it, you know.' His eyes met hers; very level, very steady, and very challenging. 'I thought you realised that I enjoy being with women just as much as I enjoy looking like one. I'm not a homosexual, *per se*.'

Kevin's story of last night flashed through her mind, leaving a trail in its wake. He had spoken of a 'Davidson type', but she had a sudden fancy that it might have been the man himself.

'I do realise that,' she said, a little nettled. 'You made it pretty obvious.' She could also remember, very clearly, the taste and feel of Davidson's cock in *her* mouth. Her female and, at the time, submissive mouth.

'I swing both ways,' he said, smiling. 'It seems to suit me.'

And me too, now, Joanna thought, her mind's eye shifting again to Cynthia, naked and beautiful, in the shower.

'It doubles my opportunities,' Davidson went on cheerfully, then he stood up and gestured towards the social area, at the other end of his office, where there was a low table, flanked by easy chairs. There was a cafetière on the table, and two large cups set out in readiness. 'Shall we sit over there?'

'Why not?' countered Joanna, needing a respite. Picking up her bag from beside her chair, she followed him over.

Davidson waited on her courteously. He poured out her coffee for her just like any perfectly ordinary – albeit handsome – man trying to make a good impression on a woman he fancied; but somehow, the very naturalness of his actions seemed unnatural. Joanna could only think of the bizarre world he represented and, when he sat down opposite her and grinned, she had to round on him.

'Why can't you tell me who's behind all this?' she said, sipping her coffee but not tasting it. She put down her cup, crossed her legs and thrust her hands into her pockets. 'I won't tell them it was you who told me,' she offered, wondering whether to try the kind of bribery she had endeavoured to use the previous day. It hadn't worked, of course, but the attempt had been delicious in itself.

'They'd find out anyway,' Davidson answered, putting aside his own cup, then studying his hands. He ran a thumb over the fingernails of his other hand, and Joanna wondered if he was looking for stray flecks of nail lacquer. 'Then *I* might be banished, as well as you. As a punishment.'

'Couldn't they just whack you with a hairbrush instead?' Joanna said flippantly.

Davidson gave her a slow, silky smile. 'I would have thought you'd know better by now,' he said. 'In the circles we move in, the hairbrush could be considered a reward, rather than a punishment.' He crossed his legs, *à la* Mistress, and clasped his long hands around his uppermost knee. 'Has it occurred to you that what happened to you yesterday might have been an incentive, a dividend for getting as far as you have done?'

The idea was outlandish, and the logic perverse, yet it glimmered before her like the jewel in a mysterious fable. And she was starting to see the pattern. Pain, and the suppression of will were not just ordeals to be got through in order to receive supreme pleasure afterwards. The ordeal in itself was a part of the pleasure; it preconditioned the body for release; it transformed it and extended its senses. One aspect could not truly exist without the other. She had seen this all along, but never quite so clearly.

'Bloody hell,' she said, almost under her breath, moving forward in her seat, uncrossing her legs, and staring into the middle distance before her. She was aware of Davidson watching her, and that he was amused, but she also knew that his amusement was benign, almost congratulatory. She could almost believe he was aware of her every thought.

'Neat, isn't it?' he said when she looked up.

'If you say so,' she replied, still thinking.

It could only be *some* people who had seen this same light, she reasoned. Or everyone would be at it. And then it wouldn't be so secret.

Or maybe everybody was at it, and she was just the last to catch on?

She frowned, dismissing that notion. It was much more of an ego trip to be part of an élite.

'Who decides, though?' she demanded of Davidson. 'Who picks out people in the first place? There *is* someone; don't tell me there isn't!'

'You'll find out soon.'

'Is it Halloran?'

'Joanna.' His voice was smooth, quiet, warning. Quintessentially 'Mistress'.

'Is it a woman?'

'Is who a woman?'

She was just about to press harder when something Louise Walker had said to her resurfaced again.

The more you try to find out the less you discover . . .

Joanna had a sudden flash of insight; her second within the space of ten minutes. If she asked one more question about the identity of whomsoever it was who commanded the Continuum, its illusory doors would never open to her again. She knew that with more certainty than she could explain or understand.

She bowed her head, and muttered, 'Sorry,' and tried to look penitent, even if she didn't feel like that at all.

'Better. So much better,' said Davidson, sounding genuinely pleased.

And it was better, Joanna thought. Her own satisfaction surprised her. She had achieved something, conquered her own will, and the reward was strangely voluptuous. She was suddenly aware of every inch of her skin; of the way her breasts pressed against the stretchy fabric of her bra; of the sensation of her jeans's seam, where it had worked up into her crotch and was lodged against her clitoris. Looking down at the coffee table before them, she pictured its surfaces cleared, and herself kneeling up on it, her jeans and knickers conveniently pushed down to her knees. She would be quiet and still. She would be obedient. She would wait.

'If I didn't have a meeting in a few minutes, I'd reward you right now,' said Davidson, making Joanna look up again. He was casually fingering his narrow leather belt, and the action made her stomach muscles quiver. 'But, alas, I'm required elsewhere,' he continued and, abandoning his belt, he reached into the inner pocket of his jacket and took out a tiny, leather-bound notebook and a slender silver pen. 'This will make up for it, though,' he said with a sudden briskness, jotting down words, then tearing out the sheet and passing it across to her. 'Be there tonight, at about nine. Maybe you'll find some of those answers you're so desperate for.'

But will I? thought Joanna later. She had a feeling that all she would find were more and more questions.

When she had arrived home, she had not looked once at the files in her tote bag, but had spent the whole day mulling over the ambiguous utterances of Davidson, and her own paradoxical reactions to them.

The address he had given her was a smart one, in Mayfair no less, not far from Green Park, but there was no indication of what was to occur there. In answer to her respectfully couched question, Davidson had replied that it was not a grand party, or a night club as such, but simply an informal get-together of like-minded people.

This is it! This is it! she had thought at the time, feeling an elation which had been, and still was close to hysteria if she didn't stringently suppress it. She had been invited to a gathering of the Continuum, most probably one of the same ones Louise Walker had described.

Something else Davidson had said had completely blind-sided her, though.

'Why not bring a friend?' he had suggested, his brown eyes twinkling.

'But – I – ' she had stammered, forgetting the dictum of polite, submissive questions only.

'You've been chosen, so *you* too can choose,' had been his reply, but he was on his feet by then, and at his desk, slipping the single file into his narrow matt-black briefcase. She had been dismissed and, feeling numb, she had got up and walked quietly to the door, wondering if she was somehow back in disgrace.

But as she had turned the handle and opened the door, Davidson had had one more suggestion to offer.

'Bring someone you think can contribute; someone who'll "fit in", if you know what I mean?'

That choice had been difficult, but easy. She hadn't the faintest idea of who would fit in, or quite what they were fitting in to; but there were only two people she could possibly consider.

Joanna had balked at leaving a message on Cynthia Russart's answerphone, because she didn't really know what it was she was inviting the artist to. That left only one other possible candidate, and if he didn't answer, there would really be nobody.

'Steel,' Kevin had answered, on the first ring, sounding just as he had done last night – cool and dispassionate until she had identified herself to him. He had listened to what she had to say without interruption, then answered her with a surprising solemnity. 'Yes, I'd like to go with you.' His words had lacked any trace of the glee and excitement she had expected. 'I'm glad you've asked me. You don't know these people, Joanna, not really. I don't think it's safe that you go there all alone.'

It hadn't been anything like the response she had anticipated and afterwards when she had rung off, and even now, when she was waiting for Kevin to arrive, it was still perplexing. There was a part of her that wanted to forget the Continuum altogether, she realised.

A Joanna who wanted to stop craving things she didn't fully understand, and settle down and concentrate on building a relationship with this man who sincerely seemed to care for her. It would be much easier, and less painful – and not at all boring, really, because even without all the

Continuum developments, Kevin had proven to be a challenge in himself.

'Damn!'

Her entryphone had trilled, making her knock over a pot of loose powder. She shot up from where she was sitting and darted away from the flying dust. Grabbing her tiny shoulderbag, she raced through the flat to answer the call, leaving a still settling cloudburst of 'Cameo Ivory' across the carpet.

'It's me. I've got a taxi outside. Shall I come up?' said Kevin's tinny voice through the speaker.

'No! It's okay. I'll come down,' she replied, knowing she was denying herself a last chance to renege, and feeling a small thrill of pleasure in that fact. She had never taken the easy path in her life.

'You look gorgeous,' said Kevin, as she reached him on the pavement.

'Thanks,' murmured Joanna, suddenly apprehensive as he helped her into the cab. She had expended a good deal of thought on her choice of clothing, and was still not sure she had selected the right outfit. Davidson had been so infuriatingly vague about the nature of the gathering.

Not sure whether she was going to be arriving at a cocktail party with just something a little special in the way of entertainment, or a fully enacted ritual scenario, as she had read described in some of the Walkers' magazines, she had used her instincts alone as a guide, and chosen a long-sleeved, close-fitting 'little black dress', worn with the red shoes she had been wearing when she had met 'Mistress'. She had noticed a glint of admiration in Davidson's eyes, as if he had coveted them.

There was a similar sparkle in Kevin's eyes now. The black dress was short, and she was wearing hold-up stockings – and, as she settled down in the taxi seat, their deep lace welts came sliding briefly into view. She did not dare to think about what he would say about the rest of her ensemble, or perhaps the lack of it, but that was an issue she would have to face when the time came.

'What's this?' he said, reaching out, unexpectedly, to touch the only other adornment she was wearing – a thin strand of black silk ribbon, tied around her neck, with its bow towards the back, at her nape.

'I-I don't know, really,' she said, reaching up to touch it herself, just as Kevin withdrew his fingers. 'It just sort of seemed right, you know – for this sort of thing.'

Kevin shrugged, and gave her a quirky, 'Are you sure?' smile. Joanna thought of the collars of leather and of steel that had first shocked her, then fascinated her, in the magazines, and wondered how long it would be before she wore one herself.

She was too keyed up to speak during the rest of the journey and, as if sensing this, Kevin was silent, too. There was so much she should have said to him, so much she should have asked him, but all the words seemed locked up inside her. When the taxi slowed to a halt, she gasped with apprehension, and wondered for how long she had been holding her breath so tensely.

'We can still turn back,' said Kevin as they ascended the broad steps towards a glossy, dark-painted door – which was anonymous but for the number '17' in polished brass numerals.

'Too late!' said Joanna, reaching out to press the entryphone button before she could have second thoughts.

A vaguely familiar voice answered 'Yes?' and Joanna said her name, then had to say it again when her first attempt was little more than a squeak. The distant voice didn't answer, but there was a click and the heavy black door swung open.

They entered through the vestibule and came out into a beautifully proportioned and subtly decorated entrance hall. There was no one around, but Joanna could hear voices somewhere nearby and, quite clearly, the tinkle of ice against a glass.

A cocktail party, then, she thought, pleased with her outfit, but feeling a moment of doubt about Kevin's. He looked wonderful, as she realised he always did, but his garb was casual rather than dressy. Jeans, very tight and very faded, made his lean legs look yards long, and a sombre, black silk polo-neck set off his fair hair and gave it a fiery, reddish cast. His plain, but very heavy black leather belt looked as if it might have a place in the dealings of the Continuum, though, and Joanna bit her lip, already imagining the sound of it being drawn out slickly through his belt loops.

'Shall we?' said Kevin, gesturing towards the sounds of conviviality, which were coming from a partially open door at the far end of the hall. Just at that moment, a figure emerged from another door, set beneath the wide staircase that led up to the first floor.

'Mercedes!' said Joanna, shocked as much by the maid's outfit as by her presence. The sultry girl was wearing what seemed to be a silk skating skirt, a transparent voile apron, and very little else at all, except for a pair of black stilettos that were far higher than Joanna's red ones. She walked towards them, her demeanour as cold as ice, and her large breasts bouncing meatily before her. Giving no indication whatsoever that she had ever seen Joanna before, she said, 'Please follow me', and gestured towards the source of the noise. As they walked behind her, they could see that her buttocks were as lush and curvaceous as her bosom was, and just as naked. Joanna glanced at Kevin and saw his eyes were as round as two blue coins. He shrugged and grinned, then stepped back so she could precede him.

In the reception room beyond, everything appeared deceptively normal at first. The party was of a modest size – with guests across what seemed to be a broad band of age and social standing – and had obviously been underway for some time, as there was a steady hum of conversation and the occasional burst of laughter. A second maid, this one more conventionally attired, brought forward a tray of glasses, and Joanna and Kevin helped themselves.

It was as she took her first sip of white wine, though, that Joanna noticed that not all was as it seemed. A rather ravaged-looking man in his sixties, dressed in a dinner suit, was standing not three yards away from her, talking expansively to a small group of other men, whilst at his heels was crouched a naked young woman. The girl's hands were shackled behind her, and her shell-pink mouth was stretched around an unpleasant-looking ball-shaped gag. Joanna felt Kevin nudge her discreetly in the midriff, and knew that he, too, had seen the girl in bondage.

Seeing one manifestation of the Continuum seemed to reveal others.

Joanna saw several more 'slaves' crouched at the feet of their masters and mistresses. A woman, half in profile, had her expensive silk skirt tucked deliberately, it was obvious, into her belt at the back. Her bottom was bare and striped with lines of pink. She was laughing gaily and seemed to be discussing a film which Joanna herself had seen a couple of weeks ago, with three other perfectly normally-dressed women.

Across the room, beside the colourful and appetising-looking buffet, a tall man with short, dark, heavily gelled hair was standing with his back to her, talking earnestly to two beautiful, olive-skinned young women – identical twins by the look of it – who were both wearing full size, authentic school uniforms. As someone moved away from between this group and Joanna, she saw that the tall man was wearing a rusty black academic gown.

There was something slightly familiar about him, too – the angle of his head, his straight-backed stance – but, just as she was about to analyse this, a familiar voice said, 'Hello, you two. I'm glad you could make it,' and a firm hand took her possessively by the elbow. Turning around, she found it was 'Mistress Denise' who had joined them.

'Oh, hello,' she said, trying to sound as normal as possible, and flicking the quickest of glances at Kevin. His jaw had dropped, and he was openly staring at their exotically-clad colleague. Clearly, the reality of Davidson's alternate persona had exceeded Kevin's imaginings by a mile.

Mistress Denise looked wonderful. She wore what looked like a real Chanel suit in a light but vivid pink, with the ruffles of a magenta *moiré* blouse tumbling out from between the edge to edge panels of her jacket. She was hatless tonight, and the heavy silky wings of glossy brown hair curved slightly inward where they brushed her broad shoulders.

'Don't look so surprised, sweetheart,' she murmured creamily, letting go of Joanna and reaching out to stroke Kevin's shocked face. Before he could stop her, she was kissing him on the mouth.

It was a long kiss, a lascivious kiss. The sort of kiss enjoyed by two lovers at the start of an affair, when the blood ran hot and the needs of the flesh were paramount. At first it was

Denise alone who was putting in the effort but, after a few seconds, Kevin began to respond, giving as good as he got, and more. Watching, Joanna felt her heart thud and, holding her glass in both hands, she took a long, reviving sip of her wine. It was either that or rub her sex through her dress.

'I never realised what I was missing,' said Denise, throatily, as she pulled away from Kevin. She reached across and rubbed a stray trace of her lip tint from his mouth. A pang of jealousy seemed to twist Joanna's gut.

'Now then, my dear Joanna, let me show you around,' Denise said, changing tack. She stepped away from Kevin and took Joanna by the arm again. 'I'm sure Kevin can amuse himself for a little while. There's plenty going on.' Denise gestured gracefully towards the shackled girl, who had been pulled to her feet, then made to touch her toes. Her grey-haired companion had an object in his hand and was twisting and flipping it this way and that, as if preparing to play a game of some kind. It looked like a tennis table bat, but Joanna knew he wasn't about to play ping-pong.

'How clever of you to choose Kevin,' said Denise, into Joanna's ear as they moved away. A maid came forward to offer more drinks, but Denise whisked away Joanna's glass and placed it on the tray without allowing her to take another. 'I'm sure he'll fit in very nicely here,' the transvestite went on, hurrying Joanna towards a partially open double door at the far end of the room.

There was a display being put on in the area beyond. A woman was kneeling on all fours on a polished oak table, her head low, her ample bottom well pushed up. She was wearing a rather ugly and old-fashioned elastane corset that had been rolled halfway up her back to expose her, and a man dressed only in a loose white shirt was toiling hard, thrusting into her from behind. All around them, people were watching. Avidly.

It took a few seconds for Joanna to realise that the woman being fucked was Louise Walker, and that the man who was servicing her wasn't her husband. Major Walker was standing to one side, his hand on the nape of his wife's neck, as if he were calming an excitable young filly. As Joanna watched, he slid his other hand down beneath his wife's chest, and eased one full breast from the bra cup of her corset, then pinched its nipple in time to the other man's thrusts. When he saw Joanna, he smiled and inclined his head in a distant greeting, but didn't pause in his manipulation of Louise.

'Are you pleased to see your friends?' whispered Denise in Joanna's ear, squeezing her arm quite forcefully and urging her further into the room.

Joanna nodded. She felt an intense urge to shake off Denise's fingers, which were really hurting her, but knew that she was no longer in a position to object to anything.

The gathered figures made way for them, and Joanna wondered just how many of these people were aware of her 'chosen' status. Or were they all 'chosen', just by being here? One thing was certain; every one of the spectators seemed to defer to Denise, stepping back and allowing her to pass. She, at least, was a member of the elect.

When they reached a position alongside Louise Walker and her unknown paramour, Joanna gasped, then pressed her knuckle to her lips to suppress a cry.

The Major's lady was not being taken in the conventional sense, as Joanna had assumed, but was actually being sodomised with a fair degree of force. Her lover, who was young and dark, and vaguely Middle Eastern in his looks, had a slender body, but an unnaturally large penis. Louise was being stretched, her anus clinging to the weapon that stroked into her. She was moaning loudly, almost glowing with delight.

'Let's get closer,' said Denise, into Joanna's ear, and pushed her forward. Joanna's pubis bumped against the table and sent a jolt of exquisite feeling through her belly. Her thigh was just inches from that of the thrusting man, and she could see that the bottom he was driving into was blotched with red. Louise had been beaten before being subjected to this ordeal.

But, of course, it wasn't an ordeal, was it? Louise was adoring every instant of what was happening to her, that was obvious. She was throwing her body about on the table, and tossing her head now, her cries rising and growing more frantic as she neared her climax. The young man who was buggering her gripped her maltreated buttocks in an attempt to steady her, but the moment he touched her rubicund flesh she shrieked and stiffened, then fell forward, one hand clasping her vulva, while her husband – at her head – supported her weight.

Unable to look away, Joanna thought for an instant that she, too, would collapse. Her knees seemed to dissolve but just as she wavered, Denise bore her up.

'Did that arouse you?' murmured the transvestite as she guided Joanna from the room, and back to the main party. They were arm in arm, but suddenly Denise reached across and lightly cupped Joanna's breast, thumbing her nipple through the fabric of her dress. 'I see it did,' she said, answering her own question while Joanna's teat tingled and engorged beneath her touch.

Joanna felt lost, off balance, disorientated. Reality seemed to have taken several shifts to the right while she had been watching Louise Walker's performance and everywhere she looked now there was lasciviousness, or some kind of shock. Dresses had been lifted, women's bottoms bared; caresses and punishments, subtle and otherwise, were being effected in all parts of the room. And there was no sign, whatsoever, of Kevin.

'This way,' said Denise, after a few moments, as if she had given Joanna a chance to regard the scene before launching her into it. She urged her forward, still massaging her tender breast.

The energised crowd seemed once again to part in front of them and, almost before she knew it, they were at the other side of the room. Joanna found herself standing behind the tall, dark-haired man in the black robes of a teacher, although he was alone now, the two schoolgirls having disappeared.

'Dale, my dear,' said Denise, almost gloatingly. 'Look who's here!' She tugged the sleeve of the man's voluminous black gown.

It was Halloran. Joanna realised she had half suspected as much when she had first glimpsed him earlier, but Denise had spirited her away, before she had been able to confirm the fact.

'Joanna. How good to see you here,' he said warmly, smiling down at her, his grey eyes scanning her face and body.

'Hello-'

Her voice petered out, her throat went dry. She had not the faintest idea how to address him in these circumstances. 'Halloran' sounded arrogant. 'Mr Halloran', flippant. 'Dale', far too intimate for their history of vague antagonism.

'Sir!' hissed Denise, from behind her, the perfect prompt, and though a week or so ago she would have died rather than comply, Joanna did so.

'Hello, sir,' she answered, her voice tiny.

'And how are you feeling this evening, Joanna?' he enquired, clasping his hands behind him, and rocking on his heels, the very picture of a stern academician.

'Fine . . . sir,' she said, somewhat thunderstruck by her own bizarre response to him. It was as if her whimsical fantasy of him as a strict headmaster – the one she had entertained outside his office whilst waiting for her reprimand – had come true. And been realised because that was what *she* wanted.

'Come this way,' he said, taking her by the arm, as Denise had done, then nodding dismissively to the transvestite. As he led Joanna away, her former companion smiled and left them.

'There's something I'd like to discuss with you,' Halloran went on, his voice quite ordinary and businesslike, just as if they were at work and on their way to a planning meeting. He seemed oblivious to the erotic ambience all around them.

Their destination was a handsome book-lined study – exactly right for the professor's gown he wore – and once they were both inside, he closed the door with an ominous 'clump'. There was a large, leather-topped desk, not dissimilar to the one in his office at Perry McAffee, and he sat down behind this in a high-backed leather-upholstered chair. It didn't surprise her that he didn't offer her a seat.

Joanna felt her heart begin to hammer. She didn't know what to do with her hands, and fiddled nervously with her little evening-bag, slipping it down off her shoulder and twisting the strap between her fingers while Halloran merely watched her, his expression mild. She didn't know what he wanted, but she knew she mustn't ask.

'Now then, Joanna,' he said at length, reaching into a drawer and bringing out – to her horror – a traditional wooden school ruler. 'What conclusions have you come to about the Côte Mystère proposals?'

She was astonished. It was the last thing she had expected him to say. He was talking shop; Côte Mystère was one of the new files she had taken from her desk this morning.

'I-I haven't had a proper look at them yet.'

'But you took them home – a highly irregular act, I might add – surely you've formed an opinion?'

'I never even opened the file . . . um, sir,' she muttered, finding it difficult to force the words from her dry, constricted throat. 'I got distracted.'

Halloran sighed heavily, picking up the ruler, then balanced it between his two forefingers. His brow was crumpled, and he looked thoroughly perplexed.

'I'm very disappointed,' he said, tutting softly and beginning to twirl the ruler. 'I was relying on your input on this project. Depending on it. Your participation in this is absolutely crucial.'

'I'm sorry.'

Halloran dropped the ruler, rose, and came around from behind the desk towards her. When he reached her side, he took the bag, with its tangled strap, out of her hands.

'Now, I don't think we need this any more, do we?' he said, his voice gently coaxing as if she were indeed the trembling, misguided schoolgirl this fantasy seemed to make her. Putting the bag aside, he sat down on the edge of the desk, and looked straight at her.

'You've let me down, Joanna,' he said, lacing his hands before him. 'And I had such high hopes for you.' His eyes were patient, and a little melancholy, as if he were truly suffering because of her shortcomings. His steady look was like a dart that pierced her loins.

'Now, do you think we can find a way to avoid this happening again?' he suggested. 'Some kind of *aide memoire;* something that would stick in your mind, so that the next time you're tempted to overlook important tasks, you'll remember it, and do what you're supposed to do?'

At the back of her mind, Joanna was laughing. How easily they found ways to get down to business. Anything, but anything, could be twisted into an excuse. Even if they didn't really need one.

She didn't answer, but just looked at the shiny red toes of her shoes, aware that Halloran had picked up the ruler again.

'And stubbornness, too, now,' he said, sadly, rising from the edge of the desk and taking a step away from her. 'I wonder if you would be good enough to lean over the desk for me, Joanna. I think we're quite ready to stop wasting each other's time.'

His voice was cool now, and professional; Joanna felt her lower belly flutter. Her legs felt weak but, making a supreme effort of will, she stepped up to the desk and pressed her pelvis against it, feeling a pang of pleasure from the unyielding texture of the wood.

As she bent over, she was aware of her tight skirt moving inexorably up her thighs, revealing her lace stocking tops and that which lay beyond them. And though the room was warm, the air felt chilly against a bare expanse of skin.

'Oh, Joanna, how could you?' said Halloran, his tone disapproving yet excited – as she revealed her naked crotch for his perusal.

He was chuckling softly as he folded back her skirt.

12

Sir Says

Is he the one? thought Joanna, in the momentary silence. The Master of the Continuum? Am I now showing my all to the very mystery man who's 'chosen' me?

'Don't you realise how foolhardy this is, Joanna?' said Halloran, his voice a little strained.

Joanna sensed him fighting urges just as compelling as those that gnawed at her. He dropped the ruler again, on the leathered surface of desk by her face and, as he leant close, his breathing was very marked, and very deep; she could almost feel it. His fingertips hovered, pleating the thin, stretchy cloth of her dress, but not yet touching either her buttocks or her vulva.

But that soon changed.

'And you're marked, too.' He traced the very faint bruising she knew still lingered; the remnants of her humbling at the hands of Mistress Denise. 'You've been letting people abuse you, Joanna, haven't you? I really thought you had much more sense than this.'

Again, the façade of aggrieved benevolence. The old-fashioned, almost patriarchal solicitude. Joanna was too tense, and too aroused even to think of laughing now, but she was still sharp enough to applaud a fine performance. He wanted to spank her, to handle her body, and perhaps even to plunge himself into it, but not even that would deflect him from his rôle.

It works, though, thought Joanna. She had always preserved a certain inner superiority in her office dealings with Halloran; she had kowtowed to him, as her boss, but had always managed subtly to let him know it was an act on her part.

Now, however, there was a facet of her that was melting to obey him, to submit to him, to feel the power of his strong arm as he chastised her. She had compartmentalised her natural defiance, and shut it away for the duration of this strange, new pleasure to which she was rapidly becoming addicted.

'I'm sorry,' she whispered. 'I'm sorry, sir,' she added, fighting the urge to wriggle.

'So you keep saying,' observed Halloran, his thumbs pressing into her buttocks now, one on either side. She almost choked as, rudely, he pulled her cleft open, then scrutinised her anus for several moments, as if checking its crinkled rim for perfect cleanliness. When he released her, the lobes of her bottom bounced.

'Very good,' he murmured inconsequentially, then pushed two fingers into her vagina from beneath, making her gasp again.

She was very wet, and the fingers had slid in easily, but she held her breath as Halloran seemed to test her inner muscle-tone by parting the digits inside her and pressing them outwards against the walls of her channel.

'Excellent,' he said, still measuring her resilience. 'Just how I've always imagined you to be. Tight, yet wet and wanton. Wickedly wanton,' he continued, bringing his other palm down in an open-handed slap across her bottom, while the fingers within her flexed and probed, exploring her tightness.

Sudden pleasure made Joanna gurgle, her mouth opening against the fragrant leather of the desk. A light, almost imaginary orgasm flashed through her loins so fast it was gone again in a second. It lasted only long enough for her vagina to clamp once on the intrusion inside it and the instant it was gone she received another slash of pain.

'Tut tut,' said Halloran, as he bent over her, giving her bottom cheek another couple of slaps. 'You weren't given permission to let that happen, Joanna. It's far too early on in the proceedings for you to come.'

But I can't help it, she wanted to shout, straining every sinew to keep still, and to keep from flexing and grinding herself on Halloran's fingers. Was he going to conduct the entire punishment with them still lodged inside her?

As if in answer, he whipped his fingers out with a swift, crude jerk, making Joanna whimper with a sudden sense of loss.

'Joanna.'

His voice was soft and warning. Joanna dug her fingers into the edge of the desk, willing herself to quieten down, then feeling a thrill of shame as Halloran took a crisp, white handkerchief from his pocket and calmly wiped the fingers he had just withdrawn from her body. When their cleanliness obviously satisfied him, he flicked the hanky significantly in Joanna's direction, and said, 'If you can't keep quiet, my dear, it may be necessary to do it for you.'

For some reason, the idea of being gagged was appalling. Joanna pursed her lips tightly and this seemed to satisfy Halloran, if only for the moment. He refolded his handkerchief, slid it back into his pocket, then retrieved the wooden ruler from where it had lain, almost touching Joanna's nose.

'I'm going to ruler you now, Joanna,' he said, moving to a position somewhere behind her and swishing the foot-long implement through the air, as if testing its weight and heft. 'I'm going to make your bottom red all over, and quite sore. Probably sorer than you would expect without the benefit of a strap or a cane.' He rested the simple strip of wood across the crown of her buttocks, and Joanna closed her eyes, screaming inside and resisting the compelling need to move herself beneath it. To grind her crotch against the desk, to reach down and rub her sex. To take her clitoris between her fingers and roughly pinch it. She wanted to pant, to gulp in breaths, but she did not dare to jeopardise her unspoken pledge of silence. Instead, she gripped the edge of the desk with all her strength.

'And while I'm tanning you, and afterwards when your bottom cheeks are as hot as fire, and I'm touching you, I want you to consider what you've done. Your misdemeanours and your responsibilities. Then, the next time you're about to transgress, you'll remember, and think again.'

It didn't make sense, of course. To think those thoughts would only make her more likely to do something she shouldn't. But as the ruler fell the conundrum itself fell away too, and with the pain came a new and perfect logic. A special sensibility; the law and reason of the finely wielded rod.

The ruler had a light and whippy quality which was deceiving. Her mind was telling her it was a childish punishment. Nothing. A mere fly swat. But her buttocks had a different tale to tell. The ruler stung. It hurt like the thin, piercing bite of electricity; it fired her, it insidiously raised a glow.

And if Halloran was her master, the Continuum Master, he was a worthy one. He circulated the blows to her buttocks with a skill and artistry which, had she been a dispassionate observer, Joanna's nascent knowledge would have caused her to applaud. Shifting the thin strip of wood in circles, in meticulous spirals, he was gradually, but comprehensively, toasting her bottom.

God, how it stung! The entire area, both the lobes, and the more sensitive areas of her thigh tops and anal cleft seemed to be on fire now. A high, bright prickling fire. She had managed to remain silent, biting her lips and grasping at the desktop with fingers turned to talons, but her intention to keep still had proved impossible. She was rocking her crotch against the surface beneath her, almost without realising it; and, when she did become aware of what she was doing, she also discovered that she was wetting the desk beneath her with her juices. Filled with desire, filled with passion and heat, she acknowledged Halloran – once so cool and soulless, it had seemed to her – to be an artist, a consummate maestro.

It is you, isn't it? she thought, as the very tip of the ruler seemed to bend impossibly and catch her right across her anus. Her body leapt on the desk, and tears trickled down her face at the spiteful jolt of pain. She realised she had been crying freely for some time now, snuffling and snorting like a strange hybrid of human child and piglet. She felt disgusting, pathetic, revoltingly weak and pitiable, yet so aroused that her sex seemed about to burst.

If I had the guts, I would just roll over, point to my crotch and make him take me, she thought, grunting as a stroke whipped inward and caught her slippery labia. She heard the soft repeating rustle of his gown as his actions disturbed the heavy fabric and in her mind she saw him strip it off, unfasten his flies, and jam his doubtless erect and marvellous penis deep inside her. From the back, from the front, in intercourse or in sodomy, she didn't care. She was just dying for relief of any kind.

When it came, though, it surprised her. Halloran surprised her. Throwing aside the ruler, he took hold of her almost gently by the hips and flipped her over on to her back, on the desk. As he parted her legs and stood between them, the pressure of her own weight on her punished buttocks made her moan; but the sound wavered in her throat, and changed to a howl of pleasure when his long, flexible fingers sought her vulva. With the utmost care and delicacy, he once more slid two fingers inside her, then settled his flat thumb squarely against her clitoris.

For a few brief seconds, Joanna stared up at him, meeting his steady grey eyes with a tearful look of gratitude. He seemed unperturbed, calm, quiet, and his whole expression was one of kindness; of almost avuncular affection. Then his thumb began to circle, rolling her tiny pearl of flesh like a ball-bearing inside a perfectly machined socket, and she closed her eyes as she orgasmed sublimely, her waving legs brushing the coarse cloth of his gown.

As the spasms subsided, Joanna remained where she was, her eyes closed, her legs wide apart, her bottom quietly throbbing. The discomfort – for that was all it seemed to be now – was a low, steady sensation that settled her rather than plagued her. She felt relaxed, sated, at peace, and not even her lewd, vulnerable position could spoil that. To her mild surprise, she discovered she was smiling. Halloran's hand was gone from her, but she sensed that he still lingered close by.

A kiss finally woke her from her somnolent state, her chastiser's lips pressing fleetingly against her own. Then Halloran stepped back, and she opened her eyes and sat up, feeling the warmth pulse in her bottom as she did so.

'Thank you, sir,' she said with a smile, seeing his mellow expression and the humour in his eyes. There was a bulge, too, in his immaculately tailored trousers, but he seemed in no hurry to assuage his own desire.

'Dale, now,' he instructed her amiably. 'Just Dale.' Suddenly, he surprised her by shrugging off his formal black gown and tossing it aside, over the back of a nearby chair. When he moved forward again, he put out his arms and helped Joanna off the desk and on to her feet.

'Is it over, then?' she asked, adjusting her stockings and smoothing her dress back down to cover their tops. The clinging fabric across her buttocks stirred her spanking a little, but the flush of heat was far from disagreeable.

'For the duration of this particular encounter, yes,' he replied, still smiling at her. There was a light in his eyes, a look of vague perplexity that bemused her as well, for a moment. Then she understood some, but perhaps not all, of its cause.

'But what about you?' she asked, letting her eyes dart to the disturbed line of his trousers. 'I've had my fun –' she lifted her hand, gesturing faintly ' – don't I owe you something in return?'

'That would be nice,' he said, a hint of regret in his tone. 'But on this occasion, not appropriate, I'm afraid.'

Joanna frowned, and Halloran quickly continued: 'Oh, don't worry, Joanna. It's no deficiency on your part. You're a gorgeous, desirable woman. In every way. There's nothing I'd like better than to sweep you off to bed right now. And to grab you by that delicious, red bottom of yours while I fuck you senseless.' He shrugged and a look of wry wistfulness crossed his face. 'But, as I said, it's not appropriate.'

'What do you mean by that?' demanded Joanna, sensing the workings of a plan afoot. A Continuum plan.

'It's not my place; not just yet,' he prevaricated, evading her scrutiny by crossing to a glass fronted cabinet and bringing out a bottle of brandy, and two heavy balloon glasses which were conveniently sequestered amongst the leather bound books there.

'Whose place is it then?' persisted Joanna as he poured a hefty measure of the spirit for each of them, then handed one to her. 'Surely you can have whatever you want, whenever you want? A man of your status?'

'And what status do you think that is? I'm only your boss.' He smiled, as if being her superior at work was meaningless and without value, then sat down in the chair over the back of which he had abandoned his gown. Lifting the brandy glass to his lips, he took a long pull at it, drinking nearly all of the fiery spirit in one gulp. Joanna had the impression it had been a drink he had really needed.

'The Master, or whatever you call it. Of all this.' She made a slight indication with her glass, knowing full well that he would realise she meant the entire establishment and all that was happening in it.

'Would that it were so,' he said, cradling the glass in his lap, its base almost touching his erection. As Joanna watched, he tapped the bowl with a single finger. 'But that position is already taken.' He seemed composed, but the tapping went on.

Joanna sipped her own brandy and studied him without speaking.

Was it a ploy, perhaps? A misdirection, to put her through yet more sexual hoops before the final *dénouement?*

'You don't believe me, do you?' he said, after a few moments.

'I don't know who to believe about anything these days,' replied Joanna, shifting from foot to foot and realising in a detached sort of way that she was quite at home, now, in her towering red heels. 'Nobody really lies to me, but you'd be amazed by the creativity of all the half-truths.'

Halloran laughed. 'Isn't it more fun this way?'

Joanna considered the suggestion, then joined in his laughter. Crossing the room, she freshened her own drink and topped up Halloran's for him. They were equals now, she realised. The transaction – her submissiveness, his dominance – was concluded.

'If you say so . . . sir.' Shaking her head, she grinned and clicked her glass to his. 'Here's to the truth. Eventually. Chin chin!'

A few minutes later, Joanna was out in the main room of the party again. She had left Halloran relaxing in his armchair, savouring his brandy and, presumably, anticipating sexual pleasure of some kind. As she had shut the door she had caught one last glimpse of him, his eyes closed, his head tipping back against the upholstery, one hand already resting on his crotch. He had smiled fleetingly, knowing that she had seen him.

The assembly of guests had thinned out a little, the participants either having gone home, or having retired to rooms Joanna had not yet seen. There was still no sign of Kevin, and Denise, too, had disappeared from view. Feeling hot, dishevelled and a little sweaty in her long-sleeved dress, Joanna decided to slip away and try to find a bathroom. As the first floor seemed the most likely location, she made her way across the room and out into the entrance hall, keeping her eyes averted from the other guests, just in case one of them should try to claim her. She felt that she had already paid her dues in full as a penitent this evening, but that some other master or mistress might not think so.

Despite her qualms, Joanna was not accosted, and the only person who did catch her eye wasn't in any kind of position to waylay her.

A slender young woman, in a tight, red leather bodice, ankle boots and nothing else, craned her head to look up pleadingly as Joanna passed her. The girl was draped across the back of a chair, and was being held there by two men while another pushed something inside her body. Joanna could not see into which orifice the object was being inserted, but the glint of lubricated black rubber, and the expression of happy anguish on the prone girl's face brought back memories of Cynthia and her dildo.

On the first floor all was quiet, and the elegant smoked glass wall lights were discreetly dimmed. Turning left along a corridor, Joanna saw a row of unmarked doors, all secretively closed, and faced a dilemma. What trysts might she disturb if she opened any of those doors?

Someone being pleasured?

Someone being made to suffer?

Or more likely, as it was in her case, someone gladly submitting to both? She walked up to the first one and listened intently, but there was only silence. She tried the next, with the same result. The one after that, however, revealed evidence of occupation. Just as Joanna reached it, she heard the distinctive and ominous crack of a lash meeting a bottom, then the rising, gurgling shriek of a woman either suffering intensely or coming to violent climax. Once again, Joanna guessed that it was both.

After passing several more doors closed on silence, Joanna was relieved to find one that was ever so slightly open. Pushing it a little, she discovered the room beyond was well lit but empty; to her relief it was the bathroom that she sought.

With a sigh, then a little yelp, she settled herself on to the toilet seat. Her bottom was gently simmering now and, though the act of sitting down brought a little jolt of pain, the polished wooden seat was pleasantly cool against her soreness. She also discovered quite an urgent need to urinate, and supposed that previously it had been lost somewhere in the mix of nervous signals. Perched on the toilet, and safe behind the bolted door, she began to giggle at the bizarre nature of her evening.

Denis Davidson dressed as Coco Chanel; Mrs Walker being publicly sodomised; Halloran revelling in his assumed rôle as an Edwardian schoolmaster. In a rational world each phenomenon defied belief. But here in the Continuum – which was where she supposed she was now – all these and more were just voluptuous diversions. Joyous, grown-up fun in a world that had become too grim, too serious, too repressive. Pulling the chain and preparing to leave the cubicle, she sent up a silent prayer of salute to the unknown manipulator who governed this strange society; she could only thank her lucky stars that he had found her.

It took only a few moments to repair her make-up and tidy her hair. Halloran's efforts with the ruler had wrung a minor torrent of tears from her, but having half expected them, Joanna had prepared her face accordingly. Her smudge-proof eye paint had barely moved at all.

Better find Kevin, I suppose, she thought, tilting her head this way and that, and admiring the chic way her curls and her maquillage had survived her ordeal in the study. Her body, too, looked luscious and proudly unbowed, and – smoothing her hands over her black-clad curves – she pinched her own bottom to remind her of its heat. The red ache flared, and she hissed between her teeth, but it was more an expression of self-congratulation than anything. Swinging her bag jauntily over her shoulder, she strode out of the room.

Out in the softly-lit corridor there was a change. One of the doors, previously so forbiddingly closed, was now open. It was ajar just a sliver, an inch or two, but to Joanna it was a sudden invitation. Slipping off her shoes, she tip-toed towards it, breathing lightly. There was no sound coming from the narrow, enticing aperture, but she clearly sensed a presence – or presences – beyond.

Careful not to block what little light would be shining into the room from the corridor, Joanna peered in and – as if on cue – there was a sudden burst of sound; a man's cry, but choking and muffled.

As her eyes adjusted to the dimness of the room, Joanna saw two partially clothed bodies in motion on the roughly stripped bed that stood at its centre. Framed by the whiteness of the sheet, their actions were jerky and unmistakably familiar. Like Louise Walker, earlier in the evening, the figure underneath was being buggered.

Joanna felt her nails flex as they dug into the leather of her shoes, and she thrust the back of her free hand against her mouth. It was not only the act being performed that was familiar to her; the two male participants she knew intimately well too.

'Denise' was the active partner, but, from her current vantage point, Joanna could no longer think of Davidson as 'she'. Though still wearing his Chanel jacket, his sheer stockings and his stilettos, he was thrusting into the submissive body beneath him with a force, and a towering, primitive violence that was archetypally and unequivocally male. His penis was drawing out and driving in, almost to the full extent of its not inconsiderable length, exhibiting its hardness and glistening slickness as it moved. He was holding his partner's hips to control his angle of penetration, and was clearly supremely dominant in this hasty, dramatic coupling, even though, to Joanna's further puzzlement, he had the broad red line of a fiery welt across his buttocks. Somebody – perhaps even the poor wretch who suffered beneath him? – had cracked the proud 'Denise' a telling wallop with a leather belt.

Poor wretch? No. Not really. The writhing sodomite who was being possessed was in pure heaven. It was *he* who was groaning with pleasure while his ambiguous friend toiled and pumped away behind him. It was *he* who was so frantic with excitement and ecstasy that he was having to bite the white pillow beneath his face to suppress his shouts of joy. It was *he*, who gave Joanna the surprise of her life, even though he had already graphically described this preference to her.

After losing him at the very beginning of the evening, she had finally found Kevin again.

As Denise's relentless pounding squashed Joanna's erstwhile escort flat against the mattress, Kevin twisted his sweating face to one side and seemed to stare towards the doorway and at her. His eyelids fluttered, and his mouth worked confusedly, as if he were trying to call out to her, to explain, or to apologise, but, just then, his whole body went quite rigid and his limbs began to spasm.

Joanna couldn't tell if just one of them was coming, or whether they were both climaxing together. Kevin's radiant blue eyes rolled up in their sockets, and he sank his teeth, once more, into the pillow. 'Denise' gave a huge shout and began to almost climb right over his lover's back, his glossy ersatz hair cascading forward like a fall to blend chaotically with Kevin's tousled blondness.

Still clutching her shoes, Joanna pulled herself away from the door, then turned and ran, no longer worried that the men in the room, or anybody else, would hear her. She had to get away from what she had seen as fast as she could, but not from any sense of horror or revulsion.

If she had stayed any longer she would have burst into their darkened enclave and joined them, adding her own body to the hot tangle on the bed.

She spent the rest of the evening participating dazedly in what could best be described as an eccentric discussion group.

Down in the main party room, a great many of the guests had disappeared – either to private encounters, like Denise or Kevin, or to their homes. However, in a rough circle that meandered over various items of furniture in the corner of the room, Louise Walker was holding court with a collection of female friends, and several bottles of fine red wine.

'Joanna, sweetheart, why don't you join us?' she cried across the room, rising from her seat with a fleeting but undisguised wince. Joanna noticed she had been sitting on a cushion.

Several of the women were sitting on cushions, too, she soon realised when she went across and joined the group. They were all fashionably and discreetly clothed now, although, earlier in the evening, Joanna had seen several of them either naked or with their breasts and bottoms on show. Smoothing down her own dress, she took a seat beside Louise.

The talk was surreal and, even if she hadn't still had the image of Denise and Kevin in her mind, Joanna would have found the topics covered quite mind-boggling.

One woman described how her lover had burnt every pair of panties in her possession, plus all her jeans and her trousers, and now required her to be completely naked beneath her skirt at all times of the day. 'He likes me to leave my skirt off too, when we're not expecting visitors,' she said with a smile. 'Sometimes he likes me to spend an hour or two kneeling up on the sofa, so he can either whip me or fuck me whenever he wants to. Or sometimes he has me sit in an armchair with my legs wide open, over the arms, and I have to masturbate for as long as I've got the energy to.'

Another woman described – in a degree of detail that made Joanna squirm her punished bottom against the chair seat – having her nipples pierced at the behest of her lesbian partner. While she was recounting what had happened, she pulled down her bodice and displayed the results.

'That's nothing,' said a young, pretty, and very poised woman, to Joanna's left. She then proceeded to raise her skirt, to reveal a narrow strap of scarlet leather that disappeared between her shaven outer labia. Standing up, she lifted her skirt at the back, too, revealing the way in which the strap emerged from her bottom cleft and was buckled – fore and aft – to a matching leather harness that dug deeply into her, around her waist.

Joanna took a long sip of wine to fortify herself, grateful for its earthy, well-rounded strength. The sight of that vicious little strap, fastened so tightly that the woman could barely get one finger between it and her skin, made her feel dizzy. She tried to imagine the constant, crushing pressure it must exert on the most sensitive part of the woman's body, and found it not only impossible, but also unbearably arousing. Her belly surged and her own clitoris seemed to throb in tingling empathy.

The rest of the stories told were equally stimulating but after a while Joanna felt her eyelids beginning to droop with a pleasant drowsiness. The sensation was one of mild intoxication, combined with a compelling need to sleep, but without any of the obnoxious nausea that usually accompanied an excess of the grape. Feeling vaguely curious, she squinted at the bottle that had ended up in front of her, on a low, marquetry table. When she had deciphered the ornate copperplate on its square white label, she experienced a sudden desire to giggle insanely. The wine was from Côte Mystère, the very vineyard she was supposed to have read a report on, earlier today.

The house wine of the Continuum, she thought, with a certain bleary satisfaction. She would have liked another glass of it but just at that moment she slipped away into the haze of sleep.

The sound of a fax machine woke her up again. Her fax machine. The one which stood on the second shelf of her IKEA telephone table, in the corner of her living room, in her flat at Sweigert Mansions.

How did I get here? she asked herself, sitting up in bed and looking down at her naked body. She swallowed, licked her lips; ever-so-gingerly shook her head. She waited for the stabs of a sickening headache; the usual retribution that over-indulgence wreaked on her. But nothing happened, her head felt clear, and her stomach calm and settled. She should be suffering, but she felt as fit and lively as a frisky spring lamb.

The only thing wrong was with her memory; a portion of it was missing. Grabbing her robe, which was conveniently draped over the end of her bed, just as she normally left it, she padded through into the lounge to collect the fax. Knowing the thought to be illogical, she began to read it, in the hope of finding answers amongst its terse, no nonsense wording.

Strangely enough, though, it did seem to offer some answers. Or, at least, a course of action that would distract her mind from brooding.

13

En route à la Côte Mystère

'Was it you who took me home last night?'

They had sat in silence for the first part of their chauffeured drive out of London, each of them supposedly reading the various papers in their files on Côte Mystère. Joanna suspected, however, that neither of them was really concentrating on the unorthodox financial status of a minor vineyard in the southern Rhône Valley.

Joanna's thoughts were chasing around aimlessly like a rat in a maze, a puzzle path that kept leading her back to the Continuum, and she had a suspicion that Halloran wasn't all that interested in performance indicators and cash flow either.

'Well, was it you?' she persisted, when he ran one long finger down a column of figures, his high forehead slightly wrinkled as if in thought.

Halloran looked up, then smiled distantly. It seemed hard to believe that last night she had been stretched across a desk while he beat her and touched her.

'No, alas, it wasn't me,' he said, his smile warming a little. 'I'm afraid I was otherwise engaged. Your friend Steel and

Mr Davidson took you home. You were fast asleep and they didn't want to wake you.'

'I was drugged!' she retorted, crumpling the edge of a memo, then smoothing it out again. 'There was something in that damned wine – this wine!' She slapped the file where it lay on her lap.

'Joanna, you're imagining things,' said Halloran easily. 'You were tired, and Côte Mystère is quite robust. It was as simple as that.' He looked at her closely, his grey eyes sharp. 'How do you feel this morning, anyway?'

'Fine!' she snapped, then realised that, physically at least, it was true. She felt no trace of a hangover, she was surprisingly well rested, and her bottom bore no trace, visible or otherwise, of what Halloran had done to it last night. She felt a sudden yen to quiz him about his involvement in the strange scene of erotic corporal punishment, and in the Continuum in particular but, when she opened her mouth again, he suavely cut her off.

'Excellent. I'm glad of that. Now, let's get down to some serious reading. You're not the only one who hasn't studied the papers.'

I bet nobody thrashed you with a ruler for not reading them, though, thought Joanna mutinously, as she turned her attention to the Côte Mystère file.

Strangely enough, the idiosyncratic data on the vineyard was deeply absorbing and, when she looked up again, the limousine was pulling into the gates of what looked like a well-kept private airfield. She was surprised, having expected that they would fly from one of the major airports, on a scheduled flight.

'I don't know why on earth we're going to this place, to be honest,' she said, closing the file and sliding it into her briefcase. She had no intention of letting Halloran know how rattled she suddenly felt. Limousines, private planes, personal visits to their continental clients; this wasn't the way in which their business was usually conducted. Well, at least not by her at her level of responsibility. She had been astounded by the content of Halloran's fax, instructing her to pack an overnight bag and find her passport, then to be waiting outside her building for his car to collect her.

'It's a pet project, isn't it?' she persisted, stepping out of the car and feeling the slim skirt of her dress rise up her thigh. Why had she put this on? Why had she given in to someone's manipulation? 'This vineyard is just a rich man's folly. It's running at a loss. I can't see what it is that we can do for it. No amount of mechanisation and streamlining is going to turn it around, and you know that!'

'You'll see,' said Halloran, his face expressionless and his long stride eating up the tarmac, forcing Joanna to half-run to keep up with him.

'Bastard!' she muttered, trying to keep her poise as she clattered along beside him in her high heels. Something was going on, she realised, as they approached the plane, a small grey-painted business jet which gleamed almost silver in the sunshine. She cursed herself for not catching on earlier. She had been too wound up in the fluster of last minute preparations for the trip, and her memories – or lack of them – of what had transpired at the mysterious 'Seventeen'. Under normal circumstances she would have smelt a rat immediately.

The passenger door lay open in readiness, with steps leading up to it and, hanging back suddenly, Halloran almost seemed to be hustling Joanna forward and up them.

'What about – ' she began to protest, about to try to turn, then halting in mid-motion and swaying precariously as she caught sight of the 'stewardess' who stood waiting to welcome them, just inside the plane's entrance.

'And what the fuck are *you* doing here?' Joanna demanded, as sure hands reached forward to take her briefcase and her bag.

'Tsk, language, Joanna,' said Denise, her eyes merry, her glossy brown hair immaculate beneath a chic, steel-blue airline cap. She wore an A-line skirt, and short, boxy jacket in the same discreet colour, with a tie-neck blouse in virgin ivory underneath it. As ever, her make up was perfect, and her deportment faultless.

'What the hell's going on? This isn't a fact-finding mission at all, is it?' said Joanna, aware of Halloran boarding the plane just behind her, and feeling shaky as the door was slammed and the engines immediately began to run.

'Oh, it is,' said Denise, moving behind Joanna, and helping her off with her coat. 'But maybe not the sort of facts you were expecting.' Preparing to stow the coat, she ran her fingers over the light, checked fabric, that matched the short, slightly fitted shift dress that Joanna still wore. 'Anna Sui again,' she murmured. 'You have wonderful taste, Joanna. This really suits you.'

Joanna frowned, thinking furiously as Denise guided her towards a seat. The Anna Sui coat and dress had been hanging on the front of her wardrobe this morning, inviting her to wear them, even though, for the life of her, she couldn't remember putting them there. Had Denise herself selected the outfit last night when she and Kevin had brought home their sleeping charge?

Kevin! I should have phoned him! He won't know where I am, thought Joanna in alarm, as Denise oh-so-gently manhandled her into a deep, comfortably upholstered airline seat, and started adjusting and buckling her seat-belt.

Following on from the first thought came an image of Kevin as she had last seen him, squashed against a white-sheeted bed, being possessed by a man wearing stockings and a pink Chanel jacket. Suddenly, almost as if she, or he, had read Joanna's mind, Denise looked up from her menial task and smiled.

'Where are we going?' asked Joanna, her pulse beginning to race as fast as the engines that were poised to fling them upward into the skies.

'To *Le Manoir Mystère*, at the heart of the Côte Mystère vineyard,' said Halloran, from across the cabin, his voice raised above the thrumming roar that seemed to surround them. 'You've been summoned, and we're your escort.' He grinned, then applied his attention to his own belt.

It's a trick, thought Joanna. A blind. He's the one . . . Or she is, she thought, returning her attention to Denise, who was still, inexplicably, fiddling with Joanna's belt.

Even as Joanna looked down, the transvestite reached beneath the arm-rests and, with two swift yanks, released a set of restraints which were far from being a standard safety feature. Before Joanna could protest, her wrists were strapped firmly into place against the rests.

Joanna took deep, deep breaths, trying not to pant. She heard a moan, a soft whimper of longing, and was astonished to realise it had come from her. Denise was crouched right down now, releasing straps somewhere in the base of the seat, and immobilising Joanna's ankles as securely as her wrists. Just as the plane began to taxi, the transvestite rose nimbly and took her own place, glancing across and giving Joanna a wink when she was settled.

No one spoke during take-off. Halloran, unperturbed, took a magazine from a holder beside his seat and began flicking through it, while Denise looked out of the window, her face alight, as if she were a child taking a flight for the very first time. Joanna suddenly found it hard to believe that the elegant, ersatz stewardess was really a hard-nosed American executive who probably travelled the world by air a score of times each year.

For some time, the cabin remained quiet. Neither of her companions moved, both lost in their own particular pastimes, but their very stillness seemed to stoke Joanna's tension.

Her mouth was dry, and her heart seemed to clamour deafeningly inside her. This was it. This *really* was it, this time. Her secret Master was shortly going to reveal himself. Or herself.

I'm going to be tested, thought Joanna, feeling her bonds – which were padded and comfortable – seem to tighten around her wrists and ankles. Everything that has happened so far will be nothing. She tried to imagine a pain – in her bottom, there was no doubt about that, her bare white bottom – which would exceed everything she had experienced up until now.

What will he use? she asked herself, feeling her buttocks tingle faintly inside her pants, as if anticipating the torment ahead. Her breasts were swollen too; they felt tight and uncomfortable against her bra.

What haven't I had? The Paddle? The Cane? The Belt? The thought of each one made her tremble; her calves and thighs seemed to be vibrating with tension. She could feel moisture gathering between her legs. It was completely irrational; she was anticipating pain – agony, even – and all her body could do was surge and rouse. Closing her eyes, she wished she could free a hand and touch her vulva through the fabric of her designer dress. She shifted her buttocks against the thickly padded seat, trying to stimulate herself without her captors noticing.

The silence, and her discomfort went on.

It wasn't until she heard a voice murmuring: 'Wake up now, Joanna,' that she discovered she had fallen asleep in her bonds. And this time without the aid of strong wine.

Blinking, she saw Denise leaning over her. 'Time for the in-flight entertainment,' said the transvestite, her eyes bright with wickedness. 'Let's get you ready now, shall we?'

Feeling horribly excited, Joanna quickly realised that, rather than the entertainment being provided for her, *she* was to provide them with a diversion.

With no hint of a warning, Denise reached down behind Joanna's back and drew down the long zip of her smart, checked dress.

'Lovely,' she whispered, working the bodice down as far as it would go, and exposing Joanna's bosom in her white lycra brassière. Almost methodically, she squeezed each firm orb in turn, then peeled the bra down too, flicking the straps off Joanna's shoulders, pushing down the cups to rest on the bunched fabric of her dress. 'So beautiful,' said the transvestite, taking hold of Joanna's breasts again, and manipulating them vigorously as if testing a fruit for ripeness.

Joanna closed her eyes again. The rough treatment made her want to groan and wriggle, as a great weight of desire settled low down in her belly. She could feel that the crotch of her knickers was wet now, soaked by her juices and, with a touch of fatalism, she knew that her arousal would very soon be uncovered.

'My darling,' said Denise, then – still holding a breast cruelly tight in each hand – she gave Joanna a swift, hard kiss on the mouth.

A second or two later, the transvestite released her, then plucked determinedly at the hem of Joanna's dress. 'Let's get those pants down, shall we?' she said briskly, performing a similar procedure with the dress's skirt as she had with its bodice. Reaching beneath Joanna's bottom, she rucked the cloth upwards at both back and front, until the whole dress was an ugly bundle around her waist. With a deft professionalism, she then tugged Joanna's panties and tights halfway down her legs and left her naked from her waist to her knees.

Uncovered, and in a particularly humiliating manner, Joanna willed herself to stay calm and in control of her emotions, which was difficult when her thoughts were wild and wilful, and seemed to bob about her mind like the fluffy clouds outside.

They could do anything to her. They could tease her, abuse her, pleasure her. They could even punish her; her bottom was unavailable but her thighs were both naked and accessible. She imagined Halloran extracting his damned ruler from his briefcase and thrashing the tender skin on the insides of her legs. He might even strike her breasts; there was nothing she could do to stop him.

The worst thing of all they could do now was ignore her. She could take any amount of pain, she believed, because at least it would guarantee their close attention.

'Are you going to hit me?' she asked quietly, as Denise rose to her feet with a smooth, balletic grace.

'Why, do you want us to?' enquired Halloran, peering at her intently, leaning on his armrest, chin on hand.

'I – I think so,' answered Joanna, her throat tightening.

'Well, we'll have to see if we have time to oblige you,' observed Denise, picking up the thread. 'But first, why don't we have a glass of wine?'

Do I have a choice? Joanna wanted to say, but she knew that pert remarks were not appropriate. The instant she had stepped on to this plane, she had also crossed the border of the Continuum and, beyond it, instinct told her she was not yet within its higher echelons.

But she would be when she finally met her Master. Or met him in a scenario in which he acknowledged his identity. Until then, she would be quiet, and compliant.

Denise opened a concealed bar, and set to work. The wine she selected was Côte Mystère, unsurprisingly, and she poured it out into three deep-bellied glasses, then handed one of them to Halloran. Taking a sip from her own glass, she put it aside and brought the third glass across to Joanna. Kneeling, she then held the fragrant, ruby-dark fluid to Joanna's lips, tipping the glass so she was obliged to drink or have the wine trickle down her chin and on to her naked breasts.

Despite the coercion, Joanna found the wine just as exquisite as she had done the night before. It slipped down her throat like a rich and warming nectar, setting light to coals of desire that were already live and smouldering.

As she sipped the intoxicating sacrament of the Continuum, Joanna peered over the crystal rim and saw Halloran drain his own glass, rise from his seat and come towards her. Sinking to a lithe, elegant crouch, he put out a hand and cupped her breast, flicking her nipple while Denise still coaxed her to drink.

The sensation of being 'fed' her wine, and of being played with at the same time was so disquieting that Joanna panicked. As she tried to cry out, the rich, red Côte Mystère bubbled from her lips and, as she had feared, dribbled down on to the very breast that Halloran was manipulating. Unperturbed, he leant further over her and began to lick it off slowly and lasciviously, sometimes massaging her nipple with his lips and tongue, and sometimes sucking his own fingers to absorb the luscious fluid.

Unbearably excited, Joanna began to struggle, and the wine went everywhere, all over her.

'Wicked girl!' admonished Denise in her ear, still tipping the glass against Joanna's lips, and steadying her head with a firm grip on the nape of her neck. 'Don't struggle. Drink your wine. Don't you like it?'

Joanna did like the wine, but, distracted by Halloran's mouth and hands plaguing her breasts, she was unable to concentrate on drinking. He was nuzzling her now, chewing gently on one nipple while, at the same time twisting the other between a finger and thumb. The brilliant wine daubed not only her chest, but his hands and his face, too. It had also stained his pristine white, sea-island cotton shirt by now, but he was so lost in his task that he seemed not to notice.

When the glass was empty Denise set it aside, but did not release Joanna's head. The transvestite's lips began to explore her cheek, her throat and her ear in the same nibbling, exploratory mode that Halloran was employing so effectively on her breasts.

'Oh, baby, yes,' teased Denise in Joanna's ear, then closed her strong, straight, perfect American teeth around the tender lobe, biting delicately, just as her equally perfect manicured hand settled on Joanna's bare thigh, a couple of inches from her vulva.

Still, Joanna wanted to move, but the bonds, and her lovers, constrained her. It was incongruous; they were kneeling while she was seated, and yet they had the power. Denise was slowly squeezing her thigh, painted fingertips edging closer and closer to her sex without yet touching it, while Halloran kissed and mouthed her breasts with a sloppy, desperate hunger that was completely unlike him. Where was the chilly aesthete now? Joanna wondered dreamily, feeling his saliva mix with the wine on her skin.

'I fucked your boyfriend last night,' purred Denise, suddenly, the words vibrating against the side of Joanna's throat. 'I had him. I made him howl with pleasure and ejaculate without even touching his cock.' She drew her tongue along the line of Joanna's jaw. 'You saw us, didn't you?'

'Yes!' croaked Joanna, feeling the fingers which had dug into her thigh grab her crotch with the same rough fervour.

'And you liked it, didn't you?' The fingers gripped and pressed, making a crude sucking sound with her freely running juices. Joanna wanted to cry out; her sex was on fire. She nodded furiously, unsure of her voice.

Halloran raised his head, briefly, and leered at her. Then he applied his lips once more, with energy, to a tingling nipple.

'You loved it, didn't you?' accused Denise, punctuating the words with a rhythmic, swirling pressure between Joanna's legs. 'The way I shafted him. Stretched him. The way I made him sob, and give it up. Just the way you're going to give it up for me – aren't you?'

A sudden image of Denise – of Davidson – mounting her made Joanna choke and spasm, the contours of her sex-flesh rippling helpless beneath the transvestite's remorseless grip. Hot waves of sudden pleasure began to lash her. Her hips bucked, her limbs strained against their bonds, she cried out loudly; a hoarse, inhuman yell that was quickly stopped by Denise's crushing mouth.

She did not black out, although a part of her expected it to happen; the part that could still think while the rest of her jerked and climaxed. Weirdly, she seemed to rise up from her physical form and float somewhere in the region of the cabin's roof; looking down she watched them work on her body.

Licking. Sucking. Rubbing. Probing. Fingers and tongues caressing wine-stained skin that smelt also of sweat and sexual fluids. Tender membranes that pulsed and leapt until she could bear no more, and begged her tormentors to stop.

Still drifting, but back in her body now she watched as they abandoned her and engaged in strange congress on the carpeted floor of the cabin. Denise's smart cap slipped off as Halloran bore down on her, top to tail, and forced his suddenly freed penis into her mouth – whilst hiking up her skirt and freeing her own engorged organ for his lips. Their cheeks bulged as they thrust and rocked in a strange but clever syncopation. Fingers grabbed buttocks, sought out anuses and palpated them. Rich, creamy fluid flowed from the corners of two suddenly slack mouths, as two male bodies collapsed in a mêlée of limbs and gasping moans of ecstasy.

Joanna closed her eyes, her own desire reborn. She knew that this time, her need would not be sated. Longing to stroke herself, she just sat and silently wept, her body sticky, unfulfilled and marked with wine.

After a period of quiet, she heard the sounds of Denise and Halloran disentangling themselves, a slow process that seemed to require many pauses for kisses and whispered endearments. Then first one, then the other of them disappeared through a door towards the aft of the cabin, which presumably contained a lavatory and facilities for washing.

Joanna did not open her eyes. She still felt numb with desire, and humiliated by her nakedness and her dishevelled condition. She could smell the sharp tang of the wine, and the pungent odour of her own bare vulva. Her Anna Sui dress was ruined; crushed and crumpled and liberally splashed with the blood-purple of the dark red Côte Mystère.

Be quiet, be calm, be patient, she told herself as she finally managed to conquer her discomfort. This flight into mystery was part of her trial, one of the tests she must pass to reach her Master. The Master. He who controlled the Continuum. And, she suspected, enduring the foibles of Denise, and Dale Halloran, was probably the very least of the ordeals she had to get through. To lose heart now was to fail before she had even really started.

She opened her eyes and looked around the cabin. Defiantly.

Denise was combing her hair, and smoothing her hand over it, after each stroke, with such pleasure that it was difficult to remember that the silky, shoulder-length curtain wasn't real. When she was finished, she pinned her flight cap neatly in place, then stood up, and slipped on her jacket. It was obvious that her immaculate uniform was a fresh one.

Halloran seemed to have changed clothes, too. He sat flicking through a file – the Côte Mystère papers, Joanna realised – dressed in a dark suit and white shirt which were identical to the ones he had boarded in, but perfectly pressed, and unmarked by wine.

About ten minutes after Joanna had opened her eyes, she got a surprise when the pilot's disembodied voice spoke over the intercom, warning them that they would be landing at their destination in a couple of minutes. Joanna couldn't quite see her watch because of the angle at which her wrist was secured, but it seemed to her as if they had been flying for an eternity. How long did it take to reach the southern Rhône valley? And where would they be landing? She imagined being escorted through a major airport in her crumpled, wine-stained dress, with her wrists shackled in heavy cuffs behind her back. The idea made her dizzy, yet excited. She would be a slavegirl being led towards her prince.

On hearing the pilot, both Denise and Halloran buckled themselves in, ignoring Joanna as if she suddenly wasn't there.

The landing was smooth and uneventful and, looking out of the window, Joanna saw they had arrived at another, relatively small, private airfield. She sagged in her seat, in both relief and disappointment, wondering if she would be allowed to dress before she got off the aircraft.

As the plane taxied to a halt, both Denise and Halloran were galvanised into action. Halloran stowed his papers in his briefcase, and then gathered the travel documents pertaining to all three of them.

Denise turned her attention strictly to Joanna. First, she freed her from all her bonds, then, taking her by her shoulders, she pulled her on to her feet. Joanna swayed a little, her body feeling light, yet cramped by its extended immobility. Uttering brief, brisk encouragements, Denise rubbed Joanna's wrists and ankles to get the circulation going, then stood back, and studied her appraisingly.

'Right, take off your clothes,' she instructed, nodding at the wine-daubed wreck of Joanna's dress, and her tights and panties, still at half mast around her knees.

Still feeling awkward, Joanna complied with as much grace as she could, kicking off her shoes first to make things a little easier. Letting each garment fall to the floor, she stripped off every last stitch and, when she was completely naked, she stood awaiting Denise's order.

The transvestite eyed her intently, as if she were monitoring the condition and resilience of each critical part of Joanna's anatomy. Her glance darted from breasts to thighs to crotch, and back again, then she walked around so she could study Joanna's bottom.

'The Master is going to love you,' she said cheerfully, drawing from her pocket a small, dark object which proved to be the narrow band of a black velvet choker. This she fastened around Joanna's neck, taking the opportunity to stroke her face as she did so.

Master? So they did actually call him that?

But is it a 'him'? thought Joanna, watching Denise open a locker and get out the rest of her 'outfit'.

Is it you? she asked silently, as Denise helped her into a pair of narrow black shoes far higher and shinier than the ones she had set off in. Will you revert to being Davidson once we get there? she thought, allowing herself to be passively dressed in an abbreviated, red PVC mac that barely covered her bottom and her crotch. Will you then bind me and beat me, then take me as a man would?

She sensed that Denise could read her questions, but was declining to answer. The transvestite simply smiled and led her, by her arm, to the door.

The sun on the tarmac was dazzling and, as Joanna put up her arm to shield her eyes, she felt the short, tightly belted mackintosh ride up and expose her. From beneath her fingers, she looked towards a set of low, white-painted administrative buildings, about a hundred yards away, and seemed to see figures there looking back towards her. She felt their distant eyes ogling her privates and her bare behind, and she tugged at the hem of the revealing red mac.

'Come along, sweetheart, don't dawdle,' said Denise, still urging her forward. 'I would have thought you would be eager to get there.'

Joanna remained silent, and continued to fight battles on various annoying fronts. The shoes she had been given were far too high to walk in safely; the mackintosh kept flapping playfully in the warm, rising breeze; she was sweating profusely beneath its impervious plastic surface. If she were to meet her Master now – if he were waiting in the long, black car towards which she realised they were heading – she would meet him at an embarrassing disadvantage.

But maybe that's the whole point? Just another part of the test.

Just then, the driver's door of the car ahead opened, and a most unexpected chauffeur stepped out and waved.

It was a woman. She had on a chic dark suit with a mini-skirt, sheer stockings, and the elegant high heels so favoured by the women of the Continuum, but wore with all this a traditional chauffeur's cap. Her eyes were hidden behind menacing, almost Mafioso-styled dark glasses, and her hair – which was red – was worn up in a severe but flattering pleat.

It was Cynthia, Joanna's lesbian lover from London. As they drew close to her, she touched her cap in a small salute. She also smiled very faintly, too, and, although Joanna couldn't see her friend's eyes through the black lenses of her sunglasses, she knew the subtle greeting was for her.

Very much the perfect servant, Cynthia had the passenger doors open in a flash, then helped Joanna into the deep shade of the back seat of the car. She also managed to covertly stroke her bottom in the process. The touch was gentle and fleeting, but full of feeling, and induced in Joanna a fierce pang of sudden yearning. They had enjoyed but a single afternoon together, yet it had been full of meaning and affection. She hoped they would soon be in a position to repeat it.

When the brief formalities had been completed by Halloran, and their small amount of luggage stowed in the boot, Cynthia put the car smoothly into motion. Joanna found herself sandwiched between Denise and Halloran on the leather-upholstered back seat, and it didn't surprise her when they began to adjust her clothing. The short skirt of her mackintosh was lifted at the back to bring her bare buttocks into contact with the leather, and prised open at the front to display her pubis. Denise fingered her for a moment, the action casual, almost perfunctory, then withdrew, lay back in her seat and closed her eyes. At the other side, Halloran had opened his briefcase.

Joanna looked out of the smoked-glass window, seeing the gentle slopes of the vineyards, where they rolled away towards some unknown mountain range in the distance, through an odd and rather menacing grey pall. The day was bright and yet, because they were in the car, a darkness lay over it, like the pain she would have to endure before the light of revelation was granted her.

Could the Master be a woman? she thought, glancing down at her own exposed femininity, then forward, through yet another division of smoked glass, at Cynthia's sleek hair where it was tucked into its pleat.

Cynthia was delicate and feminine, yet she also had strength and a talent for control. Joanna remembered how easily she had slipped into a state of compliance when Cynthia had produced, and used, her giant dildo. It hadn't been a whipping, but it had been a humiliation. Perhaps it was also a sign she should have heeded? A subtle indicator of Cynthia's true, but hidden status?

Soon. Soon I'll know, thought Joanna, surreptitiously wiping her sweaty palms against the leather of the seat. She felt an odd, weird fluttering sensation of nervousness. Would she be happy with her discovery? What would happen to her? Would she continue to live her normal life, from day to day, but have nights that were full of sensuality and debauchery? Would she even continue to live alone?

But I still want to be free, she thought, a sense of panic setting in. The idea of being a pampered pet, a kept woman, appalled her, and she suddenly realised that, whatever happened in the bedroom, or the punishment room, she would have to assert herself beyond them. Even within the strange, turned-about *milieu* of the Continuum, she would still – sometimes – have to retain her personal power.

No-one made a sound, but a change in the atmosphere inside the car broke up her reverie. Focusing on the outside world again, Joanna saw that they were turning right, and about to pass through the entrance gates of an estate of some kind. The single word 'Mystère' seemed to float above them as part of an elaborately-fashioned wrought-iron arch and, beyond it, an extended corridor of plane trees led to an unfussy, but handsomely proportioned country house built of a mellow, slightly yellowish stone.

The tyres of the car crunched on the gravel beneath them, and Joanna felt her will and her defiance being crushed too. To gain the prize, and the power she so wanted, she must suffer now. Endure quietly and in perfect humility; surrender her selfhood somewhere in this attractive, unassuming residence.

Would it be in a bedroom? A specially prepared chamber of some kind? Or maybe even a stable, or – horror of horrors – in the open air, somewhere behind the house? Before an audience of assembled guests, and perhaps, worse than that, her Master's servants and other employees too?

'Oh no,' she whimpered faintly, lost in a state of horrid anticipation as Denise helped her from the opened door of the car. Two smartly dressed maids, like historical mannequins in long, black frocks with white caps and aprons, stepped forward to assist with the luggage, but their eyes were intent and curious. They studied Joanna with matched expressions of carefully suppressed salaciousness. She could imagine them whispering to each other about her once they were out of earshot. Gloating over her fate, and vying with each other to suggest more and more demeaning and painful things that might be done to her.

Oh Master, oh Master, help me, cried Joanna silently, as, without warning or comment, Denise stripped the red mac from her body, and drew her hands behind her back and fastened them there, using a pair of cuffs she seemed to have produced from nowhere.

Oh Master, I'm so ready, thought Joanna as she was led, naked and bound, towards her fate.

14

Master

Her fate is like a dream. An intoxicating fantasy which has little to do with her Master's heady, southern wine.

The woman supposes she should think of herself as a penitent in this scenario. A student. A neophyte. A submissive. All these are appropriate, yet she knows she is at the very centre of this mystery – *ce mystère* – and without her, on this occasion, it would not exist. After some thought, she assigns herself the nomenclature 'slave'; it is an accepted convention, and the name given to a rôle established by those far more versed in the rites of pain than she is. But in her heart she knows she is far more.

Secure in her title, the slave sways dizzily on her heels as she is led through the venerable and beautiful old house. On the wall are prints and paintings which seem set on preparing her for what lies ahead. Scenes of plump and wicked maids, their pantaloons lowered, their fresh bottoms offered to their *seigneurs* to spank; ladies of the house submitting to their husbands, accepting the birch or the cane with perfect poise; other females – mistresses perhaps, or passing fancies – being belaboured, either in the casual heat of passion, or with care in cool, protracted rituals.

Hesitating before a particularly vivid reproduction, the slave is urged forward by her keeper, her protector, her own maid, you might say.

'Come along! Don't dawdle. It will only be worse for you if you're late,' says gentle, solicitous Cynthia, who has prepared her charge most carefully for what awaits her.

The slave has been bathed, her skin soaped and creamed to petal softness, her blonde curls fluffed and scented, her teeth cleaned, her breath perfumed with mint. She has been shaved – beneath her arms, and on her legs, but not in the area of her pubis – and cleansed, most scrupulously and particularly, for sexual purposes, her orifices prepared for repeated usage. She shudders still recalling the ignominy of an enema, her wastes expelled and her forbidden passage sluiced again and again so that she might be empty and pleasing, ready to receive whatever her Master chooses to insert into her, whether it be inorganic, or a part of his person.

Shuddering, the slave looks at Cynthia. Her artistic friend still wears the skirt of her smart chauffeur suit, a white silk camisole, her elegant high heels and, though the skirt is short, and the camisole delicate, almost gossamer, she is fully clothed. The slave, on the other hand, is very lightly, almost demeaningly clothed. She wears the shoes she was given on the aircraft, and the little black velvet choker. The only other thing she is wearing is a pair of perfectly plain white panties. Their cut is full, almost chaste, and the fabric a soft, very fine cotton. They hug the roundness of her bottom, and seem to adhere lewdly to the fine nest of hair at her groin. She feels far more exposed, wearing them, than she would do completely naked, wearing nothing.

They are leaving behind the lovely pot pourri smells of the upper house now, where the boudoir is, but the slave detects attractive new odours. She can smell the scents of culinary herbs, particularly thyme and rosemary, as well as the sharp, rich tang of crushed grapes that seems to permeate the entire atmosphere of Le Manoir Mystère. Blending with these is the mouth-watering aroma of spices and roast meat. A sumptuous meal is being cooked somewhere in the house, a feast, an edible celebration of a momentous event. The slave has been offered food, a light *dejeuner*, to sustain her, but she was too excited to take more than a little bread and a mouthful or two of cheese – and of course a small glass of the superb Côte Mystère.

They are passing beyond the house proper now, and moving along a corridor with rough, whitewashed walls. At the end of this is a heavy wooden door of great antiquity, and it is fortunate that Cynthia is stronger than she looks because the massive, iron ring which serves as its handle takes some turning. The slave waits, her heart pounding, knowing that beyond the door lies her Master.

The door opens on to a set of stone steps which lead down to a cellar, and the room they find themselves in, ultimately, is long, with a low vaulted roof, lit only by a faint light from small high windows, and by flickering antique lamps. There are some barrels lining the wall, but the slave reckons that they are more for effect than anything. She suspects that the real working cellar of the vineyard is elsewhere, and that this chamber has but one purpose, and that is arcane enjoyment.

At one end of the room, in the shadows, is a shallow dais and on this, enthroned in a high-backed chair of dark oak with an intricately carved back, is her Master. For a moment she re-examines an astounding notion which has just occurred to her; one that is both elegant and ironic, but also deeply pleasing to her. She wonders why she did not think of it earlier; it should have been staring her right in the face. Despite this, she has not yet committed herself to belief, as the ways of the Continuum are full of tricks and deceptions. She could be quite, quite wrong.

Although he is, as yet, little more than a suggested figure in the deep shade, she perceives that her Master is slim and lithe, and that his whole body appears to gleam. He is clad from head to foot in black leather; boots, jeans, a long-sleeved body-hugging top. A strange mask, like that of an executioner, completely covers his face, and only his mouth, his eyes and his nostrils are exposed. There may also be apertures which allow him to hear, but the slave cannot be sure. His peculiar, almost reptilian appearance is a cliché, but here in the Continuum, it is correct and relevant. He wears a belt around his slim waist also; very plain, but heavy, and this, too, the slave considers significant. More than significant.

The Master lifts his black-gloved hand in a graceful gesture of dismissal, and tapping footsteps on the stone floor behind the slave indicate that Cynthia is leaving them. The slave feels a momentary pang of fear. Cynthia was kind and protective, a possible intercessor. Those that remain can also be kind, she suspects, but, at this time, are committed to ceremonial cruelty – especially the one who now steps forward into the weak light to reveal herself. The Master smiles faintly at the slave's look of alarm; his curving lips seem to float in mid-air, disembodied by the black mask that surrounds them.

The helper is the false woman, Denise, whose long, shiny brown hair and painted face are just a clever illusion. He/

she is also clad in black, but black silk in this case. A ruffled shirt, Cossack trousers, calf-length boots. Dually-sexual, he/she cuts a handsome, dashing figure.

Between the slave and her Master stands a structure not dissimilar to a rather low vaulting horse, a plain affair, but thoughtfully fitted out with a selection of straps in places that might soon be very useful. There is also an antique table nearby, from the same era as the Master's throne, and on it a number of implements are laid out in readiness. Some of these the slave has seen before, although only in magazines; some are unknown, but evoke emotions that are disquietingly visceral.

The slave studies the horse, and the implements, to prevent herself from staring upwards towards the Master's masked face. She longs to peer intently at his eyes and his mouth, to discover if they are features she has gazed on before, but she knows that in this scenario it is not her place to be bold. She must be meek, compliant, available, calm. And long, long suffering. Her rewards – knowledge not the least among them – will come later. For now she must merely endure.

Staring at the centre of the leather-covered horse, which is slightly worn down – polished by the bodies of other slaves, of other masters, perhaps? – she senses the passing of a brief instruction between the two black-clad figures.

Sure enough, Denise approaches her and takes her by the shoulder. 'Hello, slave, how are you feeling?' whispers the false woman silkily, confirming that the slave's choice of title is correct. Her fingers are firm against the slave's skin, and dominant, but they do not hurt her. They almost caress.

The slave is led around to the other side of the horse, facing away from the serene, unmoving Master as he sits in the semi-darkness. She is not surprised when Mistress urges her to lie across the centre of the shallow, leather-upholstered body of the horse, then encircles her wrists with the stiff hide cuffs that are secured to the floor. The slave feels blood rush to her head and hears a ringing in her ears, but she senses the latter is due to fear, rather than the simple fluid mechanics of circulation. Her legs are trembling now, really shaking in a way that must be visible to the one who sits behind her. They wave about madly, even though she tries to control them, and it is a relief when Denise comes around and secures them too, at the ankle, and about twelve inches apart.

The slave is still very conscious of the white panties she wears. She imagines them beckoning to her Master like a beacon in the gloom, drawing attention to the rounded cheeks of her bottom. Saying, 'Here it is, the prize you delight in. Here it is, to use exactly as you wish.' The very idea makes her unbearably excited. She is thrilled by the concept of possession, the fact that for the duration of this interlude, she has made over the dominion of her own body and, particularly the tender lobes of her buttocks, to another.

Acutely aware of his attention, she moves a little in her bonds, shifting her thighs so her bottom jiggles attractively. Then she purses her lips to prevent a cry of triumph when she hears him rise from his chair and move towards her, his booted tread firm and even across the stone.

When he takes hold of her she does cry out. A soft 'Aah' of delight when his gloved hands grasp her crudely. Immediately, she senses another of those unspoken orders – a nod of the head, she suspects, detecting it faintly, transmitted through his arms and hands – and a second or two later, Denise is at her head, lifting it with one hand, while the other stuffs a gag into her mouth. It is a sphere of rubber on a leather thong, and the taste is terrible, but the slave, to her own surprise, is glad of it. She feels freed by it somehow. She cannot cry out now, and no longer has the responsibility of keeping herself silent. She can concentrate on her own endurance now; all her energy is confined within her flesh.

Having waited for the gag to be fitted, the Master now resumes his manipulations. He holds her buttocks briefly through the thin panties, as if exploring the layering of fabric and skin. Bottom; cotton; leather; hand. To ring the changes, he releases her for a second or two, and allows Denise to intervene and pull the panties down. They are left, suspended like an accusing white bridge, at her parted knees. The slave smells herself and knows she has already scented the garment with her lust. She wonders what her Master will think of that.

His gloved hands grip her again, more consummately this time, his long fingers curving right around each cheek and pressing the texture of the leather against its surface. Already beginning to float, the slave thinks distantly that his fine leather gloves must have cost a fortune. The hide they are made from is so thin it feels like little more than a living membrane between him and her. She can feel the shape of his hands as they grip her; the sensitive pads of his fingertips; his large, cradling palms. He lifts her flesh very gently, testing its elasticity, and the gag in her mouth performs its function most efficiently, holding in her broken cry of pure desire.

For about a minute, he simply handles her in a way that, of late, has come to thrill her. He moves the lobes of her bottom about in slow but vigorous circles; he parts them wide, stretching her anus and making it wink at him; he pushes them together, making them kiss each other and compressing her swollen inner labia. As he does this, she wishes Denise would reach beneath her and stroke her clitoris; she knows she would climax within the space of one or two seconds, such is the heat that is smouldering within her belly.

Then, as suddenly as he took hold of her, her Master releases her. Another hand, the one she was wishing for a moment ago, slides brusquely into her crotch and rummages around quickly. The cursory examination is designed to test, rather than stir, but even so the slave pushes herself against it.

'Naughty, naughty,' says Denise, her southern drawl pronounced, probably because she, too, is excited. She withdraws her fingers, then strokes the slave's bottom, anointing her hot skin with her own moisture of arousal. 'You're enjoying this too much, my darling. It's about time we made the whole thing a little more exacting.'

The slave waits, her nerves singing with fear, her mind presenting her with a dozen or more gruelling scenarios. She knows she could crane her head up and to the side, to see what her Master and Denise are preparing for her, but, instead, she dangles her head, closes her eyes and looks at nothingness, trying to intercept the silent messages between her captors.

All of a sudden, reality jerks the slave from her imaginings and, in a state of shock, she groans and gobbles around her gag. First, a thick slather of lubricant, a scented gel or ointment, is worked around her anal closure; then, without warning, something hard is being pushed into her rectum. The insertion is ruthless, and the object itself is round and cold and smooth – possibly glass, or polished bone, or alabaster – with a woven cord that dangles down a little way.

Almost as soon as she is stuffed with this thing, the slave's innards begin to protest and roil and surge. The sensation is horrible, yet wonderful, and the slave cannot keep still. Unable to control herself, she swings her buttocks around to the full extent that her bonds allow, gyrating her hips in small but energetic circles. She is both ashamed of the action, and delighted by it, because she knows full well her dancing rear will please her Master. She feels her juices begin to seep down her weaving legs.

'Be still!' warns Denise, her voice like honey.

The slave tries to obey, fighting the impulses that surge through her pelvis. She knows there is only one thing that can effectively still her, a stronger sensation than mere discomfort in her rectum.

She hears the tiny 'snicking' sound of a belt being drawn through its belt loops. Opening her eyes, the slave sees that the Master is a yard or so away from her, and his booted feet are set apart to strengthen his stance. The tail of the belt dangles down, black and plain, then rises again; she pictures him winding a couple of twists of it around his hand.

Oh no . . .

Terrified anticipation blooms in her mind, in the all too familiar dichotomy. She fears what is to come, but also yearns for it. She wants to be past it, but the only way is through.

Studying the set of her Master's stance, the slave sees a subtle alteration, a tensing, and steels herself. In the last few seconds of grace, the false woman Denise bends and kisses her brow.

A stroke of fire lands across the slave's bottom. For a second she does not recognise it as pain, and has just time to think, 'It isn't too bad,' when her nerve-ends interpret the message correctly and she shrieks. Or tries to shriek, her saliva bubbling noisily round the gag. She rocks in her bonds, feeling as if a two-inch-wide strip of her skin has been flayed, a level band across the crown of both buttocks. Her master allows her just enough time to absorb the impact, and to let the sensations entangle themselves with those inside her, around the bung; then he lets fly with another stroke, which aligns perfectly with the first one, an inch below it.

The slave is amazed at the clarity of her perceptions. Pain, by rights, should befuddle her; be just a mass of hideous, screaming heat. But it isn't. The pain is crystalline, and extremely quantifiable, both in location and in texture. She jerks and squirms freely, mewling behind the gag, but she also knows – exactly – where each inexorable stroke is landing. Rising up from her own scorched body, she seems to look down at the pure geometricality of the parallel stripes he is creating on the lobes of her bottom. Each line is laid down in relation to another, first going up, to sear the upper curve, then going down, down to the susceptible undercurve and the tops of her thighs. When he has defined the area, he begins, quite methodically, to overlap, and to extend his fiery war zone around the sides.

Even after more strokes than she can count, the slave can still feel the slamming burn of each new one. Each new impact seems to fall on virgin flesh, and to sink in through her throbbing musculature, then to wind itself disconcertingly round the object inside her rectum and make it swell and press more firmly on her innards. The slave is sobbing and snuffling, now, but, if asked, she could not specify what it is that is oppressing her the most.

The inferno in her buttocks?

The awful and continuing feeling that she needs to evacuate?

The glorious, choking jolt of desire each blow engenders?

Her vulva is engorged and running. It feels a mile wide. She wishes that, for just one moment, her Master would abandon his belt, open his trousers, and thrust himself into her. She would not mind, even, if he left the smooth, hard sphere inside her bottom at the same time. She would not mind if just the one stroke of his penis meant a hundred more strokes with the lash. She knows that whatever he demands of her in payment would be more – a thousand times more – than worth it. She knows instinctively that just one thrust would make her whole. Make her blessed. Make her come.

During a pause in her Master's virtuoso performance – he is walking around to her other side, to balance his treatment, to ensure both buttocks are equally flaming – the slave looks up briefly, through a mist of red anguish.

Although she has forgotten that Denise is in the room, forgotten, at times, that the false woman has ever lived, she derives a faint comfort from seeing her.

The watcher, too, is suffering. What Denise endures bears no resemblance to the ordeal that the slave is gladly going through, but nevertheless she, or he, still hurts.

The slave knows she must not smile, even if she could, but she enjoys the pleasure of a smile within her mind. The false woman stands, legs apart, at attention, almost, but her hand is slowly rubbing her swollen crotch. She/he is jealous, the slave realises, her delight increasing. Denise envies both the slave the attentions of her Master, and – which is even more gratifying – the Master his joys with the slave.

Another crack of the belt lands, making the slave gurgle madly into her gag, but even so she manages to make a resolution. Later, with her Master's permission, she will be kind to Denise, who has been so diligent and so clever in his service. She might even pleasure the false woman without her Master's permission, she thinks, wincing as the belt flicks her stretched and bulging anus. It might be interesting to assay certain limits.

But just as this thought occurs, and the slave wonders just how much more of these attentions she can withstand, there comes another pause, this time a much longer one.

What is he doing? the slave asks herself, pumping her legs involuntarily within the confines of her bonds. Her bottom is pulsating so hard that she can almost hear the low, drumming sound of it, and it is impossible not to try to move with the rhythm. She finds herself concentrating hard just to make herself breathe; the sensation in her rear is so consuming. The obstruction in her bottom feels like a football now, as if the regular impacts of the belt have released a valve and made it swell up with air.

Lifting her head again, and feeling the tears drip down her cheeks instead of running down her forehead, she is just in time to see Denise nod respectfully, turn on her heel and leave the room.

And, as she leaves, the black belt suddenly goes sliding away across the floor, flung forward so the slave can see it there, abandoned.

What is he doing? she asks again, her poor heart clamouring. She lets her head drop again, knowing that if she strains to see him, he could well choose to leave her.

He is very close now. She can sense his leather-clad body just an inch from her sensitised flanks. He leans over her, and she jerks as if electrocuted when his crotch presses briefly against her pain. She wills herself to be still so she can feel the small, neat movements he makes at the back of her head, then she gasps and pants as the rubber gag is drawn out of her mouth and is sent sailing away across the room to join the belt. He ruffles her hair, then passes his gloved fingers across her liberated lips. Passionately she kisses the very hand that whipped her bottom.

Being free of the gag is like being given a wonderful gift. The slave remains quiet, but to have her mouth her own again is blissful. She moistens her lips with her tongue, wishing that her Master would allow her to kiss his hand again, or even better, instruct her to fellate him.

But that is not to be. At least not yet.

He is still behind her, and now he shows her a very soft and beautiful scarf of iridescent white silk. He lets it dangle before her for a moment, so she can draw a fairly obvious conclusion, then drapes it over her shoulder. She hears more small, neat, rustling sounds, and more objects begin flying across the room.

First one glove, then the second and, finally, the baleful black hood joins the growing heap of leather on the floor.

The urge to turn round now is a torment to rival even the ache in her buttocks – but the slave masters the impulse and stays still. After a few seconds, the pretty scarf is tied around her eyes, and things are much easier.

He begins to kiss her, pressing his lips to her shoulders and the nape of her neck. She senses he is gentling her, soothing her, preparing her for something much less pleasant. She knows what it is even as it begins.

In answer to his pull on the woven cord, the intruding sphere inside her rectum is withdrawn. The slave yelps as it pops rudely from her anus, then keens loudly as horrid urges assail her. Her Master strokes her between her bottom cheeks to calm her down, stirring the pain in her inner slopes as he does so. She hears the intruder drop to the floor and roll away.

There is only one reason that he has removed the bung, she thinks, as he continues to stroke her. It is an act she has never engaged in before but, given the number of other new things she has become addicted to over the past week or so, she suddenly finds the prospect of it excitingly exquisite. She churns her bottom beneath his gentle, teasing touch.

'Please . . .' she whispers, unable to keep silent as a finger lightly probes her. His answer is another kiss upon her back.

The next thing she knows is that more of the jelly-like ointment is being smeared around her anal portal, then there is the sound, small but familiar, of a descending zip.

Her Master pushes into her, not unkindly but with a degree of measured force. His insertion of his penis into her bottom is slow, relentless and complete and when he is fully lodged inside her, as deep as he can get, she feels his pubic hair, thick and wiry, chafe her soreness. Expecting him to thrust, the slave is surprised when he just stays there, completely still.

His inaction is yet another of his gifts. It allows her to savour fully each distinct sensation. The stretching and possession of her narrow, forbidden passage; the feel of his zippered trousers pressing against her bruised buttocks; the fine trembling of his strong, straight body as, with difficulty, he maintains his self-control.

Staying still herself, she nevertheless feels her own interior passively caress him. Each nerve-ending acknowledges his presence, says, 'Hello. I am nothing. I am yours'. His answer, after a moment or so of immobility, seems to be an attempt to get inside her even more deeply. He holds her hips in his powerful hands, his flexible thumbs digging into the soreness his belt has inflicted. He feels like a poker, a bar of iron rooted into her body.

Impaled like this, the slave knows what it is to be truly mastered. She feels like a beautiful thoroughbred, tamed to the bridle by a cool, calm hand.

He kisses her again, then presses his face against her hair as he inclines his body over her. As close as this she can smell a faint whiff of his cologne, a special signature amongst the odours of sweat and sex. She smiles, realising that not only does she know him now but, at a deep level, she has known him from the very beginning, and that knowledge is a knowledge that brings her joy.

'Master,' she says softly, surging back against him, even though it stirs up the pain and the strange feelings in her bottom.

He answers with a gruff sound of appreciation, and an almost boyish wriggle of his body against hers. Still gripping her hip with his left hand, he reaches around and slips his right hand flat under her body, then wiggles his fingers through her pubic hair to find her centre.

When he touches her, the slave almost howls with exultation. Her empty vagina contracts hard, and her clitoris, beneath his touch, leaps and pulses with a supreme, dark pleasure. She feels her Master's flesh throb, too, then hears him cry out just as passionately as she does. He calls her name, his voice broken and worshipping, and together they spiral down into a luscious velvet well, their bodies melded by his penis deep inside her.

What follows is even more dreamlike than the hours and minutes that preceded it.

The Master withdraws, then begins to unshackle his slave, pausing many times in the process to kiss her and embrace her. He kisses her glowing bottom with the utmost tenderness and though even this most delicate of contact hurts her, he gentles the pain by whispering 'I love you . . . I love you . . .' over and over again against the flesh which he has punished.

When she is free, but still blindfolded, he carries her up from the cellar, through his impressive house, and to his own suite of rooms, which look out on to the garden and the vineyard. Once there, he bathes his slave and ministers to her every need with a finesse and sensibility which at times is even more feminine in character than the attentions of Cynthia before him. Then, he dresses her in a lace-trimmed night gown of the softest silk and makes love to her, with his lips and his tongue, in the same clever, yet taxing fashion he employed when they were very first together.

It is only after she has come a dozen times, and her legs are in danger of giving way, that he stands up, lets the skirt of her gown fall to cover her, and unfastens the knot of the scarf that still blinds her.

Her vision restored, the slave who is no longer a slave reaches up to tousle his familiar blond hair, and smiles happily into his brilliant blue eyes. They both laugh.

And they are still laughing as she tumbles him on to the bed, lifts her nightgown once more, and impales herself triumphantly on his magnificent erection.

Epilogue

Afterwards, she could not sleep, even though her companion was sleeping like a baby.

'Master,' she whispered, so softly it was little more than a breath. Then she rose from her bed, wincing as her well-whipped buttocks reminded her of his skills, and her sticky, sated vulva recalled his gentleness and his ability to love her.

She smiled, looking down at his recumbent form, his dear, pointed face in profile against the pillow, his naked body; strong shoulders and back, narrow waist, firm, masculine buttocks. Almost without thinking, she stretched out her hand, wanting to touch him there, to stroke his beautiful bottom and slowly explore it.

Oh, Kevin, Kevin, Kevin, she chanted silently, entranced by his smooth skin and the fact that, for the moment, he was vulnerable to her. She had learnt such a lot from him over these last months, and a lot about him, but he still retained a sweet air of mystery. There was so much yet to discover about Kevin Steel, she realised, her hand still hovering, and much, she knew, that he would never reveal, even to her. He was an enigma, but that only made him more exciting.

Indulging herself, she let her fingers settle briefly on his bottom cheek. The flesh was firm and resilient, warm still from his exertions, and a little damp, with a thin gloss of sweat. He moved slightly on the bed, but did not wake.

He was unmarked too, and Joanna had a sudden, rushing urge to change that. To pick up the belt that lay abandoned on the floor – the one he had used at her 'graduation' in France – and lash it down across the perfection of his arse. Ruefully, she reached behind her and pressed the damage that strip of black leather had inflicted on her own bottom. The pain seethed, and she bit her lip and swayed. Between her legs a fresh inferno began to smoulder.

Patience, woman! she told herself after a moment, when the desire to masturbate – or to wake Kevin – had died down a little. There would be plenty of time later. Right now, her handsome master needed his rest.

Moving quietly around the room, she retrieved her nightdress, his clothes, and the belt. Were her senses deceiving her, or was its stern surface still hot from her thrashing? She let it rest in her palm, savouring its weight and imagining the lightning crack of it impacting upon her. She seemed to hear again her own whimpers and moans.

And not only her own.

Others had suffered under this belt too. Dear friends who Kevin had punished for her amusement; the same dear friends, punished by her, to amuse him. She had seen it plied, or plied it, upon bottoms of all shapes and sizes, and of both the sexes. She had even used it, with great delight, across his own flesh.

Thrilled at that thought, she clutched the belt against her breasts, trying to absorb the memories it contained. Sparks of subdued pleasure shot through her, and she looked back towards the bed and at Kevin's exposed bottom. She thought of the first time he had knelt before her, the first time he had offered himself. That momentous night at Le Manoir Mystère.

She laughed inside, still rubbing the leather voluptuously against her body, and feeling her vulva delicately ripple in response to it. She had not used the belt on that occasion; it was only later, after some weeks of education, that she had acquired a sufficient degree of skill.

A slipper it had been, that night; and, though her technique had been sloppy, she had still managed to make him shout.

Enough already! she told herself, placing the belt over the back of a chair, on top of the clothing she had just neatly folded. She considered slipping on her nightdress again, then decided against it. Reaching for a thick, towelling robe, she slid into it, knotted the belt and sighed. The nubbly white fabric made her sore bottom tingle – which would remind her of Kevin while she made tea and considered what her next move should be.

It was time she turned the tables, she reflected, ten minutes later, as she sipped the fragrant, reviving brew. Agitated by the hard kitchen stool beneath it, her rear was still simmering, and she thought again of the black belt and Kevin's virile body. Refreshing her tea, she began to fantasise and plan.

What about something elaborate? She imagined Kevin being prepared for her by Dale and Denise. Her dear, dear friends, they would gag him and bind him with exquisite gentleness; position him in readiness, at her command. He would be revealed, yet contained. Closing her eyes, she saw a harness, some kind of demeaning rubber garment; chains, handcuffs, his buttocks, defencelessly naked. She saw his wild, blue eyes widen as she approached him, and showed him the implement – his own belt.

Within the towelling of her robe, her own buttocks burned, and her sex wept and engorged. Abandoning her tea half finished, she reached down, flipped aside one white, terrycloth panel, and found her clitoris.

As she climaxed, she pressed her hand across her mouth, her mind filled with dreams and images from the Continuum.

In a little while she would write a letter to her love. . . .

Read on for a sneak peek at the seductive

ILL MET BY MOONLIGHT

A novella from Portia Da Costa,
featured in the collection

MAGIC AND DESIRE

BLACK
LACE

1

It was a dream. She knew it was a dream. But somehow that didn't seem to matter.

She was in a warm place, and she was deliciously, tropically warm. And, even though she didn't recognise her surroundings, she felt as safe and enclosed as if someone she loved and trusted was holding her tight.

Sniffing the air, she caught the scents of pine and balsam. Woodsy odours that were both clean and earthy at the same time.

She was waiting for a man. She'd been waiting for him quite a while, but somehow that didn't seem to matter either. Just to be here, relaxed and ready, was a pleasure.

Who are you? Do I know you?

Lois wondered if it might be Oliver, her ex. But why would she be waiting for him, even in this floating unreality? They'd parted ages ago, in an easy break, and, when she was awake, she barely ever thought of him . . . so why suddenly dream about him now?

In their heyday, though, the sex had been good. So maybe that was the reason? She was horny, so her body had fixed on its last source of satisfaction – other than her by own efforts. She remembered some of Ollie's finer moments with a twinge of hot nostalgia.

The room was dark and full of deep shadows, lit only by a nightlight and the flickering of a low burning fire. There was a womblike quality to the walls, something natural and organic, and she still couldn't work out where she was. She only knew it was somewhere new to her that felt irrationally like home too.

Maybe I was here in a former life?

Now there was a peculiar notion, if ever there was one ... but, then, everything about the situation was strange and other-worldly.

Maybe I'm remembering something I dreamt once before? Now that's complicated . . . a dream within a dream. Whatever next?

Whatever it was, she couldn't deny that she felt mellow and loose and sexy.

Touching her hands to her body, she was surprised. What the devil was she wearing?

Instead of her habitual shabby T-shirt and overwashed knickers, she found the voluminous and enveloping folds of an old-fashioned brushed-cotton nightdress. Nestling into it like a small furry animal, she sighed. Who'd have thought that something so prim could also be so sexy? The long full night-gown was both cosy and erotic at the same time, and the contrast between being all chastely covered up on top, and bare and devoid of panties beneath was sinfully naughty. As her naked thighs slid against each other, her nipples stiffened and puckered, their tips chafed by the virginal white fabric in a subtle autonomic caress.

I'd rather have a man do that, but where is he? Where is he?

Someone was coming though, she knew that. He just wasn't here yet. And, in the meantime, she would make her own amusement.

Picturing a pair of hands that were long and elegant, but full of suppressed strength, she clasped her breasts through the soft cotton of the gown and teased them with light squeezes. The mind image was almost supernaturally clear.

Strong hands, sleek golden skin . . .

Graceful fingers that were gentle but strangely cool . . .

Curiouser and curiouser . . . but also mmm mmm mmm . . .

When she flicked her thumbs across the hardened peaks of her nipples, the slight contact sent streaks of sensation flashing along her nerves. She could almost see that too, like little pathways glittering and silvery beneath the white nightdress and her own skin. She watched them zip and twinkle until they popped tiny starbursts in her clitoris. Of their own accord, her hips lifted and she moaned.

Ohmigod, all I've done is touch my breasts and I'm almost there! What's going happen when I really get down to business? Or he does?

Suddenly, she couldn't wait . . . she could hardly breathe.

Wriggling against the crisply laundered sheets, she hitched up her nightgown. Up and up until it was just a scrunched-up crumpled bunch under her armpits.

She was a goddess of sex. An odalisque exhibiting herself for a hundred watching eyes. She'd kicked off the sheets as she'd pulled up her nightgown and now she was on display from her chest down to her toes, her skin lapped by the warm scented air.

Breasts. Belly. Thighs. Pubis. The Full Monty.

She could smell herself too. A new perfume had blended itself into the pine, the earth and the juniper wood smoke. Her arousal, salty and pungent and also of the earth.

She stared down at her body, pale as alabaster against the luminous white sheets, the curls of her pussy a wild sandy shock between her thighs. She could see a glint of juiciness sparkling through the hair there and, shimmying against the mattress, she clenched herself, tensing up her strong inner muscles, and felt the slow honeyed roll of her arousal.

I'm very wet, secret lover . . . very wet. I'm ready . . . where the hell are you?

Should she touch herself? Or should she save herself for *him*? For a moment, she fantasised that he'd tied her hands to the bed-rails behind her head, punishing her, preventing her from stealing that special privilege.

Then, suddenly, because it was a dream . . . her hands *were* tied!

She was lashed to the brass rails with what looked like the cords from a couple of old-fashioned dressing gowns. How bizarre was that?

Instantly, of course, the need to touch her sex ramped up to an almost agonising pitch. Unable to suppress it or ignore it, she threw herself around on the mattress, hips circling and weaving while she tried desperately *not* to imagine her legs being fastened too.

Uh oh, too late!

No sooner had she thought it than the deed was done and she was bound hand and foot with more dressing-gown cords. Had she ever had a dressing gown like that? Did she know anyone else who had one? Where the hell was all this stuff coming from? She only knew that her ankles were spread wide apart and there was no longer any way whatsoever to get ease from the ravening itch of desire.

And it was now, when somehow she'd managed to make herself totally vulnerable, that the unknown dream lover finally put in an appearance.

The door swung back just like in an old Dracula movie and a figure appeared in the doorway.

And she didn't have the slightest idea who he was.

Who the hell are you, Dream Lover? And, boy, do you know how to make a big entrance!

Dream Lover was a cliché as well as a total stranger. Your actual tall, dark and handsome, but with a twist, and dressed all in black – a long coat, close-fitting T-shirt, jeans and boots.

And he had the most amazing hair!

It was almost black, yet also blond. Like ebony frosted with gold, and cut short, but not too short. A touch of wild, natural curl set off its startling pale tipping and made it appear to glow in the dim room like a halo, its brilliance second only to the fire in its owner's gleaming, flashing eyes.

Lois blinked. There was something weird about those eyes, but their very brightness made it impossible to work out what it was. She could only stare into them, like a willing patsy totally hooked by a hypnotist's spinning coin.

Talk about a fantasy man.

This is a dream, you fool! Of course *he's a fantasy man* . . .

But still, why the hair? And the eyes that she wished she could see better.

She must have conjured him up from the very depths of memory, from some long-lost book she'd read, or image she'd once seen. A world of faeries or earth spirits, of beings of supernatural power and alchemical attraction that she'd loved in more innocent times before she'd become a techno-geek.

But, however she'd cooked him up, God, how she wanted him! Between her thighs, she grew wetter, wetter, wetter . . .

The apparition didn't speak, and Lois couldn't. But still those amazing eyes pinned her to the spot, widening with an unmistakeable hunger. He immediately zeroed in on her cunt, and his fine-cut nostrils flared as if he'd smelt her. Which wasn't surprising, because she could certainly smell herself.

And the more she stared at him, the more she thought he was a dish fit for a queen.

He really was quite something. Face broad and intelligent, and vaguely familiar somehow now. Cheekbones high, jaw firm and a mouth that was strong and manly yet ever so slightly pouty in a way that made her long to nibble his plump lower lip. Even as she hungered for him and his eyes told her he was hungering for her in return, his tongue flicked out and moistened those succulent lips. It was pointed and very pink, darting lasciviously.

Almost expiring with lust, Lois hauled in a deep breath, and began to smell Dream Lover as much as he could smell her, getting yet another surprise into the bargain.

Not for him the smells of leather and sweat. Not for him the cool blue smells of male cologne.

No, as he approached her across the cabin, soft-footed on the wooden floor, he brought with him the sweet smell of flowers.

Violets, wild roses, delicate woodland blooms . . . and, most piercingly and headily, the scent of lavender.

It was like swigging down a triple belt of some perfumed liqueur made by monks in the wilds of rural France.

Lois squirmed around against the mattress, the very quick of her body aching like the devil as if the sweet odour was stimulating it directly. She throbbed and throbbed, her simmering flesh begging for contact. Just the tiniest little touch would do it. The stranger's mouth twisted in a slow knowing smile as he drew nearer. It seemed to light his every feature like a candle.

And still they hadn't exchanged a single word.

While Lois watched like a starving beast eyeing up a prime rib, Dream Lover flung off his long dark coat and then knelt on the bed. Having braced herself for the bounce of substantially muscled body hitting the mattress, she got a shock that made her gasp. He was big – tall and broad and solid – but the sheet on which she lay barely seemed dented. It was the oddest phenomenon, and Lois knew she should be frightened . . . but in a dream, she supposed, weird stuff like this was normal.

That was, if it *was* a dream? Some of it was far too vivid to be imaginary.

Free of his coat, Dream Lover's body was shown off to perfection. His arms gleamed in the firelight as if they were fashioned from polished wood and strength shone around him like an aura. The golden glitter that dusted his thick dark hair was even more breathtaking in close proximity, and his close-fitting black T-shirt embraced the ripped contours of his torso. Beneath the tough dark fabric of his jeans, his thighs were as sturdy as oak branches, and at his crotch there was a fine chunky bulge.

Lois's fingers itched to explore him, but her bonds were disturbingly real in an imaginary situation. She simply could not move, and Dream Lover's velvety, tantalising lips curved at the sight of her struggles. His hand, so conveniently *un*fettered, reached out towards her body, hovering for several seconds over her breast, before dropping to the full curve and cupping it. Lois hissed through her teeth, as his long thumb settled against her nipple as if it belonged there. His skin was as cool as she'd imagined it to be . . .

Her hiss turned to an outright groan as he flicked and tickled her; her mystery man smiled, his passionate mouth widening in a smile that was impish and knowing. With slow calculation, he strummed her again and again, and the compulsion to thrash about and rub the skin of her bare buttocks against the sheet beneath her grew stronger and stronger by the second. She tried to stay still, because for some bizarre reason it seemed important to show a little decorum, but it was hopeless. Wriggling like a strumpet, she knew she'd never looked sluttier in her life.

Why can't I just ask you who you are?

She opened her mouth to speak, but Dream Lover put paid to all questions by tweaking the nipple quite hard now, rolling it between finger and thumb, plucking at it and pulling at it, making it stiffer and pinker than ever. He cocked his gilded head on one side as she bucked against the mattress, attempting to widen her thighs and entice him with her sticky melting sex. She'd never behaved like this before, even in her wildest moments, and her own wantonness both appalled and excited her, goading her aroused body to even greater heights of shamelessness.

Please . . . please . . . she begged him silently, still unable to speak. *Touch my cunt. Stroke me with your fingers . . . Fuck me! Please, please, fuck me now!*

The golden-frosted head cocked again, and he grinned like the sun.

You heard that, didn't you, you bastard? You read my mind!

Maybe mind-reading was standard operational procedure in dreams? Anything was possible. Watching her face, Dream Lover continued to play idly with her breast for a while, all the time watching her face with the intensity of a scientist.

I can't take much more of this.

Lois watched his face for an acknowledgement, but Dream Lover just regarded her benignly as he went on with his fondling.

But Lois didn't feel benign. She wanted to kill him, or fuck him, or even both. Between her legs tension gathered and gathered and her head seemed to be floating it felt so light. Her brain was emptying of thought. She was about to come.

Just from having her breast touched? Surely not? But anything seemed achievable in this wonderful warm place.

But just when it seemed almost about to happen, Dream Lover withdrew his hand.

'You bastard!'

So near, yet suddenly so far, Lois found her tongue at last, and Dream Lover's brow puckered. What was he thinking? Planning some devilish new sexual torture for her, no doubt. He snagged his sinful lower lip with his Colgate-white teeth, and his brilliant eyes sparkled with mischief.

Lois blinked. Surely not? It had suddenly dawned on her what was peculiar about those eyes – they were two different colours. The right one was a sharp, electrical sky blue and the left one was as warm and brown as Armagnac.

She was just about to remark on this unexpected phenomenon, or just simply beg him to fuck her now she'd finally got her voice back, when, without warning, Dream Lover scooted back to the edge of the bed, and then reached down to unbuckle his heavy boots. After kicking them vigorously away across the room, he plucked at the hem of his T-shirt and pulled it out of his waistband with equal impatience. A second later it flew away on the same trajectory as the boots, and she was gifted with the sight of the most awesome male pulchritude. Muscles rippled across his chest and abdomen as he moved, bunching and relaxing beneath skin the colour of honeyed sandstone, almost too beautiful and magnificently male to be real.

Well, I've never wanted to worship a guy before, but I do now, she thought hazily. *What are you, some kind of magical deity? A prince of the world of dreams . . . a perfect lover?*

Coming to her again, he lay over her, his chest hard and smooth against her nipples, while the coarse workaday cloth of his jeans was equally rough against the bare skin of her belly. Lois blushed furiously as he pressed his hard crotch against her mons. She was soaking wet down there and it would surely seep through his jeans and he'd be able to feel it.

But then she forgot about qualms and wetness and jeans and everything. His mouth came down on hers, and she almost drowned in his sweet floral odour.

The contact of his lips on hers was soft at first, almost ethereal, like chilled velvet. Then, after a few seconds, the kiss grew wild and his tongue pushed inside her mouth, bringing with it a taste that was as heady as his smell. Lois gasped. His lips were candy sweet, and his tongue was cool and wicked, darting like a benevolent serpent inside her mouth, tasting and probing, then powerfully devouring. The pressure of the kiss became so intense that her jaw ached a little from the effort of giving back as good as she was getting.

Big hands settled over her smaller ones where they were fastened to the bedhead. He laced his fingers between hers as he used his entire body to caress and excite her, rubbing her with silky skin and with the denim and with the hardness of his muscles and his cock. His strong hips rocked and rocked, and the bulge of his erection somehow worked its way between her thighs, spreading her sex-lips so it could stimulate her clitoris.

And suddenly it was all too much . . . and yet not enough.

Muffled by his tongue, Lois growled a garbled sound of protest, her pelvis jerking against his, commanding him to give her more, more, more.

In return, Dream Lover laughed, his glee as sweet in her mouth as his taste was. Then he slid one hand down her body, visiting her breasts and her belly. His cool skin was a satin kiss against her heat.

Touch me! Touch me down there! Masturbate my clit and make me come and make me come before I die!

But, even if he'd heard her, he was determined to do what *he* wanted.

Working blind, still kissing, he worked deftly at the button and zip of his jeans and uncovered himself. Lois couldn't see his size, but, hot damn, she could feel it. He was huge and breathtaking against her thighs, hard and determined as he sought his target. With just a little help from his hand, he navigated himself inside her. His sex was as strong and sturdy as the rest of him and just its presence, cool inside her, was a thrill.

Aroused beyond anything she'd ever known before, she was stretched around him, and the bulk of his penis almost made her come without him moving. She lay beneath him, trembling on the brink, gasping and dreaming.

But he was a man – even in the dream – and he wanted action. With barely a stroke or two he had her in rhapsodies. Her body clutched and clutched at him, clenching and contracting, the sensations twice as spicy because she was helpless and couldn't wrap her limbs around him. When he freed her lips, she peaked again, howling and whimpering. When he thrust again, her soul soared, swooping and flying.

Higher, higher, higher she arced, and then descended, barrelling back down into her body like the little shooting star she suddenly and distinctly remembered watching earlier.

And with that, she achieved oblivion.

All went dark.

'Shit!'

Lois Hillyard jerked upright, her heart lurching with the sudden disorientation of waking up far too fast and not quite knowing where she was. She stared around wildly, her eyes skittering from object to object in the unfamiliar room.

What the hell am I doing in a log cabin and why is it so bloody cold?

She scrabbled for the quilt, which was on the floor beside her bed and, as she swaddled it around herself, she started to remember things. Things like why she was here in a log cabin in the wilds of nowhere beside the sea, which she could hear rolling outside instead of traffic noises to which she was more accustomed.

And things like stray hot fragments of the dream from which she'd just woken.

'Shit,' she muttered again, burrowing even deeper into the quilt and puffing out her cheeks, still in shock.

What the hell was all that about?

She'd had sex dreams before, but never one so vivid, so strange . . . or so kinky.

Bondage with an unknown man who had gold in his hair and smelt of lavender . . . Where had that madness come from?

Dreams were weird. You usually forgot most of them within moments of waking. But not this one.

Her Dream Lover sprang into her mind instantaneously, every detail like crystal.

He'd been tall, muscular, and graceful with the most astonishing hair and eyes. What possessed someone's subconscious to cook up details like that? Still in her duvet, gripped by the shakes, she tried to analyse him.

Well, the height might have come from a TV actor she was keen on, and the long black coat and funereal garb in general was *de rigueur* for vaguely threatening men of mystery.

But the hair? The eyes? The strangely cool skin? She hadn't the faintest . . .

Face? Well, funny as it seemed, she could pin that. The basic features were her actor again, but there was a touch, just a touch, of the man sharing the beach with her as well.

But why the hell dream about *him* though? It wasn't as if there was any chance, she'd quickly discovered, of getting off with him. No holiday romance there, no way.

Neighbour Guy, as she called him, seemed to have been going out of his way to avoid her, and when they had run into each other he'd been surly at best. He was worthy of fancying, in a purely physical sense, but, in terms of conversation, he seemed to begrudge every monosyllable.

Well, sod you, she'd thought, catching sight of him once or twice, stalking the beach or the rough gravelled track to the local shop, but, somehow, she couldn't help feeling sorry for him too. Somehow, without knowing why, she'd formed a distinct impression that he was a man with a load of sorrow hanging over him. And for that she could almost forgive his chilly grumpiness.

Yes, her fantasy guy of the gilded hair and other magnificent accoutrements had resembled her unhappy neighbour ever so slightly, but otherwise they couldn't have been more different.

Dream Lover had been full of the joys of life. And rambunctiously overflowing with the joys of vigorous pervy sex!

Her body was still tingling with the aftermath, and between her legs she was humid and sticky.

Ohmigod, I must have come in my sleep!

Well, all this sea air and the woodland ambience must be good for something. It had put her in touch with her earth goddess self, or something like that. Being out here in the wild beyonds of unconnected nowhere was going to be a blast if she had a dream like that every night, and with any luck she'd not miss the internet at all. With no television, and a mobile connection that kept dropping out every two minutes, all she had for entertainment otherwise were a couple of uninspiring novels.

You knew this, didn't you, Sand!

Sandy, her friend and partner in their small web-development business, had been moaning at her for long enough to take a well-earned holiday and get away from it all for a while, and had more or less strong-armed her into accepting this offer of a seaside-cabin break from one of their grateful clients.

Unbeknown to Sandy, Lois had brought her laptop, and had planned to work anyway . . . until, of course, it had dawned on her that she was miles and miles from the nearest wi-fi hotspot!

'Twit!'

That would teach her to take the digital, technological world so completely for granted. It served her right for trying to wriggle out of the rest that Sandy had so kindly levered upon her.

It was still frustrating though. Especially when the weather was unseasonably grim and icy for the end of May and the best place to be was inside the cabin, tucked up with a steaming-hot laptop. But her mobile connection was too erratic and slow and, even if she did work, she had no way to upload anything to the testing server without tearing her hair out waiting for minute after minute after minute.

Better just concentrate on erotic fantasies then . . . They seem to be downloading just fine!

Either that or do some cleaning.

Why the hell is this stupid place suddenly covered in dust? It wasn't here earlier . . . Where is it all coming from?

The cabin had been impressively spick and span when she'd arrived but now a delicate veil of dust lay over most of the surfaces and drifted across the floor. There were even whorls of dust scattered over the bed and on the pillows, with several strange heaps against the head and the foot rails.

What the f–?

She shivered. She sniffed the air. And then tentatively, almost reluctantly, she slipped a hand down into her knickers and touched her wetness. Of which there was a lot. Far more than there ought to have been from simply playing with herself.

But it wasn't the quantity that bothered her, it was the way it smelt.

As she withdrew her fingers, a familiar odour made her head spin.

Lavender . . . It was lavender . . . Why does my crotch smell of lavender?

Pulling the quilt over her head, she tried hard not to think.

In human form, Robin crouched on the woodshed roof and tasted the flutters of fear in Lois's mind.

No, this was not what he wanted. Not at all. He'd wanted to give her pleasure, not scare the living daylights out of her. Savouring the physical sensations of sighing, he sent out his mind, and touched hers again, filling it with soothing waves of peace that granted sleep.

There, that was better. Unable to resist the temptation, he disassociated and floated through the roof of the cabin so he could be close to his new object of curiosity.

Touching down, he reassociated, and stood by the bed, just looking at her. Not that there was much to see with human eyes. She was curled up beneath the thick quilt like a hibernating dormouse, and only a few tufts of her tousled blonde hair were protruding from the top of it.

There was much to be said for being what he was though. If she woke up now, and emerged from her hiding place, she would see a man . . . but what she couldn't perceive were the powers he still retained.

He could see through the quilt to the pretty face, and even prettier body that lay beneath.

She was delightful and complex and Robin liked that. Connecting with her gave him everything that was delicious about assuming human form. Every year in the month of May, when the transformation was possible, he tasted and interacted with humans, feasting indulgently on their complicated and sometimes turbulent feelings. His own kind had emotions, true, but they were mild, bland and somewhat basic. Contentment. Satisfaction. A kind of wistful regret, occasionally. The only emotion that really stirred him while discarnate was curiosity. And, in that, he knew he was unusual among his breed.

And one of the very few to pursue the ancient privileges of merry May.

But look where it had got him!

He was addicted now, perhaps polluted somehow. Even while discarnate, he was gripped by powerful yearnings. Feelings had filtered through by osmosis into the whole of his existence and he only felt truly alive when he was 'human' . . . or as near as to that condition as he could approximate.

And tonight, with beautiful Lois, he'd almost believed for a moment that he was a man.

Dipping lightly into her mind, he relived the delicious episode, smiling at the way her own subconscious had provided all the elements of the scenario.

You didn't realise you were so kinky, did you? he told her sub-vocally, relishing the words he'd picked up from her vocabulary and from others, over the years.

Binding her to the bed and tormenting her with pleasure had stirred him mightily. And it stiffened his temporary flesh now in a way that made his spirit swirl with emotion and heady pleasure.

Now this, he thought, placing his large hand over his swelling groin and giving it a gentle squeeze, was something his own kind were really missing. Yes, they had a melding of sorts, and it was exceptionally pleasant, but it was a pale shadow in comparison to the hot, wild, sweaty, pumping chaos of human sex with its pungent fluids, its loss of control and ecstatic release.

For that alone, with a special woman like Lois, he might be prepared to lose the many powers humans lacked.

As Lois stirred, probably sensing him, he stepped back from the bed, ready to disassociate and disappear instantaneously. Her head emerged from under the coverlet, and he was struck again by the sweet appeal of her human face.

It was elegant and oval, but with a soft rounding to the cheeks and a rather snub nose that he knew she sometimes fretted about. He'd modelled his own nose a little on it, to reassure her of the attractiveness of the shape. He'd noted too that, despite her qualms, she'd also found the very same feature subconsciously attractive in the man next door, so he'd taken elements of that face too, when creating the image of his own.

His thoughts balked for a moment, troubled as the consciousness of Lois's neighbour briefly touched his own.

Now there was a human emotion he *didn't* want too much of. Grief. Intense sadness. Inconsolable loss. The man in the next cabin had lost a lover, and lost her here, in this place, to the force of the sea. Robin knew what was in the thoughts of Lois's neighbour and, though he felt he understood them, the course of action that the man was planning was anathema to him. Did he not know how precious a thing the human condition was? Even in its darkest, direst hours . . .

Shaking his head as if that might dispel the received sorrow, Robin returned his attention to the warm sleeping woman who lay before him.

Her hair, he considered, was delightful; the shimmering golden colour of sunlight. He knew, of course, that it had been tampered with to make it look that way, but who was he, an entirely artificial human form, inspired by elements from many sources, to disapprove of a bit of creative enhancement? He'd taken his cue from her in acquiring his own sunlit streaks.

She was deeply asleep again now, without dreams, but the temptation to intervene once more was vivid. His penis was hard, stiff and aching, although the sensation was deliciously pleasant, despite the discomfort. Her body was smooth and warm beneath her untidy T-shirt and panties, and the odour of her sex teased his senses and reinforced them.

How delightful it would be to ensorcell her again and plunge his borrowed stiffness into her.

He experienced a momentary qualm . . . guilt, he recognised. Guilt at exploiting the slumbering woman, and using her for his own satisfaction – even though he had given her pleasure and her subconscious had gladly welcomed him.

No, next time they joined – fucked, had sex, made love, as the humans so whimsically called it, even when they didn't love each other – next time, exquisite Lois would be an active conscious participant. That was a promise he silently made, and swore to keep.

Yet still his acquired flesh ached and ached.

Of course, the answer was to disassociate again. No body. No arousal. No physical ache. But he didn't want to do that. The month of May was precious and there were only a couple of days remaining. He wanted to remain human for as much time as he could.

Settling into his chair, he unzipped his jeans and drew out his cock.

How fine and delightful it felt to caress himself. To fuck the beautiful girl curled up on the bed was obviously the ideal satisfaction, but handling himself had its own particular charm. Curling his large fist around himself, he pumped greedily at his penis, working and working it. There was no need to take his time. No need to delay in order to increase his partner's sensations. He could rush, snatch his release quickly, come fast and hard.

But, when relief came, her name was noiseless on his lips.

For a while afterwards, he just sat there, letting his consciousness roam around the room, examining her possessions and her clothing, learning about her.

Eventually his attention settled on the device set on the rustic table, the one she called her laptop.

Robin had come to understand what the laptop was, and he applauded it as an excellent mode of communication. Humankind might be sorely limited in the way they interacted with one another, but they were ingenious in creating mechanisms to allow themselves to do the best they could, and this small computer was a prime example of what they could achieve.

He touched it and, energised by *his* energy, it sprang to life. Quickly, he rode its patterns of force and deduced the way to mute its operating noises. He didn't want to wake Lois yet. It would be better to 'meet' her for the first time in more acceptable circumstances. Finding an intruder in her bedroom wouldn't get their relationship off to a very good start!

As he played with the device, he sifted through thoughts and notions that he'd gleaned from Lois. She was vexed with her little computer, and vexed with herself over it. Out here, far from so-called civilisation, there was no way for her to connect it to the great web of energy lines she called 'the internet'. It needed something called 'wi-fi' to become a part of that matrix.

Robin smiled. It was simply a node that was required, a nexus that would focus yet another pattern of force. Swooping down, he caught up a big handful of dust and compressed it tightly in his palm.

A moment later, he looked down at a small gleaming lozenge shape that pulsed softly in the dim light of the cabin.

His kind weren't called magical for nothing, he thought wryly, as he attached the little 'hotspot' to the underside of the desk, well out of sight.

A gift, my Lois, he thought fondly. In return for the pleasure you gifted to me.

With one last longing glance at her, he disassociated and floated away.

'What the fuck?'

Staring at the screen, Lois forgot the shivering chill of the cabin. She forgot the fact that her feet were blocks of ice and she could only keep marginally warm by wrapping the entire duvet and a couple of extra blankets around her. She even, for the moment, forgot the raving hot erotic dream she'd had, that seemed to have burnt itself into her brain in lurid Technicolor detail.

She had a wi-fi connection where one was impossible.

'This is mad!' She refreshed the list again.

But there it was. She was logged into a connection designated '000000' and the signal strength was excellent and the speed frankly phenomenal!

Absently rubbing her chilled toes together to increase their circulation, she went through all the settings, and everywhere, where there should have been strings of figures, she got '000000'.

'This is mad,' she repeated, and then clicked on the icon for Google, which brought up the search engine instantaneously.

The inexplicable connection bugged her, but after a few fruitless minutes of diagnostics, she gave up.

What the hell, at least the IP address wasn't 666.666.666.6.

By the time she'd checked all her favourite pages, and even uploaded a bit of work to her testing server, the sun was high in the sky and its soft yellow rays were cascading in through the windows to warm up the cabin.

Thank heavens for an oil-fired heating system!

Lois was grateful for that small mercy as she took a shower in the tiny cubicle. It might be absolute rubbish at warming the rooms of the cabin, but at least it provided plenty of hot water.

She needed to be clean after last night. She'd felt icky and sticky and foxy after that dream. Masturbating in her sleep? Nothing wrong with it, really, nothing at all, but still sort of disturbing that she should be so horny, and not actually all that consciously aware of it.

Touching herself before she stepped beneath the spray, she'd been almost afraid she'd smell the odour of lavender on her fingers, and she'd been relieved – but irrationally disappointed – when all she'd smelt was plain old Lois-smell.

The bay was bright and blue when she stepped out on to the shared porch connecting the two cabins. Despite its convenience, the phantom wi-fi connection troubled her more than she cared to think about and, contrary to her every usual instinct and inclination, she'd turned off her laptop and decided to get out into the fresh air and do some 'nature'.

But why is it so bloody cold?

Despite the late-May sun, she was glad of her fleece and her boots as she trudged down the short packed-earth track and on to the beach. With just the two holiday cabins sharing it, the tiny bay was deserted. Lois had no idea where her neighbour was. She'd thought she'd heard him tramping about on the porch earlier, but now there was no sign of him. It would have been nice to make friends because, when she had managed to encounter him briefly once or twice, she'd rather fancied him. He was good-looking in a slightly heavy-set sort of way. But there was nothing doing. His responses had been barely monosyllabic, and a dark pall of 'touch me not' sadness seemed to envelop him.

'Poor bugger,' Lois observed as she stepped out on to the sand and made for the firmer stuff, closer to the water's edge, 'but you can't be happy if you don't give anyone a chance to cheer you up, can you?'

Yes, it would have been nice to forge a little holiday romance with her bay-mate if he'd been amenable, but maybe she didn't really need one. Not with the hyper-real sex dreams she was having! She was having plenty of erotic kink without any of the effort of the courtship dance. It was perfect. She could be as lazy as she liked, and still get satisfaction. Result!

Away from the pull of her computer, and the puzzle of the mysterious wi-fi connection, her experience of last night rushed in again to claim her.

Boy, had it been hot!

Dream Lover might have been chilly-skinned, but everything else about him was nothing short of incendiary. Just thinking about it all warmed her up inside her fleece and jeans, despite the spiteful bite of the nippy wind.

Dream Lover rose up before her in her imagination.

The tall dark powerful man out of nowhere was a classic romantic archetype, but where the hell had the image of odd eyes and gold-frosted hair come from? She had no explanation for those.

Not to mention the funky smell of lavender.

She seemed to smell it now, that rich sweet scent. And her body was growing warmer and warmer and warmer, surging and rousing with a rush of reborn lust.

The mysterious stranger advanced through her mind towards her and she felt so weak at the knees that she was forced to stagger to a scrappy outcrop of sand grass that had created a small dune at the edge of the beach.

Cowering on the little hump, she hugged her arms around her, shaken by the intensity of returned lust.

This is mad! Just mad! I'm going crazy!

For the second time in a morning, it was impossible to focus on reality. She was right back in her sweet, dangerous, nocturnal fantasy even while she scanned the bright clear sky above the bay.

A solitary bird was wheeling in the brisk salty air. It was dark, and appeared tiny so far aloft, but, as she watched it, there suddenly seemed a new purpose to its circling. It swooped, and seemed to be flying right at her, inducing a wild rush of Hitchcock-related panic.

Don't be crazy! How can it have seen you? And, if it has, why would it fly at you?

Yet still the bird, a gull of some kind, was closing, diving on dark wings, but revealing a strange mottling to its plumage as it neared. There were lighter speckles among the feathers around its head and its eyes, possibly white, possibly yellow . . . possibly gold.

Lois wanted to spring to her feet, and run back to her cabin, pack up her gear and just get the hell out of Dodge . . . but all she could do was sit and watch, locked in place as the bird began to circle again, slowly, maintaining its distance in the air over the water.

The leisurely repeated sweeps were hypnotic. Her fear ebbed, and the strange warmth in her body grew almost tropical.

And so, to her astonishment, did the low, deep, sweet welling of desire. Night and day coexisted somehow; she was in her dream, but also awake, in the sunshine.

Half her mind watched a bird. Half of it was back in the cabin, in the soft lamplight, watching Dream Lover approach, anticipating his touch.

'Oh please,' she whimpered, repeating her plea from last night.

She yearned for him, desire flickering deep in her groin for this vivid, but imaginary man. Her nipples tingled, her sex clenched on emptiness, the hunger to be filled so intense it brought tears to her eyes.

No real man had ever satisfied her like him.

Without thinking, she clasped her hand to her crotch, squeezing, trying to ease the ache. Pressing and massaging, she stared up at the strange dark gull, watching it execute a graceful diving spiral, almost in response to her action. Then she looked down again, observing her own pale hand against the stonewashed cloth of her jeans, and wishing it were another hand. One that was bigger and stronger and totally male.

Imagining him behind her, she moaned, longing for it to be his great body on which she leant while she took her pleasure, longing for his arms to enfold her and gentle her through the spasms.

'Oh! Oh, God!' Crying out, she came in a sudden rush, out of the blue, dimly hearing the gull shriek too, as if applauding her or even sharing her crisis.

Still clutching herself, she wrapped her other arm around her torso, hugging and rocking.

She didn't hear the heavy trudging footsteps until it was too late, and, when they did penetrate her haze, she looked straight up into the frowning face of her next-door neighbour.

'Are you all right?'

Hot blood flooded her cheeks. Oh, God, it must be obvious what she'd been doing, and his dour frown seemed to confirm her worst suspicions. His grim set expression spoilt what was really a very personable countenance. Any normal man would have been smirking at her, turned on by what she'd been up to . . . but not him. He appeared unutterably depressed and disapproving.

'Yes, I'm fine.' Even though it was a lost cause, Lois snatched her hand from her crotch and stuffed it surreptitiously into her pocket. 'Thanks. Just got a bit of a stitch. It's going now. Thanks.'

'Sure?' His brow was still crumpled.

She had no idea whether he believed her but, if he didn't, her little exhibition obviously left him cold. His eyes were bleak and bitter, as if he were already weary of talking to her.

'Yes, thanks, I'm fine,' she parroted, her face flaming.

'I'll be getting along then. Be seeing you,' he concluded gruffly, and, as he turned and stomped away, Lois didn't know whether to be angry or relieved.

He thinks I'm some kind of sex maniac. He thinks I'm disgusting!

'Well, screw you!' she muttered, hurling the suppressed insult at the broad retreating back that had already reached the path and was rapidly receding from view. 'Any *normal* man would be all over me like a rash.'

Attracted by a flash of movement, she realised that the dark gull-like bird had landed only a couple of yards away from her and was regarding her solemnly, its peculiarly mottled head cocked on one side.

'Yeah, yeah, yeah, birdie! I know the guy's obviously got some serious problems and I should feel sorry for him . . .' She paused, her throat tight all of a sudden, and her eyes hot with un expected tears. 'But I'm lonely. I'm used to being around people . . . but Sandy said I needed a break.' Bright avian eyes blinked and Lois blinked too. There was something very odd about this creature, and yet she couldn't stop herself rambling on to it. 'I don't know . . . when I saw him, I was sort of hopeful; it's a while since I, um, was with anybody, and I suppose I was hoping I'd get a bit of holiday nookie.'

The bird hopped sideways and flapped its wings making Lois jump.

'Oh fucking hell, I'm talking to birds now! I've had enough of this . . . I'm off to the shop to get some wine and I'm going to get drunk!'

She leapt to her feet and, as she did so, the bird took flight and seemed to hover for a moment, floating above her, before flapping vigorously and soaring away.

Lois shook her head. *I'm going nuts here . . . just another day or so, to keep Sandy quiet, and then I'm back to town, no messing.*

Wondering what kind of wine the small local shop stocked, and how much of it they had, she stomped off towards the path, her sandy footsteps blending with those of her neighbour.